Marie O'Regan is a British Fantasy Award-nominated horror and dark fantasy writer and editor. She has served as the Chair of the British Fantasy Society, and has at times edited both their publications, *Dark Horizons* and *Prism*. In September 2009, Simon & Schuster's Pocket Books imprint published her anthology (co-edited with Paul Kane) *Hellbound Hearts*, a collection of short stories based on the original novella *The Hellbound Heart* by Clive Barker that inspired the movie *Hellraiser*. Marie lives in Derbyshire, England.

The Mammoth Book of

Ghost Stories by Women

Edited by

MARIE O'REGAN

ROBINSON

RUNNING PRESS
PHILADELPHIA · LONDON

Constable & Robinson Ltd
55–56 Russell Square
London WC1B 4HP
www.constablerobinson.com

First published in the UK by Robinson,
an imprint of Constable & Robinson Ltd, 2012

A copy of the British Library Cataloguing in Publication
Data is available from the British Library

UK ISBN: 978-1-78033-024-2 (paperback)
UK ISBN: 978-1-78033-025-9 (ebook)

1 3 5 7 9 10 8 6 4 2

First published in the United States in 2012 by Running Press Book Publishers,
A Member of the Perseus Books Group

Books published by Running Press are available at special discounts for bulk purchases
in the United States by corporations, institutions, and other organizations. For more information, please contact the Special Markets Department at the Perseus Books Group, 2300
Chestnut Street, Suite 200, Philadelphia, PA 19103, or call (800) 810-4145, ext. 5000, or
e-mail special.markets@perseusbooks.com.

US ISBN: 978-0-7624-4594-3
US Library of Congress Control Number: 2011939124

9 8 7 6 5 4 3 2 1
Digit on the right indicates the number of this printing

Running Press Book Publishers
2300 Chestnut Street
Philadelphia, PA 19103-4371

Visit us on the web!
www.runningpress.com

Printed and bound by CPI Group (UK) Ltd, Croydon, CR0 4YY

For Jen, who loves the spooky stuff

Contents

Acknowledgements

Special thanks to Roland, Vivien and Portia Asquith; also Mike Ashley, Paul Kane, Stephen Jones and Duncan Proudfoot, for all their help and support.

"Seeing Nancy" by Nina Allan, copyright © 2012

"The Third Person" by Lisa Tuttle, copyright © 2012

"Freeze Out" by Nancy Holder, copyright © 2012

"Return" by Yvonne Navarro, copyright © 2012

"Let Loose" by Mary Cholmondeley, originally published in *Moth and Rust* (John Murray, 1902).

"Another One in from the Cold" by Marion Arnott, copyright © 2012

"My Moira" by Lilith Saintcrow, copyright © 2012

"Forget Us Not" by Nancy Kilpatrick, copyright © 2012

"Front Row Rider" by Muriel Gray, copyright © 2012

"God Grant That She Lye Still" by Cynthia Asquith. Originally published in *When Churchyards Yawn* (Hutchinson and Co., 1931). Reproduced by permission of Roland Asquith.

"The Phantom Coach" by Amelia B. Edwards, originally published in *All the Year Round*, 1864.

"The Old Nurse's Story" by Elizabeth Gaskell, originally published in *Famous Ghost Stories by English Authors*, (Gowans & Gray, 1910)

"Among the Shoals Forever" by Gail Z. Martin, copyright © 2012

"Afterward" by Edith Wharton, originally published in *The Century Magazine* (The Century Co, 1910)

"A Silver Music" by Gaie Sebold, copyright © 2012

Introduction

Ghost stories have always been my favourite kind of tale, especially in the short form. Recently I've read or re-read several pieces by women whose work I admire, both from the Victorian era and from today (Michelle Paver's excellent novel *Dark Matter* and Susan Hill's short novel *The Small Hand* spring to mind, as well as short stories such as Edith Wharton's "Afterward", to be found in this anthology) – while at the same time reading grumblings about the lack of "women in genre fiction". The truth is that there isn't really a *lack*, as such – women have always written in the horror and supernatural fields, and continue to do so. Proportionately, they form a smaller part of the genre as a whole. They are, however, a *significant* part, which leads me to this anthology.

I wanted to put together a collection of ghost stories – both old and new – that would showcase the talents of women in the genre, both past and present; and because there's a wealth of talent out there, regardless of the writers' gender.

These stories range from Amelia B. Edwards's "The Phantom Coach", which first saw print in 1864, through stories by such luminaries of the past as Edith Wharton, Elizabeth Gaskell, Mary E. Wilkins-Freeman, Mary Elizabeth Braddon and Mary Cholmondeley, right up to modern writers such as Lilith Saintcrow, Muriel Gray, Sarah Pinborough,

Marion Arnott and Nina Allan. The subject matter covered is wide, from ghostly children to visitations by departed loved ones both human and animal, intended to warn, scare, or even comfort – Mary E. Wilkins-Freeman offers a genuinely heartrending spectral visitor in "The Lost Ghost", while stories such as "The Fifth Bedroom" by Alex Bell (her first ghost story) show us a more malevolent creature by far.

Although the stories vary from tales of ghostly children to those of lost pets, from murder to accidental death, from rage to sorrow and back again, one thing is central to all: a slight chilling of the skin as you read. A feeling of something being not *quite* there but rather just behind you, ready to make itself known, and leaving you reluctant to turn out the light.

Enjoy the stories, and ladies – thank you for your help in bringing this anthology to print.

Marie O'Regan
Derbyshire, England, November, 2011.

Field of the Dead

Kim Lakin-Smith

Dean Bartholomew Richards saw three figures at the periphery of his vision. Sunlight filtered through the stained glass and the Lady Chapel was transfigured. He tilted his chin to the blaze. Lichfield Cathedral was the Lord's house, he told himself. It was not to be slighted by spirits.

A cold wind blew in from the direction of the altar. Dean Richards turned around slowly, the three figures shifting so that they continued to flicker at the corner of his eye. He walked past Saint Chad's shrine and felt the temperature drop. Shadows lengthened. At his back, the sun went in.

Something wet touched the dean's nose. He dabbed it with a sleeve. Staring up at the distant vaulting, he saw snow dusting down. He had heard about the phenomenon from the canons but hoped it was just the fantasies of young men left alone in a dark cathedral. But in his heart he could not deny the haunting had become more substantial. Sir Scott's renovators were reporting screams like those of the damned, shadows writhing over walls, and spots of raging heat. Ice coated the Skidmore screen, a thousand tiny diamonds amongst the gilt. And then there were the children, their arrival always heralded by the inexplicable fall of snow.

Dean Richards rubbed the bulb of his nose. Faith must keep him stalwart.

"Come, children," he whispered, fearing the words.

Snow dusted the flagstones. Silence packed in around him.

He spotted them at the foot of The Sleeping Children monument; two girls in white nightdresses – exact replicas of the dead sisters depicted in the marble monument. The elder child made the shape of a bird with interlaced fingers. The younger smiled. Snow settled on his shoulders, and he forced himself to advance to within several feet of the sisters. Kneeling on the cold flagstones, he clasped his hands.

"'The Lord's my shepherd, I'll not want; he makes me down to lie'." He heard the tremble in his voice but pressed on. The important thing was to focus on the appropriate passages. The Beatitudes for these pitiful, not-quite children? Or a parable to lead them to the light?

He fixed his gaze on his hands until curiosity got the better of him. Glancing up, he felt a jolt of fear. The girls had moved closer and now knelt side by side, their insubstantial hands joined in prayer. But the longer he stared at the ghosts, the more solid they became.

"'In pastures green, he leadeth me—'"

The youngest girl's lip curled back into a snarl.

"'The quiet waters by—'"

The older sister flinched, a blur of movement.

To the dean's horror, both underwent a metamorphosis. Eyes flickering shut, their skin turned silky white while their bodies stiffened and set.

The dean could not help himself. Forgetting the three spectres at the outer reaches of his vision, he stretched out a hand to comfort the poor dead children.

"Sleep now," he whispered, hand hovering above the youngest's exquisitely carved head. "In the arms of the Lord." He lowered his hand to bless the girl.

The ghost girl's eyes shot wide open, her sister's too – stone angels brought to life. Their mouths strained and the screams of hundreds of men issued forth.

Dean Richards leaped back on to his feet. The noise was ear-splitting and unnatural. Flames burst from the flagstoned floor and licked the walls. Shadows writhed. The snow changed to falling ash.

"'Our Father, which art in Heaven . . .'" The heat was terrible. "'Hallowed be Thy name.'" Dean Richards felt searing pain and stared at his palms to see the flesh bubbling. *Help me, my God*, he cried inside, and aloud, "'Thy kingdom come, Thy will be done!'"

He tried to run. The smell of burning bodies filled his nostrils and he tripped, his head pounding against the flagstones. His lips blistered around his prayer. The blackness set in.

Lichfield. City of philosophers. From the pig-in-a-poke cottages and elegant residences of Dam Street, to the shady sanctuary of Minster Pool, to the dung-and-fruit scented market place, Lichfield was glorious in its Middle Englishness.

Nowhere was this more apparent than in The Close. While the city walls and its south and west gates were long gone, the elite nature of the cathedral's surrounding remained intact. Grand establishments housed the ecclesiastical and the educated in a square around the magnificent red-sandstone building.

The exception was the new breed of specialist who had taken up residence there. Stonemasons crawled about the western front of the cathedral like nibbling spiders. Hammers chinked. Chisels spilled red dust into the air.

On the afternoon of Monday, 22 October 1855, the strangest figures for miles around should have been the craftsmen at work on repairing the cathedral. But that changed the instant a troupe of five men came marching past the row of Tudor townhouses opposite the western front. Dressed in feathers and rags, they wore rings on their fingers and bells on their toes, and carried patchwork packs like colourful hunchbacks.

The stonemasons would later tell their families it was a change in the air which first alerted them to the mummers' presence. Hanging off precipices many feet up, the men detected a country aroma. Their minds turned to hay ricks, windfalls, smoking jam kettles and bonfires. A few even smiled before they craned their necks to look down.

Sitting on the steps to one side of the courtyard, a set of plans across his knee, Canon Nicholas Russell detected the scent and was reminded of long summers spent at his grand-mother's cottage in Alrewas. But then he squinted over at the mummer troupe, with their multi-hued ragged tunics and sooty faces, and had visions of ungodly rituals enacted on chalk hills, of painted faces, and runes cast, and unfettered sensuality. Nicholas clutched the plans to his chest and got up.

The troupe arrived at the foot of the steps. Each man wore a variation of the rags. One had fantastically blue eyes and an embroidered red cross around his neck. Nicholas shuddered at the sight; it had a bloody and bandaged look. The next grinned like an imbecile, showing fat white teeth. This man wore a pair of stitched donkey's ears on his head, and stood running what appeared to be a pin-on tail through his hands. A third man wore a tall black hat and was exceptionally thin. These three were peculiar in their own right, but it was the two figures to the fore of the group who disturbed Nicholas the most. One was a monster of a man with blackened eyes and green-painted skin to match his rags who wore a neck-lace of dead, dried things. The second was a boy of ten or so, wearing red horns and a doublet of scarlet rags.

"Good afternoon, gentlemen." Nicholas hated the quiver in his voice.

The man in green nodded. "Isn't it?" He inhaled deeply. "Lichfield in autumn. Reminds me of my childhood."

"You're a local man?" Nicholas eyed the weird fellow.

"Once upon a time. It probably takes a city as ghost-riddled as Lichfield to produce a man of my ilk." He glanced back at his men and they shrugged agreement.

Ghost-riddled? Nicholas tensed. Had the stonemasons been gossiping? Certainly he and his fellow canons had done every-thing in their power to refute the rumours, but the apparitions would insist on appearing to clergy and laymen alike.

The leader of the troupe leaned in. That smell of mouldering fruit and damp straw . . . Nicholas almost choked against it.

"Word was put our way concerning Dean Richards's recent incapacity."

Nicholas tried to process the statement. The man's flippancy grated. But before he could respond, the boy with the horns butted in.

"Want us to warm up them working folk, Mr Savage?" The boy produced a black velvet bag held by two sticks, almost identical to the collection purses used in the cathedral.

"Good idea, Thom. Go on now, fellas. Get us a crowd going."

The devil boy and the other three climbed the stairs between Nicholas and the man in green. Leaving their organic perfume in the air, the four strode over to the scaffolded west front.

Mr Savage, as the devil boy had referred to him, called after them. "Ask after the best ale house. One with lodgings." He arched a thick black eyebrow. "Some people need guidance. Without a strong hand, we're as lost as lambs. And there are always wolves on the prowl, hey, minister?" The man's shoulders shook in amusement. Tiny bells inside his clothing tinkled.

Nicholas folded the plans and slid them into a pocket of his cassock. "It is good to see a Lichfield son return to the fold. And now, if you will excuse me." He glanced pointedly up at the late afternoon sky. "The weather sickens."

He was about to hurry off when Mr Savage brought his huge green face closer. The man's breath smelled of freshly dug soil. His eyes shone blue-white.

"Dean Richards sent word that he wishes to see me. Be a good fellow and lead the way." His heavy brow bulged. "That's a demand, Canon Nicholas."

The Deanery was a red-brick Queen Anne mansion with tall chimneys and a central pediment. Ailen, the green man, imagined an interior dedicated to stoked fireplaces, plum pie and antique furnishings. Indeed, the house provided all of these things when a bustling housekeeper let them in – in spite of her clear alarm at Ailen's costume. The comforts of the house did not extend to the dean's bedroom, however. Following the faintly sanctimonious young canon across the threshold, Ailen was disappointed to find the room in semi-darkness and the air perfumed with lavender. Disappointed because he had hoped a strong-willed man like Dean Richards would not have taken ill after his fright.

"The Shakes," Ailen muttered under his breath.

Canon Nicholas glanced back. "Excuse me?"

Ailen shook his head. "Nothing."

A lamp burned low on the bedside cabinet. By its weak light, he saw eiderdowns piled high on a large bed, wall-mounted crucifixes, dried lavender arrangements – to soothe the nerves – and long tapestry curtains drawn tight to keep the cold out. Or something other.

Sound issued from beneath the eiderdowns. Muttered prayer – or, as Ailen understood it, just another form of incantation.

"Dean Richards?" said Nicholas.

The covers were thrown back. Dean Richards stared out, wild-eyed and with a halo of white hair about his head.

"Nicholas?" The Dean scrubbed his fists into his eyes. He blinked at Ailen, mole-like. "And you, friend? Are you phantom or mortal man?" A shiver visibly passed through the man and he hugged himself.

"Mortal, if in the guise of a handsome devil." Ailen grinned – which prompted the dean to clutch the eiderdowns up to his chin.

"Forgive my crass humour, Dean Richards. It comes of a good many years spent on tour with a mummers' troupe."

"Mummers?" The dean chewed the word over. "The archbishop's people mentioned a mummer. Pied Piper of the dead, they called him."

"Aye. That'd be on account of this." Reaching into his pack, Ailen pulled out a long metal pipe. Worked in silver and brass, the instrument appeared to be a cross between an oboe and a mechanical Chinese dragon. "I blow here." Ailen pointed to the reed-tipped tail. "Notes are produced here." He indicated a series of plated "gills" along the tail pipe. "I change pitch with these." Two wing sections coruscated where the pipe fattened at the body section. "And here is the mouth." He worked a series of nodules along the neck to exercise the metal jaw.

"So you are our Spirit Catcher?" Dean Richards relaxed his grip on the eiderdowns and sat up.

"What's a Spirit Catcher?" The canon's voice was laden with fear and judgement.

"The man who will cleanse our great cathedral of its unwelcome parishioners," said the dean, rifling through the drawer of a bedside cabinet. "Ah." He produced a purse and rested back against his pillows.

"Eight shillings and ninepence for the tall spirits. A crown apiece for the two girls." He arched an eyebrow. "Half up front." Loosening the string at the neck, he handed the purse to the canon. "Count it out please, Nicholas."

The canon faltered. Ailen knew it pained the pious young man to play any part in the transaction. After all, such talk of ghosts bore more in common with the earth spirits entertained in pagan rites than with Christian doctrine. But Ailen could see many things others could not, including the canon's desire to please his seniors and progress through the church hierarchy. He wasn't surprised when Nicholas kept his concerns private and dug around inside the purse.

Dean Richards gestured to a chair off in the shadows. "Sit with me a while, Spirit Catcher. Let me tell you what I know."

An hour later, the dean slipped back into his muttered prayer and strange hugging of the eiderdowns. Ailen stood up. Coins belonging to the church jangled in his pocket. He slid the dragon pipe back inside his pack and retrieved an envelope, which he presented to Nicholas.

"Arrowroot, garlic, lilac, mint, and mercury. Sprinkle the powder on the windowsills, the threshold and at the foot of the bed."

Nicholas looked as if Ailen had handed him the severed hand of a baby.

"I want nothing to do with your witchcraft!"

"Then the Shakes will continue to pollute the dean. Leave

him be or use this." He held up the envelope pointedly then laid it down on top of the bedside cabinet. "Your choice."

The King's Head, Bird Street, reputedly opened its doors in 1495 and had since served as a coaching inn, birthed the Staffordshire regiment, and acquired its fair share of ghosts over the centuries.

Approaching the building, Ailen saw a silver-blue orb flicker at a window on the third floor. Voices came to him – men readying themselves for battle, their muskets and pikes knocking against armour as they moved. He was struck by a thick bitumen stench, felt the dry heat of flames. A woman screamed inside the public house. But the sound did not belong to the living. Instead, the scream looped back on itself and then faded.

Unlike the activities in the cathedral which the dean had described, these hauntings were moments in time caught in the King's Head's ancient footings. Even the screaming kitchen maid who had perished in a fire was just a shade. He saw her as he stepped into the bar. Most would experience her movement past them as a brief sensation of cold. Closing the door at his back, Ailen watched her sweep the floor, heedless of the patrons in her path.

He was brought back to the land of the living by a blackened face looming in.

"Cutting it close. But the crowd's nice and eager. Here." Willy Bones, part-time exorcist, full-time Fool, shoved a pint of ale into Ailen's hand. "Quaff it quick. Our Saint's about to announce us."

Ailen sank a draught from the ale glass. The King's Head had a generous quota of patrons, all gathered around the edges of the room to allow for a makeshift stage. Thom's character, Little Devil, stood to the back alongside the anaemic Doctor, Naw Jones. Playing the part of Saint George, ex-clergyman Popule Brick faced the audience and bowed.

"Greeting, good patrons, and drunkards too, a merrysome Autumn eve to you.

"Our play today is fearsome bold, a tale of quandaries aeons old.

"I am Saint George—" A patriotic cry went up from the crowd. "I like to fight."

Here Willy leaped in to deliver the rhyme. "He smites Man, wyrd worm and ass alike."

Saint George crowed over the laughter and pointed at Willy.

"Lo, the Fool who pulls a tinkers cart, brays 'eey-ore', lifts his tail and f—"

Thom's Little Devil danced in then.

"Far and wide doth search the godly saint, to fight the bad – or those that ain't.

"But no good deed goes quite right, when the devil watches from the night."

Thom withdrew. To the crowd's delight, the Saint lunged at the Fool, wielding a squeezebox as a weapon. On the run, the Fool dashed over to Ailen, who offered up the mechanical dragon pipe. While the Saint played a jig on the squeezebox, the Fool brandished the dragon pipe. Steam belched from its jaws.

The audience "oohed" and "aahed" at the oddity. Willy the Fool made no attempt to play the pipe. Instead it was paraded as the worm mentioned in the verse – a puppet with gleaming scales and tick-tock inner workings.

Performing their ceremonial dance about the floor, the Saint succeeded in overpowering the dragon; Willy mimed the creature's death throes then tossed it back to Ailen, who caught the pipe and tucked it back into his pack.

Running over to Popule, Willy announced, "Saint George has slain the worm fast and true, and now my sword will do for you."

Willy stabbed the man in the belly with his finger. Popule howled and made a great show of staggering about the stage, to the general amusement of the spectators. At last, he collapsed and lay on his back.

Willy tugged on his donkey's ears.

"Oh, Lord, he's dead! Oh, me! Oh, my! Why'd that old windbag go and die?

"I'll have to face the Queen's cavaliers, and me not yet supped all my beers."

Ailen strode out on to the stage. He stopped opposite Willy, the crowd clearly enthralled by his bulk and appearance.

"Behold! The woodland son, the Jack o' the Green," exclaimed Willy, sinking to one knee. He clasped his hands, imploring, "Oh, sacred son, do not judge me by this bloody scene. Indeed the knight deserved to die." Willy pointed to his donkey's ears. "He was a greater ass than I."

Ailen held out his arms, the feathered sleeves of his tunic fanning out like wings.

"I cannot save this Christian son, who slayed my worm for sport and fun,

"But to save thee gross palaver, I'll do away with the cadaver.

"In my wyld wood where fairies dwell, I'll make his death a living hell!"

He swooped towards the onlookers, saw a flash of fear in their eyes accompanied by nervous smiles. At his back, Naw stepped forward, tall black hat exaggerating his height.

"At peace, Green Man, you know as I, all return to your wyld wood once they die."

Naw switched his attention to Willy.

"Doctor Sham. I alchemize stone into gold, heal the sick and lame,

"Help spirits rest, clear unwelcome guests and raise the dead again."

Willy the Fool butted in, "You raise the dead? Oh, say it's so, and to the gallows I'll not go."

Naw kneeled down beside Popule, who rolled his eyes and stuck out his tongue. Holding out his arms in appeal to Willy, Naw spoke,

"This holy knight I can revive at your behest,

"For one-tenth your mortal soul – and the devil take the rest."

Thom jigged from one foot to the other at the back of the stage. He hissed in a loud aside, "I've use for a foolish man, spread on toast like gooseberry jam."

The Doctor waved his fingers over the prone Saint.

"Wake up, wake up, our noble son, there's beer to sup now the play's done.

"Arise, Saint George, with magic black, so this young fool escapes the rack."

Popule staggered to his feet, reeling about the stage so that his audience leaned away, laughing and clutching their ale glasses tight. The Fool, the Doctor and the Saint joined hands and bowed as one. Thom began to circulate the pub, holding out his black velvet purse by its twin sticks and requesting mummers' alms. Meanwhile, Ailen stepped forward and bowed. Sweeping out his feathered arms again, he delivered the final verse.

"It's story's end, night's drawn in and we must bid farewell,

"To saints and fools and wyrd worms beneath our mummers' spell.

"If we have cheered your autumn eve, please spare a coin or two; And so we take our final bows and bid goodnight to you."

Ailen Savage knew it took a special breed of man to want to assist a Spirit Catcher. He had been born to it, his great-grandfather having originated the role. In the year 1754, as a young man fascinated by elemental folklore, Tam Savage had found a way to divine a restless spirit and capture it via a multi-metalled steam pipe. At a time when religion was in decline and science us providing the answer to many of life's mysteries, Tam Savage had chosen to work alongside the local vicar as a Spirit Catcher. Perfecting his skills and instruments, he had passed the knowledge down to Ailen's father, who in turn had passed it on to Ailen. Some argued it was a brutal business to hand on to a child. Ailen himself considered it no more dangerous than a life spent in Birmingham's factories or down Leicestershire's coal mines or taking a chisel to the worn-out heights of Lichfield's cathedral.

Less obvious were the reasons why the others joined him.

"I can see the science in your method," said the young canon, Nicholas. He hugged himself against the cool air, or the awesome sight of the cathedral veiled in early morning mist, Ailen wasn't sure which. "That pipe contraption of yours . . . It has a heathen design but the science is no doubt godly."

Nicholas lowered his voice. "You are a man of breeding. Why take up with a mummers' band?" He pointed ahead to the three men and the boy, dressed in costume and paint even at that hour.

"I'll set you straight, Canon, because you aren't a man to see past his own faith or social standing. Once, mind, and then no more will be said on it. Those men might be carved from God's arse-end, but they are still of his flesh. There's living and undead aplenty outside your great and glorious cathedral, and Willy, Thom, Naw and Pop have helped me separate the two more times than I care to remember. Take Willy there." Ailen nodded at the man wearing the donkey's ears. "He's a product of Lancashire and Cajun blood. Look past the paint and you'll see his features lean towards the exotic. Turns out Willy's mother couldn't take the Lancashire climate. Back home in her native Louisiana, she contracted typhoid fever – or became possessed, as Willy tells it. In the third week, she started to cut the flesh from her own bones. Willy lent himself out to every witch around – drawing water, mending what was broken, giving up food meant for his own mouth – all in a bid to learn the way to cast the demon out."

Ailen's eyes softened. "He didn't learn enough in time to save her. After his mother's death, Willy returned to Britain and put his skills as an exorcist to good use." He placed a heavy hand on the canon's shoulder. "The others have similar tales. We sniffed out the fear in each other – not fear of personal attack by the supernatural elements we encounter, but fear that we would not save others from those same dangers."

Nicholas frowned. He took time over his words, as if adding to a stack of cards. "Please understand, Mr Savage. Dean Richards is in a vulnerable state and our cathedral . . . it houses some remarkable treasures."

"And you think we may find those too great a temptation to pass over, being the lowly vagabonds that we are?"

"Not you, Mr Savage. You are an honest Lichfield son, no doubt. But the men you travel with are a coarser breed. By your own admission, one is part-negro—"

Ailen drew himself up. In that instant, he appeared less man than something gnarled and grown tall over hundreds of years. "Do not judge a man by his skin!" he thundered. The canon flinched as the mummer moved in close. "The very fact that spirits have survived beyond death and haunt your cathedral should be enough to illustrate our worth beyond the boundaries of flesh."

A flicker of confusion crossed Nicholas's face.

They were interrupted by Naw, materialized through the mist. He smiled, an expression that exaggerated his skeletal appearance.

"Mr Savage does love a good debate on subjects of a spiritual and religious nature. But he don't always appreciate the force of his vigour." Naw's soft Welsh lilt instantly humanized him.

"Of course. It is good and right for a man to exercise his intellect. But my apologies, sir, we have not been introduced properly. I am Canon Nicholas Russell."

Naw shook his hand. "Naw Jones of Cardiff. Mummer, spiritualist, historian." He laughed kindly. "Please do not hold the latter against me."

Nicholas looked newly floored by Naw's generous spirit and evident education. Ailen almost felt sorry for the clergyman. He consulted a small brass pocket watch hidden amongst his tunic rags. "What time do the stonemasons start work?"

"At eight," replied Nicholas.

"We have an hour." Ailen pointed at the bunch of keys the canon carried. "Please accompany us inside. I will need to hear all the details you can offer on what has occurred within." He slapped Naw on the back. "And, hopefully, our historian here can go some way to explaining why."

"... very little in the way of restoration until the architect James Wyatt undertook repairs late last century. Wyatt's idea was to create a church within the cathedral – a bullish idea to my mind – which saw the interior whitewashed, the arches of the choir filled in, the High Altar removed and seating installed right through to the Lady Chapel." Nicholas held up his hands, indicating the magnificent restored interior. "Mr Scott has repaired this great building with flair and sensitivity."

"It is certainly soul-rich," murmured Naw, intent on the device he held in his palm.

The tan leather box housed a circular device with a flickering hand – not dissimilar to a compass, thought Nicholas, distracted from his efforts to demonstrate his superior knowledge of the cathedral's architectural history.

"And that device suggests as much?" He stared at it quizzically. The hand was a shard of purple crystal.

"Amethyst." Naw tapped the glass cover over the dial. "Wards off danger while protecting mental and psychic clarity." Circling slowly on the spot, he cast a long thin shadow.

"Have you located the source of the apparitions?" Nicholas felt the weight of the cathedral keys at his belt.

"The source?" Naw pointed down. "We're standing on it. One thousand Christians murdered on this spot during the Roman occupation. And what about the three spires above us – coincidental, or in homage to the three martyred kings buried at Borrowcop Hill?"

"Nothing but folklore!"

"So their prominence on the city seal is pure fancy?" Naw eyed his ghost compass intently.

Nicholas blustered, "I'm simply saying, a town as rich in history as Lichfield is bound to have an abundance of pagan lore and country legends."

"And the shrine?" Naw pointed to the far end of the nave and the High Altar with its decorative apse. "Saint Chad died in 672. But while he was originally interred here in the cathedral, the Reformation saw his bones travel as far as France and return at last, having acquired a third thigh bone. Or so legend has it." Naw inclined his head respectfully. "Yet still you believe, Canon Nicholas."

The boy stood to the fore of the south-east aisle. A bird fluttered among the ceiling arches. Dawn lent the stained glass windows a subtle glow.

"Thom?" Ailen approached slowly. The lad was so still he could have passed for a statue. He appeared absorbed in study of a large white marble monument depicting two young girls at rest in one another's arms.

"I'm not sure about this spot, Mr Savage. I think it might be colder here." Thom cocked his head. "Are the girls' bodies buried beneath?"

"Dean Richards said not. It's just a monument. Commissioned when a mother lost both her daughters and husband, who was a clergyman, inside three years." Ailen laid a hand on the cool stone of the eldest sister's forehead. A shooting pain lanced through his arm and he pulled away.

"You all right, Mr Savage?"

"Yes . . . yes, Thom. Thank you." He cradled his arm. The pain subsided.

"I touched the stone before you came and wasn't hurt." Thom sucked his lower lip.

"Could be the children sense a kinship with you. Although—" Ailen stared at the monument, half-expecting the two sisters to open their eyes and stare back. "Objects can attract and house ghosts. I'm suspicious that the sympathetic rendering of the two dead girls has attracted a poltergeist. They are drawn to the young."

"Aye. And I remember how difficult it is to trap them buggers."

Ailen smiled and nodded. "Difficult, not impossible. But I may need to use you as bait."

Thom and Naw busied themselves salting the doorways; the windows were adequately protected by their ecclesiastical stained glass depicting Saint Chad and other holy entities. Meanwhile, the sounds of stone being chiselled and idle banter filtered in from outside. The stonemasons had started work

"If you are afraid of ghosts you might want to step outside so we can close the salt line behind you."

Nicholas found he was being addressed by the mummer Knight – or Popule as the boy called him. The man had impossibly blue eyes.

"I'm not afraid," the canon lied.

"Should be." Popule dragged down his tunic at the neck, revealing a web of scar tissue across his collarbones. "Poltergeist pinned me to the floor of my church in Ashbourne. Poured blazing lamp oil all over my chest." He pushed up his left sleeve. His arm was scarred by healed burns and bites. "Ghosts lash out when provoked. They learn to throw a punch . . . or grow teeth."

"You are a clergyman?" Nicholas wasn't sure whether to find the fact reassuring or disturbing.

"*Was*." Popule put down his pack and undid the string at the neck. He talked as he retrieved a number of items. "Once the spirits had laid their marks on me I was lost to the Shakes. Know what that is?"

Nicholas thought about Dean Richards, cocooned in eiderdowns. "I think I do."

"I pray you never experience it yourself and know for certain. Even if you can find a Spirit Catcher to doctor you, the sickness never truly leaves your soul. It's always hovering, just below the surface." Popule glanced up. Surrounded by a weird cornucopia of objects, he looked like a warlock from a romantic painting. Nicholas recognized sticks of chalk, a small brass bowl, a bunch of lavender, smelling salts and a tinder box. Less familiar was a long belt fitted with cartridges of some white mineral and the gun which accompanied it.

Popule picked up the weapon and appeared to weigh it in his hand. It was a beautiful object, thought Nicholas, remembering the rusty flintlock his grandfather had used to shoot rabbits on the family estate. Popule's gun had a long silver barrel, at least a foot and a half in length, and spiralled like a hazel branch. The loading mechanism was a traditional cylinder, but larger. The hammer and trigger were cast from an intensely black metal, the stock carved from exotic deep red hardwood. Symbols were inlaid in brass wire along it; they struck Nicholas as Arabic in origin.

The ex-clergyman sensed his interest. "A revolver. A few years ago, I was fortunate enough to be able to discuss my requirements with a visiting American, Mr Samuel Colt. He was able to adapt his brand new design to fit my specialist needs. Here . . ." Popule picked up the gun and spun the barrel. "The cylinder revolves to align the next chamber and round with the hammer and barrel. Shoots cartridges of solid rock salt. I can fire the salt as a bullet, or if I close this small grid across the muzzle then the salt splinters and scatters. See?"

Nicholas flinched as Popule pointed the gun at his face. He forced himself to stare down the capped barrel.

"Salting the doorways keeps the spirits where we want them. Inside." Popule's strange blue eyes twinkled. "And this revolver helps stun them if need be. Ghosts of the sort you have here are not inclined to come quietly." He gave his weapon an affectionate pat and slid it into a holster at his waist, the long barrel running the length of his thigh. He slung the cartridge belt over his head and slid one arm through.

"If you are staying – and in these circumstances it's always good to have a man of God not as lapsed as I – then you'd better open your mind to things the church doesn't care for." He put one hand to the side of his mouth, shouting, "Seal the doors! The canon's staying put." Kneeling, he picked up the chalk, appeared to examine the patterns of light on the flagstones and began to draw.

It started out this way. Men moved stones set in place for hundreds of years, with no mind to the consequences. Sometimes a structure was depleted of spiritual energy and alterations left the ground sleeping. But for a building as entrenched in bloody history as Lichfield Cathedral, the ghosts' awakening was inevitable. Of course the disturbances could have been avoided with the right consecrations and herbal homages buried beneath the dirt at ten-foot intervals around the building's exterior. Fortunately for a Spirit Catcher such as Ailen, these rudimentary ghost traps were not common knowledge – which meant there was a profit to be made from tidying up after enthusiastic architects.

Two hours in and the chalked traps were set. The mid-morning sun shone in weakly at the high windows. Dust speckled the air. Stonemasons could be heard at work on the Gothic façade. Behind the scaffolds, row on row of ancient kings were being restored to their plinths.

Inside the cathedral, Ailen called his men to order and asked, "Canon, would you say a prayer?"

The mummers formed a circle and bowed their heads. Nicholas started to speak, the tremor in his voice betraying his nervousness.

Ailen kept his gaze on his surroundings. He caught flickers of motion from the corners of his eyes. Three figures, all exceptionally tall – and twisting up from the floor near the South Transept. Each wore something on its head – a crown? The figures disappeared when he tried to focus.

Smaller shadows danced about the walls – hundreds of them, layering over one another. The floor was patterned with them, too. Ailen knew that, for all their numbers, these were harmless shades.

"See them, Mr Savage?" Despite his devil garb, there was still innocence in Thom's eyes.

"I see them, Thom." Ailen kept his voice low so as not to interrupt Nicholas. Prayer niggled restless spirits. Used in isolation, it was a slow, unreliable method of exorcism. Combine prayer with psychic weaponry and the fight became quicker if potentially messier.

The boy swallowed and stared down the length of the nave. "We've got to clear them all?"

"No, lad. Most are harmless. We've got three ghosts to parcel up. Powerful ones. And then there's the poltergeist." Ailen pointed a finger upwards. "I think we have its attention."

Twenty or so prayer books levitated overhead. Canon Nicholas's prayer petered out.

"Everyone back up slowly." Ailen led by example, his dragon pipe trained on the floating books.

The circle of men widened.

With a tremendous crack of leather spines, the books

began spitting out their pages. A few stayed intact and careered down like black hailstones. Ailen saw Nicholas receive a cut to one eyebrow. The wound bled into the canon's eye; he dabbed at it with a handkerchief and mopped his glistening brow with a sleeve. Other books aimed themselves at Popule and Thom. The ex-clergyman fired his revolver. Slugs of rock salt punched through the books, the blast holes giving off smoke.

"I take it your prayer woke the blighter." Willy winked at Nicholas. "You all right there, friend?"

Nicholas nodded. He looked deathly pale, though.

All the books had fallen. Except for the sounds of the men working outside, the cathedral was silent.

"Which direction next?" Ailen kept his pipe close.

Naw consulted his compass. He pointed south-east. "Originated at The Sleeping Children monument. But the reading is south-west now, vestibule most likely. Also—" The historian wheeled around, checking the coordinates. "I have a second reading from the South Transept."

Ailen nodded. He had a partial view of the South Transept, a shaded arm of the cathedral at that hour.

"Tell me, Canon. What do you see in those shadows?"

The canon forced his gaze in that direction. He cocked his head.

"I see nothing."

"Good. Then you won't mind assisting Popule and Naw in investigating that quadrant."

"Oh. Oh, I see. Do I need to be armed?" asked the young man tensely.

Popule brought two fingers to his lips, kissed them and pressed them to the cross around his neck. "Faith, Canon. All the weaponry you need."

Nicholas thought he knew the cathedral intimately, but the South Transept's atmosphere seemed queer today while its shadows deepened.

"See them now, Canon?" Popule pointed to the far end of

the transept. "Blur your eyes and stare ahead. Don't try to look at them directly. They'll disappear."

Nicholas played with the keys at his belt. He wanted to call the mummers madmen and demand they leave that sacred house. But then he remembered the dean, all tucked in on himself against some unseen foe. Nicholas slit his eyes and focused ahead.

Three silhouettes came into focus, just as if they had moved to stand immediately behind him when he was looking in a mirror. The figures were wraith-thin and stooped. They wore long robes, cloaks, and spiky crowns.

"Still not scared?" Popule murmured in an aside.

Heart drumming, Nicholas shifted his focus to the ex-clergyman. Popule rested his revolver against one shoulder. His strange blue eyes coruscated.

Willy led the way and Ailen let him, knowing that Willy's failure to save his possessed mother burdened him with a lifetime's worth of guilt. Sometimes Ailen wondered if all Willy's travelling pack contained was guilt – great sticky clumps of the stuff. Which was why the man had to lead the way now, face the demon first, and strive eternally for relief from that oppression.

"What have we got, Willy?" Ailen brought up the rear, followed noiselessly by Thom. He liked to know the kid was with him. It gave him courage as the antechamber threatened to seal them in.

"Angry raggedy sprite. You see the shadows?"

Ailen looked. The shadows cast by the rippled stone of the numerous arches spiked as they passed. Bone fingers stretching.

"Air too. You get a lungful of that sulphur?"

Ailen grimaced. "One of the least appealing aspects of our job." He glanced back at Thom.

"What do you see, lad?"

Colours danced in Thom's wide eyes. "It's a cross one, Mr Savage. I see red mist coming off the stones. Waves of it."

"Aye." Ailen watched the mist tendril out. "What's at the end there?"

"Chapter House," answered Willy over his shoulder.

"A dead end."

"Not literally, I hope." Willy showed his teeth. He stepped aside. "You going to pipe the nasty inside?"

Ailen nodded. "Get ready to join in the song, Willy."

Thom stuck close, twitchy and bright-eyed. He clutched a handful of lavender stems from Naw's stock for protection.

Ailen put the mouthpiece of the dragon pipe between his lips. A small sighting lens was mounted halfway down the body; Ailen squeezed one eye shut and peered through it with the other. The mist transmogrified into clawing, fleshless arms. A hideous face loomed amongst the tangle of limbs.

"Angry is an understatement." He concertinaed out the wing sections of the pipe and sounded his first note. Long and low, a musical whisper.

Something shifted in the atmosphere. Where the poltergeist had only been playing with them before, now it began to realize these men posed a threat. The face in the mist broke open, revealing spindly teeth. Ailen didn't falter. Playing a second note, he kept the mist inches from their faces. His grandfather had calibrated the pipe at a frequency too seductive for the spirit to ignore. The men moved through the narrow arched doorway to the Chapter House and the mist followed.

"Is that the last of it?" Willy pushed back his sleeves. "All right then. I'm going to block us in." He stood in the narrow arch, raised his arms sideways and touched the stone to either side of him. He closed his eyes. "Nasty raging thing, this one. Don't leave me too long."

"I won't." Ailen flexed his large fingers around the winged extension of the pipe. Thom stared around the room, enthralled.

Willy began to chant – weird, ancient, dangerous words in the language of the dead Ailen did not want to understand. Instead he played the long, slow notes on his dragon pipe and walked in a circle around the sigil chalked on to the floor.

The mist altered, becoming more substantial and moving in

ripples. As Ailen played, a fat tendril oozed out from the wall, drawn to him. It nosed at the mouth of the dragon pipe like a cat sniffing an offered morsel. Ailen continued to weave a circle around the sigil while Thom stayed quiet nearby and Willy kept up his peculiar chant. Slowly, doing his level best not to alarm the spirit, Ailen moved the fingers of one hand on to the brass nodules along the neck of the pipe. Steam escaped the dragon pipe's opening jaws.

Ailen crushed his fingers around the neck of the pipe and the jaws slammed shut. The tendril lashed from side to side, its tip covered in suckers. Willy's voice faltered, but he struggled on, his face crumpled in pain.

Running over, Thom produced Popule's smelling salts and waved them under the man's nose. Willy showed the whites of his eyes, but managed to refocus.

Ailen touched the tip of his pipe to the floor sigil, attaching the tendril to it. He began to trace out the design with his foot-steps, and the poltergeist was forced to follow, tethered to the embroidery of lines.

It was the cry of a wounded man from the other side of the cathedral which broke the spell. The misty poltergeist quivered and reared, tearing free from the sigil. A heatwave burst around the walls, prompting Willy to utter his own cry and collapse, knocking the smelling salts out of Thom's hand. The bottle shattered on impact with the flagstones.

Naw fell back into Nicholas's arms, leaving a ghost warrior's spear slick with blood. A tremendous crack resounded; Nicholas saw a slug of rock salt punch in the back of the ghost's head. The apparition flickered and was snuffed out.

More warriors solidified out of the walls. Their flesh was crisp and black, their weapons large and brutal. A few carried swords. Most wielded axes, spears and short blades.

"What are these devils?" cried Nicholas. Lowering Naw to the floor, the canon brushed away blood from his own nicked eyebrow and tried to focus.

"Devils is the right word for them! Get Naw over to the sigil, stand inside its circle and quote your Bible." Popule flipped the grid over the muzzle of his revolver and fired. Plumes of salt exploded into the air; the warriors faded as it dusted down on them. Seconds later, they were whole again.

Fresh blood trickled from Nicholas's eyebrow. Fear threatened to liquefy his bones as he dragged Naw on to the sigil, leaving a glossy red trail behind. His conscience rebelled as he thought about the occult symbols chalked beneath his feet. But he remembered Popule's words about having to open his mind. Seeing the ex-clergyman dodge a tremendous hammer blow from one warrior, he began to recite.

"'In you, O Lord, I have taken refuge; let me never be put to shame.'"

Popule fired off more cartridges. A wave of warriors went up in flames, but still more kept materializing out of the walls.

"'Deliver me in your righteousness. Turn your ear to me.'"

Spectres lunged in Nicholas's direction but backed away when they struck the circumference of the sigil. Death's stink was in the air.

"Why haven't the other three spirits moved?" he called between snippets of scripture, pointing at the colossal wraiths visible under the large stained glass window.

It was Naw who answered, gulping in great lungfuls of air. "The three Christian kings, martyred in Lichfield in the time of the heathen Emperor Diocletian. Their burial ground is at Borrowcop."

"But that's just a legend!"

"Yet here they are," panted Naw.

"But why are their spirits here and why do these demon warriors attack?"

Ghosts charged at the sigil. Nicholas gabbled a fresh section of a psalm; the warriors' weapons struck the air overhead like hammers brought down upon an anvil. In an opposite corner of the South Transept, Popule shot a couple clean through with his salt revolver.

"The warriors protect their lords, who are linked to this site by their own spilled blood." Naw let out a sigh. "I'm blacking out, boyo. Help Popule fight the good fight." The Welshman's eyes rolled back and he slumped unconscious.

The spirit evaporated the instant Willy lost his hold on the sides of the archway.

Ailen ran over to his friend, who collapsed into his arms. He lowered Willy to the floor. Thom worried at the man's tunic collar, loosening it.

Ailen stepped away. "Check his hands," he said.

Thom turned Willy's hands palm up. They were burned red-raw.

"Stay here, Willy. Thom and I can see to the devil."

"Not in a month of Sundays." Willy sucked air through his teeth and fought his way to standing. "We've spooked the blighter now. You're going to need me to chant, to help chain it. First, though, you're going to need to coax the flibbertigibbet out of its hiding place—"

Ailen glanced at Thom. "The poltergeist likes you. I need you to lure it out." He placed a hand on the boy's shoulder. "Don't worry. It can burn down the cathedral about our ears but it can't harm you."

"Someone has been harmed, though. We heard the cry." Thom looked pained. "It sounded like Naw."

Ailen pointed through the doorway. "Let's deal with the ghost first. Then we can help our man."

They exited the vestibule to find the sun had gone in. The nave was cavernous and very dark. From the south side of the building came the crash of swords, blasts of fire from Popule's revolver and the young canon's quivering prayer.

"On second thoughts, I'm going to help Naw and the others first." Ailen pointed in the direction of The Sleeping Children monument. "I know where to find you."

Ailen arrived in the South Transept to see Popule fire off a salt spray and the five ghost warriors who had him cornered fade at their edges. He looked for the canon and found him muttering prayers and gone wild about the eyes. Naw bled at his feet.

The sigil provided them with a circle of protection, but if Popule and Ailen were to catch the spirits, they would need the trap to be empty.

"Canon!" he shouted, avoiding the arc of a ghost's axe by bending low. "I need you to exit the sigil if we're going to tie the spirits down."

"But they'll destroy us the instant we step off," answered Nicholas, close to tears.

Ailen chuckled. "How soon you adopt our wicked pagan ways, Canon." Again, he avoided the fall of the axe and, seconds later, the huge sword that was swung towards his throat. "Have faith in your own spells," he called. "Prayer will keep the ghosts at bay long enough."

The canon looked doubtful. Ailen had no choice but to trust that the man would exit the sigil in time, and hopefully drag Naw out too. Charging towards Popule like a bull elephant, Ailen cried, "I'm going to pipe them in. Salt ain't enough. These spirits are too ancient and justified."

Justified in misunderstanding the alterations to the building and wanting to keep their deathbed intact, he thought as he ran through the salt mist, tasting it on his lips. Figures came at him, their burned flesh, whited eyes and flashing weapons seemingly birthed from Hell. Ailen fought their blows with bursts of notes from his dragon pipe. Ahead, the three kings flickered beneath the stained glass window. Their crowns were thorny, their bodies elongated like men put to the rack. Ailen didn't need them to speak to sense the tremendous anger issuing from them. He would have liked to reason with the three ancients – reassure them that the stonemasons were repairing, not destroying. But he knew enough about ghosts to understand they were capable of raw emotion but otherwise inflexible.

His tune quickened as he approached the kings. Images smoked in his mind – hundreds slaughtered by Roman hands, crowns falling into pools of blood. The noise of battle tenderized his brain. Still he played, steam spilling from the mouth of the instrument. The images broke, spraying up pain and torn

flesh and death – so much death. The faces of the kings
distorted. Their bodies leaned towards him, drawn to the pipe.
Thinner and thinner they stretched, as if hypnotized. In rapid
snaps, the dragon pipe's jaw caught each by a thread.

Ailen walked backwards, towing the spirits in the direction
of the sigil. He sensed shadows lunge for him, heard the explo-
sion of salt in the air and knew Popule was keeping the warriors
at bay. The kings, meanwhile, became trailing ether. Ailen
didn't look away for a moment but kept on stepping backwards until he saw the chalked line of the sigil underfoot. He
heard the canon chanting his Bible passages a few feet away;
all he could do was trust in the man to have left sanctuary and
taken Naw with him. Stepping to the edge of the sigil, he
twisted at the waist, cast out over the chalked circle and
released the jaw of the pipe.

It took only seconds for the kings' spirits to interweave on
top of the weird symbols, like stitches in time. The instant
their masters were gone, the ghost warriors dissolved.
Returned to history.

Ailen nodded at Popule, who returned the gesture. Nearby,
Canon Nicholas hugged Naw. His face streaked with blood
and tears, the priest's eyes danced about the walls and he kept
up his muttering. *The Shakes*, thought Ailen.

He would tend to the young man later. First he had a poltergeist to catch.

A distant spectator could be forgiven for mistaking the two
young girls in nightgowns and the boy in mummer's garb for
the best of friends. Ailen, though, knew the girls owed their
manifestation to a malevolent spirit. Once upon a time he
had been interested in the origins of such entities, had studied
papers by the great spiritualists of the modern age. It was
Willy who had convinced him that there was no reasoning
with a poltergeist, no explanation which would aid his understanding or his empathy. There was only the squatting toad of
a spirit inside its chosen object, ready to scare or taunt or
main on a whim.

Yet seeing Thom conversing with the ghost girls suggested a softer, more human presence. Ailen knew that was a lie. He joined Willy in the shadows.

"The others alive?" Willy nodded sharply in the direction of the South Transept.

"Naw's wounded. Canon's got the Shakes. Popule is in one piece."

Willy glanced up. "Beautiful building, this. Shame it's built on a field of the dead." He sucked his gums against the pain of his burned hands and stared back over at Thom. "Seems almost a shame to interrupt them."

"Aye. If they were what they seem." Ailen slipped the macabre necklace from around his neck. It was one of Willy's voodoo creations, made up of dead beetles, lambs' wool, chicken claws and the dried remains of mice. He pointed at the apparitions of the two girls. "We both know poltergeists love dead things."

He rattled the necklace. The girls moved on to all fours, shoulders hunching, cocking their heads one way then the other. Hanging the necklace off his belt, Ailen adjusted his grip on his dragon pipe. He muttered: "I could use a little salt in the atmosphere."

A hand patted his shoulder. Popule's. The man's eyes shone crystal blue; the soot covering his face was streaked by sweat.

Popule fed a fresh cartridge into his revolver and spun the barrel shut. Ailen was glad of the backup as he stepped out of the shadows.

"You all right there, Thom?"

"They're very sad, Mr Savage," he replied. Ailen felt the familiar twinge of regret not to be recognized as anything more than the boy's employee. But his own feelings were secondary to the boy's safety.

"The real sisters are buried miles away, Thom. At peace, let's hope. Our poltergeist here likes the way their monument looks and has bedded down there. Now I want you to tell your friend it has the choice to leave or we can exorcise it."

Thom bit his bottom lip. "All right." He turned back to the girls, who had crawled close, their opaque white eyes rolling.

As Thom spoke to them, Ailen felt the atmosphere still like the surface of a millpond. When the ghost girls started to fade, he felt a tinge of relief. Had Thom really talked the poltergeist into leaving? *Wonderful, kind, accident-prone Thom.*

A wall of flames rolled around them in seconds, firing off a heatwave. Both girls opened their mouths unnaturally wide and the screams of Lichfield's martyred issued forth. Ailen steeled himself against the noise as Thom backed away.

The poltergeist had no intention of losing its new friend. The girls' heads morphed into a mess of silvery, mouth-tipped tentacles while the bodies remained separate. It crawled towards Thom, a crablike Medusa.

"Get away, Thom." Ailen stepped between the boy and the poltergeist, causing it to rear up on its back limbs, tentacles hissing. "Start chanting, Willy! Popule . . . keep the air full of salt!" he demanded, and put his lips to the reed of the dragon pipe.

Rock salt burst overhead like fireworks and Ailen began to play. The poltergeist tried to sink back into its marble tomb. It tugged at itself as if attempting to prise itself free from thick mud. Ailen quickened his tune and bit out at the spirit with the steaming jaw of the dragon pipe. The poltergeist arched away, a serpentine movement at odds with its crabbed lower limbs. Seconds later, it had scrabbled around to the opposite side of the chalk sigil marked out on the flagstones.

Wind blew in – red hot and scented with decay. Willy's chanting grew weaker; Ailen suspected the man's palms were freshly aflame. Blinking against the ash and snow whipped up by the vicious spirit alongside Popule's salt sprays, he fought to put one foot in front of the other. Blood trickled from his ears, his nose. Ailen pressed on against the tremendous volume of suffering and the searing heat of the funeral pyre from many centuries before. One thought gave him strength – some ghosts stay to ease the agonies of those left behind while others stay to torment those who live on. Unlike Thom, the poltergeist belonged to the latter category and needed to be put back among the demons.

Ailen ran the last few steps, lungs baking against his ribs. He grasped the neck of his dragon pipe, burned the tips of his fingers on the glowing nodules and clamped the steaming jaw around one misty tentacle. The poltergeist writhed, but Ailen held fast this time. Hearing Willy's voice harden, those ancient, occult words seeming to pepper the poltergeist's surface like hot coals, Ailen moved to the sigil's edge.

"I make you an offering. Pieces of death for peace inside this hallowed hall." Retrieving the voodoo necklace from his belt, he tossed the offering into the chalked circle. Arching at the spine, he cast out with the dragon pipe and released the jaw.

The poltergeist streamed into the sigil, a bolt of silver ether. Writhing and whipping against its bonds, it found itself dragged down over the symbols, one tentacle at a time. As the last thread of it was engulfed, the screams of the martyred ceased. The wall of flame around the men brightened then went out.

A month passed before the large man came to call at The Deanery. Mrs Rook the housekeeper would later describe the pains she was put to, trying to place the gentleman. His suit was of cheap cloth but cut well enough, while a starched collar hugged his neck. But the face – a mask of steel with scars aplenty!

The man's voice betrayed him. Nicholas recognized its deep tone from his place before the fire and on instinct gripped the blanket tucked over his legs. He forced himself to let go and call, "Mrs Rook! Show Mr Savage in. He and I have business."

Nicholas heard the housekeeper falter, perhaps afraid of the name. But then she must have ushered in their visitor because the front door closed and heavy footsteps sounded across the hallway.

A man like Ailen Savage didn't wait to be shown the way. He materialized in the doorway of the sitting room, blocking out what lay beyond.

"Canon Nicholas."

"Mr Savage. Come in, do. Sit by the fire. Mrs Rook says the weather is unseasonably bitter."

"I won't stay long." The man approached the hearth none-theless and stood before it, arms crossed, his face looking more weathered in its light. "I didn't call earlier as I was helping Naw get back on his feet. I see that you too have been nursed back to health," he said after a few moments.

"Dean Richards has gone to the seaside to continue his recovery. Very kindly, he installed me in the house under the care of Mrs Rook until his return."

Ailen's lips curved. "Seems you and the Dean had use for those herbs I gave you after all."

Nicholas shifted in his seat. "If you are asking if my mind has been opened up to the existence of the supernatural, and to magick worked outside the power of prayer, then the answer is yes, Mr Savage. And, yes, the spirits have left their mark on me." He touched a finger to the fresh scar in one eyebrow, trying to control the tremors in his hand. When the man oppo-site him nodded gravely, Nicholas knew he understood that the true scar lay inside.

Keen to change the emphasis of their conversation, he asked, "How did you dispose of the remains of the spirits?" Nicholas's mind had buckled in the aftershock of events. Glimpses of them came to him occasionally – the cathe-dral's fixtures sparkling with salt as if in a new Ice Age . . . Naw collapsed at his feet . . . the air laced with the stench of burning.

Mr Savage kept up his unwavering stare. "We washed the sigils away with holy water. Helps to have an ex-man of the cloth in the form of Popule. He blessed a good few buckets' worth and we baptised God's house anew."

"Oh. Oh, I see." Nicholas liked the sound of the cathedral being newly sanctified, even if at the hands of one of the mummers' troupe. He retrieved the package tucked in beside him for safekeeping.

"The second half of your fee, Mr Savage. And thank you."

Washed clean of rags and soot, the chief mummer looked even more intimidating. His large hand took the package and pocketed it.

"You aren't wearing your costume. Has the mumming season ended?" asked the canon, unsure how to close the conversation.

The man dipped his great head. When he glanced up, tears glistened in his eyes.

"Anniversary of my son's death. I like to clean myself up once a year, to pay my respects at his grave."

"I am sincerely sorry to hear of his passing. May the Lord keep him." Nicholas felt a twist of sorrow in his gut for this strange giant of a man.

"He ain't ready for the Lord yet," said Mr Savage. He shook back his shoulders, shrugging off the mantle of mourning.

Nicholas peered quizzically at his guest. But the mummer seemed all talked out. He walked away and filled the doorway once more.

"Goodbye, Canon Nicholas."

"Goodbye, Mr Savage."

Heavy footsteps crossed the hall. The canon heard the front door open and felt a blast of cold air across his exposed skin. Seconds later, the door slammed to.

Outside the evening air was sharp and pure. The cathedral loomed before the Spirit Catcher like a rock of ages. Sculptures burgeoned. Stained glass burned like jewels, lit by internal light. Lichfield slumbered all around.

"Come now, Thom. Let's go and meet the others," said Ailen to the ghost boy at his side.

"Yes, Mr Savage," Thom replied.

Together, father and son stepped out into the night.

Collect Call

Sarah Pinborough

In the end, there was only one person Lee could call. It was, after all, the only number he knew by heart.

He gave it to the operator and waited for the connection to be made. The line crackled. He tapped his fingers on the worn surface of the phone booth wall and breathed into the handset as the line rang. It pealed out to the point where Lee was beginning to think it would just be his luck that today of all days there was no one home, when finally someone picked up.

"Hello?"

"Hello, sir, we have a Lee Moseby on the line. Will you accept the charges?"

A pause.

"Yes."

"Go ahead, sir."

The line cleared as the operator clicked off, taking the unpleasantly sharp crackling sounds with her.

"Dad?"

"Lee?"

Another pause. This time caused by his own awkwardness. It had been a long time.

"Look, this sounds stupid, but I'm at this phone box in the middle of—" he looked out at the hick town that crept into life on the other side of the dusty road "—nowhere, and I – well – I couldn't think of who else to call."

"Do you need me to come and pick you up?"

"Yes," Lee said, surprised to find how relieved he felt. "Yes, please."

"Stay by the phone, son," his dad said, as if Lee were a teen-ager again. "I'll be there before it gets dark."

"Thanks. Look, I know—" A crackling dead tone that made his ears buzz cut him off suddenly, and he hung up. His dad clearly had at the other end.

It was a hot day and the booth was like a sauna. He pushed the door open, the squeal of its hinges loud in the quiet after-noon, and stood by the roadside. He guessed he'd been lucky the phone had worked at all. Despite the heat and the still air, he wasn't thirsty. He should have been – it felt like he'd been walking all day – but his mouth was moist. He wondered about the time and glanced down at his wrist, but his ever-dependable Timex wasn't there, just the tan line, built up nicely on the golf course, outlining its ghost.

No watch, no phone, and no wallet. Thank God for Dad. Thank God for the days of actually remembering numbers instead of storing them into BlackBerrys or iPhones or what-ever the next big thing was. He looked back at that empty space on his wrist. He never took his watch off.

A short burst of wind gusted from across the street and he looked up. Although the sun was still relatively high in the desert sky, dark shadows were stretching out lazily between the tired, abandoned buildings whose glass eyes glinted at him. He hadn't seen a town sign on his walk in, and he wondered if maybe it had been blown away in a sand storm. A lot of the road had been hidden by dust blasted across it and there had been no tyre tracks at all that he could recall.

The dead buildings were still in relatively good condition. Had this place been a salt mining outpost? It might not be the largest of towns but even from where he was, on the other side of the wide road, he could make out streets that went quite far back, and he was sure that one of those signs read "Diner", although his eyesight wasn't what it used to be. It was a garish shopfront, at any rate, with what looked like a Betty Boop-style cartoon woman running down one side. Even under the thick layer of filth her red dress was visible.

His eyes ran over the outlines of each store and house. There was a lot of dirt. The sidewalks were lost. Most of the buildings were a uniform brown as if they really had grown out of the desert earth rather than been built, in different-coloured wooden façades, by the hand of man. The winds must blow strong through here to get that much grime embedded. Either that or the town had been empty for so long that the sand had simply claimed it, inch by inch.

The sun beat on the back of his neck as he squinted. He'd burn if he wasn't careful. He was probably burned already. Some of those shadows across the way were really quite dark. It might be cooler over there, he decided. He'd still be able to see the road and he wouldn't burn. He glanced up. The sun had moved another few inches across its playground of the sky. How long had he been looking at the ghost town? No more than ten minutes, surely? He glanced down at the space on his wrist with mild irritation. He never took his watch off. It bothered him that he wasn't wearing it.

A breeze gusted sand across his shoes and he took the first step on to the road. Something scurried in the shadows on the other side. He paused, suddenly tense. What had that been? A piece of garbage, perhaps? Probably a rodent of some kind. He looked again at the buildings that stared back at him from within their strange shadows. Out here, so far from any big city, who knew what the town was now home to? Rats and probably worse. He didn't know much about the desert. What lived out here anyway?

He took a step backwards and was sure he heard the wind moan in disappointment as it slashed its way through the streets opposite. At least he hoped it was the wind. He almost laughed. He wasn't a child to be scared by dark shadows and the things that might live in them, but for a moment it had seemed as if those dark patches had stretched out suddenly towards him, as if they could grab him back. It was ridiculous, he chided himself. Simply a trick of the eyes.

Still, he thought, looking up at the windows, he was plenty glad he wasn't a boy any more. There was definitely something creepy about this place. Something flashed within the small frame of a window on the darker side of the road. He frowned and his mouth dropped open slightly. Whatever had been there was now gone, but he was sure he'd seen someone in one of the upstairs rooms of the closest building. Just for the briefest moment. Had that been sunlight reflecting or had something really been clawing at the windows? A figure? Trying to get out? Was someone really in there?

"Hey."

The voice startled him and he whirled round, going over on his ankle as he did so. Pain flared up his leg. The figure in the window was forgotten. He hobbled back to the sidewalk.

"Hey," he said. "You made me jump. I didn't think there was anyone out here." He smiled and held out his hand. "Lee Moseby."

The woman stared back at him for a moment, her brow furrowed. She was sweating under her pancake foundation and it didn't make for a good look on a woman her age.

"It's hot," she said. She didn't smile, and nor did she shake Lee's hand. That made him feel less sorry for his unkind thought. Her clothes were dusty, just as his were, but her blouse and skirt looked more uncomfortable than his chinos and golf shirt, and her high heels must have been a bitch to walk in if she'd come to town the same way he had. Weird how he hadn't seen her behind him. Just how long had he been here?

"Do you have the time?" he asked.

She shook her head and then they both looked up at the sky. The sun had moved further round and Lee realized they were now in the haze of the late-afternoon.

"I wondered if you had a quarter," she asked, and then nodded at the booth. "For the phone. I need to call someone." She chewed her lip and the warm red lipstick stuck to her teeth. "Aren't you hot?" she asked. "Why ain't you sweating?"

"Just must have got used to it," Lee said. "I've been here a while."

"A quarter?" she asked again.

"Sorry." Lee shrugged and pulled his pockets out. "I don't even have a dime." He wondered why he'd made the ridiculous gesture. Never once in all his years had he actually turned the pockets of his pants out. But then, he realized, as he looked down at the fabric, it was rare that his pockets weren't full. Change, keys, receipts, all the usual bric-a-brac of life. "But the phone works," he said. "Call collect. That's what I did."

"You got someone coming to get you?" Her heavy face lit up slightly, and she pushed a wayward curl away from her face. She had that kind of over-styled and sprayed hair that was common amongst the older southern belles.

"Yeah," he said. "My dad." He thought he should feel embarrassed about that, but somehow he didn't. "I knew his number," he added.

"Uh-uh," she said. She wasn't ready to smile at him yet, but the frown had at least abated slightly. She looked past him at the town. "I guess I'll try that. I know my folks' number too. And my sister's." She turned and wiggled on her dusty heels to the phone box. "And Adele's, but I can't see that bitch getting off her fat ass and coming all the way out here to get me."

She disappeared inside and Lee decided she was talking as much to herself as to him. He rubbed the back of his neck and found it was cool, not burned at all. Despite the way the name-less woman was sweating, he hadn't found the heat overbearing during the course of the day and he still wasn't thirsty.

With his back to the phone booth, he walked to the cross-roads and peered down the road. It was empty. Surely his dad would be here soon. In the distant shimmer he couldn't see any more walkers headed this way. Probably a good thing, he decided. He wouldn't want to be waiting out here for a ride when it had gotten dark.

He found a boulder and squatted down on it. His knees rose up almost to his chin, so he spread his legs a little wider and rested his arms on them. He felt like a cowboy. His boots, dusty and scuffed, looked like cowboy's boots. He smiled again, momentarily happy. His irritation at the lack of a watch disappeared. His dad would get here eventually, he was reliable like that, and sitting in the sunshine wasn't such a bad way to spend a lazy afternoon. He stared at the ground between his feet for so long he could almost make out each grain of sand that made up the earth. Some were dull and others shone like diamonds. He picked up a handful and let it run between his fingers. It felt good.

Eventually, she came out of the booth. He'd been so lost in his study of everything and nothing that he'd almost forgotten she was there. When he got to his feet, his legs were stiff. The air had cooled slightly. The woman, however, was still sweating.

"No one was home," she said. "Can you believe that? Not even Adele, and she's always at home watching TV."

"Did you dial the right numbers?" Lee asked. He wasn't sure what else to say. She was frowning again, sharp lines running across her forehead and forcing her eyes to narrow.

"Sure I did. Who forgets their family's number?" she snapped. "They're not in, though." Her voice softened, and she turned to look over at the town. "Weird. My mom's always in. Disabled. Doesn't get out much apart from to drive to the store."

The light was fading into gloom, and Lee followed her nervous gaze over to the ghost town. "Do you check in on her often?" The shadows were getting darker, and this time he was sure he could see flashes of eyes as small creatures scurried here and there just out of sight.

"Nah," she said. "Carrie, my sister, she does all that." Like him, her eyes were fixed on the suddenly sharp angles of the abandoned buildings and streets opposite. "I was never good with old people."

"Try again later," he said.

"Sure," she nodded. "Sure."

Half an hour later, and the sun was merely a line of fire against the horizon. Evening was falling and the wind was picking up. They stood in silence for most of the time, Lee looking out into the road and the woman staring at the town.

He didn't want to look in that direction. He'd glanced round maybe ten minutes earlier and this time he was sure – *definitely sure* – that there had been figures clawing at the windows. Momentary and gone in a breath, but he'd seen them. There had also been things scuttling in the streets. The sounds of claws on tarmac carried over to them on the wind. Other sounds too. Wet. Unpleasant. Lee wouldn't look that way again, not if he could help it.

"I don't want to be here when it gets dark," the woman said. It was the first time either of them had spoken for a while.

Lee said nothing. Over the wind and its unpleasantness, he could hear another sound, coming from the road. A familiar rattling noise that he hadn't heard in such a long time. Years. How many? Forty?

"I don't like the look of this place," she continued. "I think it gets cold at night."

Even as a silhouette against the raging death of the sun, Lee recognized the old pick-up truck. His dad's car. The one they rode to town in when his mom didn't come with them. The one she laughingly called "the boys' toy".

"Did ya hear me? I don't like this place. Not at all. Damn stupid phone."

Lee smiled, ignoring the woman, lost in the lift of his own heart as the truck pulled alongside him.

"You best get in, son." His dad smiled from behind the wheel. "It's nearly dark."

Lee did as he was told. He sucked in the forgotten and yet familiar smell of the worn leather and old cheroot smoke.

"Thanks for coming to get me, Dad." he said.

His dad's crinkled face smiled back. "No problem, son. It's been a long time."

Lee could feel his grin almost cracking his face. His dad was wearing the old dungarees he used to wear when messing around with cars out in the barn when Lee had been maybe fifteen or sixteen. They'd built Lee's first car together with his dad wearing those old dungarees. His dad looked the same as he had then too, no more than fifty. Healthy and happy.

Lee looked down at his wrist and the empty space there. His heart ached again.

"Where's my watch, Dad?" he asked, softly. "I always wear my watch." He felt fifteen again, maybe even younger. He felt of an age when your father had all the answers.

"Hey!" The woman slammed into the passenger side door, her sausage fingers with their painted tips hooked over the half-open window. Lee jumped. Her eyes glinted like the windows of the dead town.

"Hey," she said again, looking past Lee to his old man. "Can I get a ride with you? I need to get out of here. Night's coming." She smiled, revealing the patches of lipstick that clung grimly to her teeth, and Lee wondered if it was an attempt at flirtation. If it was then she needed to practise. She was panting slightly and her stale breath was bad; as if something was rotting in her mouth.

Lee's father nodded over at the phone booth, the light in it flickering on as the darkness began to take hold. "Make a call."

"I tried that," she hissed. "No one was home. Gimme a ride! You got the room. I'll go in the back."

Lee watched his father's face. His brown eyes were unreadable but his expression had softened into something that was almost pity. Almost, but not quite.

"Everyone's home," he said. "They just ain't answering." Without warning, he put his foot down on the pedal and the old truck pulled away. The woman's mouth fell open and she cursed as she lost her grip on the window. The truck turned in a wide loop, coming off the vague edges of the sandy road here and there, but Lee's father didn't stop. Once they were facing the setting sun, he cranked it up to sixty.

"Come back, you bastards!" the woman screeched after them. "You can't leave me here!" After a moment, when she'd realized that they could, her voice rose an octave. "Go to hell! Go to hell, you pair of fuckers!"

Lee flinched and twisted round in his seat.

"Don't look back, son," his father said. "It's night back there. You don't want to see that. It's not where you belong." Lee looked anyway. He couldn't help it.

The woman had lost one of her shoes and was hobbling back to the phone box as if she could find some kind of sanctuary in it. Lee thought it looked like a beacon now. One that would draw everything that lived in the dead town's shadows. What would happen to her? He thought of fingernails clawing at glass, and shivered. He sat back in his seat, facing forward. A few moments later, a short howl rang out that had nothing to do with the wind. The truck picked up speed and the sound faded.

"My watch, Dad?" he asked again. He thought he knew the answer. He'd known it all along. He never took his watch off.

"Your Ella has it, is my guess," his dad smiled. "A keepsake."

Lee nodded. He guessed that was right. Ella had given him the watch on their twenty-fifth wedding anniversary and he hadn't taken it off in the twenty years that had passed since except to change a battery and that one time it needed to be repaired.

"Will I see her again, Dad?" he asked.

"She's a good woman, your Ella." Lee's dad smiled at him. "She was a honey when you were kids and she's been a fine wife and mother and grandmother since, ain't that the truth?"

Lee nodded. "That's the truth."

"Then you'll hear that phone ringing, son. You'll hear it ringing."

The two dead men smiled at each other, content, and drove into the brightening sunlight.

Dead Flowers by a Roadside

Kelley Armstrong

The house is damnably silent.

I sit in the middle of the living room, furniture shoved out of the way, one chair tipped over where it fell, pushed too hard in my haste. Shards from a broken vase litter the floor. One is inches from my hand.

Amy would panic if she saw it. I close my eyes and imagine it. Her gasp from the doorway. The patter of her stockinged feet. The soft click of the piece against the hardwood as she snatches it up. Her voice as she tells me not to move, she'll clean it up, I need to be more careful – really, I need to be more careful. What if I'd cut myself? What if Rose had run in?

In my mind, her voice is not quite right. The cadence, the tone, are fading already. Amy's voice. Rose's voice. How much longer before they slide from memory altogether? Before I'm reduced to endlessly playing old videos that don't sound like them, not really, and telling myself they do, just so I can still hear their voices in my head.

I open my eyes and look at the ancient book lying open in front of me. Spidery writing, water-smeared ink, barely legible. The air smells faintly of acacia. That's critical, the book says. The dead will not speak without the scent of acacia to pull them through the ether.

Not true.

I know it is not true because I have seen the dead. Heard the dead. All my life they've been there, flitting past, whispering in my ear. Never once have they needed acacia.

Yet for three months, I've been trying to contact them. My wife. My child. I beg, I plead, I rage and shout for a sign, any sign. Comfort, any comfort. In desperation I turn to the books, to the acacia. But I hear only silence. Damnable silence.

I look down at the shard of glass by my hand.

Daydreaming again, weren't you? Amy laughs. *Always dreaming. Always distracted. One of these days, you're going to hurt yourself.*

I run my finger along the edge of the shard. As sharp as her ceramic knives, the ones I bought for her birthday, kept in the cupboard so Rose wouldn't mistake the white blades for plastic.

And don't you use them either, she'd said to me. *Please.*

Worried about me. About us. That was her nature. Double-checking door locks. Double-checking the stove. Double-checking Rose's car seat. Even if she'd done it herself, she always double-checked. If Rose or I so much as stubbed our toes and yelped, Amy would come running.

She'd always come running.

I take the shard, pinch it tight between thumb and forefinger. Drag the edge along my arm. Blood wells up.

"Amy?"

I cut deeper. Blood drips on to the dirty pages of the useless book.

"Amy? I need you."

Damnable silence. Always silence.

Crouched at their graves. Talking until I realize I'm only speaking to fill the silence, and I stop. I touch the marble. Cold. Always cold, even now with the late winter sun beating down.

No flowers. I took them away as soon as they started to wither. Dead flowers by a grave seem wrong. Left and forgotten. Nothing here should be forgotten.

I bring new mementoes every week. Something small.

Something meaningful. A franc from our honeymoon. A seashell from our last vacation. A button from Rose's First Communion dress. A cat's-eye marble from Amy's childhood collection. Indestructible. As memories should be.

I come here twice a week to talk to them. I know they won't hear me, but I hope others will. Other ghosts. I can see them flitting past the graves. Wandering, endlessly wandering, looking for someone to take their message to the world beyond.

That someone used to be me. I couldn't set foot in a cemetery without being besieged by the dead. Now they give me a wide berth. They know I come with a plea of my own. Find my wife. Find my daughter. Tell them I need to see them. Need to speak to them.

I want something from the ghosts, so they want nothing to do with me. I sit here and I talk to my wife and child, and I pray my words will thaw the hearts of those shades. I pray one will finally approach and say, "I'll do this." They don't. They keep their distance and they wander in silence. Always silence.

The doorbell rings. I hear it through the garage walls. Someone on the front porch. Someone come to call. I ignore it and keep working on the car.

Three months, and it's almost finished. The windshield replaced. The engine repaired. The dents hammered out.

There's one thing I can't fix. The blood on the passenger's seat. No longer red. Faded to rust brown. But still blood. Undeniably blood.

The insurance company didn't want me to have the car. Too badly damaged, they said. We've paid you; now let us dispose of it. I'd pulled out my contract and showed them the clause where I could buy back the wreck for a few hundred dollars. At least let us remove the seat, they said. No one needs to see that. But I did.

"Hello!" a voice calls.

I stay crouched by the front of the car, replacing the cracked headlight. The door opens.

"Hello?"

It's no one I know. I can tell by the voice. I consider staying where I am, but that's childish. I stand and wipe my hands on my jeans.

"Can I help you?"

It's a portly man, smiling that desperate, too-hearty smile of the salesman. I let him talk. I have no idea what he's saying, what he's selling. Just words, fluttering past.

"I'm not interested," I say.

He sizes me up. I wonder how I look to him. Unshaven. Bleary-eyed. Worn blue jeans. Grease-stained T-shirt. A drunk? Drug addict? Can't hold a job? Explains why I'd be home in the middle of the day. Still, it's a decent house, and he's desperate.

He sidles around the front of the vehicle.

"Nice car," he says.

It isn't. Even before the accident, it was a serviceable car, nothing more. Amy had wanted something newer.

Not fancier, she said. *Just safer, you know. For Rose.*

I hear BMWs are safe, I said. *You're a lawyer's wife now, not a law student's. You need a BMW.*

She laughed at that. Said I could buy her one when I made partner. I played along, but secretly made phone calls, visited dealers, planned to buy her a BMW or a Mercedes, whichever would make her feel safer. It was to be a Christmas gift.

Christmas.

That's what we'd been doing three months ago. Christmas shopping. The mall busy, the shoppers cranky, we'd left later than we expected, past dark. Cars were still streaming into the lot, circling for spots. A woman saw me putting bags in our trunk. She asked if we were leaving and I said I was. When I got in the car, Amy was still standing by the open rear door, trying to cheer up Rose, fussing, her nap missed.

Hon, there's a lady waiting for our spot.

Whoops. Sorry.

She fastened Rose's chair and climbed into the passenger seat. I started backing out.

Wait! I need to double-check the— She glanced back at the car waiting for our spot. *Never mind. I'm sure it's fine.*

"You restoring it?" The salesman's voice jerks me from the memory and I glower at him. I don't mean to. But for a second, I'd heard Amy's voice, clearly heard it. Now it was gone.

"Yes," I say. "I'm restoring it."

"Huh."

He struggles for a way to prolong the conversation. I bend and continue tinkering with the light. He stands there a moment. Then the silence becomes too much and he leaves.

A week later, the car is roadworthy. Barely. But it will make it where I want to go, all the bits and pieces intact, no chance of being pulled over.

The roadside.

I pull to the shoulder. It's dark here, just outside the city. An empty snow-laced cornfield to my right, a bare strip of two-lane highway to my left. In front of the car, a crooked cross covered in dead flowers. More dead flowers stuck in a toppled tin can. I didn't put them there. I don't know who did. Strangers, I suppose. Heard of the tragedy and wanted to mark the place. I'd rather they hadn't.

I didn't need that wretched memorial to remind me where it happened. I would know the exact spot without any marker, save the image burned into my memory.

Coming back from Christmas shopping. Dark country road. The car quiet. A good silence. A peaceful silence. Rose asleep, Amy and me being careful not to wake her. Snow falling. First snow. Amy smiling as she watches the flakes dance past.

A pick-up ahead of us. A renovation company. Boards and poles and a ladder piled haphazardly in the back.

Oh, Amy said. *That doesn't look safe. Could you . . . ?*

My foot was already off the gas, our car falling behind the truck until all we could see was its rear lights through the swirling snow.

She smiled. *Thanks.*

I know the drill.

She reached over to squeeze my leg, then settled back to snow-watching silence.

Another mile. I'd crept up on the truck, but was still far enough back, and she said nothing. Then I saw it. A figure walking down the other side of the road. A woman in a long, red jacket.

I looked over. Ghost, I told myself, and I was quite certain it was, but I'd hate to be wrong and leave someone stranded. I squinted through the side window as we passed and—

Watch—!

That was all she said. My head whipped forward. I saw the ladder fly at us. I swerved to avoid it. The car slid, the road wet with snow. An oncoming car. I saw the lights. I heard the crunch of impact. Then . . . silence.

Now, three months later, I sit by the side of the road and I hear her voice.

Always dreaming. Always distracted. One of these days, you're going to hurt yourself.

Yes, I hurt myself. More than I could have ever imagined possible.

I get out of the car. The tube is in the trunk. I fit it over the exhaust pipe, and run it through the passenger window. Then I get inside and start the engine.

Does it take long? I don't know. I'm lost in the silence. There's a momentary break as a car slows beside me. The driver peers in, thinks I'm dozing, revs the engine, keeps going. The silence returns. Then I begin to drift . . .

I wake up. The engine has stopped running. I check the fuel gauge. Half-full. I try to start the car, but the ignition won't work. I slump on to the dashboard, defeated.

Then I hear . . . something. A bird call? I look out the windshield. Fog, so thick I can't see anything else.

I get out of the car. The hinges squeak. I leave the door open behind me and walk around the front. The memorial cross is there, but it's been replaced, the flowers fresh and white, the can beneath them upright and filled with daisies.

Rose loves daisies. I smile in spite of myself and walk to the flowers. More scattered around. Still more trailing off towards the field.

As I follow them, I stumble through the fog. That's all there is. Fog. Rolling across the field. I look down at the flowers, crushing beneath my feet. I keep going, following them.

Another noise. Not a bird call. It sounds like . . .

"Amy?" I call. "Rose?"

A voice answers. Then another.

The silence ends.

The Shadow in the Corner

Mary Elizabeth Braddon

Wildheath Grange stood a little way back from the road, with a barren stretch of heath behind it, and a few tall fir trees, with straggling wind-tossed heads, for its only shelter. It was a lonely house on a lonely road, little better than a lane; leading across a desolate waste of sandy fields to the sea-shore; and it was a house that bore a bad name among the natives of the village of Holcroft, which was the nearest place where humanity might be found.

It was a good old house, nevertheless, substantially built in the days when there was no stint of stone and timber – a good old grey stone house with many gables, deep window-seats, and a wide staircase, long dark passages, hidden doors in queer corners, closets as large as some modern rooms, and cellars in which a company of soldiers might have lain *perdu*.

This spacious old mansion was given over to rats and mice, loneliness, echoes, and the occupation of three elderly people: Michael Bascom, whose forebears had been landowners of importance in the neighbourhood, and his two servants, Daniel Skegg and his wife, who had served the owner of that grim old house ever since he left the university, where he had lived fifteen years of his life – five as student, and ten as professor of natural science.

At three-and-thirty Michael Bascom had seemed a

middle-aged man; at fifty-six he looked and moved and spoke like an old man. During that interval of twenty-three years he had lived alone in Wildheath Grange, and the country people told each other that the house had made him what he was. This was a fanciful and superstitious notion on their part, doubtless, yet it would not have been difficult to have traced a certain affinity between the dull grey building and the man who lived in it. Both seemed alike, remote from the common cares and interests of humanity; both had an air of settled melancholy, engendered by perpetual solitude; both had the same faded complexion, the same look of slow decay.

Yet lonely as Michael Bascom's life was at Wildheath Grange, he would not on any account have altered its tenor. He had been glad to exchange the comparative seclusion of college rooms for the unbroken solitude of Wildheath. He was a fanatic in his love of scientific research, and his quiet days were filled to the brim with labours that seldom failed to interest and satisfy him. There were periods of depression, occasional moments of doubt, when the goal towards which he strove seemed unattainable, and his spirit fainted within him. Happily such times were rare with him. He had a dogged power of continuity which ought to have carried him to the highest pinnacle of achievement, and which perhaps might ultimately have won for him a grand name and world-wide renown, but for a catastrophe which burdened the declining years of his harmless life with an unconquerable remorse.

One autumn morning – when he had lived just three-and-twenty years at Wildheath, and had only lately begun to perceive that his faithful butler and body servant, who was middle-aged when he first employed him, was actually getting old – Mr Bascom's breakfast meditations over the latest treatise on the atomic theory were interrupted by an abrupt demand from that very Daniel Skegg. The man was accustomed to wait upon his master in the most absolute silence, and his sudden breaking out into speech was almost as startling as if the bust of Socrates above the bookcase had burst into human language.

"It's no use," said Daniel; "my missus must have a girl!"

"A what?" demanded Mr Bascom, without taking his eyes from the line he had been reading.

"A girl – a girl to trot about and wash up, and help the old lady. She's getting weak on her legs, poor soul. We've none of us grown younger in the last twenty years."

"Twenty years!" echoed Michael Bascom scornfully. "What is twenty years in the formation of a strata – what even in the growth of an oak – the cooling of a volcano!"

"Not much, perhaps, but it's apt to tell upon the bones of a human being."

"The manganese staining to be seen upon some skulls would certainly indicate—" began the scientist dreamily.

"I wish my bones were only as free from rheumatics as they were twenty years ago," pursued Daniel testily; "and then, perhaps, I should make light of twenty years. Howsoever, the long and the short of it is, my missus must have a girl. She can't go on trotting up and down these everlasting passages, and standing in that stone scullery year after year, just as if she was a young woman. She must have a girl to help."

"Let her have twenty girls," said Mr Bascom, going back to his book.

"What's the use of talking like that, sir? Twenty girls, indeed! We shall have rare work to get one."

"Because the neighbourhood is sparsely populated?" interrogated Mr Bascom, still reading.

"No, sir. Because this house is known to be haunted."

Michael Bascom laid down his book, and turned a look of grave reproach upon his servant.

"Skegg," he said in a severe voice, "I thought you had lived long enough with me to be superior to any folly of that kind."

"I don't say that I believe in ghosts," answered Daniel with a semi-apologetic air, "but the country people do. There's not a mortal among 'em that will venture across our threshold after nightfall."

"Merely because Anthony Bascom, who led a wild life in

London, and lost his money and land, came home here broken-hearted, and is supposed to have destroyed himself in this house – the only remnant of property that was left him out of a fine estate."

"Supposed to have destroyed himself!" cried Skegg. "Why the fact is as well known as the death of Queen Elizabeth, or the Great Fire of London. Why, wasn't he buried at the cross-roads between here and Holcroft?"

"An idle tradition, for which you could produce no substantial proof," retorted Mr Bascom.

"I don't know about proof; but the country people believe it as firmly as they believe their Gospel."

"If their faith in the Gospel was a little stronger they need not trouble themselves about Anthony Bascom."

"Well," grumbled Daniel, as he began to clear the table, "a girl of some kind we must get, but she'll have to be a foreigner, or a girl that's hard driven for a place."

When Daniel Skegg said a foreigner, he did not mean the native of some distant clime, but a girl who had not been born and bred at Holcroft. Daniel had been raised and reared in that insignificant hamlet, and, small and dull as it was, he considered the world beyond its only margin.

Michael Bascom was too deep in the atomic theory to give a second thought to the necessities of an old servant. Mrs Skegg was an individual with whom he rarely came in contact. She lived for the most part in a gloomy region at the north end of the house, where she ruled over the solitude of a kitchen that looked like a cathedral, and numerous offices of the scullery, larder, and pantry class, where she carried on a perpetual warfare with spiders and beetles, and wore her old life out in the labour of sweeping and scrubbing. She was a woman of severe aspect, dogmatic piety, and a bitter tongue. She was a good plain cook, and ministered diligently to her master's wants. He was not an epicure, but liked his life to be smooth and easy, and the equilibrium of his mental power would have been disturbed by a bad dinner.

He heard no more about the proposed addition to his

household for a space of ten days, when Daniel Skegg again startled him amidst his studious repose by the abrupt announcement:

"I've got a girl!"

"Oh," said Michael Bascom, "have you?" and he went on with his book.

This time he was reading an essay on phosphorus and its functions in relation to the human brain.

"Yes," pursued Daniel in his usual grumbling tone; "she was a waif and stray, or I shouldn't have got her. If she'd been a native she'd never have come to us."

"I hope she's respectable," said Michael.

"Respectable! That's the only fault she has, poor thing. She's too good for the place. She's never been in service before, but she says she's willing to work, and I daresay my old woman will be able to break her in. Her father was a small tradesman at Yarmouth. He died a month ago, and left this poor thing homeless. Mrs Midge at Holcroft is her aunt, and she said to the girl, 'Come and stay with me till you get a place'; and the girl has been staying with Mrs Midge for the last three weeks, trying to hear of a place. When Mrs Midge heard that my missus wanted a girl to help, she thought it would be the very thing for her niece Maria. Luckily Maria had heard nothing about this house, so the poor innocent dropped me a curtsey, and said she'd be thankful to come, and would do her best to learn her duty. She'd had an easy time of it with her father, who had educated her above her station, like a fool as he was," growled Daniel.

"By your own account I'm afraid you've made a bad bargain," said Michael. "You don't want a young lady to clean kettles and pans."

"If she was a young duchess my old woman would make her work," retorted Skegg decisively.

"And pray where are you going to put this girl?" asked Mr Bascom, rather irritably. "I can't have a strange young woman tramping up and down the passages outside my room. You know what a wretched sleeper I am, Skegg. A mouse behind the wainscot is enough to wake me."

"I've thought of that," answered the butler, with his look of ineffable wisdom. "I'm not going to put her on your floor. She's to sleep in the attics."

"Which room?"

"The big one at the north end of the house. That's the only ceiling that doesn't let water. She might as well sleep in a shower-bath as in any of the other attics."

"The room at the north end," repeated Mr Bascom thoughtfully; "isn't that—?"

"Of course it is," snapped Skegg, "but she doesn't know anything about it."

Mr Bascom went back to his books, and forgot all about the orphan from Yarmouth, until one morning on entering his study he was startled by the appearance of a strange girl, in a neat black-and-white cotton gown, busy dusting the volumes which were stacked in blocks upon his spacious writing-table – and doing it with such deft and careful hands that he had no inclination to be angry at this unwonted liberty. Old Mrs Skegg had religiously refrained from all such dusting, on the plea that she did not wish to interfere with the master's ways. One of the master's ways, therefore, had been to inhale a good deal of dust in the course of his studies.

The girl was a slim little thing, with a pale and somewhat old-fashioned face, flaxen hair braided under a neat muslin cap, a very fair complexion, and light blue eyes. They were the lightest blue eyes Michael Bascom had ever seen, but there was a sweetness and gentleness in their expression which atoned for their insipid colour.

"I hope you do not object to my dusting your books, sir," she said, dropping a curtsey.

She spoke with a quaint precision which struck Michael Bascom as a pretty thing in its way.

"No; I don't object to cleanliness, so long as my books and papers are not disturbed. If you take a volume off my desk, replace it on the spot you took it from. That's all I ask."

"I will be very careful, sir."

"When did you come here?"

"Only this morning, sir."

The student seated himself at his desk, and the girl withdrew, drifting out of the room as noiselessly as a flower blown across the threshold. Michael Bascom looked after her curiously. He had seen very little of youthful womanhood in his dry-as-dust career, and he wondered at this girl as at a creature of a species hitherto unknown to him. How fairly and delicately she was fashioned; what a translucent skin; what soft and pleasing accents issued from those rose-tinted lips. A pretty thing, assuredly, this kitchen wench! A pity that in all this busy world there could be no better work found for her than the scouring of pots and pans.

Absorbed in considerations about dry bones, Mr Bascom thought no more of the pale-faced handmaiden. He saw her no more about his rooms. Whatever work she did there was done early in the morning, before the scholar's breakfast.

She had been a week in the house, when he met her one day in the hall. He was struck by the change in her appearance.

The girlish lips had lost their rose-bud hue; the pale blue eyes had a frightened look, and there were dark rings round them, as in one whose nights had been sleepless, or troubled by evil dreams.

Michael Bascom was so startled by an undefinable look in the girl's face that, reserved as he was by habit and nature, he expanded so far as to ask her what ailed her.

"There is something amiss, I am sure," he said. "What is it?"

"Nothing, sir," she faltered, looking still more scared at his question. "Indeed, it is nothing; or nothing worth troubling you about."

"Nonsense. Do you suppose, because I live among books, I have no sympathy with my fellow-creatures? Tell me what is wrong with you, child. You have been grieving about the father you have lately lost, I suppose."

"No, sir; it is not that. I shall never leave off being sorry for that. It is a grief which will last me all my life."

"What, there is something else then?" asked Michael

impatiently. "I see; you are not happy here. Hard work does not suit you. I thought as much."

"Oh, sir, please don't think that," cried the girl, very earnestly. "Indeed, I am glad to work – glad to be in service; it is only—"

She faltered and broke down, the tears rolling slowly from her sorrowful eyes, despite her effort to keep them back.

"Only what?" cried Michael, growing angry. "The girl is full of secrets and mysteries. What do you mean, wench?"

"I – I know it is very foolish, sir; but I am afraid of the room where I sleep."

"Afraid! Why?"

"Shall I tell you the truth, sir? Will you promise not to be angry?"

"I will not be angry if you will only speak plainly; but you provoke me by these hesitations and suppressions."

"And please, sir, do not tell Mrs Skegg that I have told you. She would scold me; or perhaps even send me away."

"Mrs Skegg shall not scold you. Go on, child."

"You may not know the room where I sleep, sir; it is a large room at one end of the house, looking towards the sea. I can see the dark line of water from the window, and I wonder sometimes to think that it is the same ocean I used to see when I was a child at Yarmouth. It is very lonely, sir, at the top of the house. Mr and Mrs Skegg sleep in a little room near the kitchen, you know, sir, and I am quite alone on the top floor."

"Skegg told me you had been educated in advance of your position in life, Maria. I should have thought the first effect of a good education would have been to make you superior to any foolish fancies about empty rooms."

"Oh, pray, sir, do not think it is any fault in my education. Father took such pains with me; he spared no expense in giving me as good an education as a tradesman's daughter need wish for. And he was a religious man, sir. He did not believe—" here she paused, with a suppressed shudder "—in the spirits of the dead appearing to the living, since the days of miracles, when the ghost of Samuel appeared to Saul. He never put any foolish ideas into my head, sir. I hadn't a thought of fear when I first lay down to rest in the big lonely room upstairs."

"Well, what then?"

"But on the very first night," the girl went on breathlessly, "I felt weighed down in my sleep as if there were some heavy burden laid upon my chest. It was not a bad dream, but it was a sense of trouble that followed me all through my sleep; and just at daybreak – it begins to be light a little after six – I woke suddenly, with the cold perspiration pouring down my face, and knew that there was something dreadful in the room."

"What do you mean by something dreadful? Did you see anything?"

"Not much, sir; but it froze the blood in my veins, and I knew it was this that had been following me and weighing upon me all through my sleep. In the corner, between the fire place and the wardrobe, I saw a shadow – a dim, shapeless shadow—"

"Produced by an angle of the wardrobe, I daresay."

"No, sir; I could see the shadow of the wardrobe, distinct and sharp, as if it had been painted on the wall. This shadow was in the corner – a strange, shapeless mass; or, if it had any shape at all, it seemed—"

"What?" asked Michael eagerly.

"The shape of a dead body hanging against the wall!"

Michael Bascom grew strangely pale, yet he affected utter incredulity.

"Poor child," he said kindly; "you have been fretting about your father until your nerves are in a weak state, and you are full of fancies. A shadow in the corner, indeed; why, at daybreak, every corner is full of shadows. My old coat, flung upon a chair, will make you as good a ghost as you need care to see."

"Oh, sir, I have tried to think it is my fancy. But I have had the same burden weighing me down every night. I have seen the same shadow every morning."

"But when broad daylight comes, can you not see what stuff your shadow is made of?"

"No, sir. The shadow goes before it is broad daylight."

"Of course, just like other shadows. Come, come, get these silly notions out of your head, or you will never do for the work-a-day world. I could easily speak to Mrs Skegg, and make her give you another room, if I wanted to encourage you in your folly. But that would be about the worst thing I could do for you. Besides, she tells me that all the other rooms on that floor are damp; and, no doubt, if she shifted you into one of them, you would discover another shadow in another corner, and get rheumatism into the bargain. No, my good girl, you must try to prove yourself the better for a superior education."

"I will do my best, sir," Maria answered meekly, dropping a curtsey.

Maria went back to the kitchen sorely depressed. It was a dreary life she led at Wildheath Grange – dreary by day, awful by night; for the vague burden and the shapeless shadow, which seemed so slight a matter to the elderly scholar, were unspeakably terrible to her. Nobody had told her that the house was haunted, yet she walked about those echoing passages wrapped round with a cloud of fear. She had no pity from Daniel Skegg and his wife. Those two pious souls had made up their minds that the character of the house should be upheld, so far as Maria went. To her, as a foreigner, the Grange should be maintained to be an immaculate dwelling, tainted by no sulphurous blast from the underworld. A willing, biddable girl had become a necessary element in the existence of Mrs Skegg. That girl had been found, and that girl must be kept. Any fancies of a supernatural character must be put down with a high hand.

"Ghosts, indeed!" cried the amiable Skegg. "Read your Bible, Maria, and don't talk no more about ghosts."

"There are ghosts in the Bible," said Maria, with a shiver at the recollection of certain awful passages in the Scripture she knew so well.

"Ah, they was in their right place, or they wouldn't ha' been there," retorted Mrs Skegg. "You ain't agoin' to pick holes in your Bible, I hope, Maria, at your time of life."

Maria sat down quietly in her corner by the kitchen fire, and turned over the leaves of her dead father's Bible till she came to the chapters they two had loved best and oftenest read together. He had been a simple-minded, straightforward man, the Yarmouth cabinet-maker – a man full of aspirations after good, innately refined, instinctively religious. He and his motherless girl had spent their lives alone together, in the neat little home which Maria had so soon learned to cherish and beautify; and they had loved each other with an almost romantic love. They had had the same tastes, the same ideas. Very little had sufficed to make them happy. But inexorable death parted father and daughter, in one of those sharp, sudden partings which are like the shock of an earthquake – instantaneous ruin, desolation, and despair.

Maria's fragile form had bent before the tempest. She had lived through a trouble that might have crushed a stronger nature. Her deep religious convictions, and her belief that this cruel parting would not be forever, had sustained her. She faced life, and its cares and duties, with a gentle patience which was the noblest form of courage.

Michael Bascom told himself that the servant-girl's foolish fancy about the room that had been given her was not a matter of serious consideration. Yet the idea dwelled in his mind unpleasantly, and disturbed him at his labours. The exact sciences require the complete power of a man's brain, his utmost attention; and on this particular evening Michael found that he was only giving his work a part of his attention. The girl's pale face, the girl's tremulous tones, thrust themselves into the foreground of his thoughts.

He closed his book with a fretful sigh, wheeled his large arm-chair round to the fire, and gave himself up to contemplation. To attempt study with so disturbed a mind was useless. It was a dull grey evening, early in November; the student's reading-lamp was lighted, but the shutters were not yet shut, nor the curtains drawn. He could see the leaden sky outside his windows, the fir-tree tops tossing in the angry wind. He could hear the wintry blast whistling amidst the gables, before it rushed off seaward with a savage howl that sounded like a war-whoop.

Michael Bascom shivered, and drew nearer the fire.

"It's childish, foolish nonsense," he said to himself, "yet it's strange she should have that fancy about the shadow, for they say Anthony Bascom destroyed himself in that room. I remember hearing it when I was a boy, from an old servant whose mother was housekeeper at the great house in Anthony's time. I never heard how he died, poor fellow – whether he poisoned himself, or shot himself, or cut his throat; but I've been told that was the room. Old Skegg has heard it too. I could see that by his manner when he told me the girl was to sleep there."

He sat for a long time, till the grey of evening outside his study windows changed to the black of night, and the war-whoop of the wind died away to a low complaining murmur. He sat looking into the fire, and letting his thoughts wander back to the past and the traditions he had heard in his boyhood.

That was a sad, foolish story of his great-uncle, Anthony Bascom: the pitiful story of a wasted fortune and a wasted life. A riotous collegiate career at Cambridge, a racing-stable at Newmarket, an imprudent marriage, a dissipated life in London, a runaway wife, an estate forfeited to Jew money-lenders, and then the fatal end.

Michael had often heard that dismal story: how, when Anthony Bascom's fair false wife had left him, when his credit was exhausted, and his friends had grown tired of him, and all was gone except Wildheath Grange, Anthony, the broken-down man of fashion, had come to that lonely house unexpectedly one night, and had ordered his bed to be got ready for him in the room where he used to sleep when he came to the place for the wild duck shooting, in his boyhood. His old blunderbuss was still hanging over the mantelpiece, where he had left it when he came into the property, and could afford to buy the newest thing in fowling-pieces. He had not been to Wildheath for fifteen years; nay, for a good many of those years he had almost forgotten that the drear old house belonged to him.

The woman who had been housekeeper at Bascom Park, till house and lands had passed into the hands of the Jews, was at this time the sole occupant of Wildheath. She cooked some supper for her master, and made him as comfortable as she could in the long untenanted dining-room; but she was distressed to find, when she cleared the table after he had gone upstairs to bed, that he had eaten hardly anything.

Next morning she got his breakfast ready in the same room, which she managed to make brighter and cheerier than it had looked overnight. Brooms, dusting-brushes, and a good fire did much to improve the aspect of things. But the morning wore on to noon, and the old housekeeper listened in vain for her master's footfall on the stairs. Noon waned to late afternoon. She had made no attempt to disturb him, thinking that he had worn himself out by a tedious journey on horseback, and that he was sleeping the sleep of exhaustion. But when the brief November day clouded with the first shadows of twilight, the old woman grew seriously alarmed, and went upstairs to her master's door, where she waited in vain for any reply to her repeated calls and knockings.

The door was locked on the inside, and the housekeeper was not strong enough to break it open. She rushed downstairs again full of fear, and ran bare-headed out into the lonely road. There was no habitation nearer than the turnpike on the old coach road, from which this side road branched off to the sea. There was scant hope of a chance passer-by. The old woman ran along the road, hardly knowing whither she was going or what she was going to do, but with a vague idea that she must get somebody to help her.

Chance favoured her. A cart, laden with seaweed, came lumbering slowly along from the level line of sands yonder where the land melted into water. A heavy lumbering farm-labourer walked beside the cart.

"For God's sake, come in and burst open my master's door!"

she entreated, seizing the man by the arm. "He's lying dead, or in a fit, and I can't get to help him."

"All right, missus," answered the man, as if such an invitation were a matter of daily occurrence. "Whoa, Dobbin; stand still, horse, and be danged to thee."

Dobbin was glad enough to be brought to anchor on the patch of waste grass in front of the Grange garden. His master followed the housekeeper upstairs, and shattered the old-fashioned box-lock with one blow of his ponderous fist.

The old woman's worst fear was realized. Anthony Bascom was dead. But the mode and manner of his death Michael had never been able to learn. The housekeeper's daughter, who told him the story, was an old woman when he was a boy. She had only shaken her head, and looked unutterably weary, when he questioned her too closely. She had never even admitted that the old squire had committed suicide. Yet the tradition of his self-destruction was rooted in the minds of the natives of Holcroft; and there was a settled belief that his ghost, at certain times and seasons, haunted Wildheath Grange.

Now Michael Bascom was a stern materialist. For him the universe, with all its inhabitants, was a great machine, governed by inexorable laws. To such a man the idea of a ghost was simply absurd – as absurd as the assertion that two and two make five, or that a circle can be formed of a straight line. Yet he had a kind of dilettante interest in the idea of a mind which could believe in ghosts. The subject offered an amusing psychological study. This poor little pale girl, now, had evidently got some supernatural terror into her head, which could only be conquered by rational treatment.

"I know what I ought to do," Michael Bascom said to himself suddenly. "I'll occupy that room myself tonight, and demonstrate to this foolish girl that her notion about the shadow is nothing more than a silly fancy, bred of timidity and low spirits. An ounce of proof is better than a pound of argument. If I can prove to her that I have spent a night in the room, and seen no such shadow, she will understand what an idle thing superstition is."

Daniel came in presently to shut the shutters.

"Tell your wife to make up my bed in the room where Maria has been sleeping, and to put her into one of the rooms on the first floor for tonight, Skegg," said Mr Bascom.

"Sir?"

Mr Bascom repeated his order.

"That silly wench has been complaining to you about her room," Skegg exclaimed indignantly. "She doesn't deserve to be well fed and cared for in a comfortable home. She ought to go to the workhouse."

"Don't be angry with the poor girl, Skegg. She has taken a foolish fancy into her head, and I want to show her how silly she is," said Mr Bascom.

"And you want to sleep in his – in that room yourself," said the butler.

"Precisely."

"Well," mused Skegg, "if he does walk – which I don't believe – he was your own flesh and blood; and I don't suppose he'll do you any hurt."

When Daniel Skegg went back to the kitchen he railed mercilessly at poor Maria, who sat pale and silent in her corner by the hearth, darning old Mrs Skegg's grey worsted stockings, which were the roughest and harshest armour that ever human foot clothed itself withal. "Was there ever such a whimsical, fine, lady-like miss," demanded Daniel, "to come into a gentleman's house, and drive him out of his own bedroom to sleep in an attic, with her nonsenses and vagaries." If this was the result of being educated above one's station, Daniel declared that he was thankful he had never got so far in his schooling as to read words of two syllables without spelling. Education might be hanged for him, if this was all it led to.

"I am very sorry," faltered Maria, weeping silently over her work. "Indeed, Mr Skegg, I made no complaint. My master questioned me, and I told him the truth. That was all."

"All!" exclaimed Mr Skegg irately. "All, indeed! I should think it was enough."

Poor Maria held her peace. Her mind, fluttered by Daniel's

unkindness, had wandered away from that bleak big kitchen to the lost home of the past – the snug little parlour where she and her father had sat beside the cosy hearth on such a night as this; she with her smart work-box and her plain sewing, he with the newspaper he loved to read; the petted cat purring on the rug, the kettle singing on the bright brass trivet, the tea-tray pleasantly suggestive of the most comfortable meal in the day.

Oh, those happy nights, that dear companionship! Were they really gone forever, leaving nothing behind them but unkindness and servitude?

Michael Bascom retired later than usual that night. He was in the habit of sitting at his books long after every other lamp but his own had been extinguished. The Skeggs had subsided into silence and darkness in their drear ground-floor bed-chamber. Tonight his studies were of a peculiarly interesting kind, and belonged to the order of recreative reading rather than of hard work. He was deep in the history of that mysterious people who had their dwelling-place in the Swiss lakes, and was much exercised by certain speculations and theories about them.

The old eight-day clock on the stairs was striking two as Michael slowly ascended, candle in hand, to the hitherto unknown region of the attics. At the top of the staircase he found himself facing a dark narrow passage which led north-wards, a passage that was in itself sufficient to strike terror to a superstitious mind, so black and uncanny did it look.

"Poor child," mused Mr Bascom, thinking of Maria; "this attic floor is rather dreary, and for a young mind prone to fancies—"

He had opened the door of the north room by this time, and stood looking about him.

It was a large room, with a ceiling that sloped on one side, but was fairly lofty upon the other; an old-fashioned room, full of old-fashioned furniture – big, ponderous, clumsy – associ-ated with a day that was gone and people that were dead. A walnut-wood wardrobe stared him in the face – a wardrobe with brass handles, which gleamed out of the darkness like diabolical eyes. There was a tall four-post bedstead, which had been cut down on one side to accommodate the slope of the ceiling, and which had a misshapen and deformed aspect in consequence. There was an old mahogany bureau that smelled of secrets. There were some heavy old chairs with rush bottoms, mouldy with age, and much worn. There was a corner washstand, with a big basin and a small jug – the odds and ends of past years. Carpet there was none, save a narrow strip beside the bed.

"It is a dismal room," mused Michael, with the same touch of pity for Maria's weakness which he had felt on the landing just now.

To him it mattered nothing where he slept; but having let himself down to a lower level by his interest in the Swiss lake-people, he was in a manner humanized by the lightness of his evening's reading, and was even inclined to compassion for the weaknesses of a foolish girl.

He went to bed, determined to sleep his soundest. The bed was comfortable, well supplied with blankets, rather luxurious than otherwise, and the scholar had that agreeable sense of fatigue which promises profound and restful slumber.

He dropped off to sleep quickly, but woke with a start ten minutes afterwards. What was this consciousness of a burden of care that had awakened him – this sense of all-pervading trouble that weighed upon his spirits and oppressed his heart – this icy horror of some terrible crisis in life through which he must inevitably pass? To him these feelings were as novel as they were painful. His life had flowed on with smooth and sluggish tide, unbroken by so much as a ripple of sorrow. Yet tonight he felt all the pangs of unavailing remorse; the agonizing memory of a life wasted; the stings of humiliation and disgrace, shame, ruin; a hideous death, which he had doomed himself to die by his own hand. These were the horrors that pressed him round and weighed him down as he lay in Anthony Bascom's room.

Yes, even he, the man who could recognize nothing in

nature, or in nature's God, better or higher than an irresponsible and invariable machine governed by mechanical laws, was fain to admit that here he found himself face to face with a psychological mystery. This trouble, which came between him and sleep, was the trouble that had pursued Anthony Bascom on the last night of his life. So had the suicide felt as he lay in that lonely room, perhaps striving to rest his wearied brain with one last earthly sleep before he passed to the unknown intermediate land where all is darkness and slumber. And that troubled mind had haunted the room ever since. It was not the ghost of the man's body that returned to the spot where he had suffered and perished, but the ghost of his mind – his very self; no meaningless simulacrum of the clothes he wore, and the figure that filled them.

Michael Bascom was not the man to abandon his high ground of sceptical philosophy without a struggle. He tried his hardest to conquer this oppression that weighed upon mind and sense. Again and again he succeeded in composing himself to sleep, but only to wake again and again to the same torturing thoughts, the same remorse, the same despair. So the night passed in unutterable weariness; for though he told himself that the trouble was not his trouble, that there was no reality in the burden, no reason for the remorse, these vivid fancies were as painful as realities, and took as strong a hold upon him.

The first streak of light crept in at the window – dim, and cold, and grey; then came twilight, and he looked at the corner between the wardrobe and the door.

Yes; there was the shadow: not the shadow of the wardrobe only – that was clear enough, but a vague and shapeless something which darkened the dull brown wall; so faint, so shadowy, that he could form no conjecture as to its nature, or the thing it represented. He determined to watch this shadow till broad daylight; but the weariness of the night had exhausted him, and before the first dimness of dawn had passed away he had fallen fast asleep, and was tasting the blessed balm of undisturbed slumber. When he woke the winter sun was shining in at the lattice, and the room had lost its gloomy aspect. It looked old-fashioned, and grey, and brown, and shabby; but the depth of its gloom had fled with the shadows and the darkness of night.

Mr Bascom rose refreshed by a sound sleep, which had lasted nearly three hours. He remembered the wretched feelings which had gone before that renovating slumber; but he recalled his strange sensations only to despise them, and he despised himself for having attached any importance to them.

"Indigestion very likely," he told himself; "or perhaps mere fancy, engendered of that foolish girl's story. The wisest of us is more under the dominion of imagination than he would care to confess. Well, Maria shall not sleep in this room any more. There is no particular reason why she should, and she shall not be made unhappy to please old Skegg and his wife."

When he had dressed himself in his usual leisurely way, Mr Bascom walked up to the corner where he had seen or imagined the shadow, and examined the spot carefully.

At first sight he could discover nothing of a mysterious character. There was no door in the papered wall, no trace of a door that had been there in the past. There was no trap-door in the worm-eaten boards. There was no dark ineradicable stain to hint at murder. There was not the faintest suggestion of a secret or a mystery.

He looked up at the ceiling. That was sound enough, save for a dirty patch here and there where the rain had blistered it.

Yes; there was something – an insignificant thing, yet with a suggestion of grimness which startled him.

About a foot below the ceiling he saw a large iron hook projecting from the wall, just above the spot where he had seen the shadow of a vaguely defined form. He mounted on a chair the better to examine this hook, and to understand, if he could, the purpose for which it had been put there.

It was old and rusty. It must have been there for many years. Who could have placed it there, and why? It was not the kind of hook upon which one would hang a picture or one's garments. It was placed in an obscure corner. Had Anthony

Bascom put it there on the night he died; or did he find it there ready for a fatal use?

"If I were a superstitious man," thought Michael, "I should be inclined to believe that Anthony Bascom hung himself from that rusty old hook."

"Sleep well, sir?" asked Daniel, as he waited upon his master at breakfast.

"Admirably," answered Michael, determined not to gratify the man's curiosity.

He had always resented the idea that Wildheath Grange was haunted.

"Oh, indeed, sir. You were so late that I fancied—"

"Late, yes! I slept so well that I overshot my usual hour for waking. But, by-the-way, Skegg, as that poor girl objects to the room, let her sleep somewhere else. It can't make any difference to us, and it may make some difference to her."

"Humph!" muttered Daniel in his grumpy way; "you didn't see anything queer up there, did you?"

"See anything? Of course not."

"Well, then, why should she see things? It's all her silly fiddle-faddle."

"Never mind, let her sleep in another room."

"There ain't another room on the top floor that's dry."

"Then let her sleep on the floor below. She creeps about quietly enough, poor little timid thing. She won't disturb me."

Daniel grunted, and his master understood the grunt to mean obedient assent; but here Mr Bascom was unhappily mistaken. The proverbial obstinacy of the pig family is as nothing compared with the obstinacy of a cross-grained old man, whose narrow mind has never been illuminated by education. Daniel was beginning to feel jealous of his master's compassionate interest in the orphan girl. She was a sort of gentle clinging thing that might creep into an elderly bachelor's heart unawares, and make herself a comfortable nest there.

"We shall have fine carryings-on, and me and my old woman

will be nowhere, if I don't put down my heel pretty strong upon this nonsense," Daniel muttered to himself, as he carried the breakfast-tray to the pantry.

Maria met him in the passage.

"Well, Mr Skegg, what did my master say?" she asked breathlessly. "Did he see anything strange in the room?"

"No, girl. What should he see? He said you were a fool."

"Nothing disturbed him? And he slept there peacefully?" faltered Maria.

"Never slept better in his life. Now don't you begin to feel ashamed of yourself?"

"Yes," she answered meekly; "I am ashamed of being so full of fancies. I will go back to my room tonight, Mr Skegg, if you like, and I will never complain of it again."

"I hope you won't," snapped Skegg; "you've given us trouble enough already."

Maria sighed, and went about her work in saddest silence. The day wore slowly on, like all other days in that lifeless old house. The scholar sat in his study; Maria moved softly from room to room, sweeping and dusting in the cheerless solitude. The midday sun faded into the grey of afternoon, and evening came down like a blight upon the dull old house.

Throughout that day Maria and her master never met. Anyone who had been so far interested in the girl as to observe her appearance would have seen that she was unusually pale, and that her eyes had a resolute look, as of one who was resolved to face a painful ordeal. She ate hardly anything all day. She was curiously silent. Skegg and his wife put down both these symptoms to temper.

"She won't eat and she won't talk," said Daniel to the partner of his joys. "That means sulkiness, and I never allowed sulkiness to master me when I was a young man, and you tried it on as a young woman, and I'm not going to be conquered by sulkiness in my old age."

Bedtime came, and Maria bade the Skeggs a civil goodnight, and went up to her lonely garret without a murmur.

The next morning came, and Mrs Skegg looked in vain for

her patient handmaiden, when she wanted Maria's services in preparing the breakfast.

"The wench sleeps sound enough this morning," said the old woman. "Go and call her, Daniel. My poor legs can't stand them stairs."

"Your poor legs are getting uncommon useless," muttered Daniel testily, as he went to do his wife's behest.

He knocked at the door, and called Maria – once, twice, thrice, many times; but there was no reply. He tried the door, and found it locked. He shook the door violently, cold with fear.

Then he told himself that the girl had played him a trick. She had stolen away before daybreak, and left the door locked to frighten him. But, no; this could not be, for he could see the key in the lock when he kneeled down and put his eye to the keyhole. The key prevented his seeing into the room.

"She's in there, laughing in her sleeve at me," he told himself; "but I'll soon be even with her."

There was a heavy bar on the staircase, which was intended to secure the shutters of the window that lighted the stairs. It was a detached bar, and always stood in a corner near the window, which it was but rarely employed to fasten. Daniel ran down to the landing, and seized upon this massive iron bar, and then ran back to the garret door.

One blow from the heavy bar shattered the old lock, which was the same lock the carter had broken with his strong fist seventy years before. The door flew open, and Daniel went into the attic which he had chosen for the stranger's bedchamber.

Maria was hanging from the hook in the wall. She had contrived to cover her face decently with her handkerchief. She had hanged herself deliberately about an hour before Daniel found her, in the early grey of morning. The doctor, who was summoned from Holcroft, was able to declare the time at which she had slain herself, but there was no one who could say what sudden access of terror had impelled her to the desperate act, or under what slow torture of nervous apprehension her mind had given way. The coroner's jury returned the customary merciful verdict of "temporary insanity".

The girl's melancholy fate darkened the rest of Michael Bascom's life. He fled from Wildheath Grange as from an accursed spot, and from the Skeggs as from the murderers of a harmless innocent girl. He ended his days at Oxford, where he found the society of congenial minds, and the books he loved. But the memory of Maria's sad face, and sadder death, was his abiding sorrow. Out of that deep shadow his soul was never lifted.

The Madam of the Narrow Houses

Caitlín R. Kiernan

She has never called herself a medium, this furtive, brown-eyed woman who lives alone where Hull Street crosses Snow Hill Street and runs down to the glassy, slow river. She does not seek to profit from the bereaved, nor to offer solace to grieving widows, widowers, or orphans. She does not hold séances in hushed and darkened parlours, and never has she practised automatic writing, nor even once communicated with otherworldly spheres via planchettes and elaborate codes of table rapping and the cracking of knuckles. She does not call the dead, for always have they come to her unbidden, in their own time and in their own service. Rarely do they speak to her, and when they do, it is even more rarely that they share words she would dare repeat.

By day, she is a sempstress, an architect with needle and thread and thimble, clothing well-bred Boston women, and she minds her spools and stitches. She has a fondness for old hymns, and often hums them while she works, though she is not particularly religious. Religion has always seemed to her the domain of questions which will be answered in the fullness of time, one way or the other, by and by. Or they will not, in which case it hardly seems they matter very much. She lives in the high gabled house left behind by her mother and father when they passed – only one month apart, one from the other – and she imagines that she will live there until the end of her own days. She has an especial liking for yellow roses, and for mulled cider, as well, and late autumn, and the inscriptions she finds carved on slate headstones when she walks between the rows at Copp's Hill. Of the latter, she has two favourites, both of which she has copied down and pinned upon the wall near her chifforobe. They offer some comfort on those infrequent occasions when it occurs to her, in passing, that perhaps she is a lonely woman who has simply never paused to recognize her own particular sort of loneliness. One reads:

Sacred to the Memory of
MR SAMUEL WELLS,
Who resigned this life Nov. 13th,
1804
in the 26 year of his age.
Stop my friends; in a mirror see
What you who ere so healthy be,
Tho' beauty with rosebuds paint each face.
Coming death will strip you of each grace.

and the other goes:

Here lyes ye body of
MRS AMNEY HUNT
Wife of Mr Benjamin Hunt who died
Nov. 20th, 1769 aged
40 years
A sister of Sarah Lucas lieth here,
Whom I did love most dear;
And now her soul hath too its flight
And bid her spiteful foes good night.

That both Mr Wells and Mrs Hunt died in November has always seemed significant, and sometimes this sempstress who is not a medium imagines it a portent of some sort, conceivably that she herself will perish on a chill November day, only after the crisper delights of October have finished, and that thought bestows a certain solace.

She sleeps always above the blankets, for no reason in particular and following from no superstition. This bed was once her grandfather's, as was once this house the property of that same man, who made his meagre fortune importing tea and exporting tobacco. She keeps a sachet filled with dried lavender and thyme beneath her pillow, and on the bedside table she keeps a small box made from cherrywood. The lid is finely carved with a scene from Greek mythology – Narcissus gazing longingly at his own reflection while Echo watches bitterly. Inside the box, wrapped in a white linen handkerchief, she keeps her baby teeth and two she has lost as an adult. There is also the cracked arm of a china doll she found lying in the street, years ago, and there is a silver coin, tarnished mostly black, which she thinks must have come from Portugal or Spain.

She does not call them to her. Always, they find her by their own secret wiles, the spirits who come when she is sleeping or lying awake waiting for sleep. They find *her*, following whatever compass a ghost might hold, slipping in through the inevitable, stingy gaps afforded by all closed doors and windows. They rise up through floorboards or sift down through sagging ceiling plaster. Or they appear somewhere in the room without having seemed to have entered by any obvious, material route. So, she knows there must be a multitude of invisible doorways that her living eyes cannot discern. They have also risen from the scorched glass chimney of the oil lamp that sits on the table along with the cherrywood box, and from beneath the bed, too. On more than one instance, they have emerged suddenly from the brick maw of the chimney, sooty and fire-lit and scattering ash and embers across the room.

The first one came when she was only fifteen years old, and it merely sat at the foot of her bed and watched her with its sunken coal-lump eyes. She was not afraid that night, and she has never yet been afraid of them since. They come with needs, with the unfathomable and insatiable hungers and desires of all dead things, but they do not come maliciously. And though she understands, instinctively, that they are all jealous of her flesh and of her ability to taste and smell and touch, envious of her every breath, she also understands that she is an unlikely banquet, and that the loss of her would be an almost incalculable loss to these uninvited visitors.

Sometimes, they bring her gifts, though she has never asked or expected anything from them. Once, a withered bouquet of violets, found afterwards on her pillow, and on another night, a page torn from a book of poetry by Longfellow, and after still another liaison, she found a blue China bowl of milk waiting in the hallway outside her bedroom door.

She was a sickly child, prone to unaccountable fits and agues, and her parents were convinced on more than one night that she would not live to see the dawn. Certainly, hearing the grim pronouncements of the physicians who attended her, they had not expected their daughter and only child to reach adulthood. But she did, and now she has outlived them both by almost fifteen years and grown to be a fit and sturdy woman, though still somewhat thin and of a paler complexion than she'd prefer.

One of the few times she has spoken with her spectral callers, she asked, "Why was I always so sick?"

And the ghost hesitated only for a moment, then replied in a voice like winter wind along shingled rooftops, "We have ever been near to you."

Emboldened by its response, she asked, "Why, then, am I always well now, hardly ever suffering even so much as a runny nose?"

"Because," the ghost told her, and she thought possibly the tone of its voice betrayed a hint of impatience, "we are ever near to you."

Because you need me, she thought, but would not have spoken those four words aloud. If they need her, she has come to need them at least as much, and she can no longer comprehend the tedium of an existence without their nightly company. She is proud of her skill as a dressmaker and of her position in the shop on Hanover Street, but she knows that the work and the demands of her craft are hardly sufficient to give meaning to her life. She has seen and felt too much to live as others live, to be no more than a spinster and a sempstress dwelling alone in the high, old house in the city's North End. And it is not necessary that she flaunt her certainty of her visitors' need for her; it is enough to know they do, to sense, from time to time, their anxiety that they will come some evening or another and find her gone.

She has overhead whispers and gossip, in the shop and on the street, when others think she is not listening or out of earshot. "Such a shame she never married," someone will sigh, feigning pity, pretending to sympathy. Or, "An odd one, that woman, and have you heard . . . ?" and then there will be some hushed tale of strange lights from her windows or peculiar sounds heard in her presence. Perhaps the smell of dying flowers or brimstone whenever she passes by, and were it only two centuries earlier, she might be hauled before magistrates in powdered wigs to be interrogated, accused of congress with demons, found guilty of witchcraft, and then hung from the limb of a convenient tree. But, by chance or providence, she was born into an enlightened age of Science and Medicine and gas streetlights. So, usually, she ignores the whispers, because none of them even begin to suspect the truth, and none of them can steal the nights away from her.

She lies in bed, naked and unashamed of her nakedness, shivering but unmindful of the chill, and she watches the restless patterns the lamp throws upon the walls. Sometimes, they come to her as no more than shadows, and when she happens to consider the unperceived form that *casts* those shadows, there is a delicious twinge or prickling at the nape of her neck or deep in her belly. So often, it is not what she glimpses, but what she will never behold that seems to nourish the greatest revelations.

In her right hand, she cradles the page ripped from a volume of Longfellow and left upon her pillow, and she has underlined this passage:

> *Let us go forward, and no longer stay*
> *In this great picture-gallery of Death!*
> *I hate it! ay, the very thought of it!*
> **Elsie.** *Why is it hateful to you?*
> **Prince Henry.** *For the reason*
> *That life, and all that speaks of life, is lovely,*
> *And death, and all that speaks of death, is hateful.*
> **Elsie.** *The grave is but a covered bridge,*
> *Leading from light to light, through a brief darkness!*

Often, she has wondered which one of them left it for her, and precisely what those lines may have meant to them, but she has never found the courage to ask any of the visitors. Lying there with the page crumpled and brittle in her hand, worn smooth by her fingers and all the nights she has held it, she broods over the truest meaning of the stanzas and whether they might hold within them any truth beyond the pretty conceits of all poets, great and minor and those who have died completely unknown. It might be that Elsie has spoken the truth to the Prince, or it might be that the darkness of the grave runs on forever, that it is not a covered bridge at all, but a tunnel bored through solid granite, which never again emerges into the light of day. Or, she thinks, it might be a deep reflecting pool, where the weight of souls bears them down to the grey-green half-light, through murk and silt, to settle amongst the knotted roots of water lilies, disturbing only the fitful slumber of turtles and newts.

In a corner, near the bedroom door, something stirs and is still again. She watches, but only from the edges of her vision, because sometimes they are shy, especially if they have never visited before. For the moment, this one seems hardly more than a shredded slip of lightlessness, not even as solid as the fleeting wisp of smoke when a candle has been snuffed. She smiles and lets the page of Longfellow slip from her fingers to the floor, and then she rolls on to her back and raises her knees, spreading her legs in a wordless act of invitation. She turns her head until her right cheek is pressed against the blanket, until she can once again keep her indirect watch upon that corner of the room. She wants to whisper some further, slight encouragement, but keeps quiet for fear that even the softest voice might be too much. This one will come, or it will not, and she can make no more overture than the simple offering of herself that has been made already.

For an instant, a span measured in shallow breaths and the uncontrollable metronome of heartbeats, she watches as the angles of the corner become somehow more acute than their usual ninety degrees. The portal swinging open, stretching and straining that only apparently fixed intersection of the room's north and eastern walls, and she parts her knees the slightest bit more. What was only a slip or a smoky wisp has already taken on a more substantial form, flowing into this world from when- and wherever Nature or Super-Nature consigns that part of the human mind that survives death. Then the walls are merely plaster walls again, the corner no more or less than any corner in this house, but filled now with a roiling, slowly revolving material, the singularly gossamer filaments of a being sewing itself together with naught but longing and urgency and dim memories. It is not exactly translucent, nor quite genuinely opaque, and its shifting surface glints with a greasy sort of iridescence or polychromasia.

And this is when she always looks away, prudently turning to face the ceiling, instead, averting her gaze, for there is something too horribly vulnerable about her visitors at this stage of their manifestation. Neither quite here nor there, half in and half out, raw and exposed to any prying, curious eyes that might fall on them and stare without understanding or mercy. The lamp on the bedside table flares suddenly, glowing almost painfully bright, and then it gutters as if an unfelt draught is about to extinguish it. But soon enough the flame grows steady again and retreats to its former, fainter brilliance, and she is grateful that the presence in the corner has not seen fit to douse the wick and leave her blinking at afterimages and waiting in the dark.

That is kind of you, Sir or Madam, she thinks, and at once there is a dry, fluttering noise, the rattle of fallen leaves or castoff feathers blown across parched earth or cobblestones, and it may or may not have been anything meant for her ears. She knows that the apparitions hear her thoughts, sometimes, but other times, it seems her mind is closed to them. Or that they simply choose not to listen. She lies as still as she may, at ease and unafraid and open to the approach of her coalescing guest, waiting for this night's ministrations to begin in earnest. She takes a deep breath, filling herself with the air in the bedroom which has become laden with all the familiar, astringent odours of ghosts, and exhales through her nostrils.

And were there anyone alive – a sister or mother, a friend or father confessor – to whom the sempstress might ever divulge these unions, she would readily admit that while the visitors do not frighten her, the reactions of her own body to them often do. Which is to say, the unconscious reflexes of her sympathetic flesh to the appetites and yearnings of non-corporeal intelligences, and no doubt it would leave the spiritualists in awe, and surely they would deem her possessed of some mighty gift or talent. It has been her experience that people are often eager to praise or envy that which they themselves have never had to endure. The cold begins in her belly and rises quickly into her chest, that ache, that unfolding bloom of frost, as though she is about to cough up the dirty slush of a January street.

She swallows, blinks, and sees that it is standing at her bedside now — no, not *it*, but *him*, for the features have solidified into the face of a young man. There is a keen sadness to his expression, which is unusual; rarely do they show her sorrow, regardless of what the living might expect of those bereft of blood and bone. More often than not, there is relief that they have found her, that she has welcomed their arrival, and so their eyes beam and glisten for her, all gratitude and release. They wear the echoes of smiles and the faint remembrances of joy, no moaning phantoms dragging the burden of clattering chains, no weeping haunts. So this gentleman's downcast countenance is unexpected, and she almost asks him aloud to tell her, to talk if he can and if, perchance, talking might help, but then she catches herself and keeps the questions to herself. If he wishes her to know, he will explain, when and how it suits him. The ghost leans nearer, and she knows there would be tears if the dead did not, inevitably, forget how to cry.

And here is the same fact they all bring to her, and it might overwhelm or disappoint or insult another, but never yet has it lessened her enthusiasm for these encounters. The fact – they do not come to see *her*, but, rather, they come to see what she can *show* them. She is merely the instrument capable of sounding those old tones which they have dragged themselves up from pine boxes and mouldering, worm-gnawed sod to hear, just as they are merely the musicians capable of playing her. In this improbable symphony, as in all orchestrations, neither one is anything without the ability of the other. He reaches out, and she can almost feel his fingertips brush gently across and through her erect nipples, and trapped there within the bower of her ribcage, the cold has redoubled and swelled into a blizzard. She can hold it inside just so long and never a single second more.

He kisses her then, and his lips are flavoured with dust and the clicking language of ebony beetles. She does not shut her eyes, and he does not close his, and so they share this one moment between them before she can no longer forestall what he has *truly* come here for. But it is enough, and she stops fighting what cannot be defeated, as the ice inside flows effortlessly along the trough of her throat, answering his unspoken pleas and rising up to meet her visitor.

"Death," her father says, and he smiles so that the word does not seem so ominous. "When all is said and done, it is hardly more than a covered bridge."

And here she is standing down on the street, staring up at the gauzy white drapes that cover her bedroom windows like cataracts obscuring blind and aged eyes. A carriage passes behind her, the horses' iron-shod hooves throwing sparks as they strike the pavement.

And here she is only seven years old, lost in the throes of a fever, and her mother is sitting next to her bed, holding her hand and wiping her face with a cool, damp cloth.

"Life, and all that speaks of life, is lovely," her mother says, and even though she sounds very afraid, the authority in her voice will brook no argument and accept no compromise. "Do you hear me, young lady? Death, and all that *speaks* of death, is hateful. Do you understand?"

"Yes, Mother," the sempstress whispers, keeping her eyes on the inconstant shadows hunched all around, pressing in from the years she has not yet lived.

"So, you're staying *here*," her mother tells her, "with us. You're not going *anywhere*."

"No," the child replies, the child who knows what lies ahead because these are only recollections seen through the distorting glass of time. "I would never leave."

The frowning young man with sad grey eyes touches her face with intangible hands, and a glacier pours across her tongue and teeth and out of her open mouth.

"A shame she never married," mutters the greengrocer's wife, who has five children and loves none of them. And the sempstress thinks, *But I am a married woman, and my husbands and my wives and all my children are scattered across the ages and always seeking me.*

"An odd one," sighs the dour, scowling wife of a butcher or a banker or a Presbyterian minister. "You wonder what she gets up to, left all alone in that abominable old house. Oh, I've heard stories, but it's nothing I'd care to repeat, being a Christian woman."

From the shingle of a rocky beach, she watches as the day draws to its sunset end and the advancing tide rises by slow degrees from the eternal, devouring sea; her father laughs and places an especially pretty shell or rounded pearl of blue beach glass in her palm.

"She is your mother," he says and sighs. "What did you expect she would say?"

She does not know, because she cannot even remember the question.

"Fear whatever you can avoid, and be mindful where you step, sure. But death, child, is only a bridge, leading you from light to light, through a brief darkness. Fear it all you wish, and sidestep all you like, it will change not a thing in that regard. Your mother knows that as well as I."

And now her soul hath too its flight
And bid her spiteful foes good night.

As saltwater and foam rush across sandy shores and weathered stone, so, too this flood spills from her, rushing over her chin and across her bare chest and shoulders. Disregarding gravity, it flows back and upwards, as well, entirely shrouding her face, filling her nostrils, sealing her eyes. There is only a passing, reflexive fleck of panic, that initial shock when she can no longer breathe or see and before she remembers that this is not what will kill her one day, somewhere farther along, and that she has done this thing so many nights before *this* night and, always, she has lived to entertain the needs of other visitations.

"Don't waste your days afraid of ghosts," her father says, and bends to lift another piece of flotsam from the beach. The buttermilk sky is filled with dappled wings and the cries of wheeling gulls.

The viscous, colourless matter expelled from some unknown recess of her anatomy or mind or spirit has already heard the ghost leaning low over her, that sorrowful man who has come here to find something lost and not yet restored to him. Someone who still breathes, perhaps, or someone dead who has yet to cross his path, and maybe there are so many roads on the other side of death's covered bridge that souls might wander all eternity and never find reunion. And, because she was born to be a violin or cello or a penny whistle, and because she is incomplete without a melody, she has disgorged this second, telepathic skin to read his thoughts, and that membrane expands and wraps itself tightly about her body until it has been pulled as thin as any human skin. Her face is no longer her own, but is the face *he* needs to see, the face that she was birthed to show him on this night when at last he has found his way to her bedroom. The caul hides away the indecent flush and warmth of her mortality, and now he can *touch* her as though the two of them were living or both of them were not even as solid as a breeze.

He kisses her again, and the sempstress does not need to see to know that he is no longer frowning.

The Lost Ghost

Mary E. Wilkins-Freeman

Mrs John Emerson, sitting with her needlework beside the window, looked out and saw Mrs Rhoda Meserve coming down the street, and knew at once by the trend of her steps and the cant of her head that she meditated turning in at her gate. She also knew by a certain something about her general carriage – a thrusting forward of the neck, a bustling hitch of the shoulders – that she had important news. Rhoda Meserve always had the news as soon as the news was in being, and generally Mrs John Emerson was the first to whom she imparted it. The two women had been friends ever since Mrs Meserve had married Simon Meserve and come to the village to live.

Mrs Meserve was a pretty woman, moving with graceful flirts of ruffling skirts; her clear-cut, nervous face, as delicately tinted as a shell, looked brightly from the plumy brim of a black hat at Mrs Emerson in the window. Mrs Emerson was glad to see her coming. She returned the greeting with enthusiasm, then rose hurriedly, ran into the cold parlour and brought out one of the best rocking chairs. She was just in time, after drawing it up beside the opposite window, to greet her friend at the door.

"Good afternoon," said she. "I declare, I'm real glad to see you. I've been alone all day. John went to the city this morning.

I thought of coming over to your house this afternoon, but I couldn't bring my sewing very well. I am putting the ruffles on my new black dress skirt."

"Well, I didn't have a thing on hand except my crochet work," responded Mrs Meserve, "and I thought I'd just run over a few minutes."

"I'm real glad you did," repeated Mrs Emerson. "Take your things right off. Here, I'll put them on my bed in the bedroom. Take the rocking chair."

Mrs Meserve settled herself in the parlour rocking chair, while Mrs Emerson carried her shawl and hat into the little adjoining bedroom. When she returned Mrs Meserve was rocking peacefully and was already at work hooking blue wool in and out.

"That's real pretty," said Mrs Emerson.

"Yes, I think it's pretty," replied Mrs Meserve.

"I suppose it's for the church fair?"

"Yes. I don't suppose it'll bring enough to pay for the worsted, let alone the work, but I suppose I've got to make something."

"How much did that one you made for the fair last year bring?"

"Twenty-five cents."

"It's wicked, ain't it?"

"I rather guess it is. It takes me a week every minute I can get to make one. I wish those that bought such things for twenty-five cents had to make them. Guess they'd sing another song. Well, I suppose I oughtn't to complain as long as it is for the Lord, but sometimes it does seem as if the Lord didn't get much out of it."

"Well, it's pretty work," said Mrs Emerson, sitting down at the opposite window and taking up her dress skirt.

"Yes, it is real pretty work. I just *love* to crochet."

The two women rocked and sewed and crocheted in silence for two or three minutes. They were both waiting. Mrs Meserve waited for the other's curiosity to develop in order that her news might have, as it were, a befitting stage entrance. Mrs Emerson waited for the news. Finally she could wait no longer.

"Well, what's the news?" said she.

"Well, I don't know as there's anything very particular," hedged the other woman, prolonging the situation.

"Yes, there is; you can't cheat me," replied Mrs Emerson.

"Now, how do you know?"

"By the way you look."

Mrs Meserve laughed consciously and rather vainly.

"Well, Simon says my face is so expressive I can't hide anything more than five minutes no matter how hard I try," said she. "Well, there is some news. Simon came home with it this noon. He heard it in South Dayton. He had some business over there this morning. The old Sargent place is let."

Mrs Emerson dropped her sewing and stared.

"You don't say so!"

"Yes, it is."

"Who to?"

"Why, some folks from Boston that moved to South Dayton last year. They haven't been satisfied with the house they had there – it wasn't large enough. The man has got considerable property and can afford to live pretty well. He's got a wife and his unmarried sister in the family. The sister's got money, too. He does business in Boston and it's just as easy to get to Boston from here as from South Dayton, and so they're coming here. You know the old Sargent house is a splendid place."

"Yes, it's the handsomest house in town, but—"

"Oh, Simon said they told him about that and he just laughed. Said he wasn't afraid and neither was his wife and sister. Said he'd risk ghosts rather than little tucked-up sleeping-rooms without any sun, like they've had in the Dayton house. Said he'd rather risk *seeing* ghosts, than risk being ghosts themselves. Simon said they said he was a great hand to joke."

"Oh, well," said Mrs Emerson, "it is a beautiful house, and maybe there isn't anything in those stories. It never seemed to me they came very straight anyway. I never took much stock in them. All I thought was – if his wife was nervous."

"Nothing in creation would hire me to go into a house that I'd ever heard a word against of that kind," declared Mrs Meserve with emphasis. "I wouldn't go into that house if they would give me the rent. I've seen enough of haunted houses to last me as long as I live."

Mrs Emerson's face acquired the expression of a hunting hound.

"Have you?" she asked in an intense whisper.

"Yes, I have. I don't want any more of it."

"Before you came here?"

"Yes; before I was married – when I was quite a girl."

Mrs Meserve had not married young. Mrs Emerson had mental calculations when she heard that.

"Did you really live in a house that was—" she whispered fearfully. Mrs Meserve nodded solemnly.

"Did you really ever – see – anything?"

Mrs Meserve nodded.

"You didn't see anything that did you any harm?"

"No, I didn't see anything that did me harm looking at it in one way, but it don't do anybody in this world any good to see things that haven't any business to be seen in it. You never get over it."

There was a moment's silence. Mrs Emerson's features seemed to sharpen.

"Well, of course I don't want to urge you," said she, "if you don't feel like talking about it; but maybe it might do you good to tell it out, if it's on your mind, worrying you."

"I try to put it out of my mind," said Mrs Meserve.

"Well, it's just as you feel."

"I never told anybody but Simon," said Mrs Meserve. "I never felt as if it was wise perhaps. I didn't know what folks might think. So many don't believe in anything they can't understand, that they might think my mind wasn't right. Simon advised me not to talk about it. He said he didn't believe it was anything supernatural, but he had to own up that he couldn't give any explanation for it to save his life. He had to own up that he didn't believe anybody could. Then he said he wouldn't talk about it. He said lots of folks would sooner tell folks my head wasn't right than to own up they couldn't see through it."

"I'm sure I wouldn't say so," returned Mrs Emerson reproachfully. "You know better than that, I hope."

"Yes, I do," replied Mrs Meserve. "I know you wouldn't say so."

"And I wouldn't tell it to a soul if you didn't want me to."

"Well, I'd rather you wouldn't."

"I won't speak of it even to Mr Emerson."

"I'd rather you wouldn't even to him."

"I won't."

Mrs Emerson took up her dress skirt again; Mrs Meserve hooked up another loop of blue wool. Then she began:

"Of course," said she, "I ain't going to say positively that I believe or disbelieve in ghosts, but all I tell you is what I saw. I can't explain it. I don't pretend I can, for I can't. If you can, well and good; I shall be glad, for it will stop tormenting me as it has done and always will otherwise. There hasn't been a day nor a night since it happened that I haven't thought of it, and always I have felt the shivers go down my back when I did."

"That's an awful feeling," Mrs Emerson said.

"Ain't it? Well, it happened before I was married, when I was a girl and lived in East Wilmington. It was the first year I lived there. You know my family all died five years before that. I told you."

Mrs Emerson nodded.

"Well, I went there to teach school, and I went to board with a Mrs Amelia Dennison and her sister, Mrs Bird. Abby, her name was – Abby Bird. She was a widow; she had never had any children. She had a little money – Mrs Dennison didn't have any – and she had come to East Wilmington and bought the house they lived in. It was a real pretty house, though it was very old and run down. It had cost Mrs Bird a good deal to put it in order. I guess that was the reason they took me to board. I guess they thought it would help along a little. I guess what I paid for my board about kept us all in victuals. Mrs Bird had enough to live on if they were careful, but she had spent so much fixing up the old house that they must have been a little pinched for awhile.

"Anyhow, they took me to board, and I thought I was pretty lucky to get in there. I had a nice room, big and sunny and furnished pretty, the paper and paint all new, and everything as neat as wax. Mrs Dennison was one of the best cooks I ever saw, and I had a little stove in my room, and there was always a nice fire there when I got home from school. I thought I hadn't been in such a nice place since I lost my own home, until I had been there about three weeks.

"I had been there about three weeks before I found it out, though I guess it had been going on ever since they had been in the house, and that was most four months. They hadn't said anything about it, and I didn't wonder, for there they had just bought the house and been to so much expense and trouble fixing it up.

"Well, I went there in September. I began my school the first Monday. I remember it was a real cold fall, there was a frost the middle of September, and I had to put on my winter coat. I remember when I came home that night (let me see, I began school on a Monday, and that was two weeks from the next Thursday), I took off my coat downstairs and laid it on the table in the front entry. It was a real nice coat – heavy black broadcloth trimmed with fur; I had had it the winter before. Mrs Bird called after me as I went upstairs that I ought not to leave it in the front entry for fear somebody might come in and take it, but I only laughed and called back to her that I wasn't afraid. I never was much afraid of burglars.

"Well, though it was hardly the middle of September, it was a real cold night. I remember my room faced west, and the sun was getting low, and the sky was a pale yellow and purple, just as you see it sometimes in the winter when there is going to be a cold snap. I rather think that was the night the frost came the first time. I know Mrs Dennison covered up some flowers she had in the front yard, anyhow. I remember looking out and seeing an old green plaid shawl of hers over the verbena bed.

There was a fire in my little wood-stove. Mrs Bird made it, I know. She was a real motherly sort of woman; she always seemed to be the happiest when she was doing something to make other folks happy and comfortable. Mrs Dennison told me she had always been so. She said she had coddled her husband within an inch of his life. 'It's lucky Abby never had any children,' she said, 'for she would have spoiled them.'

"Well, that night I sat down beside my nice little fire and ate an apple. There was a plate of nice apples on my table. Mrs Bird put them there. I was always very fond of apples. Well, I sat down and ate an apple, and was having a beautiful time, and thinking how lucky I was to have got board in such a place with such nice folks, when I heard a queer little sound at my door. It was such a little hesitating sort of sound that it sounded more like a fumble than a knock, as if someone very timid, with very little hands, was feeling along the door, not quite daring to knock. For a minute I thought it was a mouse. But I waited and it came again, and then I made up my mind it was a knock, but a very little scared one, so I said, 'Come in.'

"But nobody came in, and then presently I heard the knock again. Then I got up and opened the door, thinking it was very queer, and I had a frightened feeling without knowing why.

"Well, I opened the door, and the first thing I noticed was a draught of cold air, as if the front door downstairs was open, but there was a strange close smell about the cold draught. It smelled more like a cellar that had been shut up for years, than out-of-doors. Then I saw something. I saw my coat first. The thing that held it was so small that I couldn't see much of anything else. Then I saw a little white face with eyes so scared and wishful that they seemed as if they might eat a hole in anybody's heart. It was a dreadful little face, with something about it which made it different from any other face on earth, but it was so pitiful that somehow it did away a good deal with the dreadfulness. And there were two little hands spotted purple with the cold, holding up my winter coat, and a strange little far-away voice said: 'I can't find my mother.'

"'For Heaven's sake,' I said, 'who are you?'

"Then the little voice said again: 'I can't find my mother.'

"All the time I could smell the cold and I saw that it was about the child; that cold was clinging to her as if she had come out of some deadly cold place. Well, I took my coat, I did not know what else to do, and the cold was clinging to that. It was as cold as if it had come off ice. When I had the coat I could see the child more plainly. She was dressed in one little white garment made very simply. It was a nightgown, only very long, quite covering her feet, and I could see dimly through it her little thin body mottled purple with the cold. Her face did not look so cold; that was a clear waxen white. Her hair was dark, but it looked as if it might be dark only because it was so damp, almost wet, and might really be light hair. It clung very close to her forehead, which was round and white. She would have been very beautiful if she had not been so dreadful.

"'Who are you?' says I again, looking at her.

"She looked at me with her terrible pleading eyes and did not say anything.

"'What are you?' says I. Then she went away. She did not seem to run or walk like other children. She flitted, like one of those little filmy white butterflies that don't seem like real ones they are so light, and move as if they had no weight. But she looked back from the head of the stairs. 'I can't find my mother,' said she, and I never heard such a voice.

"'Who is your mother?' says I, but she was gone.

"Well, I thought for a moment I should faint away. The room got dark and I heard a singing in my ears. Then I flung my coat on to the bed. My hands were as cold as ice from holding it, and I stood in my door, and called first Mrs Bird and then Mrs Dennison. I didn't dare go down over the stairs where that had gone. It seemed to me I should go mad if I didn't see somebody or something like other folks on the face of the earth. I thought I should never make anybody hear, but I could hear them stepping about downstairs, and I could smell biscuits baking for supper. Somehow the smell of those biscuits seemed the only natural thing left to keep me in my right mind. I didn't dare go over those stairs. I just stood there and called, and finally I heard the entry door open and Mrs Bird called back:

"'What is it? Did you call, Miss Arms?'"

"'Come up here; come up here as quick as you can, both of you,' I screamed out; 'quick, quick, quick!'

"I heard Mrs Bird tell Mrs Dennison: 'Come quick, Amelia, something is the matter in Miss Arms's room.' It struck me even then that she expressed herself rather queerly, and it struck me as very queer, indeed, when they both got upstairs and I saw that they knew what had happened, or that they knew of what nature the happening was.

"'What is it, dear?' asked Mrs Bird, and her pretty, loving voice had a strained sound. I saw her look at Mrs Dennison and I saw Mrs Dennison look back at her.

"'For God's sake,' says I, and I never spoke so before – 'for God's sake, what was it brought my coat upstairs?'

"'What was it like?' asked Mrs Dennison in a sort of failing voice, and she looked at her sister again and her sister looked back at her.

"'It was a child I have never seen here before. It looked like a child,' says I, 'but I never saw a child so dreadful, and it had on a nightgown, and said it couldn't find its mother. Who was it? What was it?'

"I thought for a minute Mrs Dennison was going to faint, but Mrs Bird hung on to her and rubbed her hands, and whispered in her ear (she had the cooingest kind of voice), and I ran and got her a glass of cold water. I tell you it took considerable courage to go downstairs alone, but they had set a lamp on the entry table so I could see. I don't believe I could have spunked up enough to have gone downstairs in the dark, thinking every second that child might be close to me. The lamp and the smell of the biscuits baking seemed to sort of keep my courage up, but I tell you I didn't waste much time going down those stairs and out into the kitchen for a glass of water. I pumped as if the house was afire, and I grabbed the first thing I came across in the shape of a tumbler: it was a painted one that Mrs Dennison's Sunday school class gave her, and it was meant for a flower vase.

"Well, I filled it and then ran upstairs. I felt every minute as if something would catch my feet, and I held the glass to Mrs Dennison's lips, while Mrs Bird held her head up, and she took a good long swallow, then she looked hard at the tumbler.

"'Yes,' says I, 'I know I got this one, but I took the first I came across, and it isn't hurt a mite.'

"'Don't get the painted flowers wet,' says Mrs Dennison very feebly, 'they'll wash off if you do.'

"'I'll be real careful,' says I. I knew she set a sight by that painted tumbler.

"The water seemed to do Mrs Dennison good, for presently she pushed Mrs Bird away and sat up. She had been lying down on my bed.

"'I'm all over it now,' says she, but she was terribly white, and her eyes looked as if they saw something outside things. Mrs Bird wasn't much better, but she always had a sort of settled sweet, good look that nothing could disturb to any great extent. I knew I looked dreadful, for I caught a glimpse of myself in the glass, and I would hardly have known who it was.

"Mrs Dennison, she slid off the bed and walked sort of tottery to a chair. 'I was silly to give way so,' says she.

"'No, you wasn't silly, sister,' says Mrs Bird. 'I don't know what this means any more than you do, but whatever it is, no one ought to be called silly for being overcome by anything so different from other things which we have known all our lives.'

"Mrs Dennison looked at her sister, then she looked at me, then back at her sister again, and Mrs Bird spoke as if she had been asked a question.

"'Yes,' says she, 'I do think Miss Arms ought to be told – that is, I think she ought to be told all we know ourselves.'

"'That isn't much,' said Mrs Dennison with a dying-away sort of sigh. She looked as if she might faint away again any minute. She was a real delicate-looking woman, but it turned out she was a good deal stronger than poor Mrs Bird.

"'No, there isn't much we do know,' says Mrs Bird, 'but what little there is she ought to know. I felt as if she ought to when she first came here.'

"'Well, I didn't feel quite right about it,' said Mrs Dennison, 'but I kept hoping it might stop, and anyway, that it might never trouble her, and you had put so much in the house, and we needed the money, and I didn't know but she might be nervous and think she couldn't come, and I didn't want to take a man boarder.'

"'And aside from the money, we were very anxious to have you come, my dear,' says Mrs Bird.

"'Yes,' says Mrs Dennison, 'we wanted the young company in the house; we were lonesome, and we both of us took a great liking to you the minute we set eyes on you.'

"And I guess they meant what they said, both of them. They were beautiful women, and nobody could be any kinder to me than they were, and I never blamed them for not telling me before, and, as they said, there wasn't really much to tell.

"They hadn't any sooner fairly bought the house, and moved into it, than they began to see and hear things. Mrs Bird said they were sitting together in the sitting room one evening when they heard it the first time. She said her sister was knitting lace (Mrs Dennison made beautiful knitted lace) and she was reading the *Missionary Herald* (Mrs Bird was very much interested in mission work), when all of a sudden they heard something. She heard it first and she laid down her *Missionary Herald* and listened, and then Mrs Dennison, she saw her listening, and she drops her lace. 'What is it you are listening to, Abby?' says she. Then it came again and they both heard, and the cold shivers went down their backs to hear it, though they didn't know why. 'It's the cat, isn't it?' says Mrs Bird.

"'It isn't any cat,' says Mrs Dennison.

"'Oh, I guess it *must* be the cat; maybe she's got a mouse,' says Mrs Bird, real cheerful, to calm down Mrs Dennison, for she saw she was 'most scared to death, and she was always afraid of her fainting away. Then she opens the door and calls, 'Kitty, kitty, kitty!' They had brought their cat with them in a basket when they came to East Wilmington to live. It was a real handsome tiger cat, a tommy, and he knew a lot.

"Well, she called 'Kitty, kitty, kitty!' and sure enough the kitty came, and when he came in the door he gave a big yawl that didn't sound unlike what they had heard.

"'There, sister, here he is; you see it was the cat,' says Mrs Bird. 'Poor kitty!'

"But Mrs Dennison she eyed the cat, and she give a great screech.

"'What's that? What's that?' says she.

"'What's what?' says Mrs Bird, pretending to herself that she didn't see what her sister meant.

"'Something's got hold of that cat's tail,' says Mrs Dennison. 'Somethin's got hold of his tail. It's pulled straight out, an' he can't get away. Just hear him yawl!'

"'It isn't anything,' says Mrs Bird, but even as she said that she could see a little hand holding fast to that cat's tail, and then the child seemed to sort of clear out of the dimness behind the hand, and the child was sort of laughing then, instead of looking sad, and she said that was a great deal worse. She said that laugh was the most awful and the saddest thing she ever heard.

"Well, she was so dumbfounded that she didn't know what to do, and she couldn't sense at first that it was anything supernatural. She thought it must be one of the neighbour's children who had run away and was making free of their house, and was teasing their cat, and that they must be just nervous to feel so upset by it. So she speaks up sort of sharp.

"'Don't you know that you mustn't pull the kitty's tail?' says she. 'Don't you know you hurt the poor kitty, and he'll scratch you if you don't take care? Poor kitty, you mustn't hurt him.'

"And with that, she said, the child stopped pulling that cat's tail and went to stroking him just as soft and pitiful, and the cat put his back up and rubbed and purred as if he liked it. The cat never seemed a mite afraid, and that seemed queer, for I had always heard that animals were dreadfully afraid of ghosts; but then, that was a pretty harmless little sort of ghost.

"Well, Mrs Bird said the child stroked that cat, while she and Mrs Dennison stood watching it, and holding on to each other, for, no matter how hard they tried to think it was all right, it didn't look right. Finally Mrs Dennison spoke.

"'What's your name, little girl?' says she.

"Then the child looks up and stops stroking the cat, and says she can't find her mother, just the way she said it to me. Then Mrs Dennison, she gave such a gasp that Mrs Bird thought she was going to faint away, but she didn't. 'Well, who is your mother?' says she. But the child just says again, 'I can't find my mother – I can't find my mother.'

"'Where do you live, dear?' says Mrs Bird.

"'I can't find my mother,' says the child.

"Well, that was the way it was. Nothing happened. Those two women stood there hanging on to each other, and the child stood in front of them, and they asked her questions, and everything she would say was: 'I can't find my mother.'

"Then Mrs Bird tried to catch hold of the child, for she thought in spite of what she saw that perhaps she was nervous and it was a real child, only perhaps not quite right in its head, that had run away in her little nightgown after she had been put to bed.

"She tried to catch the child. She had an idea of putting a shawl around it and going out – she was such a little thing she could have carried her easy enough – and trying to find out to which of the neighbours she belonged. But the minute she moved to the child there wasn't any child there; there was only that little voice seeming to come from nothing, saying 'I can't find my mother', and presently that died away.

"Well, that same thing kept happening, or something very much the same. Once in awhile Mrs Bird would be washing dishes, and all at once the child would be standing beside her with the dish-towel, wiping them. Of course, that was terrible. Mrs Bird would wash the dishes all over. Sometimes she didn't tell Mrs Dennison, it made her so nervous. Sometimes when they were making cake they would find the raisins all picked over, and sometimes little sticks of kindling wood would be found lying beside the kitchen stove. They never knew when they would come across that child, and always she kept saying over and over that she couldn't find her mother. They never tried talking to her, except once in awhile Mrs Bird would get desperate and ask her something, but the child never seemed to hear it; she always kept right on saying that she couldn't find her mother.

"After they had told me all they had to tell about their experience with the child, they told me about the house and the people that had lived there before they did. It seemed something dreadful had happened in that house. And the land agent had never let on to them. I don't think they would have bought it if he had, no matter how cheap it was, for even if folks aren't really afraid of anything, they don't want to live in houses where such dreadful things have happened that you keep thinking about them. I know after they told me I should never have stayed there another night, if I hadn't thought so much of them, no matter how comfortable I was made; and I never was nervous, either. But I stayed. Of course, it didn't happen in my room. If it had I could not have stayed."

"What was it?" asked Mrs Emerson in an awed voice.

"It was an awful thing. That child had lived in the house with her father and mother two years before. They had come – or the father had – from a real good family. He had a good situation: he was a drummer for a big leather house in the city, and they lived real pretty, with plenty to do with. But the mother was a real wicked woman. She was as handsome as a picture, and they said she came from good sort of people enough in Boston, but she was bad clean through, though she was real pretty spoken and most everybody liked her. She used to dress out and make a great show, and she never seemed to take much interest in the child, and folks began to say she wasn't treated right.

"The woman had a hard time keeping a girl. For some reason one wouldn't stay. They would leave and then talk about her awfully, telling all kinds of things. People didn't believe it at first; then they began to. They said that the woman made that little thing, though she wasn't much over five years old, and small and babyish for her age, do most of the work, what there was done. They said the house used to look like a pigsty when she didn't have help. They said the little thing used to stand on a chair and wash dishes, and they'd seen her carrying in sticks of wood most as big as she was many a time, and they'd heard her mother scolding her. The woman was a fine singer, and had a voice like a screech-owl when she scolded.

"The father was away most of the time, and when that happened he had been away out West for some weeks. There had been a married man hanging about the mother for some time, and folks had talked some; but they weren't sure there was anything wrong, and he was a man very high up, with money, so they kept pretty still for fear he would hear of it and make trouble for them, and of course nobody was sure, though folks did say afterward that the father of the child had ought to have been told.

"But that was very easy to say; it wouldn't have been so easy to find anybody who would have been willing to tell him such a thing as that, especially when they weren't any too sure. He set his eyes by his wife, too. They said all he seemed to think of was to earn money to buy things to deck her out in. And he about worshipped the child, too. They said he was a real nice man. The men that are treated so bad mostly are real nice men. I've always noticed that.

"Well, one morning that man that there had been whispers about was missing. He had been gone quite a while, though, before they really knew that he was missing, because he had gone away and told his wife that he had to go to New York on business and might be gone a week, and not to worry if he didn't get home, and not to worry if he didn't write, because he should be thinking from day to day that he might take the next train home and there would be no use in writing. So the wife waited, and she tried not to worry until it was two days over the week, then she ran into a neighbour's and fainted dead away on the floor; and then they made enquiries and found out that he had skipped – with some money that didn't belong to him, too.

"Then folks began to ask where was that woman, and they found out by comparing notes that nobody had seen her since the man went away; but three or four women remembered that she had told them that she thought of taking the child and going to Boston to visit her folks, so when they hadn't seen her around, and the house shut, they jumped to the conclusion that was where she was. They were the neighbours that lived right around her, but they didn't have much to do with her, and she'd gone out of her way to tell them about her Boston plan, and they didn't make much reply when she did.

"Well, there was this house shut up, and the man and woman missing and the child. Then all of a sudden one of the women that lived the nearest remembered something. She remembered that she had waked up three nights running, thinking she heard a child crying somewhere, and once she waked up her husband, but he said it must be the Bisbees' little girl, and she thought it must be. The child wasn't well and was always crying. It used to have colic spells, especially at night. So she didn't think any more about it until this came up, then all of a sudden she did think of it. She told what she had heard, and finally folks began to think they had better enter that house and see if there was anything wrong.

"Well, they did enter it, and they found that child dead, locked in one of the rooms. (Mrs Dennison and Mrs Bird never used that room; it was a back bedroom on the second floor.)

"Yes, they found that poor child there, starved to death, and frozen, though they weren't sure she had frozen to death, for she was in bed with clothes enough to keep her pretty warm when she was alive. But she had been there a week, and she was nothing but skin and bone. It looked as if the mother had locked her into the house when she went away, and told her not to make any noise for fear the neighbours would hear her and find out that she herself had gone.

"Mrs Dennison said she couldn't really believe that the woman had meant to have her own child starved to death. Probably she thought the little thing would raise somebody, or folks would try to get in the house and find her. Well, whatever she thought, there the child was, dead.

"But that wasn't all. The father came home, right in the

midst of it; the child was just buried, and he was beside himself. And he went on the track of his wife, and he found her, and he shot her dead; it was in all the papers at the time; then he disappeared. Nothing had been seen of him since. Mrs Dennison said that she thought he had either made away with himself or got out of the country, nobody knew, but they did know there was something wrong with the house.

"'I knew folks acted queer when they asked me how I liked it when we first came here,' says Mrs Dennison, 'but I never dreamed why till we saw the child that night.'

"I never heard anything like it in my life," said Mrs Emerson, staring at the other woman with awestruck eyes.

"I thought you'd say so," said Mrs Meserve. "You don't wonder that I ain't disposed to speak light when I hear there is anything queer about a house, do you?"

"No, I don't, after that," Mrs Emerson said.

"But that ain't all," said Mrs Meserve.

"Did you see it again?" Mrs Emerson asked.

"Yes, I saw it a number of times before the last time. It was lucky I wasn't nervous, or I never could have stayed there, much as I liked the place and much as I thought of those two women; they were beautiful women, and no mistake. I loved those women. I hope Mrs Dennison will come and see me sometime.

"Well, I stayed, and I never knew when I'd see that child. I got so I was very careful to bring everything of mine upstairs, and not leave any little thing in my room that needed doing, for fear she would come lugging up my coat or hat or gloves or I'd find things done when there'd been no live being in the room to do them. I can't tell you how I dreaded seeing her; and worse than the seeing her was the hearing her say, 'I can't find my mother.' It was enough to make your blood run cold. I never heard a living child cry for its mother that was anything so pitiful as that dead one. It was enough to break your heart.

"She used to come and say that to Mrs Bird oftener than to anyone else. Once I heard Mrs Bird say she wondered if it was possible that the poor little thing couldn't really find her mother in the other world, she had been such a wicked woman.

"But Mrs Dennison told her she didn't think she ought to speak so nor even think so, and Mrs Bird said she shouldn't wonder if she was right.

"Mrs Bird was always very easy to put in the wrong. She was a good woman, and one that couldn't do things enough for other folks. It seemed as if that was what she lived on. I don't think she was ever so scared by that poor little ghost, as much as she pitied it, and she was 'most heartbroken because she couldn't do anything for it, as she could have done for a live child.

"'It seems to me sometimes as if I should die if I can't get that awful little white robe off that child and get her in some clothes and feed her and stop her looking for her mother,' I heard her say once, and she was in earnest. She cried when she said it. That wasn't long before she died.

"Now I am coming to the strangest part of it all. Mrs Bird died very sudden. One morning – it was Saturday, and there wasn't any school – I went downstairs to breakfast, and Mrs Bird wasn't there; there was nobody but Mrs Dennison. She was pouring out the coffee when I came in. 'Why, where's Mrs Bird?' says I.

"'Abby ain't feeling very well this morning,' says she; 'there isn't much the matter, I guess, but she didn't sleep very well, and her head aches, and she's sort of chilly, and I told her I thought she'd better stay in bed till the house gets warm.' It was a very cold morning.

"'Maybe she's got cold,' says I.

"'Yes, I guess she has,' says Mrs Dennison. 'I guess she's got cold. She'll be up before long. Abby ain't one to stay in bed a minute longer than she can help.'

"Well, we went on eating our breakfast, and all at once a shadow flickered across one wall of the room and over the ceiling the way a shadow will sometimes when somebody passes the window outside. Mrs Dennison and I both looked up, then out of the window; then Mrs Dennison she gives a scream.

"'Why, Abby's crazy!' says she. 'There she is out this bitter cold morning, and – and —' She didn't finish, but she meant the child. For we were both looking out, and we saw, as plain as we ever saw anything in our lives, Mrs Abby Bird walking off over the white snow-path with that child holding fast to her hand, nestling close to her as if she had found her own mother.

"'She's dead,' says Mrs Dennison, clutching hold of me hard. 'She's dead; my sister is dead!'

"She was. We hurried upstairs as fast as we could go, and she was dead in her bed, and smiling as if she was dreaming, and one arm and hand was stretched out as if something had hold of it; and it couldn't be straightened even at the last – it lay out over her casket at the funeral."

"Was the child ever seen again?" asked Mrs Emerson in a shaking voice.

"No," replied Mrs Meserve; "that child was never seen again after she went out of the yard with Mrs Bird."

The Ninth Witch

Sarah Langan

This was back in the old days, when women weren't worth anything. First came the wars, then the floods. Molluscs made homes out of rotted dolls. After that came the plague; moss worms riddled all the animal lungs. By the time things began to clear, and the sun burned out from its sulphurous pocket, everyone was hungry and cold. They'd forgotten what it meant to be human, and had no sympathy left to spare.

Like all witches, Jane was born the ninth daughter of a ninth daughter. This was rare, because back then, few women carried anything but stones to term. What Jane didn't know, and what no one remembered, was that the line carried farther: she was the ninth daughter of a ninth daughter nine generations back. With each generation, the magic got stronger until the last ninth was born with a misshapen womb that could only expel animals, so that no tenth would compete with God.

Though ninth of nines, nine back, were prophesized to change the world, most squandered their birthrights. They were women, after all, and rarely met their potential. Some, rejected by their families, wandered the borders of Sudamorstralia like lunatics, shouting of visions. Others were murdered because of their third eyes. Some denied they were different. Jane was like these last. As soon as she was old enough, she clotted closed her third eye with beetle fat, and if she'd been sure it would not grow back, she'd have cut it out.

Because her mother's power was nearly as strong as Jane's, each of her eight siblings was also born with a special talent. These varied from music to words to grace. Strength and beauty were obvious; those less obvious didn't tend to get expressed. Jane's third eye was a blue freckle high up in the centre of her forehead. A black cowlick covered it, and it only opened, its skin parting to reveal a cornflower blue pupil, when she was sleeping. Her father might have sacrificed her to Ve for this strange affliction, but the kind spirits of her ancestors began combing the skeletons in the Perth fallout for offerings on her behalf. They left trinkets such as round, metal bands affixed with rocks so shiny they reflected rainbows, and hunks of gold shaped like teeth, which the family traded for food. Other, less kind spirits rocked the child too hard in her crib, and knocked her out. When that happened, Jane's sixth sister, the healer, would pick her up and rock her, crooning a popular lullaby so softly that none of the other children could hear:

> *Sleep child.*
> *Close your eyes.*
> *They covet our miseries*
> *Because we are alive.*
> *Darling dear,*
> *The end is near.*
> *Do not fret.*
> *Soon we'll all disappear.*

Because Jane's mother died in childbirth, her father's heart had dried and shrivelled inside his chest. He worried about his payments to King Herod IIXX, who raised taxes every year. He worried about the price of radishes and potatoes, which kept falling. He put the girls to work. They toiled during hours of light, bare-backed and slick with sweat like men. The eldest, who at night made music from jars filled with water, quickly died. The second and smartest ran away. The third, querulous and lazy, who could track the stars by fractions of millimetres and ought to have lived on a boat, he married off to a grey-haired priest, just to be rid of her. The fourth, a rare beauty, he sold, parading her on the town auction block with her dress lifted, so the men could admire her muscular thighs. The fifth, he kept by his side, because she was strong, never complained, and had the disposition of a horse. The sixth, and Jane's favourite, made a career of medicine by studying the books she'd found in the bombed-out library. There was a room deep underground filled with untouched texts that she translated from Latin, then ate each page one by one, so that it would become part of her, and because she was hungry. She saved her father and three sisters when plague passed through the countryside, boiling down willow bark and feeding it to them as a stew, along with two-week-aged mould from bread. She stayed until Jane was old enough to speak, so that the youngest child might defend herself. *Momma*, Jane called her when she was twelve months old. *I love you.* With a heavy heart, the sixth packed her unguents and left that very day, before her love for the child overpowered her. Jane mourned her absence, standing vigil at the space on the floor where she'd slept, like a wild animal missing its poached mother.

Taxes came due on the farm. The old man and his five remaining girls got down on their knees and begged for a reprieve, but the soldiers, dressed in rusted, cut metal sheets from dismantled old-world buildings, refused. They were thrown out, their house chopped down and used for Herod's castle.

Because the farm had been in the man's family since before the flood, and even before the continental drift, he went a little mad. He murdered the seventh child and peeled off her skin, then hung it from a blue spruce tree, like the legends told him. Then he made his wish, and prayed all night to Fulla that his prayers would be answered, and the child's hanging husk would be filled by a living boy-child, who would save them from starvation. But by the next morning, something had stolen the child's dangling husk. He considered lighting what remained, her flesh and bones, over a fire to quell his rumbling stomach, but by then his daughters had buried her, and would not tell him where. For this, he beat them. Each bore the whip silently. Six lashes apiece. The strong fifth child, having never complained, did not tell them that a child had quickened inside her. Their father was the father, though not even the fifth child knew this. They'd never seen animals or the sex act, except when perpetrated upon them, and did not know what it meant. At the sixth strike, something broke inside the stalwart daughter and she fell dead. The life ran out between her legs, a perfectly formed boy-child, unbreathing and too small.

The eighth and most courageous child stripped the whip from her father, and used it to lash him. He took it back, of course, and hit her until she fell beside her sister, barely breathing. To release her from this horror, if only for a short while, Jane's third eye cracked open. Her skin wrinkled and parted like hot milk at the top of a boiling pot. The eye blinked, and showed her a glimpse of the past, where metal machines on wheels zoomed down smooth rock roads, and humans were tall and stocky from eating animal flesh. A world where fathers loved their daughters, and mothers sang lullabies. A dead world.

At last, there were only two children left. The woods were dark, and so scavenged that all they ate was dirt and ants that they lured with their monthly blood. Weeks passed, and they travelled in circles while the old man raved. The eighth child said to the ninth, *Let's run away while the old man sleeps*. But spirits had come to Jane, and told her that she would not find a better life beyond her father's thumb, and that the world was a cruel place. So the courageous eighth ran away in the night, and Jane stayed. She and her father trudged through snow like wretches. The dirt by then was frozen, and there was nothing left to eat but their own boots. Barefoot and in snowy weather three days later, they passed a band of robbers, who largely ignored them, because their clothes were tatters. But then Jane noticed, just like her dream had told her, that the tallest robber wore the eighth daughter's flaming red scalp over his flea-bald head. He and the others looked well fed, though the forest was cursed, and no animals on four feet roamed.

For the first time in all her twelve years, Jane screamed out loud.

The band looked at the wraiths more closely. The father had withered inside his flesh from years of misery, but Jane had grown strong and beautiful. Wearing the eighth daughter's flaming red hair, the lead robber wiped Jane's face with snow until it was clean, then offered to buy her for three gold pieces.

But if you take her, I'll have nothing, and everything I've ever lived for will amount to ashes, the father said. *I cannot part with her. She is my suffering to bear. And I must admit, now that there is only one left, I am lonely for the rest, and her value has accrued.*

Take six gold pieces, the robber with false red hair said, *and you will both live for at least another year. Or take nothing, and die tonight of hunger.*

The father took the deal.

The cabin in the woods where the robber and his brother lived was small, with an apple cellar in its basement, a wood stove that kept them warm, and eighty-one scalps hanging from the front door, to warn away strangers. When he took Jane home, he fed her meat, even though this forest was cursed, and live animals had not run its woods in centuries. She thought that night that she would gag or die from shame, but she did not. Instead, her third eye opened, and took her to the old place, where houses leaned row on row, and upon each lawn were flowers. *This is beauty,* she thought. *It lives inside us, trapped.*

Two and then five years passed. The robber loved her in his way, and Jane loved him in return, because she was lonely and young and did not know the difference between a whip and a kiss. At night when he and his brother were away and the wind howled, she listened to the spirits of the woods, who had died there, and lingered. Their stories were worse, for at least she had survived, and no one had loved her so deeply that she missed them.

As she grew older, Jane's beauty became so great that the robber sewed eyeholes inside a burlap bag, which she wore over her head to market, so that no one would steal her. He also branded his name into her thigh and coached her to walk with a limp, so that men in town thought she was a worthless cripple. After each hunting expedition, he and his brother returned with fresh meat despite all the rest of the countryside, that was starving, and nailed another scalp to the door. Life is ugly, Jane thought, but it's better than nothing.

When she reached sixteen years old, Jane had still not borne a child to the robber. He came home one night and sat down heavily. *I love you,* he told her, *but if you don't quicken with child within the year, I'll have to kill you and marry another. I will peel off your flesh and hang it from a spruce, so that my wish is fulfilled, for I cannot go on each day, knowing I might die without an heir, or a taste of the eternal.*

Weeks passed. Jane plied the robber with drink every night, and fulfilled her wifely duty even when disgusted by his scent. Months passed, and still her blood ran. She sopped this with dry leaves stuck high inside her cavity, but always they leaked, and he discovered her. She said prayers; she begged the impassive spirits, but her ancestors had burned up with the old house, and the murdered ghosts that haunted these woods were not kind. Eleven months passed. At a loss, she stole into town looking for her father. An imp disciple of Loki led her to a brothel, where whores without teeth or hair lounged on stained piles of hay, and a drunk old man swept the stable.

Father, she said to him, taking off her burlap cloak, and revealing her face. *Help me. I'm to be killed tomorrow, for I do not have an heir inside me.*

The old man turned to her. His eyes had been gouged. Her third eye informed her that he'd done it to himself the day he sold her. *Child,* he said. *We all suffer. When I was young I was foolish, and murdered my family. The one wish I made was eaten by the same robber who stole my heart. You must tie yourself with stones and dive into the river. Or stay here, and spread your legs.*

The girl left disheartened because her father had not recognized her and there was no one in the world who loved her. *I will go home,* she thought, and *join my red-headed eighth sister on the wall.* On her way, her third eye opened and she got lost. The woods folded and unbent. She came upon a log cabin with a fire burning from its chimney. Flowers adorned boxes under its windows. She knocked on the door. A fat old woman with warts and missing teeth answered. Behind her, the house was full of jars and tinctures and children's cauls. And on the kitchen table, Jane smelled a fresh, hot pan of something soft as cotton that made her mouth water.

She'd heard of witches, and even been told that she was one. They ate children and bathed in blood to stay young. But the smell was so good here, and she had no place else to go. *I'm lost,* she said. *I'm to be killed tonight because I have no child.*

The old woman nodded and took her in. Strange animals scurried on four legs. Jane only knew they were cats because of her visions of the old world. They purred along the sides of her legs as she ogled at the cotton blobs fresh from the oven. The old woman took one and handed it to her. *Eat this,* she said. *It will blossom inside you.*

Jane picked up the biscuit. She'd never eaten fresh bread before, and already her stomach rumbled like a spiked, spinning mace was inside it. *Is it poison?* Jane asked.

The woman cackled. *I should hope not!* she said. *You summoned me, remember?* Then she looked closely at Jane, and tsk-tsked: *Poor child, you don't even know what you are.*

Jane couldn't restrain herself. She bit into the biscuit. Sweet, red juice ran down her chin.

But, remember, the witch said. *It will give you what you truly wish for, so be careful. This is the only pregnancy you will ever have.*

Jane gobbled the rest, for she knew what she wanted: twin boys to raise, who would set her free from her robber husband, and keep her fed and happy. Blood ran down her chin and stained her throat. When she finished eating, the woman was gone. So was the cottage. All that remained was a single black cat.

When she got home, she hid the cat in the apple cellar, then told her robber husband to stay his knife for she was pregnant.

The robber was overjoyed because he'd grown to love the kindness inside the woman, and had not wanted to skin her.

Nine months later, Jane bore two daughters. One was stunningly beautiful. The other was so ugly that the midwife spat. Her feet were webbed; her hips wide. Her double joints and long arms pressed her centre of gravity against her knees and elbows, as if fit only for walking on all fours. The robber took aside the beautiful daughter and kissed it. Then he tucked the ugly daughter under his arm, to slaughter it.

Jane, still dizzy, pushed the midwife aside and stopped her husband. *It's my duty*, she explained. *I must be the one.* So, still bleeding, with neither placenta yet expelled, she carried the newborn to the apple cellar, nursed it, and stuffed cotton too big to swallow in its mouth, so the rest did not hear its cries. Then she slaughtered the cat in its place, and brought back its heart to her husband, who ate it raw, for strength and good luck. *We'll have more children*, he reassured her. Sons.

But the sons did not come. The beautiful child was enough for the robber, for even monsters can be moved. The family of three lived happily for some time, in the woods, until another blight took hold of the town. Hunger travelled like a wave, so that each could hear the other's stomach, growling. They gagged and wept and beat their breasts. The robber killed his brother and they ate him. Jane visited the cellar often, in secret, and when there was no food left, began to feed the abomination her own blood. Then she opened her third eye, and carried them both away to the old place, where life mattered. They saw libraries and universities and crowds of dancers wearing soft shoes who pranced in tiny circles. That ugly child grew up without the knowledge of suffering. Jane had only ever showed it love. When it spied on the family, it pitied them.

With the famine, the robber of human life lost his muscle and could no longer hunt. His accomplices left him. The family became destitute. *I must sell our daughter to the whorehouse*, he told his wife. *Then we will live another winter, and you will bear me a son who will help me earn her back.* Jane fought and cried and prayed, and chanted meaningless words, hoping to cast spells, but their situation did not improve. The night before the child was to leave, a murder of goblins tore south through the woods, and knocked down their door. Hungry and too weak to stand, the family saw that they would be eaten.

The cellar door opened just then. With a war-cry so loud and terrifying that their nerves retracted inside their bodies, leaving their arms and legs numb, the abomination lifted her father's scythe and sliced through the necks of all eighteen men-monsters, then hung them upside down by their feet to drain, so the family could cure and eat them. She'd grown wide-backed over the years, and walked on all fours. She was stronger than any man. Her face was the same as the robber's.

The robber did not recognize his daughter, for it had been twelve years, and women did not matter anyway. *We owe you a great debt,* he told her. *Name anything it is within my power to give you, and it is yours.*

I want my sister's freedom, the abomination said. *For you will be well fed now, and have no need for her prostitution.*

He understood then that he'd been tricked and he raged, slamming his scythe against the walls of his house and opening them to the wind. But he was superstitious: the gods curse those who break oaths. At last, he agreed.

You are free, the abomination told her sister. In that moment, the beautiful sister's back opened up into enormous white wings. She flapped, bursting through the top of the house, and was gone. While the robber screamed obscenities, Jane smiled. A tiny fire ignited inside her for the first time in her life.

As punishment for stealing his most valuable possession, the robber kept the abomination chained to his cellar wall. He beat her daily, until her skin slid from her bones. A week passed, and the moaning became intolerable. The wife missed her children. She missed her sisters. She missed the mother whom she'd never met. The spirits reminded her of the priest her lazy sister had married: smug and full of rage. They reminded her of her sixth sister, who had abandoned her. They reminded her that life could be worse: she could be dead. *Don't fight,* they told her.

The alternative is almost always worse than what you already have.
Tearing away hooves from goblin legs to stave the rumbling in
her belly, she curled herself small on the floor, and listened to
the *smack!-smack!* of the whip. The sound hurt her breasts especially, because the child had suckled there for two years.

The abomination did not fight her father. Unfamiliar with
violence, and young, she assumed she deserved it. The whip
was not nearly as bad as the exile from Jane, whom she missed
so enormously that she could not think about her without
weeping. Finally, during the third week, she cried out: *Mother!
Why have you abandoned me?*

Jane remembered being twelve years old, and sold to the man
who'd murdered her sister. She remembered working the fields,
bare-backed and whipped. She remembered the feeling of life in
her belly and the old woman in that cottage, who'd surely been
a witch. She walked down the stairs, and charged. The robber
did not turn in time. She gutted him with his own scythe.

Then she unchained her daughter. They held each other
and it was sweet and good, and she knew then that she'd loved
her sixth sister, and been loved, too. She knew then that things
unsaid have a way of being forgotten. *Though you are ugly and
not human, I love you*, she told the child.

Together, they axed down the house of human scalps and
warmed themselves by its fire. Then, carrying the robber's
corpse, they set out to the place where the woods folded. It was
dirt now, dry and barren. On the ground, panting and nearly
lifeless, was Jane's other daughter. Her white wings had
retracted into her back. Jane took her husband's carcass and let
the blood drip to the north, south, east, and west. From the
depths of each spot, stones pushed up into corners, and made
a house. It surrounded them, warm and full of food and tinctures and children's cauls.

This place will be a beacon, Jane told her daughters. Far and
wide, my winged one will travel, and spread the news. My strong
one will protect us. We will let the world know that places and
people used to matter. One day, they will matter again.

After her daughters had rested and fed, they rose up and

fulfilled their duty. Jane made daily offerings with her husband's bones, and the scalps she'd saved from the old house, including the red-headed one. The house became more houses, that became a village. Small animals returned. The people who inhabited these houses ceased to eye each other's flesh with desolate grins. They built things of beauty, and carved flutes from trees. The daughters and Jane did not marry, but stayed in the house as years and centuries passed, until the town became civilized, and they seemed strange and frightening. *The three witches*, they were called. *The weird sisters*. By then, only the desperate who wanted children and requited love visited. Jane collected drops of blood from their fingers for potions. She cackled, deep-throated, with a strange, otherworldly joy.

Jane's reflection in the mirror by then showed a stout woman with warts and missing teeth. On her deathbed, with her children at either side and the sun shining bright, her life flashed before her, and she knew that she'd summoned herself all those years ago, and she'd gotten exactly what she'd wished for in her daughters: strength and freedom.

Sister, Shhh . . .

Elizabeth Massie

Charity did not look back. She did not slow down. Her thin white sneakers, meant for sandy pathways and wooden floors, were savaged on the rock-strewn, hard-packed earth. Her yellow dress caught at her legs and threatened to throw her on to her face.

The heat of the desert was cooling quickly, the sun reduced to an orange smear atop the mountains to the west. The sky was starless and the colour of water in a deep well. Charity did her best to keep pace with her sister-wife, who was several yards ahead, but Fawn was older by a year and taller by nearly a foot.

Though she could not hear anything but her own footfalls and raspy, desperate breaths, she was sure the Prophet had roused a posse and they were thundering along behind in the darkness, truck tyres biting the ground, dogs and correction rods at the ready.

Heavenly Father, help me! God, please do not curse me!

"Fawn!"

Fawn did not look back. She did not answer.

The Prophet and his men would catch them and take them to task, dragging them by their hair to show others what happened to backsliders, claiming any punishments they received at the hands of the elders were mild compared to their punishments in hell were they to escape to live among the Outsiders.

Charity's foot caught a stone and she fell, wailing, and came up with her mouth and hands embedded with grit. She scrambled up a cactus-covered slope and skidded down the other side. The small Bible she'd pocketed before running thumped her hip, reminding her it was there, reminding her of the vows she was breaking, the chance she was taking, and the hope she might be protected anyway. Up ahead, Fawn's pink dress flapped like the wings of a terrified bird.

It was forbidden for girls to leave Gloryville. Females were to remain at home in the protection of God and the Fellowship. They were not to travel, nor even to speculate as to what lay beyond the borders of their holy, isolated town. They were to be submissive daughters and brides and mothers. They were to do as they were told, to surrender their bodies and souls to the men in their lives – their shepherds – who had spiritual and bodily charge over them.

"Fawn!"

Fawn called back, "Come *on!*"

An engine revved far behind in the blackness. They were coming. Charity glanced over her shoulder and saw nothing but the outlines of boulders and brambles and the quarter moon, hovering like a cat's eye in the near-black sky.

The engine sound faded, disappeared. *Maybe it was thunder,* Charity thought. *A storm coming in over the desert.*

Baring her teeth, she pushed on. Her heart hammered, her lungs drew in and out like bellows against a fire.

Then Fawn slowed. She bent over, clutching her knees, wheezing, spitting blood. Charity reached her and grabbed her arm.

"Are you all right?"

Fawn nodded.

"No, really!"

"I bit my tongue."

"Oh!"

Fawn glanced up; her eyes were creased at the edges,

terrified, flashing white in the faint moonlight. But she nodded again. "I'm all right."

"We should rest. Somewhere. We can hide."

"They'll catch us, certainly. But Flinton isn't too far, I don't think. Just a mile, maybe."

Mile? I can't run another mile!

"Can you run with me? Can you be free with me?"

Can I, God? Will You hate me for leaving Gloryville? Will You punish me forever?

Charity whispered, "Yes." Fawn took her hand and they ran, into the blackness, zigzagging across the Arizona desert, heading for Flinton. Heading for freedom.

Flinton had a reputation for sin. Whoring. Gambling. Murders. Loud music, televisions, and a movie theatre that showed films glorifying violence and sex. People dressed in clothes that revealed shoulders, midriffs, and bare thighs. Children running without supervision. Women out of their homes unescorted, drinking with each other and with men into the wee hours of the nights. Charity had heard all these things in passing, whispered stories that skittered through the sanctified compound of Gloryville like thorny tumbleweeds on a foul breeze.

The men of Gloryville went to Flinton to trade, sell, and buy. It was the closest Outsider town. It had stores and banks. And so they went. But they always stamped their boots clean of Flinton's foul dirt before they re-entered their own town.

And though Charity had dreamed of escape as she lay trembling on her cot at night, she could not reconcile her longing with the fact that the only place to run to would be Flinton.

It was Fawn who first spoke the dangerous words. She had sneaked to Charity's bedside one morning before the rest of the household was awake, kneeled down and whispered, "I'm going to run away, dearest. Come with me."

Charity had pulled her pillow over her head, pretending to be asleep. Fawn had poked her in the shoulder and whispered again, "Friday. After prayer meeting. We can pretend to go looking for Pips."

Charity whispered into the pillow, "Why would we look for Pips? He's a faithful dog. He would never leave Rufus."

"We can hide him, tie him up so he looks to be missing. That will give us the time we need before anyone wonders where we are."

Charity was silent, though her heart pounded so hard the cot shook beneath her.

"All right? Charity? Please? I don't want to go alone. We'll be safer together. And I don't want to leave you behind. You're the only person who loves me."

Charity felt herself nod. Fawn slipped away, back to her room, a whisper of slippers on bare floor. And Charity slept not at all until dawn, trying to breathe, staring at the wall, thinking of the dangers in Flinton, seeing images of Satan and the Prophet glaring at her, one with eyes of blazing orange, the other with eyes of ice-cold blue, wrangling over her soul.

But she wanted to leave as much as she wanted to live. And life in Gloryville had become unbearable.

Over the days that followed, Charity fought hard to keep from letting the rest of the family notice her nervousness. She was certain the fear of the impending escape was obvious, etched on her cheeks and mouth like the scars cut into Fawn's shoulders from the beating Rufus gave her when she resisted him on their wedding night. Yet, as the fourth and youngest wife of Elder Rufus Via, Charity was overlooked most of the time, her ranking in the expansive family just a little higher than that of Pips.

Charity had married Rufus, a smelly fifty-eight-year-old goat farmer, brother to the Prophet though a lesser church elder himself, thirteen months before on her fourteenth birthday. She had looked forward to the marriage and the assurance of a place in the highest realm of heaven for obeying the expectations of her sex. She thought she knew what would be expected of her, having grown up in a family with three sister-wives and nineteen children. But her own father, a carpenter who worked hard and said little, was quite different from Rufus Via, who didn't work very hard and said quite a bit.

Rufus stomped and yelled, then would disappear for several days, expecting not only the housework to be done but all the farm work, as well. If it wasn't done, and done to his liking, there was hell to pay.

The first two sister-wives, Prudence and Faith, were humble women, busy with their babies, and with little time to help Charity adjust. They assigned the youngest sister-wife the most tedious chores, as was to be expected. Laundry. Scrubbing the floors. Mucking goat pens. Gathering eggs. Cleaning the dishes. Changing the diapers of their growing brood – eleven and counting, as all of the other sister-wives, including Fawn now, were expecting. Fawn, however, had taken Charity under her wing. The two girls had known each other before the marriages, had lived in adjacent homes. They'd played together when there was time to play. They'd sat near each other during the long church services that all Gloryville residents were required to attend in the windowless chapel in the centre of town. Occasionally they dared pass notes back and forth, snickering silently over which boys were cute or which woman had a hole in her stocking or a bug in her hair.

So when Charity wed Rufus, Fawn was quick to give her advice on how best to submit to him when he wanted her and how best to stay out of his way when he didn't.

"He wants to make you scream when he takes you," she said. "If you are silent, he thinks you aren't paying attention. If you lie still, he thinks you are in contempt of him. It's best to writhe and scream and call out to God. He may spank you with a belt, or make you do things with your mouth. Oh, Charity, just say yes to it all. Then he will be done with his business more quickly and will leave you alone."

And so Charity screamed. She writhed. She prayed she would never have his child. She prayed he would die, then she prayed she would die. Then she prayed God would forgive her for her prayers. She didn't really want to die. She wanted to be gone, gone far from the man and his brutal hands and body.

She peeled carrots and potatoes. She washed. She minded the others' babies. She bent over in the shed when Rufus found her there. She bore his beatings when he came to her and found she was in the midst of her unclean days. She endured his curses when she did not conceive.

And she cried on her cot in the pantry behind the kitchen. How could she stand this for another sixty years? If this was God's plan, then God was as cold and cruel as Rufus. Maybe Satan would be kinder. He certainly couldn't be much worse.

According to the whispered rumours, Satan lived in Flinton. The road to Flinton was likely the road to hell.

And it was also the road to freedom.

They reached the outskirts of Flinton and stumbled along the shoulder of the road, at a walk now, panting, sweating. Charity's hair had long since fallen free from its pins and lay like a tangled brown shawl about her shoulders. Each time a vehicle whizzed past, they shuddered and prayed it was not the Prophet. Each set of receding tail lights looked like glowing devil's eyes, daring them to follow. Along the roadside were flat-roofed houses, tangled chain-link fences behind which dogs snarled and howled. They passed an abandoned building with rusted gas pumps, and trailers set like litter carelessly tossed, their porch lights winking. Inside, there was loud and rowdy laughter. Charity could not help but weep. Her feet were hot with blood, her face hot with dread. There was nothing left in her body but the agony of the escape, nothing left in her heart but the fear of what lay ahead.

"Sister, shhh," said Fawn. She leaned close and nuzzled Charity's cheek. "It will be all right. We just get into town, find a telephone, and call the authorities. We tell them we are runaways from Gloryville and that we need help."

"How do you know they'll help us? How do you know they won't just send us back to Rufus?"

"I've heard tell that laws of the Outsiders forbid men to marry girls our age. They believe it's criminal for men to beat their wives."

"Whose laws? Not God's laws, surely! God's laws are above the laws of man!"

"No, no! God doesn't want us beaten . . ."

"But if we disobey we *should* be beaten!"

"You're tired, Charity. Shhh, now. You want to be away as I want to. Trust me. We'll be all right. I have some coins in my pocket that I took from Rufus's dresser. We just need to find a phone, we just need to . . ."

And in that moment, there was a rumbling on the road, a roaring from behind, a dark growl bearing down on them, and Charity turned just in time to see a truck without its headlights on aiming for them, swelling in the darkness like an enraged monster. She felt the heat of the machine before it struck her, knocking her up from the shoulder and out into the sand. And then darkness covered darkness and everything flew away.

"Careless, Rufus," said a man's voice. The sound cut through Charity's brain and she flinched. "Knew you took chances but never thought you'd be so careless."

Even with her face pressed into a mattress, she knew the men who were with her. Her husband. The Prophet. She could feel the sticky crust of the sheet, could smell stale sex in the fabric. In a room next door, there was muffled music, talking, laughter.

Fawn, where are you?!

"Damn women," said Rufus. He huffed and hawked, and it sounded like he spat on the floor. "What gets into them, you know? What makes them think they can run?"

There was a moment of silence. The Prophet was likely pondering the question. Then he said, "Satan grabs a few of them and off they go. Think something's better out here."

"Out here? In Flinton? Hah!"

"Seems so."

"Bitches."

"I won't have those words, Rufus. You're an elder and ..."

"I am who I am and have always been that. Don't get high and mighty with me, Walter. I know you and I've heard your babblings ever since I was born."

"The past is past, brother. I've put up with your shenanigans for much too long. Coming to Flinton once a month for your floozies and your drink! Staying away for days, leaving your wives and children while you do God knows what with unholy women! I should have corrected you earlier, should have not allowed you to take four wives, should have . . ."

"Should have what, Walter? Used the law of placing against me? Or hauled me to the front of the body during worship to dress me down? Or would you have my blood atonement? Oh, I have shenanigans, all right. I come to Flinton for my fun, but I keep it away from Gloryville. I never sully our holy town. I never sully your holy name."

"Rufus! Enough."

"Enough? For who? For me? For you? Let me tell you, Prophet, should you share what I do on my own time with the flock, I will tell them of *your* sins. I will tell them of the boys you have sent away from Gloryville when they reached the age. You claimed they were listening to rock music, or were caught smoking. Off they went, banished! And I have no problem with that. We've not enough girls as it is for all the men to marry their required three. Yet what no one knows but you, me, and God is that you had your way with all the boys before you set them adrift. You blessed them with your lust, rammed them into the wall of your private prayer closet, left them limping, bloody, and torn."

"Rufus!"

"I tell the truth, brother. Shall I share that truth with the body of believers? Shall I tell the congregation?"

There was a sharp slapping sound and a grunt. Then a tussle and thud. Charity tried to turn over but her body screamed with the attempt.

"Hold! I think she's awake."

"You're no prophet, Prophet! You're as full of sin as the rest of the world!"

"I said hold! Stop it! She's awake, Rufus. Take care now."

"More care than your driving?"

"Not another word from you."

The bed sank and squealed. A beefy hand took hold of

Charity's chin, and turned it around. "Open your eyes!" It was Rufus. Charity tried to look but could not find the energy. Though the mattress was no longer sinking, she felt herself continuing on without it, spinning, floating downward towards a soft sound of crying. A faint sound of scratching ...

"I said, open your eyes! You're going to listen to me, and listen well. You got yourself in trouble, girl. You're hurt and we've got a doctor coming to look at you. He'll . . . I said, open your eyes. Now!" A flattened palm slammed against her cheek, though she only knew it from the sound. There was no feeling of pain. Something warm spread out around the base of her gown. She thought she had wet herself, but couldn't be sure and didn't really care because ...

"Damn it, Walter, help me get her to sit up."

. . . because her body was fading away, draining like water down into hot sand, down towards the piteous crying, the scratching—

"Listen to me!"

. . . and all was going soft, softer ...

"Sit *up*!"

. . . until all was calm.

All was dark.

She opened her eyes to the dark, musty confines of a closet. A slice of light pooled through the crack beneath the door. Scents of pine shavings, cigarette butts, and body odour stung her nose. She worked her shoulders, her neck, stretching against a stiffness that didn't want to be loosened.

"Uh," she grunted, and then snapped her jaws shut. If they knew she was awake again, they would . . .

What? What will they do?

She tipped her head, listening through the door.

Are they still here? Did they tell the doctor not to come? Did they leave me to suffer alone?

There was no sound beyond the closet door.

Slowly she looked around. Against the back wall was a folded ironing board with the words, "Property of West End Motel,

Flinton, Arizona" stencilled into the grimy fabric. A handful of wire hangers dangled from the rod above. Dead flies lay on the floor beside the dried husk of a scorpion. Little spatters of sand sparkled dimly in the carpeting.

She waited.

She closed her eyes.

Somewhere nearby she heard soft crying and a sound of scratching. She tried to speak, to ask who it was, but her voice was nothing more than cool breath on hot air.

She waited.

The motel room door was unlocked. Someone came in, pulling something with wheels that rattled.

Who is it? Rufus? The Prophet? What do they have planned for me? Is it Fawn, here to help me?

A vacuum cleaner turned on and run back and forth for a few minutes, the sound of water running in the bathroom, then the door opening, closing again.

Where are Rufus and the Prophet? How long have I been here?

She tried to open the door but her hands were too weak to work. Up on her knees, she leaned her weight against the door and shook the knob, but it did not turn.

"Help me!" she cried, but no one heard her, and no one came to help.

And so she closed her eyes and waited.

She came around when she heard the motel room door opening again. Two sets of footsteps, one heavy and certain, one light and shuffling.

Rufus? Are you back? Who is with you? It doesn't sound like the Prophet. Why are you leaving me here? Please let me out!

Voices. One man, one woman.

The man sounded young. He said, "Lay here, Julie. And don't you worry a bit. I'll be right back."

The bedsprings squealed. She groaned, then said, "Don't fucking leave me, Bob."

"I got to. You wait here. I'll get help and everything will be OK."

"I don't feel OK!"

"Just cut it out. Don't panic. Jeez."

"I hurt! Damn you for doing this to me!"

"You did this to you, too, don't forget!"

"My stomach hurts so bad, Bob!"

"Yeah, and the sooner I get out of here, the sooner I'll be back. Here's my cell. In case ..."

"In case what? I want to order a pizza? *Owwww!*"

"Damn it, Julie! I'm leaving!"

"Fine! Get the hell out of here."

"Get some sleep."

She groaned and cried out, "Fuck that! I hate you!"

The door opened, shut. Charity angled her head, listening. The woman on the bed was panting, sucking air through her teeth.

"Hello?" Charity called, but the woman did not hear her. The panting grew louder, more anxious. Then, weeping, moaning, cursing. Then the panting grew softer, slower.

Then silence.

Charity tried the door but was still unable to open it.

So she waited.

The man came back. He coughed, called Julie's name, then said, "Ah, shit." He left, slamming the door. The door rattled on its hinges.

Charity waited. Then she said, "Hello?"

There was a long pause, then a tremulous "Hello" in return.

Charity's heart leaped.

"Julie?"

"Yes, who are you?"

"Charity. I'm in the closet. I can't open the door from in here. Can you help me?"

Julie was silent, then said, "I don't know. Let me try."

A whisper-soft movement across the rug outside the closet. Then, "I can't seem to grasp the handle. What's wrong with me?"

"I think you're hurt. I heard you and that man. Bob. You were angry, and you were in a lot of pain."

"I was?" There was a pause. "Yes, I was. Bob left me, didn't he? The bastard!"

"Are you still hurt?"

"Ah . . . no, I don't think so."

"What was the matter?"

"He'd made me have an abortion. He gets me pregnant, then takes me to some fly-by-night asshole friend of his who claims to be a nurse and can do it, no cost. No cost? Too good to be true, I tell Bob. He says the guy owes him for something or other. So I figure, I don't want a kid anyway, and the guy's got a medical degree. Or nursing degree. Whatever."

"Oh."

"But then I start cramping, and bleeding like crazy. He brings me here to this shit-bag motel 'cause he doesn't want to take me home to my place, or to my mom's, or, Lord forbid, to his mom's, 'cause you know fuckin' moms, how they can get."

"I suppose."

"I tell him, you took me to some butcher to save a hundred bucks? He says it'll be OK. He says he'll go get some real help. Gives me his cell phone. Why didn't he call 911? I'll tell you why, 'cause he wanted to skip town and leave me alone to ..."

There was a long, dry silence.

"To what?" asked Charity.

"Like he wanted to skip town and leave me to die or something."

"I'm so sorry, Julie."

"What are you doing in that closet anyway?"

"I'm not sure."

"What's your last name?"

"Via."

"I don't know no Vias in Flinton."

"I'm not from Flinton."

"Out-of-towner, huh? In for a one-night stand? Get dumped by your man, too?"

Dumped by my man? I guess that's what happened. Knocked down by his truck and left here until he decides to come back.

Charity hesitated, then, "I'm from Gloryville."

Julie laughed abruptly. "You're kiddin' me, right? That creepy place with all the polygamist fundamentalists? Where the women wear those prairie dresses and puff their hair up high?"

"Yes."

"You running from there? Running away?"

"I was . . ." *Fawn! Wait! What happened to Fawn?* "I was running from there, yes! They were after me, Rufus and the Prophet!" Her words picked up speed as she remembered the truck on the dark road, the impact of the metal on her shoulders, landing in the sand. "Julie, you have to get me out of here. If they come back they'll take me home. I can't go home! Oh, my God, I think they killed Fawn!"

"What? Who's Fawn?"

"Get me out, please!"

"I can't! The doorknob won't turn. I can't seem to get it with my fingers."

"Try again!"

"I can't!"

"They could be back any minute!"

"I can't! I can't! I *can't!*"

"Shhh!" Charity held up her hand to silence Julie, as if the other girl could see her.

"Shhh, what?"

"Listen. Do you hear that? Scratching? And somebody crying? Really soft, though, but don't you hear it?"

"Where?"

"I'm not sure. It's not in here. Maybe out where you are?"

"I don't think so."

"Just listen."

"I *am* listening! Damn, but I'm sick of people telling me what to do!"

"Sorry."

Then Julie said, "Yeah, I do hear it. Maybe it's in the other room, you think? Or the TV?"

"I've heard it before. It's the same sound over and over."

"Maybe somebody's renting the same porn film. Some of that S and M shit."

"What's that? S and M?"

"Never mind. You're from Gloryville, so how would you even know? Wait. Your name's Charity?"

"Yes."

"That's funny."

"Why?"

"Did you know that other Charity? The one who ran away from Gloryville, I dunno, six years ago?"

Charity frowned and put her hand to her mouth. "Who was that? I don't remember. There are a couple of Charities in Gloryville."

"Girl about fourteen . . . fifteen. It was in the news. Found her . . . shit, it was in this same motel. In a closet. She was dead, all banged up. Said it looked like she'd been hit by a car or something."

"No . . ."

"Never found out who did it, I don't think. Went out to that Gloryville, talked to some folks. Seems she ran off. Musta gotten hooked up with some bad sorts who ran her down then hid her."

"No."

"One of the cops said she looked like she was real pretty once, in that yellow dress and all that brown hair and a little squashed Bible in her pocket. He even cried a bit on the TV. Now for a cop to cry, who's gonna forget that?"

No.

"I think the people in Gloryville said another girl ran off with her, but they never did find her. You remember the Charity I'm talking about?"

I am her.

"Do you?"

Oh my God, I am her!

She'd heard about ghosts. Some of her brothers talked about them privately, when they were choring outdoors. She'd overheard them, talking and giggling nervously. Ghosts were leftovers from dead people. They were stuck on earth for some reason. They came out at night and shook windows and rattled doors. They could pass through solid walls and scare you to death if you looked at them. They had magic numbers they used to their advantage. Thirteen. Seven. Three. Each had a purpose that Charity did not stay to hear, because at that point her mother was calling her.

"Hey, Charity?"

Slowly, she stood, held her hands in front of her, and placed them on the closet door. *Am I a ghost, then? Is that what has happened? Did I die here? Has it been six years?*

Her palms flattened against the splintery wood. She felt it grow cold at her touch, and then she pushed against it. Leaned into it. And it gave way. She tumbled forward though the door and out into the room.

Julie leaped to her feet, her eyes huge. "Oh, shit! Oh, shit!" Her blonde hair was grimy and limp, her jeans soaked in blood down to her knees.

Charity straightened and stared at her hands. They looked the same to her. She flexed them. They felt the same but for the chill.

Julie backed towards the bed. "Get away from me," she snarled.

"I . . . I won't hurt you," said Charity. "I never hurt anyone in my life."

"Get away!"

Charity took a step forward, wanting to console Julie, for she saw in the girl the fear and terror that she knew had been on her own face when Rufus came at her with his correction rod or belt. And in that moment saw herself in the mirror.

She screamed.

Gone was the recognizable, sunburned face, the narrow shoulders, the slim body, and the yellow dress. Her dress was torn away at the waist, revealing ravaged undergarments. The ragged remnants of cloth were covered in black streaks and blackened blood. Her body was mangled, one arm bent with a bone protruding, her legs flayed along the shins and thighs. Her face was purpled and her jaw could be seen through a hole in her cheek.

Charity fell to her knees, clutched the remaining clots of hair on her head, and sobbed. And somewhere nearby came the sound of someone else crying softly, accompanying by a persistent scratching, clawing.

"We're both dead, then," said Julie. She sat on the bed, her hands folded in her lap, her brows drawn, her lip trembling.

"Yes. I died at the hands of Rufus and the Prophet. You died at the hands of the nurse your boyfriend recommended you go to."

"So we're ghosts."

"Yes."

"I don't know how to be a ghost. What do we do now?"

Charity sat on the chair at the desk. She could not feel the seat beneath her. She ran her fingers along the buttons of the phone but could not push them. She and Julie had tried several times to leave the room, only to find they were unable to step through the door. "I don't know. Have you read about ghosts?"

Julie shrugged. "Some. Not much. We have unfinished business. I guess since we both got murdered, in our own ways."

"I guess so."

"How long have I been dead, I wonder? I would call the front desk and ask the date but we can't dial, can we?"

"I can't. Maybe you can. I've heard tell ghosts can move things sometimes."

Julie crawled off the bed and went to the desk. She lifted the receiver and gave Charity a look of surprise. She pushed the 0 on the dial pad. A moment later, a voice said, "Yes?"

Julie said, "What is today?"

"Hello? Is someone there?"

"Yes, I want to know the date."

"Hello? Hello? Who is there in room six? No one's been in that room for weeks!"

"Please, I just want to know today's date."

"I'm coming down there, whoever you are! Intruders! Pranksters!" There was a click. Julie put the receiver down.

"She couldn't hear me. She's coming to the room. Are we supposed to spook her?"

"Do you think we should?"

"I don't know. She's probably an OK lady, just worried is all."

"Then let's leave her alone."

Julie and Charity went into the closet. The woman from the front desk entered the room just moments later, and they could hear her grunting as she kneeled down to look under the bed, peeked in the bathroom. Then she opened the closet door. They held still as she stared right through them. Then she muttered, "Must be crossed wires. Must be last night's storm." She went out. Julie went back to the bed. Charity went back to sit at the desk.

"Are we stuck here? Forever?" asked Julie. "Do we have to haunt the place where we died?"

"Maybe. I don't know. I wish I did. My brothers knew a bit about ghosts. I should have paid closer attention. Oh, I hope Fawn has gone on to heaven! I don't want her wandering in the desert, all alone!"

"Shhh, listen," said Julie.

There was the soft crying again, beneath them. The sound of scratching, clawing.

"What do you think that is?" Julie asked.

Charity shook her head. "It's what I've been hearing off and on. I thought it might be a dog beneath the motel, scampered there out of the sun maybe."

"No, it's a human sound."

They both listened. Whimpering, scraping. Under the floor.

Charity kneeled down on the rug. She put her face to the floor. "Who are you?"

More weeping, louder now. More scratching.

"Are you hurt? Do you need help?"

A soft, tiny voice. "Help."

"How can I help you?"

"Help."

Instinctively, Charity put her hand to the floor, through the floor into the crawl space, and felt about. Her fingers brushed against some fine, soft hair, and she gasped.

"What is it?" asked Julie.

"I don't know." Her fingers traced the hair, down to a soft jaw line, a small chest, and bony shoulder. She felt about and grasped an arm.

"What are you doing?"

"Wait."

She pulled. Slowly, carefully, drawing her hand back up out of the floor, ready to let go of the arm should it refuse to move through with her. But it didn't. The body came through, huffing, shuddering.

It was a small boy, no more than five. He had raven-black hair and brown eyes. He was dressed only in a pair of short trousers. His feet were bare. There was blood at the corners of his mouth, and his chest appeared sunken, and dirt and small bits of gravel were embedded in places along his skin.

"Hi, there," said Charity. "What's your name?"

He sniffed and rubbed his nose. It was then Charity saw the nubs of his fingers. He had been digging, clawing, and had worn them clear to the bone.

"Honey," said Charity. "We won't hurt you. What is your name?"

He looked at Julie, then back at Charity, not seeming terrified by their appearances. He said, "Nantan."

"Is that an Apache name?"

He nodded.

"How did you get down there under the motel?"

The boy shrugged.

"How long have you been down there?"

The boy's face creased up and he began to cry again. His words were broken, desperate. "He threw me in the hole. Covered me up. Said I was nothing but trouble!"

"What man?"

"The man that build this place."

God . . . and how old is this motel? Thirty years, maybe?

Charity tried to hug him but there was little of substance to hold. Nonetheless, she remained there on her knees, her arms encircling the boy, trying her best to replicate what had been easy in life.

Then Julie said, "Would he sleep? Could we put him to bed? Perhaps he would at least rest."

"We can try."

Charity sat back on her heels and held out her hand to Nantan. He took it. Julie grasped his other hand.

And they all felt it. A strange and sudden surge between them, a blue, undulating energy that took their dead hearts and set them pounding.

Julie almost let go but Charity said, "No, don't! Don't let go!"

"Why?"

"Just don't, please. Let's get up together."

"Why?"

"Please?"

"I guess," said Julie.

The three of them stood then, a young woman, a girl, and a little boy. Charity's brothers had said there were magic numbers ghosts used to their advantage. One was three. And here they were, three ghosts, holding hands. There was something special there. There was power.

She led Julie and Nantan to the door.

"What are you doing?" asked Julie.

"Trying something." Charity closed her eyes, thought about Fawn, dead, her body God only knew where now. Perhaps her spirit lingered on the outskirts of Flinton, not knowing what happened or what to do about it all.

"Come with me," said Charity. "And don't let go of each other, OK?"

"OK," said Julie.

Nantan nodded.

She pushed through the door. The others came with her, sliding silently out on to the uneven concrete walk then across the night-darkened parking lot.

Yes! Yes!

Together, they could go where they needed to go. Together, they would take care of the business each needed to take care of. They had all the time in the world to figure it out and get it done.

You will be avenged, sister. I may see you again. I may not. But you will be avenged. You will be freed!

Flinton wasn't so much hell as hellish. Not so much owned by the devil as bedevilled by humans and their cruelty. Charity led the others down the road, heading westward through the shadows, casting none of their own. She imagined herself shaking the town's foul soil from her feet.

And as the silver moon rose over the desert and dogs barked behind chain link fences, she smiled her first smile in years, savouring the expressions she would see on the faces of Rufus and the Prophet when she took them to task back in Gloryville.

The Fifth Bedroom

Alex Bell

Meet Chloe Benn – a bitter, bitter divorcee at the tender age of twenty-two, with no qualifications, no job, no interests, no passions, no dreams and no hopes. She'd had most of those things once but they had been stripped and stolen from her, with her permission and with her blessing. She had wasted five years of her life, and she knew it. Made all the wrong choices, and trusted all the wrong people. She'd known – deep down – for at least a year that her husband no longer loved her, and yet she had fought viciously against herself to deny that wicked truth, even though she was not happy any more, even though that internal struggle almost tore her apart.

Perhaps there had never been anything real between them at all. She had enjoyed the lifestyle he had given her very much: the champagne bubbles and the designer underwear and the private yachts and the exclusive parties. And he had loved her beauty – worshipped it, almost. He had loved the fact that every man who saw him with her would envy him; loved the way that every man's eyes would go to Chloe as soon as she walked into a room; loved to feel that she was the best and that she was his. She was petite and graceful with a delicate, almost ethereal beauty. Like a bare-footed fairy who had danced straight out of a fairy tale. She had creamy white skin and huge, huge eyes the colour of dark chocolate. Sweet and shy and scared – like a gazelle. That was what he used to call her. A beautiful, fragile gazelle. But beauty fades and dies. A delicate thing that can so easily shatter into a hundred heartbroken pieces. And when that happens, love – or what passes for love – dies too. Dies and rots into something twisted and ugly and bitter.

Chloe's looks had been stolen from her prematurely by the car accident. That drunken bastard had even snatched those from her before he chewed her up and spat her out – ruined and broken, to be abandoned at the side of the road like an unwanted puppy. Although the right-hand side of her face remained flawless and lovely, the left-hand side was scarred and burned – creating a horrible contrast between what she was now and what she once had been. If she stood in just the right way in front of the mirror, at precisely the right angle, all she could see was the untouched side of her face. A strange optical illusion – like a fantasy that the accident had never happened at all. Skilled doctors and expensive plastic surgeons had managed to fix some of the damage, but they could not eradicate it completely – they could not get rid of all the scars or fix her drooping eyelid. They could not give her back the perfection she had lost.

In truth, it was not as bad as Chloe believed it to be. But the fact remained that she was now utterly unable to see any beauty whatsoever in her own reflection. All she saw was the disfigurement, and the lines already starting to form around her eyes and mouth – the mental and emotional scars from five long years of pain and heartache and disappointment and disillusionment. Clear evidence stamped across her skin of all those times the world had hurt her – written across her scarred face in permanent ink for everyone to see, and to point at, and to laugh at.

From the age of ten Chloe had been a striking beauty who only seemed to become more and more beautiful with every passing year. But then she made the fateful choice of getting into the car when her husband told her to, even though she knew he was drunk, even though she knew that she shouldn't.

But she was an obedient wife and she always did as she was told. And after that, for the first time in her life, Chloe felt what it was like to be something less than startlingly stunning. She felt what it was like barely even to be beautiful at all. She felt the cold hard bite of self-conscious inferiority and inadequacy when she saw another woman in the room who was clearly more attractive than she was. And the realization hit her hard and hit her fast: her delicate, lovely beauty was gone. It was gone and it was never coming back. Her career was over, too – she would never model again.

She soon realized that her husband was no longer attracted to her. He recoiled at the thought of touching that ruined flesh. It was only a matter of time before he sought out a replace-ment. The divorce had been finalized for over a year now and yet, still, all Chloe could do was brood and agonize over how much time she had wasted. And in doing so she only wasted more. Her life had always seemed such a full one back in London but her husband had been the one underpinning it all. The places that she went, the things that she did – sometimes even the clothes that she wore and the words that she said – were all formed by him. Like she was his doll. His dancing puppet on invisible strings. Even her friends were his friends. His friends first, and hers second. How could she continue to move in those circles when he might be there with *her*? With that new one. The younger model. The unruined one. The teenager who looked almost as pretty as Chloe had been before the accident.

So, finally, she made a decision – an actual decision that she took for herself and by herself, for the first time in her life. She would leave London. Money was not a problem. Aside from all the earnings she had saved back when her supermodel career was still going strong, she had received a handsome settlement in the divorce. Her ex-husband had made no attempt to deny or to hide his infidelity. He did not want a disfigured wife, and he was quite willing to pay through the nose to be rid of her. Chloe could live wherever she liked.

But what *did* she like? She had grown so used to thinking

and saying that she liked something just because she knew it was what he liked. She had lived with him from the age of seventeen, and been married to him from the age of eighteen. She had been a weak-willed girl – impressionable and eager to please and afraid to disappoint. So she had moulded herself to him as well as she was able, and now she was no longer sure how much of herself was really her, and how much of it was him. Now that it was her choice – and only hers – where did she want to live? Not a modern, brand new loft apartment like she had shared with him, she knew that. But then where?

It had taken her a long time but she had finally found the place. As soon as she saw the photos on her computer screen, she knew it was the one. A red-brick Georgian house that had been standing empty for almost two years since the owner had moved abroad. No doubt the prohibitive cost had put people off but Chloe had to have something to spend her money on. She liked the thought of all those elegant, airy, empty rooms, waiting to be filled with her choice of décor and her taste in furnishings. While the purchase had been going through, Chloe had scoured Christie's and Sotheby's looking for appropriate period furniture by Hepplewhite or Chippendale – all via their websites, of course; she never left the house now if she could help it because she didn't want people staring at her ruined face.

But she enjoyed acquiring the furniture. Here, at last, was something to do with her time, to take an interest in, and to work towards. The house was a promise – her promise to herself – of a new beginning and a new Chloe and a new attempt actually to *live* instead of allowing other people to live for her. Or, at least, that was the promise she made to herself in a rare burst of optimism on one of her good days – before she sank back down into bitterness and self-loathing and that brooding hatred towards *him* that she derived a perverse sort of pleasure out of fostering and nurturing. A pointless sort of promise made with the best of intentions but which Chloe would never be able to keep. Even if her life depended on it.

She arrived at Arietta House on a cold, drizzly morning in

mid-February. As she drove down the drive, the elegant, red-brick façade slowly materialized out of the mist that drifted in shredded ribbons about the house's square, symmetrical lines and tiled, sloping roof, almost hiding the paired chimneys from view. The sash windows with their small eight-by-eight panes were neatly lined up in rows across the front of the house, dark and cold and unwelcoming. She parked and got out of the car. The slam of the door closing seemed to echo strangely in the silence as she stared up at the empty house. Her house. A big place for a small person to hide away from the world.

Her boots crunched on the gravel as she walked up to the front door, complete with canopy and pediment and a filigree fanlight above it depicting a single ballerina dressed all in white against a dark green background of trees. Chloe took the key from her pocket, unlocked the door and stepped inside.

The house was empty and quite silent, and smelled of dust and damp and cold. She put her bag down and walked slowly from room to room. The house still had its original floors, and the wooden boards creaked beneath Chloe's weight in a way that she liked. As well as a bathroom and kitchen, there were three living rooms on the ground floor. They were all currently empty but Chloe paused to admire the walls, panelled to dado height, with chipped painted plaster above. She also admired the ceilings, intricately adorned with mouldings of ribbons and swags, ballerinas and trees. In fact, the ballerina was a common motif within the house. Chloe remembered reading something about a famous ballerina who had lived here once.

Fireplaces dominated each room, flanked with pillars, and elegant with cast-iron backs and decorated fronts. These, too, were adorned with the ballerina motif, along with swans and forests and lakes and stars. After touring the downstairs rooms, Chloe climbed the original wooden staircase to the second floor where she inspected the bathroom and the four bedrooms – three of which she would have no need of whatsoever. She lingered a while in the largest one and looked out of the window at the grounds below, still shrouded in mist, the sky grey with the promise of more rain. The lawn swept away towards a line of trees, broken only by a small lake filled with murky water and the remains of a disused stone fountain.

Chloe turned away from the view and went back downstairs. She had noticed brass bell pushes fixed to the walls in most of the rooms and, here in the kitchen, high upon the wall, was the bell board – used back in the days when the house still had servants so that they would know which room required attention.

The old teak cabinet contained ten windows in two rows upon a black glazed panel with red-and-white striped flags. The top windows were labelled: Front Door, Back Door, Dining Room, Breakfast Room, Parlour. In the second row the windows were labelled Bedrooms One, Two, Three, Four and Five – which was odd since the house only had four bedrooms. Chloe assumed it must have been a standard board and that they had simply never set up the bell for the non-existent fifth bedroom.

While she stood staring up at the board, a bell suddenly sounded – a harsh, shrill sound that echoed through the empty rooms and made her jump. The flag for the front door moved back and forth within the cabinet, indicating that was the bell that had been rung. She went to answer it and found that the removal men had arrived right on schedule.

Chloe spent the rest of that day overseeing her old possessions and new furniture being brought into the house. By the time the oriental rugs had been laid upon the wooden floorboards, and the wing chairs had been placed before the fireplaces, and the kettle had been plugged into a socket in the kitchen, the house was starting to have a more homely feel about it.

Finally all of Chloe's things were inside the house, and all the furniture was right where it ought to be. It had been a wearying task and she decided to unpack the remaining boxes the next day. It was later than she'd realized – the light had already drained from the sky outside, and darkness pressed in softly against the windows as if the house had been wrapped up in black velvet. Chloe cooked herself dinner for one and ate alone at the kitchen table.

Shortly after nine o' clock, a bell rang somewhere within the house.

Chloe had just finished her meal and laid down her knife and fork when the shrill ringing caught her unawares and made her jump. She looked up at the bell board in surprise, thinking that one of the removal men must have forgotten something and must now be at the front door. But it was not the front-door flag that was moving behind the glass. It wasn't the flag for the back door either. It was for bedroom five.

Even as Chloe looked, the bell rang again and the red-and-white striped flag waved back and forth even more rapidly in the little window. Chloe sat and watched the flag for a full minute, until it was quite as still as the others once again. Then she slowly stood up from her chair, picked up a rolling pin just in case, and searched the house from top to bottom. It was quite empty. There was no one there but her. The bell board was old and obviously faulty. Chloe decided she would have to get someone in to fix it because she'd be extremely annoyed, and perhaps a little unnerved, if the bell started ringing in the middle of the night and woke her up. She needed her sleep now more than ever. It was the only time she didn't hurt.

But in order to get it fixed, she needed to know which bell was faulty – which of the four bedrooms upstairs was bedroom five. She went up and pressed the brass bell push in the first bedroom, then went downstairs to check the bell board. The flag for bedroom one was swinging back and forth within the window. She repeated the same process for the other three bedrooms and moved the flags for bedrooms two, three and four. But the flag for bedroom five remained quite still.

Chloe then tried all the other bell pushes in the downstairs rooms but each bell was linked to the correct room on the board, and no bell that she pushed could move the flag for bedroom five, which remained completely still in its dark window. Finally, she decided to climb up into the attic in case there was a bell push up there. She switched on her torch and at first saw only spiders and cobwebs. Then the beam of light sliced into one of the dark corners and fell upon a strange old wicker chair in a wooden frame, coated in dust and spun with webs.

Chloe took a step closer, believing it to be an old armchair at first because of the adjustable arm and foot rests, but then she noticed the big spoke wheels and realized that it was an antique wheelchair. An ugly thing – unwanted junk that some past owner had decided to shove up into the attic instead of disposing of it properly. It seemed to pull her forwards like a magnet and she found herself brushing the cold wheels with her fingertips, leaving deep marks in the thick dust.

Irrepressible sorrow. Blistering anger. Abject misery. Unreasoning hatred.

Inanimate objects don't give off feelings, of course, every sane person knew that – and yet those were the emotions Chloe felt when she touched the chair. It was like drowning in someone else's desperate depression. Chloe snatched her hand away as if she'd been burned. She shook herself and stepped back. She suddenly felt a strong, unreasoning desire to get away from that chair, so she turned and went back towards the hatch leading downstairs.

The incident with the bell for bedroom five was an odd thing, but these were old bells and an old bell board and an old house. Chloe had known before she came here that there would be restoration work to be done. This was just one more job to add to the list.

She went to bed and spent her first night in Arietta House dreaming of ringing bells and decrepit wheelchairs.

The bell for bedroom five rang several times over the next few days, always at night when the house was empty but for Chloe. No one ever heard it but her. There was so much to do in the house and in the grounds she told herself that was why she hadn't got around to finding someone to fix the bell yet. But the truth was that she had made no move to start on any of the work that needed doing. The first job she had decided to tackle was painting the chipped plaster on the walls above the dado rails. She had the paint and the brushes and the step ladder all ready but she had made no move to begin.

Instead she had spent her first morning in the house lying in bed crying. Crying for her disfigured face, and her ruined marriage, and her broken heart. And when she did drag herself out of bed, she spent most of her time walking around the chilly, misty garden brooding over how much she hated her ex-husband and how fiercely she wished all sorts of miserable suffering on him and his new pretty puppet. Perhaps he would have another car crash and die this time, and good riddance. Or perhaps he would fall down the stairs and break his neck. Or perhaps he would slip into the Thames and drown.

A little smile played about Chloe's lips as she gazed down at the murky water of the lake. How she would love to be the one to force his head beneath the surface and hold him there until he stopped struggling. Until he stopped breathing. Until there was nothing left of him, just like there was now nothing left of her. The temperature seemed to drop suddenly. Chloe shivered and turned back to the house. She noticed instantly that she'd left a light on in one of the upstairs rooms – it glowed softly through all the neat little panes of glass. Which was odd because it wasn't her bedroom – that room was at the end of the house and this one was in the middle. It couldn't be the bathroom either because that faced the other side of the garden. It had to be one of the other bedrooms but Chloe hadn't set foot in them since that first night when she had been looking for the faulty bell.

She trudged back to the house, walked up the creaking wooden staircase and checked the bedrooms. They were dark – all four of them. When she went back outside there were no lit windows in the house's façade but something seemed . . . changed. Wrong. As if there were suddenly fewer windows than there had been before. When Chloe walked into the kitchen and looked at the bell board on some sudden whim, she saw that the flag for bedroom five was still moving slightly, as if the bell had been rung unheard while she'd been out in the garden.

She stood still for long, long moments, her heart thumping in her chest, her own breathing suddenly loud in her ears. The bell and the light could both be down to faulty electrics, she decided. Yes. Faulty electrics. That was the explanation.

Chloe made herself a cup of tea because she suddenly needed something normal to do. She took her steaming mug – and another glass of wine for good measure – into the living room instead of drinking it at the kitchen table. She found she did not want to sit in the same room as the bell board, waiting for that red-and-white striped flag to start waving back and forth, as if it were mocking her – just like the rest of the world.

As she sat down in a very elegant, very uncomfortable, tall, wing-backed chair before the dark hearth, it occurred to Chloe that perhaps the house had once had five bedrooms some time in the past. On a whim she turned her laptop on and googled Arietta House, thinking to get back to the old estate agent's page if it was still up. But instead the house instantly came up in a different context – as the former residence of Giselle Girard, a prima ballerina in the late-nineteenth century.

Giselle had been one of the most naturally gifted ballerinas the world had ever seen. Her career was like a shooting star sparkling across the sky in bursts of cold fire and flashes of twinkling diamond lights. She was on the verge of being awarded the rank of prima ballerina assoluta – an almost unheard of honour – when the theatre where she was working was burned down in a great fire. Giselle survived but a falling wooden beam crushed her legs. She would never dance again. She would never even walk again. So at the age of twenty-five she left France and retired to Arietta House, where she lived out the rest of her days confined to a wheelchair. Giselle had died in 1940 at the age of eighty.

Two black-and-white photos accompanied the article. One was of Giselle before the accident, dressed in a white tutu with a bell-shaped, free-flowing skirt made of tulle; her thick black hair pulled back into a severe ballerina's bun; her chin high and her eyes shining with a sort of grim pride. The second photo was dated just two months before Giselle died and showed her in the grounds of Arietta House, an old, bent woman, her face wreathed in bitter lines, a look of sullen resentment in her eyes that was almost identical to the look that sometimes came into Chloe's own eyes, only Giselle had had many more years to work upon her bitterness.

The second photo startled Chloe, not because she recognized her own misery on another person's face, but because of the wheelchair. The elderly Giselle was sitting in a wicker chair with a wooden frame and large spoke wheels. Chloe was quite sure it was the same chair that was upstairs in the attic. That photo had been taken here in the grounds. When she peered closer she could see that the lake had been much clearer back then, and had had swans on it.

The moment Chloe read of Giselle's sad story and saw her unhappy face, she felt an instant connection – a sympathy and an empathy – with a kindred spirit. For had they not both lost that which they cherished most, right at the very prime of their lives, through no fault of their own? Chloe had been a model who had lost her looks; Giselle had been a ballerina who had lost the use of her legs. They'd even been of similar ages when their respective disasters had struck. Chloe felt an instant affinity with the dead ballerina. A powerful, unreasoning rush of feeling. Other people might offer vapid commiserations and empty condolences, but here at last was a woman who could have truly understood what Chloe was feeling because she must have felt exactly the same. Chloe found herself wishing forcefully that she could have met the ballerina just once – that she could have spoken, just once, with someone who could have understood how she felt inside.

As Chloe stared at the computer screen and yearned for a meeting – a connection – that could never take place, a bell rang again, and she knew that it was from bedroom five. Before the last echoes of the bell had faded, music began to play from somewhere within the house. Softly at first, and muffled, as if coming to her through a dense fog, so that Chloe had to strain to hear it, but gradually becoming louder and clearer until each sad, sweet note was crystal perfect. It was the aria from the second act of *Giselle*, when the grief-stricken duke mourns at the tomb of the girl he has himself driven to madness and to death. Chloe had been to that ballet several times with her ex-husband. The last time had been after her accident and she could remember sitting there, twisting her handkerchief into knots, knowing that her marriage was almost over and that this was the last ballet they would ever attend together. That this was one of the last times they would ever do anything together.

The notes of the solo oboe seemed to fill the house with exquisite melancholy – beautiful and terrible – and the sadness of that music was so intense that Chloe wept where she sat. Giselle was communicating with her – reaching out to her – she was sure of it. Trying to touch her with ghostly fingers because they were the same. They had both suffered and lost – they had both been grossly mistreated and abandoned. Chloe sat in her high-backed chair and wept for them both until her eyes dried up and she had no more tears to spill for either of them. Then she fell into bed, spent and exhausted.

The next morning she wondered whether she had imagined the whole thing. Or perhaps hallucinated it in a drunken haze. There *were* a fair few empty bottles around the kitchen the next morning, after all. Perhaps no ghostly music had filled the empty house. Perhaps it had only been in her head. Her ex-husband had told her she was sick but that was probably only because she'd gone at him that one time with a knife outside the court house. And what did he know anyway? What did anyone know? No one could understand her pain. Not like Giselle could, if only she were still here.

When Chloe heard the same music again the next night, she was almost beside herself with delight. It was real, after all. Giselle was still here. She was here and she was reaching out to Chloe. Night after night, the score from *Giselle* filled Arietta House, always heralded by the bell ringing from the fifth bedroom.

On one occasion, on the exact stroke of midnight, Chloe looked from one of the windows and saw white shapes flitting between the trees at the end of the garden. She was certain they were *wilis* – the female spirits described in the ballet as risen from their graves at night, to seek revenge upon men by dancing them to death. As Chloe stood and strained her eyes to peer into the darkness outside, she wished that she could become a *wili* herself so that she could entrap her ex-husband in a dance that would kill him as he so richly deserved. How hard it was to be merely a mortal woman who could do nothing to right the wrongs she had so unjustly suffered.

These thoughts depressed her and she spent almost the whole of the next day in bed. She was drained and so very, very tired. No doubt that was why, upon opening her eyes some time the next afternoon, she gazed along her pillow and saw hair spreading out upon the fabric that wasn't hers, for this hair was thick and black instead of silky and chocolate-brown. She jerked upright in the bed, clutched a length of hair between her fingers and examined it in the afternoon sun streaming through the small, square windowpanes, only to find it was exactly the colour that it ought to be. A trick of the light, no doubt. Merely a trick of the light.

But she began to notice the black hair around the house at other times too. One day she bought a cupcake while out shopping. The sort of cake she never could have bought before when she'd been working as a model because she knew then that she could not afford to be anything other than carrot-thin. This was a rich, buttery cupcake, with thick lashings of cerise-pink icing covering the top, resplendent beneath blood-red cherries and crystals of sugar.

When she took her first bite of this cake it was creamy and delicious and sweet and sugary, and everything she had thought it would be. It melted in her mouth and fizzled upon her tongue. She closed her eyes to savour the taste, and then the bell rang and she knew, even before she opened her eyes, that it was the bell for bedroom five.

At almost the exact same second she felt the presence of something odd and alien inside her mouth – something that did not belong to the cake and did not belong to her, tickling the back of her throat in a way that made her want to gag. She spat the mouthful out on to the table in front of her, and her fingers scraped across her tongue until she found the thing and pulled. A long thick black hair came dragging out of her mouth – so long that it seemed it would keep on going forever. When Chloe finally had it out, it curled round and round itself on the kitchen table, black and shiny and sleek, glistening with her saliva. She threw the rest of the cupcake away, uneaten.

That night she picked up her brush, only to find that the bristles were all tangled up with that same black hair, as if someone else had been using her hair brush. Chloe raised the brush and sniffed it, and it smelled to her of powdered make-up, and silken costumes, and the sputtering gas lights of a theatre, and she knew that it was Giselle trying to reach her.

The night after that, Chloe was sitting in her uncomfortable wing-backed chair before the fireplace when the sad oboe music began to drift through the house once again. She was glad to hear it – almost as glad as she might have been to hear an old friend's voice calling to her through the empty rooms, and she sighed a contented sort of sigh where she sat. Then a lock of hair tickled her cheek and she reached up to tuck it behind her ear. Or, at least, that was what she thought she was going to do.

But instead of stopping at her face, her hand continued rising, until it was stretched up above her head, seeming to bring the rest of her body with it, like a puppet dragged up by its strings. She stood away from the chair, thinking that she would stretch her stiff limbs. One arm curled above her head, the other twisted elegantly in front of her, as Chloe reached up on to the very tips of her toes. *En pointe.* Naturally, fluidly, wonderfully, her left leg lifted up off the floor and stretched out behind her, perfectly in sync with the notes of the oboe, leaving her trembling right leg to take all her weight as she threw back both arms and tilted her head, allowing the music to glide around her, wrapping her in a sad, soft, safe embrace that was far more satisfying than any man's clumsy touch could ever be. Her leg, stomach, back and shoulder muscles all screamed in protest, but her soul sang out with joy as she felt her body hold the flawless beauty of the sylph-like pose.

Then she caught a glimpse of herself in the full-length mirror on the opposite wall and saw the firelight flickering in soft golden patterns over the beautiful shape she was making with her body. But Chloe didn't know how to stand upon the tips of her toes like that. No sooner had the startled thought crossed her mind than her trembling foot collapsed, her toes crunching horribly under themselves as she fell heavily to the ground, all that lovely grace draining from her limbs like water flowing through a sieve.

The music stopped and Chloe cried out in pain and tore off her slipper, only to find that her sock was spotted with blood. She huddled on the floor for some moments, cradling her throbbing foot and wondering what on earth had just happened to her. And wishing that it hadn't stopped. Those moments when her body had been stretched out like that – strong and beautiful – had felt so wonderful. So right. Already, Chloe felt she would do anything to get that feeling back, and black frustration bubbled up in her chest that she had only been able to hold the position briefly.

Chloe found herself spending more and more time down by the lake. She'd sit on the bench there and stare into the muddy water and think about her ex-husband dying a horrible death. Or she would think about drowning herself in those dirty depths and putting an end to her suffering. It would be so easy. One strong thrust of the wheels and her chair would tip into the water and she would be dead before her nurse could drag her out. The thought always made her feel so happy – so relieved – and she played it over and over in her head since there were few enough things that brought her pleasure nowadays. She clung to the dark fantasy desperately, even though it confused her – because, of course, she didn't have a wheelchair. That had been Giselle.

One afternoon, after what seemed like hours spent staring at the water, dreaming of drowning, Chloe found herself phoning her mother. She sounded surprised to hear from Chloe, and why shouldn't she? It wasn't as if they ever really spoke. Chloe couldn't even have explained to herself why she had called.

"Hi, Mum," she said, sounding strained and unlike herself. "No, nothing's wrong. I just wanted to . . . I don't know. I just wanted to hear your voice."

When her mother asked how she was, Chloe barely knew how to answer her. "I don't miss him. But I miss my career. The way I felt when the stage lights were on me and— What? Oh. I meant the cameras. I miss the way I felt when the *cameras* were on me. I don't know why I said stage lights ..."

At the other end of the line, her mother started to say that she didn't understand but Chloe cut her off. "Mum, can I ask you something? Do you think I'm a chameleon? That's what *he* used to call me. He said I had no thoughts or feelings that were my own. Mum, I think maybe he was right. I can't find myself under . . . under all this pain and heartache and anger. Sometimes I think I have but then it's like smoke I can't hold on to and it drifts away from me. I can't always tell if my thoughts are mine or if they're hers . . ." Chloe paused and in the silence her mother said, once again, that she didn't understand. "It's Giselle," Chloe said. "Giselle's thoughts. She's ... she used to live here in this house. I think she reaches inside my head sometimes— Mum, please . . . stop saying you don't understand and just listen to me! I'm . . . I'm trying to tell you that I need help!"

But her mother just kept repeating that she didn't understand. Over and over again like a broken record. Then Chloe heard her father's voice ask something in the background and she heard her mother's fraught response: "I can't understand a word she's saying! She's been speaking in French for the last five minutes."

"I'm *not* speaking in French!" Chloe exclaimed, but as the words came out of her mouth she heard them properly for the first time and they *were* French. Chloe said something else but she couldn't understand it herself because she spoke those words in French too, and Chloe didn't know a single word of French – not one single word.

Her hand gripped the phone, tight enough to crack the

plastic casing, and a cold sweat formed at her hairline as she babbled incoherently, quite unable to understand herself any more than her mother could. A dreadful, appalling sense of isolation pressed down on her as she found herself suddenly unable to communicate in any human language. All those words she'd taken for granted all her life and had unthinkingly used to shape the world and shape herself were now gone, leaving her no different from and no better than the lowliest animal. But then, finally, something clicked – shifted savagely in her head – and Chloe could understand her own words once again.

"Mum, Mum, am I speaking English now?" she gasped. "Am I speaking in English or in French?"

She breathed a sigh of relief at the answer, then went rigid with indignation a moment later. "No, I haven't been drinking!" She wiped the clammy sweat from her brow as she listened to the stern voice at the other end of the line. Finally she said flatly, "All right, Mum. Yes. Yes, I will. Yes. Bye."

She hung up and stared at the phone for long moments before turning away from it, trying to shake the strange feeling that this was the last time she would ever speak to her mother.

She went upstairs to take a shower – as if the feeling was one she could wash away with hot water and soap. Steam filled the room as Chloe stripped off her clothes and stepped into the bath, the water from the showerhead pummelling her back and shoulders for a moment before she turned her face directly into the oncoming jets. She picked up the vanilla shower gel and slowly, methodically, began to wash herself from head to toe, the sweet, sugary smell mixing pleasantly with the hot steam. She breathed deeply and felt herself start to relax a little.

Chloe was almost finished in the shower when the bell rang. Her head jerked up and she froze, listening. It could have been the front door, of course, that was a definite possibility, but it was one that Chloe did not even consider. She was sure it was Giselle, ringing the bell in the fifth bedroom as she often did – as if she wanted to be found, as if she was calling out for help in the only way she could.

"I don't know where you are," Chloe whispered. "I'm sorry. I don't know how to get to you."

She listened out for it but the bell didn't ring again so she squeezed some more shower gel into the palm of her hand and leaned down to finish washing her legs and feet. The vanilla gel glided over the smooth skin of her thigh, down her shin, towards her ankle. And then Chloe's fingers made contact with the skin of her foot and it was not smooth and supple as she had expected but old and leathery and tough. She jerked her hand away with a cry, causing flakes of something crusty to lodge beneath her fingernails as she pulled back to stare down at her feet.

They were the feet of an old, old woman. An old woman whose feet had been permanently deformed through years of rigorous point dancing. The thick, yellow toenails were sorely in need of a cut; the skin between the toes was flaky and had split in places, exposing the raw, red flesh beneath. There were hard calluses on the outsides of both little toes, like barnacles clinging to a sunken ship, and she could feel swollen, pus-filled blisters threatening to burst beneath both her heels.

Chloe screamed and jerked away from those hideous feet that were hers and yet weren't hers at all. She immediately slipped on the wet surface of the bath, feeling several blisters pop beneath her weight, smearing yellow pus and thin blood across the white ceramic. Her flailing hands gripped the shower curtain and she tore it down, rings and all, as she fell out on to the cold tiled floor in a pool of water. The impact jarred her horribly but she hardly felt the pain since she was struggling too desperately to sit up and examine every inch of her body, horrified at the prospect of finding that the rest of her had shrivelled up into wrinkles and calluses too.

But her body was still smooth and supple and young. Her body was hers – even her feet had gone back to normal – pretty and neat and dainty with pink-painted toenails and not a callus or a blister in sight. Chloe scrambled to her feet and wiped the steam from the mirror with the palm of her hand to reveal her own wild-looking face staring back at her. Her face and no one else's.

Two days later – almost two months after moving into Arietta House – Chloe woke up in the middle of the night to find herself sitting outside in the garden. The cold was like a hundred icy knives stabbing into her flesh and the soles of her feet as she gazed down upon the still water of the filthy lake. Night-time mist slid past her skin like wet velvet, making her shudder, and she wrapped her arms around herself, stood up and turned back to the house. The single light shone from the middle upstairs window again. Chloe counted them and was sure this time that there were too many windows – almost as if another room had appeared inside the house while she'd been out. The non-existent fifth bedroom.

She started forwards so eagerly that she didn't look where she was going, and instantly stubbed her toe upon something hard and cold. She's assumed she'd been sitting on the stone bench as usual but when she looked down she saw the old wicker wheelchair right there before her, and for long moments she stared at it, wondering whether she could really have taken it down from the attic and brought it outside in her sleep without waking up. But then a shape passing across the lighted window upstairs drew her attention and she tore her gaze from the wheelchair. Giselle was there inside the house, Chloe knew it. She was there in the fifth bedroom, waiting for her.

Almost tripping over herself in her anxiety, Chloe abandoned the wheelchair by the lake and practically ran back into the house, throwing the front door open just as the bell rang, the red-and-white striped flag waving frantically in the dark little window for bedroom five. Chloe's bare, frozen feet slapped loudly upon the wooden boards as she thumped up the stairs, and she saw the new door as soon as she reached the landing. She knew that it had not been there before, and she would have known it was the door she was looking for even if the music for *Giselle* hadn't been drifting out of it, sweet and sad and soft. It wasn't smooth as silk like it normally was. This time it sounded scratchy and rough – like a damaged record playing on an old gramophone. A thin beam of light glowed beneath the door that should not have existed.

Chloe placed a trembling hand upon the cold brass knob, took a deep breath, and twisted it quickly before her nerve could fail her. The door swung open soundlessly upon well-oiled hinges as the melancholy oboe continued to drown itself in guilt-stricken grief.

The first thing she saw when the door opened was the rack of costumes. Luscious fabrics in pinks and whites and blues, muslin, and tulle, and velvet, and voile, trimmed with the finest lace and the smoothest silk. Fitted bodices and powder-puff skirts – exquisite costumes, all lovingly cherished and preserved. Soft leather and pink satin ballet slippers were lined up beneath the rack, tied up with slim ribbons. By the light of a single candle placed in the window, the sequins and beads of the costumes sparkled and shone.

The room smelled of perfume and powder, and Chloe saw the glass bottles neatly positioned upon the dressing table, along with a silver-backed mirror and hairbrush – long, thick black hairs caught up within the bristles. Above the crackle of fine music playing on a scratched record, Chloe said softly, "Giselle?"

Her heart hammered with anticipation. She was going to see her. At last, she was finally going to see Giselle and to talk to her. She stared around the room wildly, wondering whether Giselle would appear to her as she had been before her accident – a young, strong, graceful prima ballerina – or whether she would look as she had when she died – a feeble old woman confined to a hated wheelchair.

But Giselle was not in the room. No eyes – young or old – met Chloe's as she gazed around. There was just an empty bed and an empty wheelchair by the window, pushed right up against the wall, fixed to which was a brass bell push. And that was when Chloe realized that there *was* someone in the room after all.

The tip of one gnarled finger rested lightly upon the bell

push. The liver-spotted hand rested on the arm of the wheel-chair, one finger still laid upon the bell, as if someone was sitting there, but all Chloe could see was that veined old hand. The rest of the chair stood in a pool of darkness but it wasn't so dim that Chloe couldn't see that the chair was quite empty except for a hazy, smoky shadow that might almost have been human-shaped. If she really squinted, she thought she could see the dark silhouette of a head, but it was only for a moment before the image melted away and all that was left was that hand, pale and stark in the dimness.

As Chloe stared, the hand lifted itself from the arm of the chair, seeming to float in mid-air as it turned palm upwards and the bent old fingers curled back and then forwards again. The meaning was unmistakable – she was being beckoned closer.

This was not what Chloe had expected, and disappointment coursed through her. She could not talk to a hand, she could not receive the sympathy and understanding she so desperately craved from a hand, and yet she found herself moving forwards uncertainly anyway. When she stopped directly in front of the wheelchair, the hand stopped beckoning and reached up a little further, still palm upwards.

After a moment's hesitation, Chloe reached out and took the lined, frail, bony hand in her own. The moment her fingers closed around it, she felt a jolt pass through her whole body. She gasped and tried to pull back but her fingers seemed to be glued into place for the briefest second, and then she found she couldn't move her hand because she didn't have one any more.

She tried to open her mouth to scream but she no longer had a mouth and so she could not utter a sound. She had no body whatsoever. All she had was a strange sense of lightness, as if she was floating. And when her eyesight cleared and her vision focused she saw her own face staring down at her, only it was not the face she knew from the mirror. The features were identical but this face was colder, harder, and looked strangely and horrifically triumphant as the red lips parted and the white teeth were bared in an awful smile.

Chloe was forced to watch in silence as, without a word, her body pirouetted on the spot with a sort of terrible grace before a cold laugh bubbled up from the imposter's throat, and then, with one last glance in the direction of the chair, Chloe's body turned and walked from the room, head held high, slamming the door behind her. Chloe struggled and struggled to scream and shout at her to come back but she couldn't so much as whisper. When she looked down, she saw that there was nothing left of her. Just a smoky hazy outline of nothingness – the wisps of feelings and memories and emotions that had made her who she was before, all floating about loose like gases released from a sealed container. She could feel herself dispersing and dissipating already, becoming weaker and weaker – more and more like nothing every second.

In a burst of panic and horror, Chloe mustered up enough strength to drag all the pieces of herself tightly back together, putting all her energy and willpower into keeping herself whole. After what felt like hours of ferocious concentration, she thought she could see the faint outline of one of her fingers. The bell push on the wall gleamed at her sullenly in the candle-light – just about within reaching distance – and, with an exhausting effort of will, she managed to push it, causing the din of the bell to echo through the now-empty house.

A short while later, the whole world marvelled as ex-model Chloe Benn took the world of ballet by storm. It was unprecedented for someone so late to ballet to dance with such exquisite perfection. She was a phenomenally gifted natural, they said, the like of which had never been seen on the stage before. She was expected to be awarded the rank of prima ballerina before her twenty-third birthday, and there were even murmurings of the possibility of the prima ballerina assoluta rank – an almost unheard of honour …

In the aftermath of her newfound success she was approached by her ex-husband, cautiously seeking a reunion.

"You look well," he said. "Different. Have you dyed your hair? Perhaps we could get a drink some time? Catch up … ?"

His voice trailed off uncertainly; he seemed unnerved by the look on his ex-wife's face. She stared at him in chilly silence for long, long moments before she finally opened her mouth and said in a voice that sounded unlike her own, "So you're him? You look just like I imagined. Come here." She beckoned with one slim finger. Something about her definitely seemed odd, but at least she hadn't told him to go to hell as he had expected. Chloe's ex-husband approached with cautious optimism, a foolish grin already starting to form itself on his foolish face.

"I thought we could—" he began, but didn't get the chance to finish the sentence before Chloe grabbed the front of his shirt in a surprisingly strong grip and dragged him closer to press a kiss to his mouth.

He remembered Chloe's kisses being sweet and soft and warm and gentle, but there was nothing gentle about this kiss. Her lips and tongue were shockingly cold and dry, like a corpse's – or a reptile's – and that coldness seemed to spread all the way through him at her touch. Her nails dug into the back of his neck hard enough to draw blood – he could feel the warm trickles running down his skin to stain his collar. It felt as if she was trying to suck his soul out through his mouth. He could barely breathe with her clamped to his lips like some terrible succubus, hissing a little with gruesome pleasure as he struggled madly in her tight grip.

He finally managed to detach himself from her, although she tore a piece from his lip as he pushed her away as hard as he could. He staggered back from her, his chest heaving with a nameless horror. For he knew, with a dreadful certainty, that whoever this woman before him was, she was not the woman who had been his wife. His blood dribbled down her chin and he watched in terrified fascination as she slowly, seductively, licked smears of it from her teeth, not bothering to clean it from her face before smiling brilliantly at him and saying, "Chloe sends her regards."

Trembling in every limb, with a terror that he had not known since childhood, Chloe's ex-husband barely noticed the warm, wet patch spreading down his trousers as he stumbled blindly away and ran from the room. The cold, creeping, delighted sound of Chloe's laughter behind him was one that would haunt him in nightmares for the rest of his life.

Meanwhile, back in Arietta House, the bell for bedroom five continued to ring frantically, day and night. No one ever heard it, since Chloe Benn had decided that the house should be torn down and a block of flats built in its place. The lost room would soon become part of a lost house. Just as it was supposed to.

Scairt

Alison Littlewood

The piper stood on the hill, all alone, his dark green kilt blowing in the breeze. Rannoch Moor was broad and windswept, great mounds disappearing into the distance, punctuated by the glisten of water.

Amanda couldn't hear the bagpipes, only the continual grind of the car's engine that had accompanied them for mile after mile. She saw the back of her grandma's head in the passenger seat and Granddad's sticky-out ears. There were white hairs growing out of them.

"Can't we stop?" she asked.

Her grandma turned and Amanda pointed. Now she saw that the piper was standing in a lay-by. There was a line of parked cars, but there didn't seem to be any people: only the piper.

Her granddad slowed, indicated, pulled in. There were brown spots on his hands. He parked the car and they sat there.

"Here, Amanda," said Grandma. She opened her window, winding the handle around and around. Cold air and the sound of wind and the strange, strident call of bagpipes came in. Amanda twisted and looked out of the back.

"Here," Grandma said again. She fumbled with her purse, undid the snappers and pulled out a coin. She pressed it into Amanda's hand. It was twenty pence.

"For his hat," said Grandma, gesturing. "There's always a hat."

Amanda slipped out of the car, jumping down on to the tarmac. Beyond the lay-by was nothing but tufts of grass, a line of green that gave way to burned orange and purple. The clouds were low and rippled and went on forever.

She walked towards the piper hearing a wheezing sound, a constant groan under the notes and the gulps of breath he took. She didn't look at him. She saw only his legs, sturdy and bare. They were covered in curling hairs that shivered in the wind. She looked for a hat and saw a large black case with the shine of coins inside. She put down the twenty pence and walked away, feeling his eyes on her back. Still he played on, different notes each time, a tune she didn't know.

Amanda climbed back into the car. The grind of the engine started and they drove away, onward, towards home.

"Well, isn't that nice?" said Grandma. "A welcoming committee." She started chinking china cups, putting them into saucers, her hands shaking.

There were three of them. They were Amanda's new neighbours. She didn't know if she wanted new neighbours. She wanted her old room, the house that was sold, the house that didn't have a family in it any more. Now she had her grandparents, and this place: a white house with a low roof, a room under the eaves with a faded carpet and a musty smell.

"Scotland will be good for you," Grandma had said. "A new start for us all. Plenty of fresh air."

And here were friends for her already. Mrs McBride was the mother, and here were the two daughters. Morag leaned against the dresser, swinging her foot like a ballerina. She had brown hair and a long, pinched face. Kitty was older. She sat down at once on the sofa, sitting up straight, looking at Amanda with a direct gaze.

"What do you say, Amanda?" Grandma nodded towards the girls.

Amanda tried a smile. She couldn't think of anything to say;

then she saw that pointed foot, swinging and swaying. "Do you like ballet?" she asked.

Morag's lips twitched and she shot a sidelong glance at Kitty. "Ballet?" she said. "No, I don't like ballet. D'ye not know Scottish dancing?"

Amanda shook her head and watched as Morag skipped a few steps across the floor.

"Have ye no been to a ceilidh, Amanda?" asked their mother. Her tone was kind. "We'll have to teach ye, won't we, Morag?"

Morag pursed her lips.

"Have you heard o' the ceilidh? Ye'd like it." Mrs McBride laughed. "Ye'll no be used to the accent. D'ye ken?"

Amanda frowned. "My name's Amanda," she said, and everyone laughed.

"Come on," said Kitty, jumping up from the sofa and holding out a hand. "We'll show ye where to play, won't we, Morag?"

There were encouraging sounds from the adults. Amanda rose to her feet and Kitty grabbed her hand. The next moment they were heading up the lane towards a wooded hill, Morag and Kitty in front, Amanda following.

"We'll go to the lochan," said Kitty. "Ye do know what a lochan is?"

"No."

They hurried on, past more small white houses, past a tiny store, past a cottage that was thatched in what looked like old heather. Water dripped from it. The sky was darker now, the clouds weighed down.

"Why're your parents so *auld*?" The question came from Kitty.

"Why so *auld*?" said Morag.

Amanda knew she would have to explain: that they were her grandparents, not her parents, because her parents were gone. There was an accident, and only she was left. She imagined the words, held in her mouth only, never reaching her insides. Just going out into the cold air where they would disappear.

"Here," Kitty cut in. There was a low bridge and the start of a wood. A path wound its way into the trees, fallen leaves lying wetly on the ground. The gold and red of tall trees mingled with the dark green of pine.

Amanda trailed after them, her smooth soles slipping on the leaves, revealing streaks of black mud. Dribbles of lichen hung from the trees. Away from the path the ground was covered in little mounds, old branches maybe, covered in moss and tight, star-shaped leaves. Everything dripped.

"A boy disappeared here once," said Kitty. "But we're not scairt, are we, Morag?"

"No."

"Are ye scairt, Amanda?"

Amanda looked at them.

Kitty turned and smiled. "How old are ye, Amanda?"

"I'm eight."

"He was eight, too. He was eight, wasn't he, Morag? When he disappeared?"

Amanda frowned. "I don't believe there was a boy."

"Aye, there was. A long time ago. An' he vanished. They all thought he ran away, but we know he's here. Don't we, Morag?"

Morag nodded.

"We'll show you."

Amanda glanced back; saw the pathway winding towards the house. Thought of going home on her own, without her new friends, and everyone asking why. She nodded.

There was a man standing by the lochan. He stood by a small green hut, a wooden creel at his feet. He twisted a length of blue rope in his hands, around and around.

The lochan was a small lake, still and grey and edged with rhododendrons that weren't in flower. A wide, even pathway circled it. "It's pretty," Amanda said.

Kitty snorted. "Come on." She led the way to another path, narrow and dark, leading up the hill into more woodland.

The man watched them go. His face was heavily lined and he had a white beard like Santa Claus. He smiled at Amanda and she smiled back.

"Don't look at him," Kitty hissed. "He's mad, he is. Everyone knows it."

She stomped up the path, leaving peaty footprints. Soon they were stepping over branches, and mounds and grooves cut into the earth by run-off from the hills.

"Look," said Kitty.

Amanda looked about. There were just trees with silver trunks, scarred here and there with black patches.

"Ye can see his face." Kitty pointed.

There was a shape in the trunk of a tree, a growth sticking out. "It's nothing," Amanda said. "Just a bole."

"Oh, is it now? Just a be-owl," said Kitty.

"A bowl, a *bowl*," Morag echoed.

But Amanda saw that it wasn't a bole, at all. It was a face; the face of a young boy with closed eyes, the mouth slightly open, his two front teeth missing. His skin was smooth apart from deep grooves that ran through the bark like scratches.

"He was kilt here, tha's wha' I think. An' they never found him."

Amanda frowned. She reached out to touch the face. It wasn't carved. It was growing in the wood, a living thing, damp and lightly greened with moss.

"Don't touch it!"

Amanda turned and saw Kitty's face, her eyes wide open.

"Ye mustn't touch it. It's bad luck."

It was too late. Amanda's fingers rested, lightly, on the bark.

"That's bad luck, now." Kitty marched off, back the way they had come, Morag trailing at her heels.

After a moment, Amanda followed.

Kitty and Morag had told her to meet them in the woods. Amanda glanced out of the window, seeing the empty lane, a formless grey sky.

"We're your friends," Kitty said. "We'll play by the lochan. *Above* the lochan." And Amanda saw the way she and Morag glanced at each other.

What if she went, and they didn't meet her after all? What if they went, and she didn't? She sighed. Soon there would be school, and the girls would catch the bus together, share the journey every day. If she didn't go to the woods – but no. It had to be them who didn't show, if anyone. And maybe they would be there; maybe they really meant to be friends.

Amanda's footsteps were loud on the pavement. She paused at the bridge, looking down into the white froth, listened to it crashing on the stones. She sniffed. Grandma was right; the air was clean here. It didn't smell of anything at all.

She went in under the trees, kicking fallen leaves that stuck to her boots in wet clumps. The woods were damp, droplets of water clinging to strands of moss and lichen. She glanced down. There was a groove in the ground where water trickled through a carpet of pine needles. Something moved.

Amanda started, and then saw the velvet body of a vole, its tender nose twitching. She imagined the voices in her ears: "Are you scairt?" "Ye *scairt*?"

She shook her head and went on.

The man by the lochan had his back to Amanda. He was clad in a light blue shirt, bending over a fishing rod that was set out over the lake. She stepped quietly, her boots scraping just slightly on the path, and began to climb up the hillside. She glanced back and could see his legs, ending in brown boots, the feet now pointing towards her.

She slipped and put out her hand. It plunged into leaves and pine needles and came away black. She looked towards the lochan once more. Now she couldn't see the man at all.

She went on, watching for the special tree. She wondered if the boy would still be there, looking out at nothing. Whether his eyes would still be closed. She swallowed.

"Kitty? Morag?" she called out, but her voice was a whisper. "Kitty?"

The wind soughed in the branches. Behind her, a branch snapped.

Amanda whirled about, seeing only silver bark, the black shadows of branches. And then something else, through the trees: something that looked like a pale blue shirt. It was there, and then it was gone. She drew in her breath, turned back, and saw the boy. His eyes were closed. They were two smooth, blank ovals.

"Kitty?" she breathed.

"Kitty?" the call came back. It wasn't a girl's voice. It wasn't a child's voice. Amanda's stomach constricted. There was nothing but trees, all around.

"Kitty?" It was a man's voice.

Amanda walked quickly onward, up the hill. The path became more irregular and she found herself picking her way between green mounds. She slipped, felt her ankle turning, but caught herself. It was all right. Her ankle smarted, but nothing more. She looked back into the wood and saw the man. He was below her on the slope. He held a blue rope in his hands. He was turning and turning it, over and over. He looked back at her. He didn't smile.

Amanda started to run as best she could. "Kitty!" she called. "Morag!"

She slipped and almost fell, recovered, ran on. She ducked under branches that snagged her hair and clothes. She pulled free, not crying out as hair was yanked from her head. The hill grew steeper; she hardly seemed to be running at all. She glanced back. She couldn't see the man.

Amanda stopped, her breath catching. Warm, stinging tears came to her eyes. Was he there? Was he waiting for her to go back down? She looked about. The trees were all the same. She could edge around him, maybe, try to get back to the lochan.

She looked left, then right. There was something through the trees. Not the man, though, not a pale blue shirt; something red. As Amanda watched, it moved.

She let out a little cry, a sound that started way back in her throat.

The thing moved towards her and resolved itself into a boy. He wore a red jumper. He was about her height. The boy jerked his head, indicating that she should follow. Amanda glanced back once more over her shoulder, and then she did.

The boy led her over the hillside. Amanda listened for

anyone following but heard only the wind, her own breath, and twigs crackling under her feet. She pushed branches aside and crawled under a fallen tree, bits of wood clinging to her hair and clothes. She could hear the man again, his deep, quick breathing, the heavy tread of his boots. The boy stopped and turned to her, put his finger to his lips. Then he pointed, two sharp stabs.

Amanda went up to him. His jumper was muddied and torn, his hair so long she couldn't see his eyes. He nodded down the slope and she saw what he meant. There was a narrow gully. It was damp, and covered with pine needles, but the way down was clear.

The boy gestured again and then he smiled. His two front teeth were missing. He wore a short twist of blue rope about his neck.

He left her, heading back towards the man. Amanda didn't wait any longer. She lowered herself into the gully and half climbed, half slid down towards the lochan, pine needles muffling the sound of her steps.

Grandma's knee was hard and bony. Amanda shifted on it and leaned back. Her grandma stroked her head, making "shhh" noises. Her hand was shaking. Amanda's granddad was at the door, seeing the policemen out, talking with them in a low voice.

Grandma began to pick bits of bark and leaf from Amanda's hair. She had not told them about the boy. She could still see his face, though, the grin as he disappeared into the trees.

They found a man, the policeman had said. *Lying against a tree. Heart attack, most likely. Had a piece of rope in his hands.* He glanced at Amanda as he said this. *A piece of blue rope.* There was something in his eyes Amanda didn't like. She wanted him to go away. Now she heard the door close.

She slipped her thumb into her mouth and began to suck it, the way she used to, back when she was really small.

"Wha', the new girl? Aye, she's our friend."

Kitty stood at the bus stop. Morag was next to her, her hair pulled into thin plaits. Two other children waited there, a boy and a girl with the same pale yellow hair.

"Here she is."

They all watched Amanda's approach. When she looked at them, they looked away.

"So you're from England?" It was the new girl who spoke. Amanda nodded.

Kitty leaned in and whispered, "We're to say sorry. We forgot. About playing. Tha's all."

"So wha' happened?" said the new girl, and the questions began, pouring out one after the next.

Amanda told them. But all the time, she thought of the boy: a boy in a red jumper, lacking two front teeth, and about her height. But she never spoke of him at all.

Amanda walked once more up the hillside, away from the lochan. Her grandma hadn't liked her going, but Amanda said it would do her good. A new start, she told her. Some fresh air. And the unspoken thought hung between them that the man who had followed her was dead.

Her trainers gripped the slope. The earth was soft and silent under her feet; Amanda could hear only the constant sighing of wind in the trees. She found she liked it. The cold air made her ears tingle.

I'm not scared, she thought; but it came out *scairt*. It was funny how that happened. Earlier she had asked Kitty to lend her a pen, but it came out "Could ye—", and she paused, hearing the strange sound. Kitty had smiled, but Amanda had only been able to think of her mother's face: sudden and clear and stricken.

She found the tree easily enough. The shape of a face stuck out of it, but something had changed. Amanda went up close and saw that the grain had split, the cracks widening, changing the shape. It wasn't a face any longer. It was just a bole.

She sat for a while, looking out over the lochan and further, seeing mountains and lochs and sky, stretching on and on. *Scairt*, she thought. *Scairt*. No, she wasn't scairt. She whispered it anyway, trying out the sound. Maybe her mother would have liked it, hearing her say it like that. It might have made her laugh. *Scairt.*

After a while she stood and began to make her way back down the hillside. She was going to Kitty's later. Morag was going to teach her Scottish dancing.

Amanda looked back only once before the tree slipped out of sight. And she saw that the boy wasn't entirely gone, after all: she could still see the gap of a partly open mouth, the space where his two front teeth should have been. Deep cracks ran down either side of his lips and on, down the trunk. *It's only a bole*, she thought. *Only the grain. That's all.* But for just a moment, it had looked as though the boy was smiling.

Seeing Nancy

Nina Allan

I'll ne'er blame my partial fancy;
Naething could resist my Nancy;
But to see her was to love her,
Love but her, and love for ever . . .
"Ae Fond Kiss", Robert Burns

I liked the house as soon as I saw it: a narrow 1930s villa at the end of a long cul-de-sac with allotments on one side and a former Methodist chapel on the other. The chapel had fallen out of use in the eighties. It stood derelict for a while, then someone had bought it and converted it into a music studio. From the outside it still looked like a church and I liked that, too.

The house had pointed gables, and was painted yellow.

"It's perfect, isn't it?" Roy said. "Don't you just love it?"

"Yes," I said. "I love it." Our offer was accepted the same day. By the time contracts were actually exchanged, though, Roy was back in Helmand, and I had to organize the removals myself. I didn't mind. Roy had no patience for things like that. It was something we had joked about in the early days; the ATO with a short fuse, the trained perfectionist who was fine with roadside bombs but who would lose his rag completely if the van with our stuff in it got held up in traffic.

I knew his rages were just a safety valve and in the beginning I found no problem in tolerating them. I even felt a kind of pride that I was the only person who could calm him down. In time that changed. I came to feel that I had been tricked somehow, that the man I married was not the man I ended up living with, although I knew myself that this wasn't entirely fair. The problems had been there all along, and I had chosen to close my eyes to them. I had tricked myself.

He was granted an extended leave after his second tour but if anything his flare-ups were worse. I knew he had seen someone killed, a soldier from his own unit, but he never told me any details of what happened and I knew better by then than to ask.

He seemed to have lost all interest in the house. He moved through its rooms like a ghost, not commenting on the changes I had made, never expressing an opinion one way or the other. Sometimes I would find him in the upstairs room we had planned to set aside as his photography studio, sitting cross-legged on the bare boards and sorting through a cardboard folder of snapshots. The photos were of men on the base, young recruits mainly, soldiers ten years younger than him or even more.

They fooled around for the camera, snatching each other's berets and making rude gestures.

"Is one of these the lad who died?" I once tried asking. Roy stared up at me, blankly at first and then with an expression of such rage I thought he was about to hit me.

Go on, do it, I thought. *Then I can leave.* I was lonelier by then than I had ever been. I was single for some years before meeting Roy and had grown accustomed to living alone. But sharing a house with a man who had become a stranger to me was something different and awful because I was forced to keep up a pretence that there was nothing wrong.

Worst of all was the fact that I had no one to talk to. There were friends of mine, people who had warned me against marrying Roy in the first place and who would have been only too happy to meet for coffee and a round of sympathetic bitching, but the thought of such disloyalty sickened me. I knew deep down that those friends who disparaged Roy were less interested in helping me than in being proved right. I would probably have felt the same in their position.

The only person I wanted to talk to was Roy, the Roy I had met and married and whom I now missed terribly. Sometimes in the pale grey hours around dawn I found it easy to imagine that the old Roy was still out there somewhere, longing for me as I longed for him. The man in the bed beside me was someone else. I wondered if he dreamed of hurting me, or of simply packing his things and walking away.

I told myself he would come out of it eventually and when he did we would talk and everything would get back to normal. But in the meantime it was like being in prison. Later that made me think of Allison Rand, and the bars across the windows in the hospital canteen.

I tried to concentrate on the new book, but could not get started. It was not just the problems with Roy. The move had disrupted my routine, and what I was now faced with was a kind of mental blankness. I had lost touch with myself, with the things that interested me. The sense of dislocation was profoundly unsettling. I suppose it was a kind of writer's block, something I had never suffered from before. I took to sitting on a wooden bench up on the allotments, staring across at the yellow walls of my own house and trying to make up a story about the people who lived there.

I liked the allotments, and quickly came to recognize the people who tended them. They were creased and faded, characters from pre-war novels, figures in the landscape of a sepia postcard. There was a Polish woman in a red kerchief, a pair of elderly Oxford spinsters, a man with a Jack Russell terrier, rake-thin and with two fingers missing from his right hand. I used to think about him a lot, wondering if he had been injured in World War II and if talking to him might help Roy.

I dreamed up various schemes for bringing them together but knew I would not dare try any of them. It was all too easy to imagine things going wrong; Roy's rage and contempt for me afterwards if it turned out, after all, that the man had lost his fingers in an accident at work.

As well as the Polish woman and the Oxford spinsters I often saw a young girl in a grey skirt and a baggy green cardigan – shapeless, too-big clothes, hand-me-downs no doubt from an elder sister. She stood out on the allotments because she was so much younger than the other people who went there. She had a curious way of walking, heel-to-toe along the narrow pathways, as if she were on a tightrope. Sometimes she picked up stones and put them in her pockets. She was always by herself. The other allotment regulars appeared to ignore her.

She was eight years old perhaps, ten at the most. She seemed young to be there all alone. She should have been in school, though I supposed lots of children truanted. I wondered if she had problems at home.

One day she came and sat beside me. She sidled up, squinting at me from the corner of her eye then plumping herself down on the bench, squarely and decisively, as if carrying out a dare she had made with herself.

She drew her legs up beneath her, and began tapping together two stones I had watched her grub up from the soil of the Polish woman's allotment. It was only then that I noticed how pretty she was. It was not just the snub nose and freckles, the youthful glow that haunts all children, even the plainest. There was a life in her, an animated curiosity that seemed to light her features from within.

She banged her stones, skewbald flints, and darted her eyes to where mine had been looking, up towards the first floor of my house.

"There was a murder there," she said. "Right there in that house. Do you know about it?"

She had a Scots accent. I felt surprised by this without knowing why. I wondered if she had been watching me, noticing my presence over the weeks as I had hers.

"A murder?" I said. "Aren't you a bit young to know about things like that?"

She looked at me as if I were stupid, which I suppose I was. "It happened *ages* ago," she said. "There's nothing there now." She gave her stones another bash then dropped them in the dirt at her feet.

"I'm there," I said. "That's my house."

She turned and gawped at me. Her eyes were bright with amazement, as if what I'd just told her was the most incredible thing she'd heard in her short life.

"No way!" she said.

I nodded. "There aren't any ghosts, though; it's just an ordinary house."

"Do you believe in ghosts, then? I mean, *really*?" She edged towards me along the bench. I felt her hand brush the seam of my jeans. Roy and I had discussed having children once or twice but it seemed a long time now since we'd had a proper conversation about anything. I remembered Roy had been keen on having kids, though. I was less sure.

"I don't know," I said. "But I know I've never seen one." I thought of Roy and me, the remnants of our past that stalked us daily. But these were not the kind of ghosts the child was after.

"Here, ghosty-ghosty!" she cried. She raised her hand and waved up at my window, her fingers spread like the limbs of a small white starfish. Then suddenly and without warning, she jumped off the bench and ran away down the main path that cut through the allotments and then joined the road. The man with the Jack Russell was coming. I watched the girl circle the dog, then dart in to pat its chocolate-coloured head. The man with the missing fingers did not look up.

A sheet of newspaper flapped across the ground by my feet. *Rig Disaster Claims More Lives.*

That story was three weeks old. For the people who made the papers it was already over.

When I looked back down the hill the Jack Russell man was still there but the girl was gone.

What she'd said, though, that preyed on my mind. I knew children made up stories constantly but I knew also that these rarely came out of nowhere and I wondered if there might be some truth in it. If she had not known where I lived when she first spoke to me, why would she invent things about my house?

No one had said anything about a murder when we first bought the place, but it's hardly the kind of thing an estate agent is likely to advertise. I felt a flicker of something, a stir of interest, like a piece of string uncoiling deep in my gut.

I thought I might finally have found my next book.

Roy was out when I got home, as he so often was. When he wasn't staring at his photographs in the front bedroom he was on one of his walks, endless, meandering rambles along the roads and country lanes that skirted the town. On those days it was as if he was afraid to be inside, as if our house had become a symbol of confinement and oppression. I had worried about this at first, concerned he might cause or become the victim of an accident. Now I was simply relieved to find him gone.

I booted up the computer and googled our address. I was amazed by how many results there were. The usual estate agents' adverts and map references, but the majority of hits seemed to relate to a woman named Allison Rand. I had never heard of her before, but a few quick searches found me the information I needed. She was forty-five years old, and had taught history at one of the local secondary schools. She had been convicted of the murder of her two infant daughters.

There was a verdict of cot death on the first child, but when the second had died eighteen months later and in identical circumstances Allison Rand was arrested and charged. Steven Rand, her husband and a teacher at the same school, divorced her and sold the house. Allison Rand protested her innocence throughout.

The case had an air of desperate tragedy about it but Allison Rand seemed more like victim than villain, and in any case it didn't feel right. The girl on the allotments had said the murder had happened a long time ago, yet the Rand case was in the relatively recent past. My first reaction was of disappointment, but the more I read, the more I wondered if there wasn't an article in it at least, something I could sell to a magazine on the back of my last novel.

"How I Came to Live with a Murderess", that kind of thing.

It was a cheap trick but at least it was something. It might even help me break out of my block.

If Allison Rand would talk to me, that was. The idea of making contact with her was strangely exciting, and once again I felt that stirring, that sense I was on to something. I felt better than I had done in weeks.

I wrote to Allison Rand, care of the governor of the secure mental hospital where she was being treated, and asked if I could come and see her. There was no reply so I wrote again. After about a week I received a terse reply from the governor's office, informing me of the visiting hours and that I was free to put in a formal request. I had the feeling I was in for a long wait, so I took a chance and wrote to Allison Rand personally. As an afterthought I enclosed a copy of my latest novel. Not long afterwards I received a brief note from her, telling me she had added my name to the list of approved visitors. I sent her a postcard by return, informing her that I would come the following week.

I didn't tell Roy what I was doing. He was due to return to his unit in a couple of days. On the day I confirmed my appointment with Allison Rand, he returned to the house after dark, stinking of beer and cigarettes. He looked sheepish, almost guilty, and for the first time since he'd come home he seemed eager to talk.

"I'm sorry, Marian," he said. "I've been acting like an arse-hole. I don't know who I am any more."

He was always conciliatory when he wanted sex. I had come off the pill while he was away, and felt a rush of annoyance with him for his thoughtlessness, for the selfish way he assumed I would be ready to patch things up the moment he felt he needed a little comfort. Where had he been when I needed comfort? I didn't refuse him, though. I told myself it was because I couldn't face another row, and that was true.

But mainly it was because I still loved him. I supposed I always would.

"We should have kids," he said before he fell asleep. His arm lay across my shoulders and for the first time in many months he seemed fully relaxed. "Wouldn't that be great? A house like this needs kids in it."

I had been on the verge of sleep myself, but his words had me wide awake again. For some reason I found it disturbing, shocking even, that he should make a connection between the house and having children. For a moment I considered waking him, telling him about the Rand case, but I didn't do it. I knew how crazy it would sound if I did, and Roy had enough craziness in him for the two of us.

I thought instead of the girl on the allotments, her baggy cardigan and too-big skirt. I wondered if her mother knew she was skipping school.

"You write about murder, then? That's what you do?"

We were in the hospital visitors' lounge, a large, light, square room overlooking open countryside. We had been talking for about half an hour, the usual introductory pleasantries followed by my own vague questions about hospital routine. It was all basic stuff, background material at best, and I found the constant presence of the male security staff disconcerting. Yet in spite of these restrictions I found myself enjoying the conversation. The newspapers had portrayed Allison Rand as a plain-faced, mousy little woman, the archetypical dried-up blue stocking. In reality she was much more attractive, with small hands and firm cheeks, her grey eyes articulate and clear. She was like a bird, I thought. A wren perhaps, or a hedge sparrow. She was dressed simply, in clean faded jeans and a check cotton shirt. If I hadn't recognized her at once from her photograph, I would have assumed she was an off-duty nurse.

She was clearly an intelligent woman. Her question about murder came completely out of the blue.

"I write crime novels," I said. "I don't suppose I can tape this?" I had been obliged to leave my phone at reception, along with my purse and my car keys, but I still had my iPod, which also had a Dictaphone function. Rand glanced furtively in the direction of one of the uniformed male nurses and then raised an eyebrow. I lifted my hand to push back my hair and, as I lowered it again, I brushed my fingers against the iPod's tiny 'on' switch. Rand's neat, lipstickless mouth curled in a half-smile.

"I don't mind what you do," she said. "But I don't think I'll be much use to you."

"Why do you say that?"

"Because I haven't committed a crime. I've never even stolen stationery from the school supply cupboard." She gave a harsh laugh, and for the first time I saw the brittleness beneath her apparent composure. "I enjoyed your book, though I didn't expect to. Perhaps it's true what they say, that deep down we're all in love with violence." She folded her hands in her lap and clenched them together. "I don't know why I'm telling you this, but I'm going to anyway. I didn't want children. I don't mean I actively disliked them, but I enjoyed my studies and I enjoyed my job and later on I enjoyed being married. I didn't want children to change things, as I knew they would. But Steven was keen, and I didn't want to disappoint him. We didn't conceive, though. Years went by and nothing happened and in the end I stopped thinking about it. Then suddenly there Sophie was.

"I loved her from the moment I knew I was pregnant. One day there was my old life, and the next there was this new one, something I had never guessed at, something that swallowed the entire world as I had known it, but I didn't care. What I cared about was Sophie, and when she died I stopped caring about anything. Even when I got pregnant again with Alana I didn't care, because I knew already that I would lose her too. Perhaps there's a writer out there somewhere who can convey what that feels like, but I doubt it."

She took off her glasses. The round, wire-framed lenses reflected the red Formica surface of the table, twin versions of Mars. Without them she looked both younger and more desperate.

"What do you mean, you knew you would lose her, too?" I said. I felt she was holding something back, either because she felt guilty or because she didn't judge me worthy of knowing. I wondered if it was this way she had of acting superior even when she didn't mean to that had turned the jury against her. I knew the actual evidence had always been minimal.

"It was the house," she said. "Don't tell me you haven't noticed?" She pulled a handkerchief from her pocket and began polishing her glasses. It crossed my mind then that she was guilty after all. That she had killed her two baby girls, and doing it had driven her insane.

"Noticed what?" I said. In the whole of the hour I'd spent with her she had not made a single reference to the fact that I was living in what had once been her home. Now it seemed it had been at the forefront of her mind all along.

"Why do you think I agreed to see you, to talk to you like this? I did it because I felt I should warn you, that I could do that at least. There's something in that house, and it killed my daughters."

"You're not serious?"

"Believe me or not, it's up to you. Just don't bring any more children into that house."

She put her glasses back on, becoming the sane and matter-of-fact ex-teacher I had met when I first arrived. What she was saying was so out of kilter with the way she looked I found myself wondering if her madness wasn't contagious.

"I'm not sure what to say," I said. "Are you talking about ghosts?" I remembered the child from the allotments, calling up at my window and waving her hand. Ghosts were just a game to her.

Rand smiled.

"Ghosts have no physical power over reality. All they can do is manifest themselves, cast an influence. That's what the experts will tell you anyway. I know you only came here for a story and I suppose you think you've got your money's worth. Don't think I don't know how I sound. But I've done my best to warn you and that's all I can do." She paused. "All life's disasters sound insane if you try and explain them out loud, have you ever noticed that? I would never have believed a word of this if it hadn't happened to me."

Soon afterwards the bell went and I had to leave. I told her I would come and see her again, not knowing if I meant it or not. I passed along the corridor to the exit, where a member of the security staff stood ready to claim my visitor's pass. The view from the first floor was a swoon of greenness, and when I learned later that the building had won several industry design awards I wasn't surprised. But when all was said and done it was still a mental hospital. There were security guards at all the entrances, and every outside window was barred.

I drove home slowly, taking the back roads to avoid the rush-hour traffic. As I turned into the narrow lane that led to our house a child dashed across the road in front of the car. I slammed on the brakes, swerving instinctively, but when I stepped out of the car there was no one there. I cooked supper then made coffee and began playing back the tape of my interview with Allison Rand.

The house was quiet, so quiet, and when a knock came at the back door it startled me so much I almost fell off my chair. Roy and I had never mixed much in the town, and I had no idea who my visitor might be. For a moment I found myself wondering what I would do if I opened the door to find Allison Rand standing there, a knife in her hand, her lips stretched in a tight little smile. Such things were not unheard of. You read about them in the papers every day.

It was not Allison Rand though; it was the girl from the allotments. I had not spoken to her since the day she had mentioned murder in my house, although I had seen her up at the allotments a couple of times since, playing with the Jack Russell terrier on the unkempt patch of grass behind the man with the missing fingers' wooden shed. She was wearing different clothes: a floral summer frock in printed cotton. There was something old-fashioned about it, and once again I had the feeling it had been altered to fit her. She had no coat on, no cardigan, though the evening was not particularly warm.

"I brought you something," she said. "Look at this."

She thrust something at me, a piece of paper. It was a newspaper cutting. I expected to see some faded headline about Allison Rand but I was mistaken. The cutting showed newspaper coverage of the trial for murder of a woman named Lorna Loomis. Part of the article was missing.

"You should have some warmer clothes on," I said. "You'll get goose bumps."

She made a face, and I noticed that in spite of the evening chill her skin showed no sign of gooseflesh. It was the colour of chalk, sprinkled with pale brown freckles.

There was no photograph of Lorna Loomis. She had lived in the town though, the article said so. She was what used to be called *a widow of independent means*.

I shivered, then realized the back door was still open.

"Come in and I'll make you a sandwich," I said to the girl.

She lounged at the kitchen table, all elbows and knees. I noticed the way she looked at my iPod, her eyes wide, as if it were an alien artefact.

"Don't touch that," I said. I didn't want her erasing Allison Rand's interview by mistake. The girl started back at once, folding her arms beneath the table, and I realized I must have spoken more harshly than I'd intended. I supposed she might be accustomed to getting hit. Her reaction suggested it, though I hated to believe it was so.

"Do you like cheese?" I said. "Marmite?"

"I lo-o-ve Marmite," she said. She stretched the 'o' lengthwise, twanging the vowel in midair like a piece of elastic. "All my friends hate it, but that only makes me like it more."

I laughed at that. The girl was clearly sharp as a flint. It wasn't late, not yet, but it was getting later. I wondered who knew she was out, if anyone cared.

"Why did you bring me this?" I said. I picked up the cutting from where I had placed it, on the kitchen table. It crackled between my fingers, brittle with age, and I realized that if I didn't handle it more carefully it would disintegrate.

The girl bit into her sandwich and began to chew. "I thought

you wanted to know," she said. "About the murder, I mean."
She shifted in her seat. "It's different in here," she said. "It was
darker before. A horrible green colour." She stuffed the rest of
the sandwich into her mouth and gulped it down. "I'd better
go now."

She left as she had arrived, through the back door. I stood at
the sink and washed up her plate, feeling vaguely worried
about what she might be going home to and wondering when
she had been in the house before. The kitchen had not been
green when Roy and I bought the house; the young couple
we'd bought from, the property developers, had drowned the
whole place in magnolia.

Perhaps Allison Rand's kitchen had been green. I read the
clipping again, the words about Lorna Loomis, *who had been
seen by three reliable witnesses outside the Gilmore public house,
holding tightly to the hand of a child dressed in her school uniform
of grey skirt and green cardigan answering to the description of
Nancy Creel.*

The Gilmore was still there, a heavy-set, half-timbered
building at the end of the High Street. One of Roy's favourite
haunts. Nancy Creel, I supposed, must have been the murder
victim.

Suddenly I remembered the incident in the lane earlier that
evening, the child who had rushed across the road in front of
my car. At least I thought that was what I had seen, but when
I'd climbed out of the car the road had been empty. Empty of
traffic and empty of people. I had dismissed the whole thing at
the time, probably because I was still preoccupied with Allison
Rand, but all at once it seemed sinister and frightening.

I went all round the house, putting the lights on in every
room and checking the doors and windows.

A fat lot of good that's going to do. I thought. *Ghosts are famous
for walking through walls, or haven't you heard?*

I should have found the thought amusing but I didn't.

Information on Lorna Loomis was hard to find. In view of
what I discovered later I still find that odd. It is as if her crime

was considered so terrible that everyone who found themselves involved with it, however tangentially, became locked
in some silent agreement to keep it secret. In any case, there
was nothing on the internet. One afternoon shortly after my
interview with Allison Rand I drove into Oxford and spent
an afternoon in the newspaper archive attached to the Central
Library, but the records were all still on microfiche and
without a date for when the crime had occurred it was next
to hopeless.

I thought of writing to Allison Rand and asking her if she
had heard of the Loomis case. She was a historian after all, or
at least she had been. But if the two crimes were connected, it
seemed odd that Rand hadn't mentioned Loomis during the
course of my visit.

I decided not to contact her unless I had to. Allison Rand
was clearly a disturbed person, and I wasn't sure how far I
could trust her. It wasn't just that, though. I knew by then
that Lorna Loomis would be the inspiration behind my next
novel and I didn't want to spoil things by talking about them.
As far as was possible, I wanted to solve the Loomis mystery
by myself.

I contacted our building society and asked if I could have a
copy of the house deeds. It gave me a shock to see that the
Rands had lived at our address for less than four years, that
they had moved in just a couple of months before Sophie was
born. Before the Rands the house had been the property of a
Mr Dennis Michaels; before that the owner's name had been
Tillyer. I paged backwards through the document, jotting
down the names in my notebook. I couldn't help noticing that
nobody had stayed in the house for very long.

Anthony Loomis, a GP, had bought the house in 1953. In
1955 the deeds had been altered to designate Mrs Lorna
Loomis as the sole owner. It was strange to see her name in
black and white at last, strange to see she really had lived here.
Strangest of all was that it was not that long ago. I had expected
some long-dead mystery, but there would still be people in
town who remembered the Loomises. I imagined the girl from

the allotments had heard about them from a parent or most likely a grandparent. How could she have known about them otherwise?

I realized I didn't know her name. I hadn't seen her since the evening she had brought me the newspaper cutting. I hoped nothing had happened to her.

The house became strange to me. I assumed Lorna Loomis was dead, but her presence seemed all-pervasive. I had never given more than a passing thought to the previous owners of other houses I had lived in, but as the days passed I found myself dwelling on Lorna Loomis almost obsessively. I tried to imagine how she had arranged the rooms, what colours she liked.

I still had only the vaguest notion of what she had done.

I started to hear noises at night: the faint murmur of a radio, the muffled thump of footsteps on the upstairs landing. Once or twice I felt someone push past me on the stairs. I was writing by then, so I was less bothered by these occurrences than I might have been otherwise. When I'm working on a novel there is scarcely any divide between the world I am creating on paper and the world outside, especially at the first draft stage. The book was going well and that was all I cared about. I told myself the rest was all in my mind.

The room I used as my study was one of the things that had attracted me to the house in the first place. It ran directly off the bedroom, no more than a box room really, the kind of odd little space that might normally be used as a nursery or an en suite bathroom. It overlooked the garden, and I liked it because it had a feeling of being separate from the rest of the house.

I kept the door closed at night, though. I didn't like waking up in the dark and seeing a yawning black gap in the wall, a minor phobia that Roy found hilarious.

"What do you think might be in there?" he said when I first told him about it. "Zombies?"

He'd disappeared inside the room and then emerged moments later, shambling towards me with his arms outstretched, like one of the living dead in the George Romero movies. That was during our first week in the house, and I laughed so hard I had tears in my eyes. Later though he stopped going anywhere near my study, even when I was in there working. I put it down to his claustrophobia, the same impulse that induced his marathon walks, but during the weeks of his absence I became less sure.

On one particular night I awoke in the small hours to see a light shining from beneath the door. I kept perfectly still, flattening myself against the mattress. I was terrified of what I was seeing, but I was even more afraid to turn on the bedside lamp because then I would no longer be able to see what the light inside my study was doing.

I stared at the glowing yellow line, clinging to the panicky hope that looking directly at it might cause it to disappear. In fact the opposite happened. As my eyes adjusted to the darkness I saw that the sliver of light was intersected by darkness in two places. Someone was standing directly behind the door.

I lay there for what seemed like hours, too frightened to move. Eventually, though, my fear outwore itself. I got out of bed and tiptoed across the carpet towards the study door. Logic told me there was no one inside. The room had been empty when I went to bed and it was empty now. But my palms were sticky with sweat, and my pulse was throbbing so loudly it made me feel faint.

I grabbed the handle and threw open the door. Bright light poured out in a rush, soaking the bedroom in colour. For a moment I thought I saw someone standing there, a dark apparition that in my enervated state I felt certain was the girl from the allotments. I reeled backwards in surprise and horror, colliding with the side of the bed. I sat down heavily, almost collapsing. When I dared to look again there was no one there.

Through the open doorway to my study I could see the corner of my desk, starkly outlined in the light from my desk lamp, which was on.

I must have forgotten to turn the lamp off before I went to bed. It was not something I would normally do but it was the only explanation that made sense. I turned it off and stood there for a moment, just listening. The room was silent, and as far as I could see nothing had been disturbed, but being there was making me nervous, all the same.

I went back to bed, but for the first time ever I left the study door standing open. When I woke the following morning the door was closed. I felt convinced I had shut it myself, after all.

I opened it again and went in. The papers on my desk – some photocopied news articles about Allison Rand, a map of the town the way it had been in the 1950s – had not been touched. I glanced around the room, trying to see if I could spot anything that seemed different.

There was a pencil on the floor under the chair. I bent to pick it up. It was bright red and dotted with flowers, a schoolgirl's pencil. The irregular paring marks around the nib showed it had been sharpened with a pen knife and not a pencil sharpener.

It was not mine and had never been mine. I felt certain of it.

Quite suddenly I wanted Roy. I wanted the man who had called the house perfect, who thought my ritual with the study door was a load of nonsense but who would do anything to protect me or save me from fear. At least, he would have done once. I felt tears start in my eyes at the way he had changed since we had first come here, my own helplessness in the face of that.

It came to me that I had no idea really of what his life was like from day to day, just as I had no idea of what it was that had traumatized him during his last tour of duty. I didn't agree with the war in Afghanistan and so I had dismissed the life Roy had chosen as none of my business.

Had I dismissed Roy also as not my business? Had he changed at least in part because of my indifference?

My friends said I was stupid to marry a soldier, that his interest in photography was simply a hobby.

I wished I could phone him, just to hear his voice: broad Lancashire, so sexy. I knew it would do no good though, that even if we could speak it would end in an awkward silence or a row. He had forgotten how to talk to me, just as I had somehow forgotten how to talk to him.

The only way we could make things work now was by meeting as different people and starting again.

I was out of milk. I slipped the pencil into my pocket then walked to the bakery and convenience store that stood on the junction with the main road out of town. By the time I got there I had stopped thinking about Roy altogether. My mind was back on the book. I couldn't work out if what I was writing could still be called a novel or whether it had mutated into something else. I picked up a carton of milk and a copy of *New Scientist* and two fresh croissants. It wasn't until I was standing in line to pay for them that I noticed the girl from the allotments was in the queue ahead of me, back in her school uniform and clutching a copy of *Jackie* magazine.

I hadn't known that *Jackie* still existed. The girl fumbled in her cardigan pocket, searching for coins. A fifty-pence piece dropped to the floor and as she bent to pick it up I saw she had a large brown bruise, high on her thigh and a sickly greenish-yellow around the edges. As she came past me on the way to the door I held out the red pencil, the polished wood the queasy, urgent colour of blood oranges.

"I think this might be yours," I said. "I saw you drop it."

The child beamed. "Oh, thank you," she said. "I thought I'd lost that. I've been looking everywhere."

She took the pencil from my outstretched fingers. I opened my mouth to ask what her name was but then decided not to. I was afraid, you see, even then.

I was afraid she was going to tell me her name was Nancy.

"Well then, I'm glad I found it," I said instead. The girl smiled at me again and left the shop. I paid for my things and followed, but by the time I got outside there was no sign of her. When I got home I put the milk in the fridge then telephoned the admin office of the school the Rands had worked at. I asked if I could speak to Steven Rand. I wasn't sure if he still worked there even, but it turned out that I was in luck.

"I think he's on a free period," said the woman who answered. "I'll see if he can come to the phone."

There followed a few minutes of silence before Rand himself came on the line.

"How can I help you?" he said. "Who is this?" He sounded testy, put out, though whether it was my call that was the irritant or the stress of trying to teach mathematics to a bunch of sixteen-year-olds I could not have said.

"Mr Rand," I said. "Steven. My name is Marian Pritchard. I was wondering if I could ask you a couple of questions." I told him my address then held my breath and waited. I heard him sigh.

"I'm sick of journalists," he said. "It's been three years. Why can't you leave me alone?"

"I'm not a journalist," I said. "I'm a novelist. It's your house I'm interested in, not you."

"It's your house now," he said. "Bad luck. I've got nothing to tell you." Some of his initial hostility was gone, though. I even thought he sounded intrigued.

"You should speak to my wife," he said. "She's the one who believes in ghosts."

"I've already done that. I'd like to hear your own thoughts, if you'll share them."

There was silence, and I thought he'd put down the phone. When he eventually spoke again he sounded resigned.

"I don't suppose it can hurt," he said. "God knows what Allison's told you."

We arranged to meet the following afternoon in a café we both knew near the centre of town.

"I like it because the kids hate it," he said. "They think it's poncey."

"I googled you," he said. "You really do write books, then."

He was different from what I'd expected. I had imagined Allison Rand being married to someone like herself, buttoned up and a little staid. Steven Rand was confident and expansive. He was even good-looking, in an aquiline, ageing-maths-professor kind of way, and I imagined he was popular with his pupils. I thought he and Allison must have made an interesting couple, that they must once have been happy. I wondered how he felt about her now.

We ordered coffee. I watched Rand spoon brown sugar into his cup and wondered how I ought to begin. He solved that particular problem by himself.

"You might not believe this, but I'm glad you called me," he said. "It's the loneliest thing in the world when someone dies. People are all over you at first, but eventually they get bored. They're tired of hearing the story and they're sick of your feelings. It's as if there's a sell-by date, and once your time is up you're supposed to be over it. Apart from school stuff and conversations with shop assistants, I've hardly spoken to anyone in months."

"That must be terrible."

He looked at me sharply, inquisitorially almost, as if he was trying to judge the sincerity of what I had said. "It is terrible actually, if you want to know. It makes you doubt your own existence. I've lost my two daughters, just at the point where I was coming to understand what it means to have daughters, the terror and the joy of it. They were alive, and now they're dead. And here I am, still marking quadratic equations." He sipped his coffee and made a face. "It's the algebra that keeps me going, actually. It's odd how things are, isn't it? It's the things that first enthral you when you're young that turn out to be your survival kit later on."

"It's always been that way for me," I said. "I started writing stories when I was five."

"Is that all my life is to you then, a story?"

I hesitated. "Only if you think of mine as a quadratic equation."

"Touché," he said, then laughed. "My God, you're as bolshie as Allison. I bet you two got on like a house on fire."

"If you're asking me if I liked her, then yes, I did."

"I'm glad." He took a sharp, nervous breath, as if he were about to dive underwater. "Allison's mad, you know. I didn't know that when I married her. Perhaps I would never have known, if we hadn't had children. Did she tell you her theory about the house?"

"In a way she did. She said there was something in the house that harmed Alana and Sophie. I got the feeling she didn't like to talk about it."

"Well, you'd be wrong about that." He spooned more sugar into his coffee. His movements were automatic, absent-minded. I knew he'd forgotten having done the same thing only minutes before. "For the final year of our marriage it was all she would talk about. Allison did a lot of research into our house's history. She did that with all our houses. It's something that gives her pleasure, the way I get a kick out of maths problems and you enjoy stories. Anyway, she discovered there'd once been a murder there. It wasn't some common or garden domestic incident either, it was something horrible. I didn't see that it mattered much. Everyone involved in the case was dead and that included the murderer. But Allison was quite upset by it. She started saying we should never have moved there, that we'd been *lured*. She'd never come out with anything like that before and I didn't believe a word of it. To be honest, I thought it was hormonal. She was pregnant with Sophie by then, and the murder victim had been a little girl. I thought Ally would get over it but she didn't. She was convinced the dead child was still in the house and trying to make contact with her. After Sophie was born things got worse. Allison started saying that the other girl – the murdered girl – was jealous of the new baby.

"I hate to say this but I was worried for my daughter. It wasn't that Allison didn't care for her – anyone could see she was besotted with the baby. But there was something else, something I couldn't put my finger on. I felt I didn't know her any more."

"You're talking about the Loomis case, aren't you? The name of the murdered child was Nancy Creel?"

"You know all that already, then?"

"Actually I hardly know anything. There's no information anywhere. All I've been able to discover is their names."

"Allison was always good with information. She had problems at first as well, but then she managed to turn up this grotty little true-crime book from somewhere that described the whole case from A to Z, even down to the court transcripts. It had Ally hooked from day one."

"Did Lorna Loomis kill Nancy Creel?"

"In a manner of speaking she did. She kidnapped her and tied her up, then locked her in an upstairs bedroom. Then she took off to Chester to visit her cousin. Nancy Creel starved to death in her absence. It was a month before they found her body."

"That's appalling," I said. I knew without having to ask that it was the box room Nancy Creel had died in, the room I had commandeered as my study. "Why on earth did she do it?"

"It was all on account of a man, if you can believe that. Lorna Loomis had been having an affair with Nancy Creel's father. Tony Creel wanted to break it off, but Lorna Loomis was having none of it. She threatened to tell his wife, but Creel got there before her and confessed everything. Apparently the wife forgave him. He'd had affairs before and they never came to anything. Loomis was furious. She started telephoning the house at all hours of the day and night, making threats and shouting insults. If she hoped to drive a wedge between the Creels it didn't work. Then suddenly the phone calls stopped. Six months later Nancy Creel went missing. Loomis knew Creel doted on Nancy. The child was probably the main reason he decided to break off the affair."

"She killed the daughter to get back at the father?"

Rand nodded. "Her defence was that she never intended for Nancy to die, that she always meant to return to the house and release her. She just wanted to scare Tony Creel a bit first. But she fell and broke her leg while she was in Chester and her cousin insisted on keeping her there until the plaster came off. Loomis couldn't think of any reasonable excuse not to stay, and the more time passed the more terrified she became of having to admit to what she'd done. Finally she convinced herself that Nancy's kidnapping had all been a dream. That's what she claimed anyway. You can imagine what the jury thought of that. She got life without chance of parole. If it had happened a decade earlier she'd have hanged for it."

"Is Loomis still alive? She'd be old now."

"She died eight years into her sentence. Allegedly of natural causes, although there was a story about one of the other inmates managing to sneak some arsenic into her food."

I realized that I liked Steven Rand. I admired the way he had managed to hang on to himself in spite of his tragedy. Also I liked the way he told stories. Sitting in the café listening to him tell me about Lorna Loomis made me realize that the events as they had happened made a more compelling narrative than anything I could invent, and in spite of the horror of the thing I was tense with excitement.

Later, once I was home, a strange thing happened. I was in the bedroom, changing the sheets, when suddenly and out of nowhere I was overcome with desire for him. I wanted to know what it felt like, to be with him here in this room, to perform the sexual act in a place that still resonated with the terrible things that had happened there. I imagined Rand's sinewy arms, the long lean rake of his body. He had told me there had been no one else in his life since Allison and I wondered with a tremor inside if that would bring an extra urgency to his lovemaking.

I shuddered and sat down on the bed. I was disgusted by my thoughts, yet still aroused by them. The house was still and silent as it always was, and yet I sensed something hovering on the outer edge of my perception: the haunted, broken laughter of Lorna Loomis.

Allison Rand had told me the house was not safe for children. Could it be that it was not safe for lovers, either? Roy and I had been so happy when we bought the place. I had blamed our problems since on his war experiences, but what if the house itself was the cause of our breakdown? The house working on us and through us, the same as it had with the Rands.

I dismissed the idea as so much rubbish and tried to put it from my mind but I went to bed still thinking about it and that night I had a horrible dream. I was in the study drawing the curtains, but each time I looked away they would open again. It was dark outside, and I was afraid to look out of the window. I became increasingly agitated, because I knew Roy was waiting for me downstairs, only I was scared it would not be him I found when I went down there. I went to the wardrobe to fetch my evening dress, and found the girl from the allotments curled up inside. She lay quite still, her bony knees drawn up to her chest. She was staring right at me, but I knew she was not really seeing me, and when I shook her by the shoulder I discovered she was not the real girl at all but some kind of copy, papery and weightless and balloon-like, reminding me of the pleated orange fruits of the *Physalis francheti* that grew in my parents' front garden, years and years ago when we lived in Birmingham. Chinese lanterns, they were called. I hadn't thought of them in ages.

I closed the wardrobe door and then woke up. I was breathing heavily, and I had the feeling I might have called out in my sleep although there was nothing to prove this either way. I turned on the bedside lamp and got out of bed. It was still dark, still early. I tiptoed out on to the landing. There were shadows bunched in every corner but no human presence, at least none that was visible to me.

I used the toilet then returned to the bedroom. The girl was lying on the bed, looking right at me as she had in my dream, only this time she was seeing me, I was sure of it. She had on the same grey school skirt and green cardigan she'd been wearing on the day she disappeared.

In the yellow light from the lamp her eyes gleamed like glass marbles.

I began to shiver, my teeth chattering in my head as if it were November and freezing. Yet it was warm in the room, warm enough to sleep naked, although this was something I rarely did when Roy was away.

"You shouldn't be here, Nancy," I said. "It's time you went home."

If you're thinking it was brave of me to say that, you don't know how scared I was. I spoke mostly to see if I still could speak. I said the first thing that came into my head.

"I don't want to," said the child. "I like it here. You've got lots of books. The soldier said I could read them, if I wanted."

She rolled on her side, drawing her knees up to her chest the same way she had when she was in the cupboard. I felt my back muscles stiffen.

"What do you mean, the soldier?" I said. "There are no soldiers here."

"He was crying," Nancy said. "He thinks it's all his fault that the other man died." She smiled a secretive little smile that reminded me unpleasantly of Allison Rand. "The other man was going to die, though, anyway. So it wasn't the soldier's fault at all, really. The soldier was just trying to help."

"What do you mean? What are you talking about?"

"I have to go now." She unfurled her legs and slipped down from the bed. When her feet hit the floor they made no noise. "We can look at the books soon though, can't we? I like the books with trains in. And animals."

"If you like," I said. There was a ringing in my ears, and I felt overcome with a feeling of faintness, the same feeling I experienced if I happened to cut my finger while chopping vegetables. It's the sight of blood that does it. Roy always thought that so funny, a crime writer who can't stand the sight of the red stuff.

She flowed past me and out through the door. The moment she was out of sight I felt certain she had never been there, that the whole thing had been in my head, an after-effect of my nightmare. I got back into the bed and pulled up the duvet. You will think I kept the light on, but I didn't. I wanted darkness around me, the deep kind of darkness that makes it impossible to see anything.

The call came the following morning. For a moment I thought the man on the other end of the line was Steven Rand, and felt a sharp, sweet lurch of the heart, that he wanted to phone me. Then I realized it wasn't Rand at all. The man asked me if I was alone in the house and if I had any friends or neighbours that I could call. I remember thinking: *what the hell business is it of yours?* Then he told me that Roy was dead.

I thought he was going to say it was one of Roy's bombs that had done it. *He was a brave man, but his number finally came up.* What he actually said was that Roy had shot himself.

"We're not sure yet what led to this tragedy," he said. "But you can rest assured there'll be a full enquiry."

I could tell he was embarrassed, that making a phone call like this was a job he dreaded. Absurdly, I told him not to worry.

Three months later one of the men from Roy's unit drove over to see me. He brought some things of Roy's: the folder of photographs he was always looking at, the wallet made of dark green leather I had given him for his birthday the year before. The wallet's silk lining was torn. There was a photo inside, a picture of the two of us on holiday in the Lake District. We'd stopped a passer-by and asked her to take it. Both of us were grinning like fools.

I asked Roy's comrade if he would like a cup of tea. He said no at first but then changed his mind. "I'd love one," he said. "But only if you're sure it's no trouble."

He told me Roy had shot a man, a young soldier who had been caught in an ambush and injured so badly that all they could do was move him to the side of the road and wait for him to die.

"His face was mostly gone," he said. "He was screaming like a man on fire. Roy had real guts to do what he did. It was like none of the rest of us could move, and only he was able to do what needed doing."

I was starting to show by then, and the man kept darting worried glances at my belly. I leaned back against the kitchen cabinets, gripping the edge of the worktop in both hands. My limbs sometimes felt heavy and throbbing during those later months of my pregnancy. My blood pressure was up slightly, but my doctor said that so long as it didn't get any worse it was nothing to worry about.

I could tell that Roy's comrade was wondering whose child it was.

"Don't you think you should sit down?" he said. He jumped up from his own chair and shoved it towards me, almost knocking over his mug of tea.

"I will in just a moment," I said. "It's good for me to keep moving, though. It stops my ankles swelling."

I wanted to reassure him that the baby was Roy's, that she had been conceived the night we made love during Roy's last leave. To tell him that in a sense Roy was still alive in me and always would be. In the end though it was not his business, and I knew he would be embarrassed if I tried to explain.

Thank God I had stopped taking the pill. I don't think I believe in God actually, but you know what I mean.

I glanced at Nancy. She was sitting quietly at the kitchen table, cutting pictures out of a magazine to stick in her scrap-book. Her tongue poked from the corner of her mouth as it often did when she was concentrating on something. I could smell the glue she was using, Gloy gum from a plastic tube.

"Will you stay for supper?" I asked the officer. "You've had a long drive."

"It's good of you to offer, but I won't," he said. "I promised the lads I'd be back before ten. We've got this card thing going."

He flushed scarlet then, as if the mention of a card game might make him guilty of some particularly heinous brand of callousness. He seemed nice enough, but I was glad he was leaving. Nancy wasn't keen on people who couldn't see her. They made her nervous.

Aside from that I wanted to keep the evening free to work on the book. With any luck I could still deliver the manuscript before the baby was born.

The Third Person

Lisa Tuttle

When she got Rachel's text suggesting lunch, Imogen was thrilled into immediate agreement, although the short notice, and her friend's choice of venue, meant a rush, and her colleagues' displeasure that she was taking the full hour for the second time that week.

For once, Rachel wasn't late; eye-catching as ever with her long, red hair and dramatic style, she waved from a booth at the back and announced that she'd already ordered for them both.

"You're going to love the cauliflower cheese soup. And it gives us more time to talk if we don't have to faff around with menus." She was glowing, radiant, bubbling in a way Imogen had not seen in months. It reminded her of the old days, when they'd shared a flat, before Rachel married Andrew.

Marriage changed everything. Everybody knew how it was: married couples had different priorities, and when they weren't alone together, liked to be with other marrieds. Add to their new status a starter house in a distant suburb and two demanding jobs, and there wasn't much left for their singleton friends. Imogen had thought she might be the exception: after all, the three of them had lived together for nearly a year, so comfortable a threesome that they joked about their Mormon marriage, if too conventional to go farther than flirting with the idea of a sexual *ménage à trois*. Andy's undemanding yet undeniably masculine presence had added a bit of spice to Imogen's life, which she missed. She recalled the pleasures of lazy Sunday morning fry-ups over three different newspapers, late-night take-aways and horror movies viewed from the sagging, second-hand couch – even a boring, stupid thing like doing the laundry was almost fun as a threesome. But maybe that was only her. Maybe they would always have been happier without a third person in their life.

She looked at her friend through the steam of soup too hot to touch. "What's up? I can see you're dying to tell me something."

Rachel compressed her lips. "I need you to promise you won't tell anyone."

She was stung by this distrust. "Who would I tell?"

"Not anyone. If it ever got back to Andrew—"

"Oh my God."

"Promise?"

Imogen scowled. "Asking me to promise *now* is a bit stable-doors. You're having an affair?"

Rachel grimaced. She could not deny it, only quibbled over the wording. It was nothing so definite as an "affair". Love didn't enter into it. It was just sex.

"But . . . why? Why take the risk?"

"Oh, Immy." She shook her head and looked chiding. "I didn't mean to. I didn't go looking for this. It just happened."

"Yeah? Where, on the bus to work? Oh, I'm sorry, sir, it's so crowded, I seem to have impaled myself upon your manly tool. As we've started, may as well continue."

Rachel nearly choked on her soup, giggling. "OK, OK. I am a weak and horny woman who cannot resist temptation. I was feeling frustrated and half-dead – Andrew, bless him, is just not up for it that often. He's less . . . *driven* by sexual needs than I am. I always knew it might be a problem someday; I just didn't expect it to be so soon. But when Mr Hotbody came along and woke me up—" She gave a fatalistic shrug.

"Who is this Mr Hotbody?"

"You don't know him," she said quickly. "Nobody does."

"That sounds spooky."

"Nobody *we* know. There's no reason Andrew would ever hear anything. He's a total stranger I met in a pub."

Imogen shivered, and took a careful sip of her soup.

"It wasn't a pub I'd ever been in, either. A client had suggested it, and after she left, he came over and offered to buy me a drink. I'd noticed him watching me, and gave him the look . . . it was just like the old days, picking out the sexiest guy in the room, to see if I could pull."

"So you can still pull. Amazing. Did you tell him you were married?"

"After he put his hand on my leg. He just smiled and said he liked married women the best, because they didn't confuse sex with love, and he sort of walked his hand up my leg, right up to my crotch, and started to rub me there, through my pants, looking me in the eye the whole time while he brought me off."

It was not the heat of the soup that brought Imogen out in a sweat as Rachel continued to describe what followed. "Sex in the toilet! I don't know what possessed me – I hadn't done anything like that since I was eighteen. And this was much, much dirtier."

"And that wasn't the end of it?"

She shook her head, eyes glazed over. "I didn't even know his name. I told Andrew I had to go away overnight, on business, and booked a room in a Travelodge. He met me there. We were at it all night. Never slept. I did things I'd never done before. He made me do things—"

Imogen pushed her bowl to one side, her appetite gone. "That does not sound good."

"Are you kidding? It was the best I've ever had."

"Not good for your marriage."

"Oh, no, there you're wrong, my friend. Sometimes a bit of danger, the risk of another lover, is just what a couple needs. I went home and bonked the living daylights out of Andrew. He loved it! For a little while, I had my Randy Andy back. Plus, I'm so much nicer when I'm not feeling frustrated. I've stopped being such a bitch at home. What's good for me is good for him."

"Good for you. You've saved your marriage. End of story."

"It's not the end."

"You can't go on sleeping with this guy."

"I have no intention of sleeping with him, or going out to dinner with him, or knitting little booties, or falling in love. This is just sex. So much spicier than I can get at home. A bit on the side. That's all I want from him."

"So what do you want from me? A seal of approval?"

"We need a place to go."

"Oh, no." Imogen's stomach clenched. "You can't go to his?"

"He lives with someone. And anyway, I don't want to get involved with his life."

"So rent a room . . . Travelodge was good enough before."

"It would be good enough again, if I could afford it . . . or if he could. Please? It won't be very often, I'm sure. Just a few more times, 'til I get him out of my system."

"Or out of your pubic hair. Where am I supposed to go while this . . . delousing . . . is taking place?"

Rachel's face tightened. "Don't be nasty."

"You're the one talking about how wonderfully dirty it is." Before Rachel's hurt, angry glare, she caved. "I'm sorry. I just don't understand why you need to do this thing."

Imogen's hand was seized and held in a warm, strong grip. "Of course you don't, my sweetheart, because you're *normal*. This is some kind of madness, but I can't get over it without going through it. And you are the one and only person who can help me, who I can talk to. I don't want to put you out. But you go to the gym and out for a meal with your friends from work every Thursday, am I right? What time do you get home?"

"About nine-thirty," she said, although ten was closer to the mark.

"I'd want to be on the nine-forty-seven for home anyway," said Rachel. "We'd be out by nine-thirty. I promise you, Imogen, you won't know we were there. One evening a week, a time when you wouldn't be there anyway – is that really too much to ask?"

She understood she could not refuse; not unless she was prepared to lose their friendship.

Rachel came by that evening to pick up the spare key, and Imogen was a little stiff with her at first, feeling she had been bullied into abetting a crime, but instead of hurrying away like a guilty thing, Rachel hung around, diffident and awkward, until Imogen thawed and suggested she stay for dinner.

"There's a kebab shop just around the corner. I could run down for something—"

Rachel checked the contents of the fridge. "I'll cook," she said. "Spaghetti carbonara sound all right?"

"I don't have any cream."

"We never did, and I don't recall any complaints in the past, so long as there was plenty of *this*." With a wicked grin, she produced a bottle of wine from her capacious shoulder-bag.

Every remnant of ill-feeling vanished as she whipped up a quick supper. It was like old times again. She phoned Andrew to warn him she'd be home late, and put him on speaker so Imogen could hear and join in a joking, friendly, three-way conversation. When they were doing the washing-up, Imogen said wistfully, "We should do this more often."

"I don't know about you, sweetheart, but I wash up after *every* meal."

Imogen laughed. "Idiot. I've missed you. Missed *us*."

"Me, too."

Walking through her front door on Thursday night (9.56 by her phone), although it was dark and still, Imogen felt another presence there.

"Ray?" she called sharply. "Hello?" Her skin prickled; what if it was *him*?

With the light on, she could see into every corner of the sparsely furnished, open-plan living room and kitchen. There was nowhere to hide, unless – looking one way – behind the half-open door of the bathroom – or, at the other end, in the bedroom. She scarcely breathed until she had checked both rooms thoroughly, even peering inside the built-in wardrobe in the bedroom, and the narrow airing-cupboard in the kitchen. But she remained tense, even knowing she was alone, so she phoned Rachel.

"How'd it go?"

"I'm on the train."

"I wasn't expecting the porno version." At the familiar sound of her friend's snorting laugh, Imogen relaxed at last. "I just wanted to check that everything was, you know, all right."

"Mmm, good question. Not sure what to say."

Suddenly suspicious, she demanded, "Is he with you?"

"What? No, of course not! I said, I'm on my way home. There's the tunnel."

"Catch up tomorrow?" She was talking to a dead phone.

The abrupt end to that unsatisfactory conversation left Imogen feeling on edge, but she went through her usual routines, tidying the already tidy flat, and put herself to bed before eleven o'clock.

She was tired, and her thoughts soon drifted into the surreal jumble that presaged sleep. Turning on to her left side, she snuggled deeper into her pillow, and caught a faint whiff of Jo Malone's Pomegranate Noir – Rachel's signature scent.

By now her own body-heat had warmed the space between the sheets, and with that warmth, other smells were released from the bedding: body odours that were not her own, sweat and musk and ejaculate, the unmistakable smells of sex.

And then she could hear them – laboured breathing, low grunts, the slap of flesh against flesh – and feel them, too, a woman and a man in bed with her, one on either side of her—

It wasn't real, of course. It couldn't be. If she'd suddenly found herself in bed with two other naked people she would have been repulsed by it, felt disgust, or fear. But instead, half-asleep and knowing she must be dreaming, it was safe to become aroused. These two people, so focused on their own sexual pleasure, stirred desires she kept buried, hidden from her conscious mind. The man behind her was a stranger – it didn't matter who he was. The woman whose soft large breasts pressed against her own was Rachel.

This was Rachel as she'd scarcely dared to imagine her, yet knew she must be, powerfully erotic, sexually voracious. As Imogen allowed herself to be overwhelmed by the power of the fantasy, she heard her friend whispering to her, words she'd actually said once when talking about masturbation.

"You shouldn't feel guilty. That's crazy! It doesn't matter *what* you think about while you're doing it – whatever gets you off is fine; it doesn't matter what crazy, sick thing turns you on, so long as it stays inside your own head. Nobody ever got hurt by a private fantasy. It's the safest sex there is."

In the morning, though, Imogen was not so relaxed. The first sip of coffee seemed to curdle in her stomach, and she felt sickened by herself, and then angry with Rachel. Why couldn't her friend have followed her own advice, and kept her fantasies locked inside her own head? Why did she have to soil Imogen's bed with them?

She poured the rest of her coffee down the sink and, although there was scarcely time for it, hurried back to the bedroom, intending to strip off the dirty sheets, rather than leave them festering with their alien stains and smells for another day. But as soon as she saw her bed she realized it wasn't necessary. Rachel had changed the bed after using it. The dirty sheets and pillowcases were in the washing machine in the kitchen – a fact she had noticed before going to bed, and then forgotten.

She leaned down and sniffed the pillow. She could just about pick up traces of herself – skin oil, face cream, shampoo – but nothing remotely like Rachel's perfume. When she put her head under the covers she smelled the lavender scent of her fabric conditioner, and nothing else.

Those smells that she thought had triggered an erotic fantasy had been part of the fantasy – part of the dream. It had been a dream, of course, with no conscious desires behind it at all. The knots in her stomach loosened. Dreams were nobody's fault. You couldn't blame yourself for what your unconscious got up to while you slept.

Text messages flew back and forth between Imogen and Rachel over the next few days, but despite reiterated declarations that they must meet, or at least talk, their busy schedules made it impossible before Thursday came around again.

There had been no repeat of that disturbingly erotic dream, and Imogen had almost managed to repress the memory of it until that morning, when she woke up thinking about Rachel and her faceless, nameless lover, who would soon be going at it like knives in this very bed, between her own, used sheets.

She didn't know if knowing his name or what he looked like would have made it better, or worse, but she was tormented by the sense of being unfairly used. Maybe she had no right to judge Rachel for the betrayal of her marriage vows, but wasn't more respect due to their friendship? Changing the sheets was the merest gesture; all that frenzied passion must leave traces that could not be easily washed away, a charge in the atmosphere, a kind of miasma in the bedroom that affected Imogen's sleep and gave her bad dreams. She wished she had made more of an effort to talk to Rachel; she should have insisted on seeing her. It was too late now, of course, but she decided tonight was the last time. She would ask Rachel to give her back the key.

Mounting the deserted concrete stairs that rose through the large, quiet building, at a quarter to ten, Imogen tingled with anxiety, again plagued by the feeling that someone was waiting for her inside. Not even the sight of the clear, empty vista of the main room was enough to calm her nerves, and she was obliged to check out the bathroom and empty bedroom thoroughly before she could relax.

This time, she did not miss the fact of clean sheets on her bed, and deliberately took several deep, calming breaths of the soothing scent of lavender as she settled down to sleep.

But it happened again. As her own body heat raised the temperature within the warm cocoon of the bed, something else was released, as if memories of what had taken place in that space a few hours earlier had left spores ready to blossom into life under the right conditions. All the smells of sex wafted over her and she heard the animal sounds of vigorous fucking, and while a small, civilized part of her was repulsed, and a little frightened, by this activity going on in her own bed, her body was melting, yearning, opening with the longing desire to be a part of it.

They were so close, so close, but at the same time impossibly distant, their desires never meeting hers, so completely focused on each other that they didn't even know she was there. They were all in the same space, but separated by time. And so, although she found herself between them, they were blissfully unaware of any impediment, intent only on satisfying themselves through each other, as if Imogen did not exist, as if she were of less substance than a ghost.

Maybe she was only a fleeting thought passing through Rachel's mind, a weightless fragment of gratitude and guilt, gone before it could be acknowledged, as the other woman hurtled, with single-minded intensity, towards her own satisfaction.

Imogen could not connect. The other two made love through her, without her, and although she was unbearably close to them, forced to witness their coupling, to smell and hear and *almost* feel their moving bodies on either side of her own, she could not make them feel her. She could only join in, steal a share of their pleasure, by pretending. This was no guilt-free dream, no dream at all. They were in her bed, but she was alone, tensing her muscles, arching her back, opening her mouth wide, nothing to fill it, nothing to assuage her emptiness and bring satisfaction but the quick, impatient movements of her own fingers, angry and dissatisfied with her own, too-familiar flesh, but still practised enough to know what they must do.

She made herself come again and again until at last her bed was empty and she could fall asleep.

She didn't want to see Rachel again. But they were going to have to meet. Rachel had the key to Imogen's flat. Even more importantly, she thought she had permission to use it. Imogen could not be like the evil landlord who changes the locks without warning. Even if she couldn't tell her the real reason, she was going to ban her friend from using it, and demand the key back. She didn't care if they fell out over it and never spoke again; that would only prove that Rachel had never been such a good friend as Imogen had thought.

They met on Saturday morning, at a Starbucks in a mall, in the middle of a heaving mass of shoppers hunting for a bargain.

"I have to meet Andrew at Ikea in thirty-five minutes, but that should be plenty of time for a coffee," Rachel said, with a hug and kiss Imogen was not quick enough to avoid. She was as beautiful and bouncy as ever, and Imogen felt like a coward, evading her direct and happy gaze. She ordered a skinny vanilla latte for the look of the thing, but knew by the roiling in her stomach that she would not be able to drink it.

"What's up? Your text was so—"

No point wasting time. She blurted it out: "I want my key back."

"Oh." Rachel's shoulders slumped. She stared down at her hands. Her wedding band made its own comment. "Well. Of course. In fact, I'd already decided . . . decided to end it. It's crazy – I love Andy, we have a good marriage, I don't want to risk everything for a bit of . . . well, *sport*."

Imogen's tension began to ease as she realized she wouldn't have to argue. "Good sense wins the day. Did you bring it?"

"Bring what?"

"My key."

"Oh! God, no, I didn't think – that's not important, is it? I mean, it is a spare, right? And somebody ought to have it, in case you lock yourself out or something happens while you're away – you shouldn't have both keys yourself."

Imogen recognized the wide-eyed, honest gaze that went with the perfectly logical argument. She'd seen her friend use it on others to get something she wanted. When she was hiding a lie. Her stomach clenched again.

"Ray, this is not about a stupid key. I don't want that man in my flat again."

"What happened? Did he do something? What did he do? Have you talked to him?"

Imogen felt her ears get hot and prayed she wasn't blushing. "Talk to him? Of course not! I don't know who he is. You won't even tell me his name."

"Only because I don't want you involved in this."

"But I *am* involved. You involved me, by using my flat. You've done it in my bed! You can't do that any more."

Something flared in her friend's eyes and for a moment Imogen thought she'd guessed; somehow Rachel knew exactly what she'd experienced—

"Just once more. Please, darling. I'll finish with him this week. I promise."

"Good. Break up with him in a pub. Or have your final fling in the Travelodge."

Rachel shook her head. "It's not that easy. I can't get in touch with him before Thursday. But this Thursday will be the last, I promise. And then, if you really insist I give your key back—"

"I do."

Rachel made a dramatic gesture. "Next week, same time, same place. I promise I will bring it. And I can provide all the sordid details you like."

The following Thursday night, at 9.47 precisely, Imogen turned the key and stepped inside. Refusing to let herself be driven again by the now-expected impression that there was someone else in her flat, she did not waste time looking around, but went straight to the bedroom to put away her gym gear.

The light was on and there was a man there, kneeling on the floor. He had been crouching, apparently examining the carpet, but when she opened the door he straightened, although still on his knees.

Her mouth dried. She looked past him, to the bed, which had been roughly re-made, but Rachel was not there.

He was not someone she would have picked out as the hottest guy in any pub. He had a muscular upper body, but his face was forgettable, and his thinning grey hair straggled down as if length could make up for what was missing on top. He was older than she had expected, a forty-something clinging rather foolishly to the style of his youth. Most surprisingly, he didn't look surprised to see her, but smiled seductively.

"What are you doing?" She spoke sharply, annoyed with Rachel for leaving this strange man alone in her flat.

He looked down at the carpet again. "She lost her necklace – chain broke. Gold chain. Had to leave . . . couldn't miss her train . . . but so upset, I said I'd find the missing bit."

Imogen peered down at the thick pile of the carpet, knowing immediately what necklace it must be, a diamond and amethyst pendant on the finest of thin gold chains, a twenty-first birthday present from Rachel's grandmother.

"She could have asked *me* to find it," Imogen muttered, and then was startled to notice the man, still on his knees, had moved closer.

He pushed up her shirt and rubbed his face against the bare skin of her midriff. The shock of it froze her in place. She caught a familiar whiff of dried sweat and hair grease at the very moment that his wet, warm tongue darted into her navel.

She opened her mouth to protest, but the incoherent sound emerged sounding more like encouragement. Her arms did not want to push him away. Her muscles seemed to have turned to jelly, and she might have collapsed entirely without his support. She seemed to have fallen into a helpless dream as he touched and rubbed and kissed her from the waist down. When he unhooked and unzipped and pulled down her trousers, she did nothing to help or hinder, and they fell to her ankles, followed soon by her pants, and hobbled her. He carried on with his more intimate explorations as she closed her eyes and surrendered to whatever he would do to her with his hands or his mouth. He sucked and licked, rubbed and poked and prodded, sometimes hurting her with a rough touch, but generally skilful, increasing her arousal to an incredible pitch.

This was no dream. He was doing it all. Doing everything to her that he had previously done to Rachel, things she could only imagine before now. Her own hands, unoccupied, hung at her sides, now loose, now clenched. Her breath sighed and whistled and caught in her throat. She moaned softly and tried to open her legs wider, wanting more, but she was trapped by her own clothes. As she tried to kick free of them, her knees buckled and she almost fell, but he caught her, and lifted her – so easily; his arms were even more powerful than she had guessed. He quickly and efficiently freed her from shoes, pants and trousers, and dropped her on to the bed.

Remembering Rachel's description of how he'd looked into her eyes the whole time he'd caressed her to orgasm that first time in the pub, Imogen waited for him to look at her, but he was absorbed in the task of removing his own shoes and socks and jeans, and when he came back, wearing only his shirt, he stared at only one part of her, so fixedly that she wondered uneasily if he found her hairy pubes disgusting. (Rachel was religious about depilating, but Imogen could not be bothered.) She was disturbed to notice his penis was flaccid, not even half-erect, but that changed as he pulled it, still staring, so it was obviously not a turn-off.

With unexpected suddenness, still without a word or even an affectionate look, he plunged inside her and began thrusting away with an odd, jerky rhythm. She was just starting to get comfortable with it when he suddenly withdrew and ejaculated on her shirt.

She gave a startled, disappointed cry.

He stood up and backed away, looking at her now with a smile that was more of a sneer. "You slut," he said, without heat. "You didn't think I'd let you have my baby?"

He began putting his clothes on. She lay where he'd put her, afraid to say or do anything that might provoke him, and wondering what had been going on inside his head while she'd been caught in her own fantasy. She was grateful when he left without another word, and sat up when she heard the definitive closing snick of the lock on the front door.

She felt sick, and desperate for a wash. She wanted to wash away every trace of that awful man. She stood up. About to cross the room, she saw something glinting on the floor, and bent down to find two gold links, snapped from a chain.

Holding them, looking at the miniscule circles lying in the palm of her hand, she had an image of Rachel's necklace, broken as it was brutally yanked from her neck, and shivered as she touched the skin across her own collar-bone. Then, closing her hand on the tiny bits of gold, she went through to the main room, where she stopped just short of colliding with Rachel.

She only just managed not to scream. Rachel had been in the flat the whole time. She must have been in the bathroom at first – she should have realized her friend wouldn't have left that man here alone – but when she returned to the bedroom – had she seen them? Looked in, and seen Imogen standing with her trousers around her ankles? And said nothing? Was it a total shock, or something she had suggested or engineered, perhaps pursuing her own fantasy of a threesome—

If so, it clearly had not turned out as she'd dreamed. She had not interrupted them or tried to join in, and her continued silence now, and the expression on her face, frightened Imogen. She had never seen Rachel with such a terrible, staring face, and such a murderous look in her eye.

"Hey, Ray," Imogen said softly, her heart in her throat. "We need to talk."

Rachel's fixed, hideous glare did not soften, and Imogen saw something that froze her heart. Yes, that was murder in her eyes. In one hand, half-hidden by her side, Rachel held the longest, sharpest knife from Imogen's kitchen.

"Don't." The word jumped out, hot and urgent, forced through the lump of ice in Imogen's chest, and then she ran for the safety of the bathroom. She slammed the door and locked it; then, leaning her head against the cool tiled wall, she began to cry.

But she soon regained control. She wouldn't risk opening the door, but she spoke through it, yelling at Rachel that she was sorry, but that jerk wasn't worth it, and couldn't they please at least *try* to have a civilized conversation? Nothing at all in reply from Rachel, so Imogen took her time about having a shower. She knew her friend was no killer. Give her a few minutes to calm down, and then they'd talk.

When she came out of the bathroom, reeking of strawberry shower gel, the flat was empty. She knew it instantly, could tell from the atmosphere that she was alone, but went through the motions of searching, just in case. The long, sharp knife was back in the wooden block where it belonged. Rachel had gone without leaving a note.

She slept that night on the couch. It was not very comfortable, but she preferred a broken night of restless dozing to the company of the ghosts in her bed. When she woke at three, four, five and six, she phoned Rachel, and left humble, apologetic messages begging her to call back, regardless of the time.

At seven-thirty, as she dressed for work, Rachel's phone was still switched off. At eight, she rang the landline number, and Andrew picked up.

"Andy, I need to talk to Rachel."

There was a silence. "Imogen? I thought she was with you."

She swallowed hard. "She left last night. It was after ten, after her usual train, but there's a later one, isn't there? She didn't say, but I assumed she was going home."

"What do you mean, she didn't say?"

"She – she was upset when she left."

"What was she upset about?"

Her eyes fell on the tiny gold links she'd brought through from the bathroom. "You know her gold necklace? From her nan? It broke."

"She stormed out because she broke her necklace?"

"There was more to it than that, but it was my fault. I couldn't get her to stay and talk about it." Imogen touched one of the links with the tip of a finger, staring across the counter to the wooden knife-block on the far wall of the kitchen, all four black handles sticking out. "She was pretty mad – I was sure she'd go home, but maybe she has another friend she stays with sometimes."

He didn't reply.

"Look, if you see her . . . I mean, when she comes in, or calls, would you please ask her to call me?"

"I was going to say the same to you."

She said a rather awkward goodbye, and then, as she broke the connection, felt the hairs rise on the back of her neck, and knew she was no longer alone.

There had been no sound, and the door had not opened, but even before she turned she knew who was there.

Rachel, looking just as she had the night before: same clothes, same ghastly expression, even the knife in her hand, although there had been no time for her to take it from the kitchen. She could only be a ghost.

Then the small, metallic click of a key in the lock, and the door opened. He came in and shut the door behind him, glaring, holding Rachel's black-and-silver Nokia, which looked ridiculously tiny in his large hand.

"Why'd you keep calling?" he asked. "You think she'll forgive you for what you did with me last night?"

She realized then that the murderous look in Rachel's eyes, and the knife in her hand, had never been meant for *her*. She could only hope, as she sprinted for the kitchen, that her own attempt at self-defence would be more successful.

Freeze Out

Nancy Holder

Ghosts moved up and down the aisles of the funeral home chapel. Ghosts of grief, anger, despair.

The ghosts didn't touch Cody.

What touched him was the cold smell of roses, icy and strangely fleshy. A spray of white roses lay like a sleeping ghost on his mother's closed casket. Florists chilled their flowers so they wouldn't rot as fast. It was minus seven degrees outside on the prairie of Minnesota. They should have kept the roses in the graveyard; their outer petals were beginning to brown.

Florists made funeral sprays out of the oldest flowers, the ones that were going to wilt the soonest. Those flowers didn't have to endure until the last dance. The last dance was already over.

Cody sat with his father in the first pew of the funeral home's non-confrontational, non-denominational chapel. The pew was cordoned off; there was a golden braided rope connected to a hook at either end, and in addition a rectangular ivory cardboard sign with "family" written in silver capital letters. The family was tiny, just three Magnusens – or there would be three, when Cody's sister, Elle, got back from talking to the funeral director.

Cody sat beside his father, nervously watching him out of the corner of his eye. His father was very tall and thin, with taut, tanned skin – good Scandinavian genes – and rheumy blue eyes. Cody and Elle were afraid Kenneth Magnusen was going to make a scene. Kenneth had dementia; he wasn't in his right mind. He did things now he would never have believed himself capable of. Sometimes he yelled. He lost control. But today there was no expression on their father's face. No tears of grief. Or of anything else.

He was frozen.

Cody's sister, Elle, had picked the funeral home because it was reasonably priced, there was no flashiness, and the director didn't try to talk them into extras. "Mom wouldn't have wanted frills," Elle had said. Cody had said nothing, although he suspected that his mother would have wanted something more than the basics – a wooden coffin, a few flowers, a service. It was the way of their family not to argue or disagree.

Cody watched his father, and waited for Elle to come back from talking to the funeral director. He was aware of people trickling into the chapel. A quick glance told him it was some of the old ladies who had been his mother's friends. He could hear their heavy footfalls as they heaved down the centre aisle. His mother had not seemed to know any thin old ladies.

He glanced over his shoulder at them. The organist of the Lutheran church headed the procession, followed by some of the members of the quilt ministry. There were three of them. His mother had stopped attending church three years before. None of the Magnusens knew why, and Cody and Elle hadn't been going since their teens. It became an issue only when she died, and the siblings weren't sure if they should ask Pastor Nylund if they could hold her funeral there. Elle had decided that it would cause less of a stir if they kept everything at the funeral home, but invited Pastor Nylund to preside. He had told them that unfortunately he was booked that day.

And also on the next date they tried.

"Kenneth, Cody," the church organist said in a wilted, sad voice. Cody couldn't remember her name. "We're all so sorry for your loss." The other three women looked sad.

Kenneth Magnusen said in a loud voice, "Let's turn up the heat. Mom is cold."

The organist blanched. Cody and Elle had had a long discussion about bringing their father. His dementia had stolen his sense of decorum; it wasn't so much that they were embarrassed for themselves, but for the man he once had been. He was so unpredictable. But what would people have said if Lucile's widower had not attended her funeral?

Cody cleared his throat. "Thank you," he said to the organist.

The ladies looked from him to the coffin, faces drawn, then took their seats.

"Those flowers look terrible. They should get their money back," one of the women whispered in a loud voice. The others shushed her.

The chapel was tasteful, nothing fussy, and the coffin was closed, as Cody and Elle had requested. Who would have thought that someone who had frozen to death would look so . . . They had decided that painting her up wasn't appropriate and even though Mr Paulson, the funeral director, had assured them that the make-up would make her look more natural, they had stood firm.

More ladies came into the chapel, and a few men. There were about a dozen, more than he had expected. Cody knew that most of them hadn't seen his mother around much of late. Her hips had been bothering her. She said the winter had seeped into them, making them ache. They got brittle. She was afraid of falling. She sat in a recliner nearly all day, holding the remote, telling Cody and Elle to bring things to her, take things away. She'd given up on ordering their father around.

"You don't understand a word I'm saying, do you, Kenneth?" she would snap at him.

"Beg pardon?" he would say. At least, at first. A few months ago. Before the dementia really took hold.

She would sit in the recliner except for when she put on her old work boots and a heavy jacket, and went outside in the dead of night. Neither Cody nor Elle could figure out what she did out there. The chicken eggs were gathered by daylight, and there were no longer any cows to check on. She didn't even take a flashlight.

It was icy in the chapel, and redolent of roses. Goosebumps ran up and down Cody's arms. His new button-down shirt and black sports jacket smelled like the plastic bag from the department store. Cody found himself remembering walking into the Lazy Daisy Flower Shop on the night of the prom to pick up Tiffany's corsage. That was nearly twenty years ago. Tiffany had sent the little wreath of white and yellow flowers from Montreal, where she lived now with her husband and two children.

Tiffany had never told him why she'd broken up with him. Later she had emailed him:

You didn't even try to stop me.

"Dad," Elle said. She had come back from the office, and she was standing beside her father, who was sitting at the very end of the inner aisle section of the pew. "Can you scoot over, please?"

Their father didn't respond. Elle waited another couple of seconds, then huffed and walked the length of the pew, unhooking the golden cord at the far end. She sidestepped and sat down next to Cody.

"Graveside is all set," she said. She had a funny look on her face. "Mr Paulson told me the weirdest story." She lowered her voice. "There was a funeral here yesterday. The widow came in before the service to see her husband in his coffin. To see if he looked natural and all." She hesitated.

Cody nodded, waiting.

"The woman said he looked great. She started to leave. Then she turned back around and looked down at her dead husband. She said, 'This is for twenty-seven years.' And she slapped his cheek as hard as she could."

Cody's lips parted. "Her *dead* husband? She slapped her dead husband?"

Elle nodded. "Right there in the viewing room." She pulled out a tissue, and clutched it in her hand.

"That's so weird," Cody said. Then he looked at his father, to see what he made of that. His father didn't react.

Elle didn't use her tissue. She didn't cry during the service. None of the Magnusens did. They would never cry in public. There was some sniffling in the other pews. Cody wondered what the old ladies were thinking – *I miss my husband; life is so fleeting; she was such a dear woman. What does she look like?*

After the funeral, Cody's father turned to him. His blue eyes were dry and his eyebrows were very thin and completely white.

"She slapped me," he said.

Cody flushed. He looked over at Elle, who had not heard.

"OK, Dad," he said.

"*Hard.*" He nodded slowly. Then he lifted a trembling hand and laid it against Cody's left cheek. "Right there."

"What is he saying?" Elle asked.

"I think Dad should skip the graveside," Cody said. "I'll take him home and I'll get everything ready for the reception."

Elle considered. She was probably wondering what people would think if the deceased's widower didn't come to the cemetery.

"He's old, and there's snow everywhere," Cody said.

Elle inclined her head, coming to a decision. "You're right," she said. "Take him home. People will understand."

"I'll get out the potato salad and the cold cuts," Cody said.

"We should have had warm food." Elle put her tissue, still unused, into her purse.

Exhaust fumes from the family Subaru flew out of the car ghost-like. Ghosts of escape, protection. These ghosts clung to the car. Cody's father had forgotten that he used to be the one who drove. Cody and Elle had waited until it was time to renew Kenneth's licence, and then quietly destroyed the form. Their father had always obeyed all laws. He would no sooner have driven without a licence than murder someone. Their mother had asked about it for a while, narrowing her eyes at Cody and Elle, making comments about how strange it was that she had called the DVS several times and had been assured that a duplicate form had been sent. Then another duplicate form. Also, that they could renew it online.

Rather than confront the issue head on, Cody and Elle just let each conversation drop. They made a point of driving Lucile everywhere she needed to go. At first, they submitted to an orgy of errands. Church, the beauty parlour, the grocery store, the shop for quilting supplies. Three months into the new regime, she stopped asking after the licence renewal and began encouraging their father to stay home "to get his rest". He never asked about his licence, not once. Maybe he knew that he had forgotten how to drive. Or maybe he had forgotten that he'd ever known how.

There were quilts on the walls of the living room, abstract shapes in forest green, hunter green, tree-bark brown, and shades of grey and charcoal on ash black on burned black. Elle had thrown out Lucile's lap quilt. There were so many food stains on it.

At the reception in their small home, the ladies from the quilt ministry admired Lucile's fine work. Cody's father kept wandering over to the thermostat and pushing it higher. "Mom's cold," he kept saying. He would glance over at the recliner like a dog that has lost its owner and is keeping vigil for her return. Of course Cody's mother would not have stirred from the chair to turn up the thermostat herself. She would have told one of them to do it.

With the fire in the fireplace and the heater blazing away, perspiration beaded on everyone's foreheads. Cody assumed that the funeral reception guests became uncomfortably hot, and that was why no one stayed long. That was fine with Cody. He was exhausted from monitoring his father. Cody had been afraid he would do something like take off all his clothes or dip his finger in the punch. But Kenneth had wandered back and forth from the thermostat to the fireplace, fretting and half-broiling everyone.

"No one ate anything," Elle said, but the truth was that no one had stayed long enough to put a dent in the food. Elle had bought too much, and the church ladies brought covered dishes. People did things like that in the Midwest.

Cody and Elle saved everything they could, refrigerating the cheese logs and dip five seconds after the last guest had shut the front door. The sooner they got the cold food colder, the longer it would last. They froze the casseroles. Elle said they would have sandwiches for breakfast, lunch, and dinner until the cold cuts were gone.

That done, the dishes washed, Kenneth, Elle, and Cody went into the living room to watch the news on TV. Brother and sister traded looks when their father sat in Lucile's recliner. It creeped Cody out. On the sofa, Elle distractedly went through the contents of her purse. She threw her unused tissue in the fire.

No one really watched the news. No one spoke. Cody was thirty-seven. He had gone to college, then came home to help his father work the farm. But two years in, his parents figured out how to apply for subsidies for not planting any more of this, then that, and that; and as the dairy cows died, they were not replaced. Soon, there was no farm. There was fallow land and subsidy money. His parents owned their house and they drew social security. He could have left, but by then, they had begun to develop health issues. He found that caring for them took up most of his time.

Elle, who was older than Cody by three years, was the one who had left. She'd been a librarian in a high school in Milwaukee. Then the economy had taken its toll, and she had come home while she job-hunted. Six months stretched into a year, and then into five. Cody thought Elle was relieved that she'd been forced by circumstances to retreat. She said that high-school students were messy and rude. Cody thought there was a failed romance somewhere in there, too. He didn't know, though. They never talked about it. Now she did copyediting online. She was always on her computer, with her door shut.

Ghosts of happier times did not linger in the house. They realized they were in the wrong place, and faded away.

A death in the family could have been messy, but Elle made all the arrangements. Cody's task was to watch their father. Their father didn't have a task.

They went to bed. Cody was sweating, wrapped in his sheets like a shroud. Their mother had been found frozen. The morgue had been refrigerated. He hadn't asked if there had been a procedure to defrost her but there must have been. Was it important to do it in some special way? How long did it take? It must have worked; otherwise the funeral director wouldn't have been so eager to make up her face.

It bordered on sick, this train of thought. But he couldn't stop thinking about it. He wondered what was happening in the graveyard. If the flowers on top of her grave were freezing. If below the piles of snow, inside the coffin, *things* were happening to her body. He found a symmetry – he beneath his pile of quilts; she beneath the ground. If she'd died just five years ago, they would have had to wait until spring to bury her. But the funeral parlour had invested in the equipment to cut through the frozen ground. People who didn't live anywhere near the parlour were getting buried in the local graveyard.

Lucile's clothes had not been returned. The old jeans with the stretch waistband, a large black-and-red flannel shirt, her sheepherder's jacket, were gone. The funeral home had given them back her big boots. Elle had put them in a white plastic trash bag, then into the trash.

Cody peeled back layers of quilts. He was so hot he felt a little ill. The Magnusens paid for their oil at the beginning of winter. With the heat up this high, they were going to have to buy a refill. Cody got up to turn it down, and heard his father talking behind the closed door of the master bedroom.

Cody pressed his ear to the door.

"OK," Kenneth was saying. "I'm coming."

Then Cody heard the whine of the mattress springs, his father shuffling through the room. Cody glanced down. There was no sliver of light beneath the transom. His father was moving through the darkness, alone.

"Dad?" Cody called.

There was no answer, just more shuffling.

Cody knocked softly. "Dad?"

Nothing.

Cody turned the knob and pushed the door open. Moonlight spilled into the room, shining on his father's hair as he stood in front of the bedroom window.

His mother's ghost was staring through the glass. Her skin was mottled blue, grey, brown. Her blue eyes were bloodshot and shone like mirrors as she glared at Cody's father.

Kenneth's hand was on the window latch, preparing to open it.

"OK," Kenneth said. "OK, OK."

"Oh, God. Oh my God, Dad," Cody whispered. His heart stuttered as he stood on the threshold. Then as he took a step forward the ghost disappeared. There was only moonlight on the snow, and beyond that, the heavy wooden fence.

"Cody?" Sounding uncertain, Kenneth lowered his hand from the latch.

"Dad," Cody said, rushing into the room. Trying not to look at the window; unable to do anything but look at the window.

I didn't see that, he told himself.

"She's so cold," Kenneth fretted.

Cody didn't know what to do. It had to have been a waking dream. A trick of the light. A guilty conscience.

"Come to bed, Dad. You had a bad dream."

Cody glanced uneasily around the room. It was chillier than the rest of the house. He could almost see his breath.

"What's going on?" his father asked. He looked around as if he had just woken up, blinking his rheumy, icy eyes.

"You were dreaming." Shaking, Cody stood beside him. His father blinked several times, glancing at the window, then down at his hands, then back at the window.

Cody didn't remember the last time he'd touched his father, or the last time his father had touched him. He couldn't remember a handshake. He lightly brushed his father's arm, surprised by how thin it was.

Cody hadn't seen her face there. It had been a trick of the light. A bad dream of his own. His heart pounded. His hands shook.

"Now climb into bed, Dad," Cody said. Cody's back was to the window. He could almost feel someone looking at him.

Her, looking at him.

"I'm so cold," Kenneth said sadly. "I'm cold to my bones and I'll never be warm again."

"Here, get under the quilt." Cody peeled back the bedclothes. For one heart-stopping moment he thought he saw a leg; then he realized it was his mother's "body pillow", purchased to help her with her hip aches.

He glanced back at the window. All he saw was the moon on the snow, the fence, and some trees. More times than he could count, he had gone outside in the early dawn, trying to find his mother's footprints so he could figure out what she was doing at night in the frigid darkness. He had tried to talk to Elle about it. She had pursed her lips and said, "She's just as crazy as he is."

Now, as his father stiffly sat on the edge of the bed, Cody realized that he couldn't leave him in this room, unattended, when his mother's face might reappear in the window.

It wasn't there. I imagined it.

But still, he couldn't. And he wouldn't stay in this room himself.

"Dad, let's go watch TV," he said, because he didn't know what else to do. "We've got all those great leftovers."

He flicked on the light so that his father wouldn't be tempted to lie down. The window absorbed the reflection, so that Cody couldn't see anything in it except the painting of birds on the wall above the bed. He'd turned on the light so that he could fool his father into forgetting that he had been planning to go back to bed. It worked; Kenneth shuffled barefooted down the hall. Usually the floor in winter would be too cold to walk on barefoot, but the thermostat was up so high that it was like walking on freshly turned summer earth.

Cody headed for the kitchen. But his father went into the living room and sat in the recliner. Cody opened the refrigerator and recoiled from the chill. Everything in there was rotting, slowly.

"What's going on?" Elle asked, belting her robe and yawning as she came into the kitchen. She looked younger without her make-up.

"Dad had a bad dream," he said, avoiding her gaze.

"I guess that's to be expected," she replied. She reached out a hand towards the refrigerator and he saw that it was shaking. Like his.

Tell her, he thought. But it was too complicated, and he didn't want to upset Elle. He hadn't really seen his mother.

"Cody," she said, and sat down at the kitchen table. She looked down at her hands. Then she said, "I'm going back to bed."

Tell her. But he never told her anything.

"Good night," he said.

He pulled out a casserole, then put it back and shut the refrigerator door. He glanced at the blank kitchen windows. What if his mother's ghost went to Elle's window next? He hurried down the hallway to his sister's door and knocked softly on it.

"Come in," she said.

The dark blue drapes were pulled across her window. He tried not to imagine his mother's mottled face, her shiny eyes, on the other side the glass.

I didn't see her.

Elle looked at him. Then her gaze slid down to the floor.

"Cody," she said again.

He took a deep breath. "Did you see her?" he asked.

She cocked her head. "When? The night it . . . happened?"

The night it happened, their mother had gone out into the dark forest without her flashlight. It had been snowing. She was found in the morning beside the fence, the gate frozen open. Cody had found her.

She had been lying face down. He hadn't turned her over. He had kneeled in the snow to check her pulse. But he already knew. He could tell. Her skin was shiny, like ice, and—

"I went into Dad's room," he began, meaning tonight. Just now.

"So did I." She clenched her jaw. "I saw."

He suddenly had the feeling they were talking about two different things. He glanced at the closed curtains.

Then he smelled the smoke. It was thick and oily, and it was rolling down the hallway.

"Dad!" he shouted.

Together he and Elle ran back down the hall. The quilts on the living-room walls were on fire. The recliner was ablaze, and Kenneth was staggering through the smoke, coughing hard.

"I'll get water," Elle said, as Cody ran for his father. He took his hand and hurried him to the front door. He threw it open and—

She was standing there. His dead mother, skin blue and brown and red. Her dark blue polyester top over a long black skirt he didn't recognize. Her eyes were like cracked marbles. Her mouth hung slightly open, revealing only blackness.

"She's cold," Kenneth said.

"The ceiling is catching!" Elle cried. "We have to get out!"

The house was making a whum-whum sort of noise as the fire grew, flames crackling and snapping. Cody heard the kitchen door slam shut. His sister had made it outside.

Lucile faced Cody and Kenneth, her face a rictus stare. Heat brushed against Cody's back.

His mother took a step forward. Her eyes blazed with fury.

"She slapped me," Kenneth murmured. "Hard."

She headed for them.

Before he knew what he was doing, Cody grabbed his father's hand and raced back into the living room. The recliner was going up, and all the quilts. The skin on his arms began to pucker. He felt as if someone was pressing heated spoons on his arms.

"Hot, hot," Kenneth wailed.

Cody stepped on something burning. His foot cramped and sizzled. He raced into the kitchen. The ceiling was burning. Smoke slammed into his throat and expanded into his lungs.

Hacking and coughing, he clung to his father's hand. He reached the kitchen door and threw it open. They ran into the snowy backyard. Snow tumbled down; ghosts darted and swirled among the clots of white: the ghosts of secrets.

"Elle!" Cody shouted. "Elle!"

The fence gate was open, as it had been the morning he had found his dead mother.

Because he had opened it himself, about two hours before then.

After he had unlocked it.

"Cody!" Elle cried.

She was waiting on the other side of the fence. When Cody and Kenneth ran through the gate, she grabbed Cody in a hug. She was sobbing.

"Wait for Mom," their father said, turning back to face the house. It was an inferno; flames shot up through the roof, surrounding the chimney.

"Cody," Elle said into his ear. "Cody, I followed her out. I-I locked the gate. Cody, she was hitting him. Hurting him. I saw the bruises. I hated her." She threw back her head. "I hated you!"

Cody's father shuffled towards the blazing structure. Cody and Elle caught up with him. Each took a hand, restrained him.

"I'm so cold," Kenneth said.

"I locked it, too," Cody said to Elle. "It was unlocked, then. But I didn't know what you know."

"Then . . . why?" Elle asked. "Why did you do it?"

"My feet are stinging," Kenneth informed them.

"I knew I had to," Cody answered. He felt a fierce sort of joy. He hadn't known why he was locking her out. He had hated her, but he didn't have a reason to, as Elle did. He just knew she was the force that kept them frozen.

But now he had a reason. The best of reasons.

The ghost of his mother appeared before them in the snow. Elle started screaming.

"I'm sorry," Kenneth said. "I'm so sorry." He lifted his hand, taking Cody's hand with him. He pantomimed locking the gate.

The ghost took a step towards the three Magnusens. And

then . . . she turned to steam. Her body drifted apart, floating in the snow; the ice crystals hissed as they collided with her.

The house burned all the way down to the foundations, to ashes. Nothing left. By then, the fire trucks had clanged into action and the Magnusens were wrapped in thick yellow blankets. They were wearing dark blue mittens and drinking hot cocoa out of Styrofoam cups. Elle and Cody were hanging on to their father, holding him, Elle kissing his grizzled cheek over and over again.

"Daddy." She sounded like a little girl.

"We'll have to move," Cody said, feeling dizzy. "Make some decisions."

The wind whistled through the dark shapes behind them, forest green, hunter green, and tree-bark brown. The ghost glided among the trees, grey and charcoal on ash black on burned black. That ghost did not touch Cody either.

"I'm so cold," his father said.

"We're done with cold, Dad. It's done," Cody said.

"All done," Elle agreed.

And his father gave them the ghost of a smile.

"All done," he agreed, and drank his hot chocolate.

Return

Yvonne Navarro

Mara goes back to the only place she can think of.

She doesn't know how she gets there, but the house is suddenly right in front of her – tan brick split-level with a black shingle roof, big picture window in the front that, like the rest of the windows, is always dirty because no one will take the time to wash it. No one will take the time for a lot of things in this house, but she has nowhere else to go, no one else to whom she can turn. All she has is old memory and deeper instinct, a compulsion in her bones that won't let her keep on going past the driveway; she *has* to turn, has to go down the steps to the back door which she knows will be unlocked during the day. It's as if she has only one eye and she's pushed it tightly against one end of the discarded cardboard tube from a roll of paper towels – there is nothing beyond that small circle of light at the end and whatever images fill it.

The steps.

The door, brown and dusty.

The doorknob.

Her own hand – such an amazing thing – reaching for it.

She stops and stares at it for a few moments, turns the palm upward, checks for non-existent dirt under the finger-nails. It looks . . . OK, about the same as it did back then. What about her face – does that look the same, too? She is wearing the same clothes, but is her hair still light brown, does her nose tilt upward, is her mouth too wide, are the eyebrows she'd always wanted to arch still straight across? Is she still *pretty*? She's been gone a long time, and she wishes she had a mirror so she can check, because it won't do to have any big surprises. Well, any *more* – she is certainly going to be one all on her own, isn't she?

She opens the door and steps inside the house.

Nothing has changed, at least in the utility room. It's still too dark and full of cobwebs and dust along the concrete floor, still lightens up a bit by the double laundry sink. The air down here is cooler than in the rest of the house. She sees that across from the sink the dog's bowls are there, where they are always kept, and that there is fresh water in one and bits of dog food scattered on the floor around the other – for an old, small dog, a Pomeranian, Greepers always had been a messy eater.

And there he is, standing in the doorway at the other end of the utility room, staring at her.

They've shaved him for the summer and he looks like a puppy, enticingly soft and cuddly. It seems like it's been years since she felt any warmth and she can't wait to pick him up ... but there is something in his stance that makes her hesitate, even though he's old and he's been hers for over thirteen years. How has he been all these months, when she was always the only one to give him affection, to keep him company? She tries to speak his name and her voice is an unintelligible croak, so she clears her throat and tries again, takes a small step forward.

"G-Greepers."

He growls at her and backs away.

She freezes, and now it's her turn to stare at him. Greepers keeps backing up until he bumps into the short flight of stairs that leads up to the kitchen, then he gives a single, shrill bark.

She hears footsteps then, overhead and hurrying down the upstairs hallway to the stairs, going to the living room, turning the corner to come down to the utility room—

And she sees, at last, her mother, at the same time as her mother sees her.

And screams.

"You need to come home," Amber O'Shannon says into the phone. Her voice is shrill, louder than it's been in eight months. That's how long it's been since— "You need to come home right *now!*" Her fingers are closed around the receiver in a death grip, as though the cold plastic has become some sort of lifeline, the only thing anchoring her to the world. If not for that, perhaps she would float away, simply drift up into the clouds. The notion is about as realistic as anything else going on here in her well-kept home.

"I'm in the middle of an important meeting," she hears her husband say. "For God's sake, Amber—"

"*I don't care!*" she shrieks, then realizes what she is doing and makes a conscious effort to regain control. Already it's starting, she thinks. *Already.* "I can't tell you why – just do it. It's an *emergency.*" She will pay for it later, but she slams down the phone before he can argue further, because she can't deal with this, can't deal with him and his questions, and most of all, she can't deal with—

She turns.

Her daughter Mara still sits, silent and patient, at the kitchen table.

Amber doesn't know how the young woman got there, or what happened in the moments between seeing her standing down in the utility room and now, what was said to get her from there to here, sitting at the kitchen table like some kind of speechless question mark. It figures that she would be home all by herself when something like this happens – an absurd thought to begin with, because who would have expected something "like this" ever to occur anyway? She wants to ask a question, *the* question, but she is nervous and afraid. Maybe it would be better to wait until Bill gets home, or Andy. Even Brianna, although God knows what help that girl could give.

So she says nothing.

Instead, she sits across the table and she and her daughter stare at each other and wait for the others to arrive.

"Yoh, Mom!" Andy O'Shannon shoves open the basement door and barrels into the house, making sure that the noise level goes up along with his bellow. He likes it when his mother comes hurrying down the stairs to meet him, to make sure he had a good day, ask if he's hungry, whatever. It's a standard routine perfected over the last six months and—

He frowns.

Car's in the driveway, but where is she? He drops his stuff on the dryer and climbs the stairs to the kitchen. "Mom?" Then he sees her, sitting quietly at the table with someone else. He starts to walk towards her, then she turns a shocked gaze on him. But any explanation she might have mouthed is forgotten the instant he focuses on the other person.

"Jesus God," he breathes. "I—" He can't think of any words to finish the sentence and so he doesn't, just stops and lets his back push up against the kitchen wall. Finally he slides down, settles on the floor, and stares.

Brianna walks in on it without warning.

She is the only one who insists on using the front door "like civilized people" and never mind the extra work it makes for her mom, because that's not the point, damn it. So she comes through the other doorway from the living room and, even so, she recognizes the back of her older sister's head immediately and is not pleased. "What is this?" she demands. "Some kind of sick joke? A mind fuck?" She turns to her mother accusingly. "This is so not funny."

But her mother doesn't even say anything about her language. "No," she says slowly. "I don't know what it is . . . but I don't think it's a joke."

Brianna scowls and steps up to Mara. "You . . ." she begins, but then they all hear the slam – intentionally hard – of the basement door. "Daddy's home," Brianna says instead, with as much sweet sarcasm as she can muster.

Her mother nods. "I called him."

Brianna gives an unladylike snigger. "What – like you think he's gonna *fix* this?"

Bill O'Shannon storms into the kitchen of his home purposefully, the same way he storms into the boardroom in the real estate firm of which he is president. He is a controlling man and it angers him to the core that his wife has had the nerve to call and demand that he come home, without even giving him a reasonable explanation. It can't be one of the kids – she would have simply told him. What the hell could be so important that she would interrupt his Friday status meeting to—?

And there, sitting with the rest of them around the table, he finally sees the reason Amber called him.

Mara sits at the table and watches her family watch her, but she feels nothing. No love, no fear, certainly no comfort. The closest thing she's felt to emotion was that fleeting desire to pick up Greepers, and that died with his nasty little growl – of all the things in her life, he had been the only one she'd always believed she could go to for comfort. But, like everything and everyone else, even he has failed her.

"So," her father asks her now, "you want to tell me how this happened?" He waits expectantly.

She says nothing.

"Mara, you can't just waltz in here like this without some kind of explanation about—" For the first time, he hesitates. "About where you've been," he finally finishes.

"Why not?" Brianna cuts in. Her voice is high. "It's what she always did before. Why should this be any different?"

"Well, *duh*!" Andy snorts.

"Shut up!" Brianna shouts. "I wasn't talking to you!"

"Like I need your permission," he shoots back.

Mara sees Brianna's face flush, as it has countless times

before. There is a difference though – the last eight months have made a subtle difference in her younger sister's appearance, filled out her face and given it a hard edge that Mara doesn't recall seeing before. Still, Mara sees a lot of hard edges in the faces of her family that may or may not have been there. Some she remembers, others she doesn't – they might be new. Not surprisingly, there is no softness when they look at her.

"You two keep your mouths closed," her father says, and there is no mistaking the *don't fuck with me* tone of his voice. "I want to know what the hell is going on." He glares again at Mara. "How do I know you're even my daughter? You might be some kind of imposter, or a con artist."

Mara still doesn't say anything. She still doesn't feel anything, and that surprises her. She remembers all the pain and the hurt and the humiliation – especially that – from before, and when she'd realized where she was, when she'd sort of *come to* herself, and found that she was going back home, she'd expected it to all come slamming back, as if she'd gone through some kind of cosmic rewinding machine and somewhere a supreme being had leaned over and pushed the play button. But it wasn't the same, and if there is any kindness at all to be attributed to the universe and whatever powers it, it is that this time around they've left the emotional track off her life tape.

"I don't believe this," Amber says suddenly. "What are we going to tell the neighbours? What are they going to *think*?" Her hands, so carefully manicured and creamed, flutter around her face like panicking humming birds. "What am I going to do about her now – Jesus, how do I get her back in school and back into a normal life? How do I *explain* her?" Her attractive face is pale and fragile, her expression crumpling beneath a problem too huge to cope with. "People will think we let her run off or something, that we lied about where she was and didn't even care enough to hire a private investigator to find her. My *God*." Her crystalline blue eyes fix on Mara. "That's what you want, isn't it? You want everyone to think we were bad parents, that I'm a bad *mother*."

It's an interesting question and rather than answer her, Mara ponders it. *Is* this something she wants? To let the neighbours, friends and all the other relatives know how truly dysfunctional this family is, what abysmal parents she has, all the dark and dirty little secrets? To point fingers and condemn? And, oh, but they had some real, honest-to-God putrid pond scum hidden in O'Shannon daily diaries, didn't they?

But . . . no. She really doesn't care. She doesn't know why, but she doesn't.

Before Amber can demand an answer, Mara's father steps close to her chair. His shadow towers over her, and it seems to her that it has always been this way, as far back as she can recall. She doesn't think there was ever a time when she looked forward to seeing him at the end of the day or over the course of a weekend; he is like the fantasy king who wields a brutal sword of justice. The peasants always know their great ruler is looming somewhere, but would rather not cross his path. Is this the way fathers are in other families? Maybe in some of them. She doesn't know.

Bill's face is grim as he stares down at her, doing his best, as he always has, to make her feel insignificant. His lips are drawn so tight that his words are almost difficult to understand. "We'll have to start this all over again," he says. He is looking at her, but talking to the others. "We'll have to watch her constantly to make sure she doesn't get back into the drugs and start running with her dope-addict friends. Make sure she isn't sneaking out to go to parties in the middle of the night." He shoots a glance at his wife and she cringes a little before he fixes his gaze on his daughter once more. "You know how she is. It better not interfere with my work like it did the last time. My work is very important, and this isn't going to be a repeat. I damned well won't stand for it." He leans closer, and now he does speak directly to her. "Do you hear me, young lady?"

Mara expects to feel something, *anything*, but she doesn't. Certainly not fear, although she knows that is what her father wants most. It is an interesting thing, this . . . state she is in, this *condition*. It's vaguely like being wrapped in a protective cocoon, insulated from anything and everything that might affect her. She can't even smell the cinnamon mints that her father is always chewing because he thinks it makes his breath smell good. For that she might feel gratitude, if she could feel anything at all beyond the mild surprise at her current predicament. She always hated that smell.

Something crashes against the floor and Mara's head swivels until she locates the source of the sound – Brianna has slammed her books flat against the golden wood. Another lie, that wood – picked specifically by her mother to give the illusion of warmth, but Mara remembers how it felt against the skin of her cheek and knows there is nothing warm about a wooden kitchen floor at 3 a.m. on a winter morning.

"Well, this is *great*," Brianna says. "I can't believe you're going to let her waltz in here like it's just another day in the life of anything *normal*. Just slide right back into the groove and make the rest of us have to fit our lives around it. Around *her*. Oh, and let's not forget that disgusting little dog of hers – we should have put that damned thing to sleep back in December." Her younger sister's voice is full of the hatred she has built up for Mara over so many months, perhaps years. "*Thank* you for coming back and making me miserable all over again, Mara. I suppose you'll want your room back now. And your clothes and stuff, too. I guess God, or what *ever*, sent you back to punish me because I was *glad* when you—"

"Brianna!" Amber sits up straight for the first time since her husband came home. "You watch how you speak to your sister!"

"I'm sorry." If anything, her tone is even more venomous. "Am I being a little too honest here? In fact, am I the *only* one being honest?" She pushes herself to her feet and takes a step towards Mara. "You were always the one who got all the attention, weren't you? Well, it's *my* turn now, so why don't you just fuck off and go away!"

"Boy, I hear *that*," Andy says before either of Mara's parents can respond to Brianna's fury. He is still on the floor and now he runs his fingers through his hair, something he has always done when he is feeling guilty. There was a time after her eleventh birthday when he did that a lot, but only Mara noticed. And only Mara knew why. "And don't be thinking I'm gonna be driving you around like before, you know. I got stuff of my own to do now— I got a summer job and a girlfriend, a football scholarship to college. My coach says I'm good enough for the pros."

Mara considers this as she looks at him. He can't meet her eyes, and she realizes what he's doing – trying, in his own, inept way, to reassure her, to give her an unspoken promise that things will be different now, he won't repeat the sins of his past, it was all nothing but a big, terrible mistake, one of those nasty and dark O'Shannon secrets. Andy looks left and right, up and down, but eventually he meets her eyes, and when he does, he is pinned, the once-proud predator frozen and knowing doom on some instinctive level within the sight of the hunter's rifle.

He begins to cry.

"I'm *sorry*, Mara. Jesus, God, I am so *sorry*." Tears course from the corners of his eyes and flow over his cheekbones and strong jaw, that chiselled look the girls began to notice in his sophomore year in high school. "I should never have done that to you, I didn't *mean* to, I don't even know why I did it and then I couldn't stop—"

He goes on and on, babbling and blubbering, and now, of all the times since she walked into this house, Mara thinks she should feel something, she *should*.

Across the kitchen, her brother is wailing, unable to stop himself from releasing the poisonous guilt bottled inside for the last four years. "You should've told on me, you should've exposed me for what I was, I should've been *punished*!" He sobs again, and he isn't just running his hands through his hair any more, he's actually pulling on it. "Everyone thinks I'm such a nice guy . . . I'm *not* a nice guy, you could tell them that. You could've told them any time. I'm *not*!"

"Wait a damned minute." Silent until now, shocked, Bill O'Shannon finally finds his voice. He strides across the kitchen and pulls his teenaged son to his feet, then grasps the front of the boy's jersey with both hands like a man about to shake an enemy. "What are you saying, Andy? What . . . *what did you do?*"

"*I made her have sex with me when she was eleven!*" Andy screams into his father's face. "*For months and months and months! And I took pictures of it and swore I'd tell everyone at school she was a slut if she told anyone!*"

"Oh my God," Amber O'Shannon whimpers. "Oh. My. God."

William O'Shannon throws his son across the kitchen like he is tossing away something he no longer wants.

Then he turns and walks to one of the kitchen chairs, where he sits down with all the grace of an improperly strung marionette. A very *heavy* one.

Andy has landed in a heap against the front of the refrigerator. He picks himself up, then wipes his bleeding mouth on his sleeve. He studies the blood but doesn't see it, then goes back and sits in the same place he'd been before his ugly confession.

"Pervert," Brianna suddenly hisses. "You're so lucky you never tried that shit with me." Before anyone realizes what she's going to do, she reaches over and gives Mara a stinging, loud slap across her bare left arm. "You're an idiot, you know that? Why couldn't you open your mouth? Oh, no – instead you held it all inside and let it drive you crazy."

Mara glances down and sees Brianna's hand print clearly against her skin. It's OK, because it didn't hurt. She still has that sensation of insulation, or maybe it's something stronger, an unseen force field. This is a good thing, because she thinks there is more coming.

"All these years," Amber says softly. "I thought she was over it. I thought the parties and the drugs were a school thing, she was running with the wrong crowd, and if we could wait it out, she'd get better. She'd . . . *forget.*" Somehow over the last fifteen minutes Mara's mother has grown deep purple shadows beneath her eyes. "But she didn't get over it, did she? Not ever.

All that stuff, every pill and joint and needle, it was her trying to get away from the memory of what Andy did. It was just her trying to *escape*."

Andy sits up suddenly. "Wait – you knew? Mom, you *knew* and you didn't do anything?" His voice is rising, climbing back towards the scream it had been before Bill threw him. "Why? *Why didn't you put a stop to it*?"

"Because I thought this . . . this dirty little *problem* of yours would just go *away*!" Amber's voice is shrill, painful. "Sometimes teenaged boys do things they shouldn't, but it all gets better – I thought that's what this was!"

"I can't believe I'm hearing this," Bill says hoarsely. "My son rapes my daughter and my wife knows it's happening and doesn't *do* anything about it? What—"

"Oh, like *you* would have done anything if we'd have told you," Brianna sneers. "Mr I Can't Be Bothered With Anything But Money And Work."

Bill O'Shannon stumbles to his feet, not noticing when his chair tumbles backwards. "Are you saying that you knew, too?" He has gone from shock to rage, just that quick.

But thirteen-year-old Brianna will not be cowed. "Yes, I knew!" she shrieks. "I wasn't sure *what* it was, but I *knew*!" Mara watches as her little sister's finger jabs in her direction. "Were you *deaf*? Didn't you hear her when she cried every night? Before and after, like clockwork – you could hear her through the door to her room. And you didn't do *anything*!"

"So you're what?" Andy asks bitterly. "Little Miss Holier Than Thou? You're better than all of us?"

Brianna whirls. "Me? Oh, sure, I'm great. Just put me in Mom's corner, where we sit and wish it would all go away. Where we wished *she* would go away."

Now no one can look at her; no one can say anything else. Through all of it – their confessions, their anger at her, their self-hatred – Mara has felt nothing, thanks to the insulating layer of . . . *something* around her. Now she finally knows what that something is.

It is the secret shame of her family.

There is guilt here, lots of it, but it is not hers. Yes, it was her own hand that tied off the vein and held the needle, her own decision to try a score from an unknown dealer, a guy too new to the street trade to know he should cut his junk a few more times before passing it down to the high-school crowd. But what she did that night in mid-December was a consequence not a cause, the result of a family so corrupted by selfishness that no one but she felt enough pain to search for a way to avoid it.

Mara still doesn't know why she has come back, or where she has been since the night she died right here on this supposedly "warm" kitchen floor. She doesn't recall wanting to come back, and she certainly never had any desire to bring out the dreadful truth that had been her true existence – it simply doesn't matter to her any more. Whatever the reason, now her being here is done ... for the second time. And when the compulsion to leave takes her, she doesn't fight it.

She rises and feels their gazes on her, but she has no desire to say goodbye. She takes one step, then two, and something tickles her ankle. When she looks down, she sees Greepers; the old dog sniffs at her ankle then gives it an affectionate lick before looking up at her and wagging his tail.

Mara reaches down and picks him up.

He is as soft and warm as she remembers, wonderfully so, and he wiggles with joy and tries to lick her face. She has one quick moment of confusion as she realizes that even though she is holding him, she can still see his body on the floor, eyes open and chest still, small and silent next to the chair on which she had been sitting.

She glances at each member of her family in turn. Her mother is pallid, crying quietly; for the first time that Mara can ever remember, she looks at her daughter with something close to longing. Her father seems to have shrunk on his chair, a man broken by the hideous truth of what has transpired, unseen and unstopped, in his own home. Her brother and sister stare first at her and the soft bundle of fur in her arms, then at the cooling corpse of the family pet. Their expressions are tight with self-recrimination and remorse.

But Mara doesn't care.

She hugs Greepers close and walks out of the kitchen, going down the steps and into the utility room.

It is filled with white light, and somewhere at the end of that light she knows she and Greepers will find a long-awaited peace.

Let Loose

Mary Cholmondeley

The dead abide with us! Though stark and cold
Earth seems to grip them, they are with us still.

Some years ago I took up architecture, and made a tour
through Holland, studying the buildings of that interesting
country. I was not then aware that it is not enough to take up
art. Art must take you up, too. I never doubted but that my
passing enthusiasm for her would be returned. When I discovered that she was a stern mistress, who did not immediately
respond to my attentions, I naturally transferred them to
another shrine. There are other things in the world besides art.
I am now a landscape gardener.

But at the time of which I write, I was engaged in a violent
flirtation with architecture. I had one companion on this
expedition, who has since become one of the leading architects of the day. He was a thin, determined-looking man
with a screwed-up face and heavy jaw, slow of speech, and
absorbed in his work to a degree which I quickly found
tiresome. He was possessed of a certain quiet power of
overcoming obstacles which I have rarely seen equalled. He
has since become my brother-in-law, so I ought to know;
for my parents did not like him much and opposed the
marriage, and my sister did not like him at all, and refused

him over and over again; but, nevertheless, he eventually married her.

I have thought since that one of his reasons for choosing me as his travelling companion on this occasion was because he was getting up steam for what he subsequently termed "an alliance with my family", but the idea never entered my head at the time. A more careless man as to dress I have rarely met, and yet, in all the heat of July in Holland, I noticed that he never appeared without a high, starched collar, which had not even fashion to commend it at that time.

I often chaffed him about his splendid collars, and asked him why he wore them, but without eliciting any response. One evening, as we were walking back to our lodgings in Middeburg, I attacked him for about the thirtieth time on the subject.

"Why on earth do you wear them?" I said.

"You have, I believe, asked me that question many times," he replied, in his slow, precise utterance, "but always on occasions when I was occupied. I am now at leisure, and I will tell you."

And he did.

I have put down what he said, as nearly in his own words as I can remember them.

Ten years ago, I was asked to read a paper on English Frescoes at the Institute of British Architects. I was determined to make the paper as good as I could, down to the slightest details, and I consulted many books on the subject, and studied every fresco I could find. My father, who had been an architect, had left me, at his death, all his papers and notebooks on the subject of architecture. I searched them diligently, and found in one of them a slight unfinished sketch of nearly fifty years ago that especially interested me. Underneath was noted, in his clear, small hand – *Frescoed east wall of crypt. Parish Church. Wet Waste-on-the-Wolds, Yorkshire (via Pickering)*.

The sketch held such a fascination for me that I decided to go there and see the fresco for myself. I had only a very vague

idea as to where Wet Waste-on-the-Wolds was, but I was ambi-
tious for the success of my paper; it was hot in London, and I
set off on my long journey not without a certain degree of
pleasure, with my dog Brian, a large nondescript brindled
creature, as my only companion.

I reached Pickering, in Yorkshire, in the course of the
afternoon, and then began a series of experiments on local
lines which ended, after several hours, in my finding myself
deposited at a little out-of-the-way station within nine or
ten miles of Wet Waste. As no conveyance of any kind was to
be had, I shouldered my portmanteau and set out on a long
white road that stretched away into the distance over the
bare, treeless wold. I must have walked for several hours,
over a waste of moorland patched with heather, when a
doctor passed me, and gave me a lift to within a mile of my
destination. The mile was a long one, and it was quite dark
by the time I saw the feeble glimmer of lights in front of me,
and found that I had reached Wet Waste. I had considerable
difficulty in getting anyone to take me in; but at last I
persuaded the owner of the public house to give me a bed,
and, quite tired out, I got into it as soon as possible for fear
he should change his mind, and fell asleep to the sound of a
little stream below my window.

I was up early next morning, and enquired directly after
breakfast the way to the clergyman's house, which I found was
close at hand. At Wet Waste everything was close at hand. The
whole village seemed composed of a straggling row of one-
storeyed grey stone houses, the same colour as the stone walls
that separated the few fields enclosed from the surrounding
waste, and as the little bridges over the beck that ran down one
side of the grey wide street. Everything was grey. The church,
the low tower of which I could see at a little distance, seemed
to have been built of the same stone; so was the parsonage
when I came up to it, accompanied on my way by a mob of
rough, uncouth children, who eyed me and Brian with half-
defiant curiosity.

The clergyman was at home, and after a short delay I was

admitted. Leaving Brian in charge of my drawing materials, I followed the servant into a low panelled room, in which, at a latticed window, a very old man was sitting. The morning light fell on his white head bent low over a litter of papers and books.

"Mr er—?" he said, looking up slowly, with one finger keeping his place in a book.

"Blake."

"Blake," he repeated after me, and was silent.

I told him that I was an architect, that I had come to study a fresco in the crypt of his church, and asked for the keys.

"The crypt?" he said, pushing up his spectacles and peering hard at me. "The crypt has been closed for thirty years. Ever since—" And he stopped short.

"I should be much obliged for the keys," I said again. He shook his head.

"No," he said. "No one goes in there now."

"It is a pity," I remarked, "for I have come a long way with that one object"; and I told him about the paper I had been asked to read, and the trouble I was taking with it.

He became interested. "Ah!" he said, laying down his pen, and removing his finger from the page before him. "I can understand that. I also was young once, and fired with ambition. The lines have fallen to me in somewhat lonely places, and for forty years I have held the cure of souls in this place, where, truly, I have seen but little of the world, though I myself may be not unknown in the paths of literature. Possibly you may have read a pamphlet, written by myself, on the Syrian version of the Three Authentic Epistles of Ignatius?"

"Sir," I said, "I am ashamed to confess that I have not time to read even the most celebrated books. My one object in life is my art. *Ars longa, vita brevis*, you know."

"You are right, my son," said the old man, evidently disappointed, but looking at me kindly. "There are diversities of gifts, and if the Lord has entrusted you with a talent, look to it. Lay it not up in a napkin."

I said I would not do so if he would lend me the keys of the crypt. He seemed startled by my recurrence to the subject and looked undecided.

"Why not?" he murmured to himself. "The youth appears a good youth. And superstition! What is it but distrust in God!"

He got up slowly and, taking a large bunch of keys out of his pocket, opened with one of them an oak cupboard in the corner of the room.

"They should be here," he muttered, peering in, "but the dust of many years deceives the eye. See, my son, if among these parchments there be two keys: one of iron and very large, and the other steel, and of a long thin appearance."

I went eagerly to help him, and presently found in a back drawer two keys tied together, which he recognized at once.

"Those are they," he said. "The long one opens the first door at the bottom of the steps which go down against the outside wall of the church hard by the sword graven in the wall. The second opens (but it is hard of opening and of shutting) the iron door within the passage leading to the crypt itself. My son, is it necessary to your treatise that you should enter this crypt?"

I replied that it was absolutely necessary.

"Then take them," he said, "and in the evening you will bring them to me again."

I said I might want to go several days running, and asked if he would not allow me to keep them till I had finished my work, but on that point he was firm.

"Likewise," he added, "be careful that you lock the first door at the foot of the steps before you unlock the second, and lock the second also while you are within. Furthermore, when you come out, lock the iron inner door as well as the wooden one."

I promised I would do so and, after thanking him, hurried away, delighted at my success in obtaining the keys. Finding Brian and my sketching materials waiting for me in the porch, I eluded the vigilance of my escort of children by taking the narrow private path between the parsonage and the church which was close at hand, standing in a quadrangle of ancient yews.

The church itself was interesting, and I noticed that it must have arisen out of the ruins of a previous building, judging from the number of fragments of stone caps and arches, bearing traces of very early carving, now built into the walls. There were incised crosses, too, in some places, and one especially caught my attention, being flanked by a large sword. It was in trying to get a nearer look at this that I stumbled, and, looking down, saw at my feet a flight of narrow stone steps green with moss and mildew. Evidently this was the entrance to the crypt. I at once descended the steps, taking care of my footing, for they were damp and slippery in the extreme. Brian accompanied me, as nothing would induce him to remain behind. By the time I had reached the bottom of the stairs, I found myself almost in darkness, and I had to strike a light before I could find the keyhole and the proper key to fit into it. The door, which was of wood, opened inwards fairly easily, although an accumulation of mould and rubbish on the ground outside showed it had not been used for many years. Having got through it, which was not altogether an easy matter, as nothing would induce it to open more than about eighteen inches, I carefully locked it behind me, although I should have preferred to leave it open, as there is to some minds an unpleasant feeling in being locked in anywhere, in case of a sudden exit seeming advisable.

I kept my candle alight with some difficulty and, after groping my way down a low and of course exceedingly dank passage, came to another door. A toad was squatting against it, who looked as if he had been sitting there about a hundred years. As I lowered the candle to the floor, he gazed at the light with unblinking eyes, and then retreated slowly into a crevice in the wall, leaving against the door a small cavity in the dry mud which had gradually silted up round his person. I noticed that this door was of iron, and had a long bolt, which, however, was broken. Without delay, I fitted the second key into the lock and, pushing the door open after considerable difficulty, I felt the cold breath of the crypt upon my face. I must own I experienced a momentary regret at locking the second door again as soon as I was well inside, but I felt it my duty to do so. Then, leaving the key in the lock, I seized my candle and looked round.

I was standing in a low vaulted chamber with groined roof, cut out of the solid rock. It was difficult to see where the crypt ended, as further light thrown on any point only showed other rough archways or openings, cut in the rock, which had probably served at one time for family vaults. A peculiarity of the Wet Waste crypt, which I had not noticed in other places of that description, was the tasteful arrangement of skulls and bones, which were packed about four feet high on either side. The skulls were symmetrically built up to within a few inches of the top of the low archway on my left, and the shin bones were arranged in the same manner on my right. *But the fresco!* I looked round for it in vain. Perceiving at the further end of the crypt a very low and very massive archway, the entrance to which was not filled up with bones, I passed under it, and found myself in a second smaller chamber. Holding my candle above my head, the first object its light fell upon was – the fresco, and at a glance I saw that it was unique.

Setting down some of my things with a trembling hand on a rough stone shelf hard by, which had evidently been a credence table, I examined the work more closely. It was a reredos over what had probably been the altar at the time the priests were proscribed. The fresco belonged to the earliest part of the fifteenth century, and was so perfectly preserved that I could almost trace the limits of each day's work in the plaster, as the artist had dashed it on and smoothed it out with his trowel. The subject was the Ascension, gloriously treated. I can hardly describe my elation as I stood and looked at it, and reflected that this magnificent specimen of English fresco painting would be made known to the world by myself. Recollecting myself at last, I opened my sketching bag and, lighting all the candles I had brought with me, set to work.

Brian walked about near me, and though I was not other-wise than glad of his company in my rather lonely position, I wished several times I had left him behind. He seemed rest-less, and even the sight of so many bones appeared to exercise no soothing effect upon him. At last, however, after repeated commands, he lay down, watchful but motionless, on the stone floor.

I must have worked for several hours, and I was pausing to rest my eyes and hands, when I noticed for the first time the intense stillness that surrounded me. No sound from *me* reached the outer world. The church clock, which had clanged out so loud and ponderously as I went down the steps, had not since sent the faintest whisper of its iron tongue down to me below. All was silent as the grave. This *was* the grave. Those who had come here had indeed gone down into silence. I repeated the words to myself, or rather they repeated them-selves to me.

Gone down into silence.

I was awakened from my reverie by a faint sound. I sat still and listened. Bats occasionally frequent vaults and under-ground places.

The sound continued, a faint, stealthy, rather unpleasant sound. I do not know what kinds of sounds bats make, whether pleasant or otherwise. Suddenly there was a noise as of some-thing falling, a momentary pause and then – an almost imperceptible but distant jangle as of a key.

I had left the key in the lock after I had turned it, and I now regretted having done so. I got up, took one of the candles, and went back into the larger crypt – for though I trust I am not so effeminate as to be rendered nervous by hearing a noise for which I cannot instantly account; still, on occasions of this kind, I must honestly say I should prefer that they did not occur. As I came towards the iron door, there was another distinct (I almost said hurried) sound. The impression on my mind was one of great haste. When I reached the door, and held the candle near the lock to take out the key, I perceived that the other one, which hung by a short string to its fellow, was vibrating slightly. I should have preferred not to find it vibrating, as there seemed no occasion for such a course; but I put them both into my pocket, and turned to go back to my work. As I turned, I saw on the ground what had occasioned the louder noise I had heard, namely, a skull which had evidently just slipped from its place on the top of one of the walls of bones, and had rolled almost to my feet. There, disclosing a few more inches of the top of an archway behind, was the place from which it had been dislodged. I stooped to pick it up, but fearing to displace any more skulls by meddling with the pile, and not liking to gather up its scattered teeth, I let it lie, and went back to my work, in which I was soon so completely absorbed that I was only roused at last by my candles beginning to burn low and go out one after another.

Then, with a sigh of regret, for I had not nearly finished, I turned to go. Poor Brian, who had never quite reconciled himself to the place, was beside himself with delight. As I opened the iron door he pushed past me, and a moment later I heard him whining and scratching, and I had almost added, beating, against the wooden one. I locked the iron door, and hurried down the passage as quickly as I could, and almost before I had got the other one ajar there seemed to be a rush past me into the open air, and Brian was bounding up the steps and out of sight. As I stopped to take out the key, I felt quite deserted and left behind. When I came out once more into the sunlight, there was a vague sensation all about me in the air of exultant freedom.

It was already late in the afternoon, and after I had sauntered back to the parsonage to give up the keys, I persuaded the people of the public house to let me join in the family meal, which was spread out in the kitchen. The inhabitants of Wet Waste were primitive people, with the frank, unabashed manner that flourishes still in lonely places, especially in the wilds of Yorkshire; but I had no idea that in these days of penny posts and cheap newspapers such entire ignorance of the outer world could have existed in any corner, however remote, of Great Britain.

When I took one of the neighbour's children on my knee – a pretty little girl with the palest aureole of flaxen hair I had ever seen – and began to draw pictures for her of the birds and beasts of other countries, I was instantly surrounded by a crowd of children, and even grown-up people, while others came to their doorways and looked on from a distance, calling to each other in the strident unknown tongue which I have since discovered goes by the name of "Broad Yorkshire".

The following morning, as I came out of my room, I perceived that something was amiss in the village. A buzz of voices reached me as I passed the bar, and in the next house I could hear through the open window a high-pitched wail of lamentation.

The woman who brought me my breakfast was in tears, and in answer to my questions told me that the neighbour's child, the little girl whom I had taken on my knee the evening before, had died in the night.

I felt sorry for the general grief that the little creature's death seemed to arouse, and the uncontrolled wailing of the poor mother took my appetite away.

I hurried off early to my work, calling on my way for the keys, and with Brian for my companion descended once more into the crypt, and drew and measured with an absorption that gave me no time that day to listen for sounds real or fancied. Brian, too, on this occasion seemed quite content, and slept peacefully beside me on the stone floor. When I had worked as long as I could, I put away my books with regret that even then I had not quite finished, as I had hoped to do. It would be necessary to come again for a short time on the morrow. When I returned the keys late that afternoon, the old clergyman met me at the door and asked me to come in and have tea with him.

"And has the work prospered?" he asked, as we sat down in the long, low room into which I had just been ushered, and where he seemed to live entirely.

I told him it had, and showed it to him.

"You have seen the original, of course?" I said.

"Once," he replied, gazing fixedly at it. He evidently did not care to be communicative, so I turned the conversation to the age of the church.

"All here is old," he said. "When I was young, forty years ago, and came here because I had no means of mine own, and was much moved to marry at that time, I felt oppressed that all was so old; and that this place was so far removed from the world, for which I had at times longing grievous to be borne; but I had chosen my lot, and with it I was forced to be content. My son, marry not in youth, for love, which truly in that season is a mighty power, turns away the heart from study, and young children break the back of ambition. Neither marry in middle life, when woman is seen to be but a woman and her talk a weariness, so you will not be burdened with a wife in your old age."

I had my own views on the subject of marriage, for I am of the opinion that a well-chosen companion of domestic tastes and docile and devoted temperament may be of material assistance to a professional man. But my opinions once formulated, it is not of moment to me to discuss them with others, so I changed the subject, and asked if the neighbouring villages were as antiquated as Wet Waste.

"Yes, all about here is old," he repeated. "The paved road leading to Dyke Fens is an ancient pack road, made even in the time of the Romans. Dyke Fens, which is very near here, a matter of but four or five miles, is likewise old, and forgotten by the world. The Reformation never reached it. It stopped here. And at Dyke Fens they still have a priest and a bell, and bow down before the saints. It is a damnable heresy, and weekly I expound it as such to my people, showing them true doctrines; and I have heard that this same priest has so far yielded himself to the Evil One that he has preached against me as withholding gospel truths from my flock; but I take no heed of it, neither of his pamphlet touching the Clementine Homilies, in which he vainly contradicts that which I have plainly set forth and proven beyond doubt, concerning the word *Asaph*."

The old man was fairly off on his favourite subject, and it

was some time before I could get away. As it was, he followed me to the door, and I only escaped because the old clerk hobbled up at that moment, and claimed his attention.

The following morning I went for the keys for the third and last time. I had decided to leave early the next day. I was tired of Wet Waste, and a certain gloom seemed to my fancy to be gathering over the place. There was a sensation of trouble in the air as if, although the day was bright and clear, a storm were coming.

This morning, to my astonishment, the keys were refused to me when I asked for them. I did not, however, take the refusal as final – I make it a rule never to take a refusal as final – and after a short delay I was shown into the room where, as usual, the clergyman was sitting, or rather, on this occasion, was walking up and down.

"My son," he said with vehemence, "I know wherefore you have come, but it is of no avail. I cannot lend the keys again."

I replied that, on the contrary, I hoped he would give them to me at once.

"It is impossible," he repeated. "I did wrong, exceeding wrong. I will never part with them again."

"Why not?"

He hesitated, and then said slowly: "The old clerk, Abraham Kelly, died last night." He paused, and then went on: "The doctor has just been here to tell me of that which is a mystery to him. I do not wish the people of the place to know it, and only to me he has mentioned it, but he has discovered plainly on the throat of the old man, and also, but more faintly on the child's, marks as of strangulation. None but he has observed it, and he is at a loss how to account for it. I, alas, can account for it but in one way, but in one way!"

I did not see what all this had to do with the crypt, but to humour the old man, I asked what that way was.

"It is a long story, and to a stranger it may appear but foolishness, but I will even tell it; for I perceive that unless I furnish a reason for withholding the keys, you will not cease to entreat me for them.

"I told you at first when you enquired of me concerning the crypt, that it had been closed these thirty years, and so it was. Thirty years ago a certain Sir Roger Despard departed this life, the Lord of the Manor of Wet Waste and Dyke Fens, the last of his family, which is now, thank the Lord, extinct. He was a man of a vile life, neither fearing God nor regarding man, nor having compassion on innocence, and the Lord appeared to have given him over to the tormentors even in this world, for he suffered many things of his vices, more especially from drunkenness, in which seasons, and they were many, he was as one possessed by seven devils, being an abomination to his household and a root of bitterness to all, both high and low.

"And, at last, the cup of his iniquity being full to the brim, he came to die, and I went to exhort him on his death-bed; for I heard that terror had come upon him, and that evil imaginations encompassed him so thick on every side that few of them that were with him could abide in his presence. But when I saw him I perceived that there was no place of repentance left for him, and he scoffed at me and my superstition, even as he lay dying, and swore there was no God and no angels, and all were damned even as he was. And the next day, towards evening, the pains of death came upon him, and he raved the more exceedingly, inasmuch as he said he was being strangled by the Evil One. Now on his table was his hunting knife, and with his last strength he crept and laid hold upon it, no man withstanding him, and swore a great oath that if he went down to burn in Hell, he would leave one of his hands behind on earth, and that it would never rest until it had drawn blood from the throat of another and strangled him, even as he himself was being strangled. And he cut off his own right hand at the wrist, and no man dared go near him to stop him, and the blood went through the floor, even down to the ceiling of the room below, and thereupon he died.

"And they called me in the night, and told me of his oath, and I counselled that no man should speak of it, and I took the dead hand, which none had ventured to touch, and I laid it beside him in his coffin; for I thought it better he should take it with him, so that he might have it, if some day after much tribulation he should perchance be moved to stretch forth his hands towards God. But the story got spread about, and the people were affrighted, so, when he came to be buried in the place of his fathers, he being the last of his family, and the crypt likewise full, I had it closed, and kept the keys myself, and suffered no man to enter therein any more; for truly he was a man of an evil life, and the devil is not yet wholly overcome, nor cast chained into the lake of fire. So in time the story died out, for in thirty years much is forgotten. And when you came and asked me for the keys, I was at the first minded to withhold them; but I thought it was a vain superstition, and I perceived that you do but ask a second time for what is first refused; so I let you have them, seeing it was not an idle curiosity, but a desire to improve the talent committed to you, that led you to require them."

The old man stopped, and I remained silent, wondering what would be the best way to get them just once more.

"Surely, sir," I said at last, "one so cultivated and deeply read as yourself cannot be biased by an idle superstition."

"I trust not," he replied, "and yet – it is a strange thing that since the crypt was opened two people have died, and the mark is plain upon the throat of the old man and visible on the young child. No blood was drawn, but the second time the grip was stronger than the first. The third time, perchance—"

"Superstition such as that," I said with authority, "is an entire want of faith in God. You once said so yourself."

I took a high moral tone which is often efficacious with conscientious, humble-minded people.

He agreed, and accused himself of not having as much faith as a grain of mustard seed; but even when I had got him so far as that, I had a severe struggle for the keys. It was only when I finally explained to him that if any malign influence had been let loose the first day, at any rate, it was out now for good or evil, and no further going or coming of mine could make any difference, that I finally gained my point. I was young, and he was old; and, being much shaken by what had occurred, he gave way at last, and I wrested the keys from him.

I will not deny that I went down the steps that day with a vague, indefinable repugnance, which was only accentuated by the closing of the two doors behind me. I remembered then, for the first time, the faint jangling of the key and other sounds which I had noticed the first day, and how one of the skulls had fallen. I went to the place where it still lay. I have already said these walls of skulls were built up so high as to be within a few inches of the top of the low archways that led into more distant portions of the vault. The displacement of the skull in question had left a small hole just large enough for me to put my hand through. I noticed for the first time, over the archway above it, a carved coat-of-arms, and the name, now almost obliterated, of Despard. This, no doubt, was the Despard vault. I could not resist moving a few more skulls and looking in, holding my candle as near the aperture as I could. The vault was full. Piled high, one upon another, were old coffins, and remnants of coffins, and strewn bones. I attribute my present determination to be cremated to the painful impression produced on me by this spectacle. The coffin nearest the archway alone was intact, save for a large crack across the lid. I could not get a ray from my candle to fall on the brass plates, but I felt no doubt this was the coffin of the wicked Sir Roger. I put back the skulls, including the one which had rolled down, and carefully finished my work. I was not there much more than an hour, but I was glad to get away.

If I could have left Wet Waste at once I should have done so, for I had a totally unreasonable longing to leave the place; but I found that only one train stopped during the day at the station from which I had come, and that it would not be possible to be in time for it that day.

Accordingly I submitted to the inevitable, and wandered about with Brian for the remainder of the afternoon and until late in the evening, sketching and smoking. The day was oppressively hot, and even after the sun had set across the burned stretches of the Wolds, it seemed to grow very little cooler. Not a breath stirred. In the evening, when I was tired of loitering in the lanes, I went up to my own room, and after contemplating afresh my finished study of the fresco, I suddenly set to work to write the part of my paper bearing upon it. As a rule, I write with difficulty, but that evening words came to me with winged speed, and with them a hovering impression that I must make haste, that I was much pressed for time. I wrote and wrote, until my candles guttered out and left me trying to finish by the moonlight, which, until I endeavoured to write by it, seemed as clear as day.

I had to put away my manuscript and, feeling it was too early to go to bed, for the church clock was just counting out ten, I sat down by the open window and leaned out to try and catch a breath of air. It was a night of exceptional beauty; and as I looked out my nervous haste and hurry of mind were allayed. The moon, a perfect circle, was – if so poetic an expression be permissible – as it were, sailing across a calm sky. Every detail of the little village was as clearly illuminated by its beams as if it were broad day; so, also, was the adjacent church with its primeval yews, while even the Wolds beyond were dimly indicated, as if through tracing paper.

I sat a long time leaning against the window sill. The heat was still intense. I am not, as a rule, easily elated or readily cast down; but as I sat that night in the lonely village on the moors, with Brian's head against my knee, how, or why, I know not, a great depression gradually came upon me.

My mind went back to the crypt and the countless dead who had been laid there. The sight of the goal to which all human life, and strength, and beauty, travel in the end, had not affected me at the time, but now the very air about me seemed heavy with death.

What was the good, I asked myself, of working and toiling, and grinding down my heart and youth in the mill of long and strenuous effort, seeing that in the grave folly and talent, idleness and labour, lie together, and are alike forgotten? Labour seemed to stretch before me till my heart ached to think of it, to stretch before me even to the end of life, and then came, as the recompense of my labour – the grave. Even if I succeeded – if, after wearing my life threadbare with toil, I succeeded, what remained to me in the end? The grave. A little sooner, while the hands and eyes were still strong to labour, or a little later, when all power and vision had been taken from them; sooner or later only – the *grave*.

I do not apologize for the excessively morbid tenor of these reflections, as I hold that they were caused by the lunar effects which I have endeavoured to transcribe. The moon in its various quarterings has always exerted a marked influence on what I may call the sub-dominant, namely, the poetic side of my nature.

I roused myself at last, when the moon came to look in upon me where I sat, and, leaving the window open, I pulled myself together and went to bed.

I fell asleep almost immediately, but I do not fancy I could have been asleep very long when I was wakened by Brian. He was growling in a low, muffled tone, as he sometimes did in his sleep, when his nose was buried in his rug. I called out to him to shut up; and as he did not do so, turned in bed to find my match box or something to throw at him. The moonlight was still in the room, and as I looked at him I saw him raise his head and evidently wake up. I admonished him, and was just on the point of falling asleep when he began to growl again in a low, savage manner that waked me most effectually. Presently he shook himself and got up, and began prowling about the room. I sat up in bed and called to him, but he paid no attention. Suddenly I saw him stop short in the moonlight; he showed his teeth, and crouched down, his eyes following something in the air. I looked at him in horror. Was he going mad? His eyes were glaring, and his head moved slightly as if he were following the rapid movements of an enemy. Then, with a furious snarl, he suddenly sprang from the ground, and rushed in great leaps across the room towards me, dashing himself against the furniture, his eyes rolling, snatching and tearing wildly in the air with his teeth. I saw he had gone mad. I leaped out of bed and, rushing at him, caught him by the throat. The moon had gone behind a cloud; but in the darkness I felt him turn upon me, felt him rise up, and his teeth close in my throat. I was being strangled. With all the strength of despair, I kept my grip of his neck and, dragging him across the room, tried to crush in his head against the iron rail of my bedstead. It was my only chance. I felt the blood running down my neck. I was suffocating. After one moment of frightful struggle, I beat his head against the bar and heard his skull give way. I felt him give one strong shudder, a groan, and then I fainted away.

When I came to myself I was lying on the floor, surrounded by the people of the house, my reddened hands still clutching Brian's throat. Someone was holding a candle towards me, and the draught from the window made it flare and waver. I looked at Brian. He was stone dead. The blood from his battered head was trickling slowly over my hands. His great jaw was fixed in something that – in the uncertain light – I could not see.

They turned the light a little.

"Oh, God!" I shrieked. "There! Look! Look!"

"He's off his head," said someone, and I fainted again.

I was ill for about a fortnight without regaining consciousness, a waste of time of which even now I cannot think without poignant regret. When I did recover consciousness, I found I was being carefully nursed by the old clergyman and the people of the house. I have often heard the unkindness of the world in general inveighed against, but for my part I can honestly say that I have received many more kindnesses than I have time to repay. Country people especially are remarkably attentive to strangers in illness.

I could not rest until I had seen the doctor who attended me, and had received his assurance that I should be equal to reading my paper on the appointed day. This pressing anxiety removed, I told him of what I had seen before I fainted the second time. He listened attentively, and then assured me, in a manner that was intended to be soothing, that I was suffering from a hallucination, due, no doubt, to the shock of my dog's sudden madness.

"Did you see the dog after it was dead?" I asked. He said he did. The whole jaw was covered with blood and foam; the teeth certainly seemed convulsively fixed, but the case being evidently one of extraordinarily virulent hydrophobia, owing to the intense heat, he had had the body buried immediately.

My companion stopped speaking as we reached our lodgings, and went upstairs. Then, lighting a candle, he slowly turned down his collar.

"You see I have the marks still," he said, "but I have no fear of dying of hydrophobia. I am told such peculiar scars could not have been made by the teeth of a dog. If you look closely you see the pressure of the five fingers. That is the reason why I wear high collars."

Another One in from the Cold

Marion Arnott

For one moment, for one awful moment, she thought Gavin
was going to say, in that clipped and brooking no argument
way he had, "We're not putting up with any of this nonsense."
But of course he was talking to BBC Scotland, not to her; and
the busy BBC man was more than his equal in not brooking
argument. Their time slot, he said firmly, would be on 11
November, sandwiched between the dipping of the flags, and
the Last Post. Gavin smiled as if satisfied, but grumbled all the
way across the glossy polished paving which ran the length of
the Cloth Hall.

"They really don't have much idea, do they, Kate? Patrick's
story should be a feature on its own, not just a mention in the
Armistice Day slot. We've come all the way to Ieper for his
burial. We should read parts of his letters – letters from ninety
years ago. Ninety! It's so short-sighted to keep the ceremony
so . . ." he flapped a hand ". . . general and unspecific when they
could make it more personal and . . ." flap, flap ". . . specific."

"The ceremony is supposed to represent everyone," she
said mildly, "and we're laying a wreath, Gavin. They're going
to film that. And they'll be at the funeral next day."

"Yes, but . . ." He broke off. "Well, you have been rather
underwhelmed by the whole thing from the start. Surprising
considering he was your relative."

His breath in the cold air formed little puffs of cloud, like smoke signals. I-AM-REPROACHING-YOU, the signals read. She responded with a white puff of her own, sighing out I-DON T-CARE on a long breath, but derived no satisfaction from it since he didn't notice. His arm swung up, pointing. "Look! This is where Patrick stood. You remember the photo – Patrick and the mule, halfway between the buttresses? Of course the water jets weren't there then. Go and stand in front of them. I'll take your picture."

She did not want to stand where Patrick had; it did not matter that she would stand before a rebuilt magnificence of creamy stone and fluttering pennants; in her mind's eye she saw smashed ruins and hillocks of broken stone, sullen grey fading to colourlessness, and Patrick grinning and holding a mule by a rope. *The Famous Kicker*! he had written in flowing copperplate on the back of the photo postcard.

> *This mule today kicked a Private, then a Corporal, then a Sergeant, then a Second Lieutenant. I always stand well to the front!*
>   *Cheer-ho!*
>   *Patrick*
>   *March, 1917*

She blinked away the image and stood half-paralysed by the same creeping unease which had squirmed inside her since their arrival in Ieper. It was like nausea, only warmer. She had felt it on the Ramparts, at the Flanders Museum, and now at the Cloth Hall, and it made her want to run away, to run and run and run. She had told Gavin about the squirmy feeling but he said that at only two months gone, nothing could possibly be moving yet, that she mustn't get broody. She mustn't.

"Kate!" He flapped his hand at her.

She steeled herself and crossed to the rectangular pond sunk into the stone. Its honour guard of thin water jets arched high and crystal cold into brilliant blue sky; she stood in front of them, trying to smile, but she could *feel* the gothic façade of the Cloth Hall pressing close behind her, its pointed churchy windows and gilded curlicues much too close and not how they should be. They were not *right*: too whole, too new, too clean. Where was the mist of dust which had thickened the air and lain fine in the creases of Patrick's tunic? It had hung like a thin sepia veil over the ruins of the great hall in 1917, and again on the day they arrived in Ieper. She had seen it.

"What mist?" Gavin had said when she mentioned it. "The air is clear as a bell."

Then she had known and understood; now she struggled to stand still for the photo. She wanted to run. She wanted to be sick.

"Say cheese, Kate! Smile a while!"

In a sudden light wind, the tall jets hunched over, shivered, and broke into icy rags and tatters. Bright water sprayed across her face, startling her into laughter. Gavin's camera whirred happily.

"That's more like it, Kate. You don't laugh often enough. Not much at all these days."

He slipped an arm round her as they walked away. "You have diamond droplets on your eyelashes." He fished out a handkerchief and dabbed the spray from her eyes. "You're the prettiest girl in town when you're smiling and sparkly." He drew her closer. She was embarrassed by a surge of relief at the return of tenderness. "By the end of next week it will all be over and everything back to normal."

He was quietly insistent. All-be-over was scheduled for next Friday lunchtime, a quick and unremarkable medical procedure, but he did not trust her acquiescence. He did not want children; neither did she. But still he must constantly be reassured that she was going through with all-be-over; that they would continue with the life they had planned together, their cycle of travelling, meeting up with friends, lounging at their summer house in Eire, buying expensive items for their stately Victorian flat in Glasgow. The flat and its pale deep rugs and polished floors were his major arguments against children: imagine sticky fingers! Roller blades! The danger to the Rennie McIntosh glass! He laughed to prove the joke, but he meant it all, and watched her constantly, looking for changes in her, wordlessly demanding that she be as she had always been.

"You should have a special time next weekend," he said, to reward her smiles. "What kind of pampering would you like?"

I would like, she thought, to be allowed to be a little affected by about-to-be-over, just a little; and I would like not to be affected by this place. But neither was likely and she could not share the unease with him.

They were still walking in the shadow of the hall, a shadow deep and dark, even on this bright day. The chill seeped up through the paving, wrapped round her and slid inside the collar of her jacket.

Mum, Patrick had written, *Thanks for the scarf and mittens. Just the ticket out here. The cold gets everywhere. March, 1917*

"You've gone quite pale," he said.

"I'm cold."

"There's a café," he said. "Let's have a hot chocolate. Warm us up."

She smelled the chocolate in the air, wafting round her face, warm and rich; she felt fingers of cold ruffle the hairs at the nape of her neck. She retched. Gavin let go of her suddenly.

"Morning sickness. You haven't had that before," he said accusingly.

"It's the chocolate. The smell is over sweet."

He swept her past the café. "I thought we'd agreed we're not having any of that nonsense!"

But it wasn't *that* nonsense, of course. It was something else entirely, something that only Great-Great-Auntie Rowan would understand.

★ ★ ★

Rowan lived in a white croft which dreamed by the side of the loch at Inverash. Kate visited her for a month every year in the summer holidays. There she could look up to the sky and study the frail white elegance of trailing clouds, and down at still water and see the pale shadows of sky; she could look into Rowan's eyes and see traces of a blue clear as the summer loch, clouded now by great old age, and hear her say, "Patrick had the same blue eyes, like mine, like yours."

As a child, Kate, standing on tiptoe, had puzzled over the old photographs ranged along the tall wooden mantelpiece, trying to see the blue. But the smiling boy in the stiff new uniform was a composition in shades of shadow; even the tartan trews and diced cap, which she knew to be bright coloured, were grey and greyish and darker grey. The eyes, though, had a curious lightness, and smiled mischief directly at her wherever she stood in the room. The other brothers, Alexander and Charlie, stared sightlessly into the distance, but Patrick sought her out. Even aged seven, she knew that Patrick knew her. And being only seven, she thought nothing of it; Rowan was comfortable with Patrick and Charlie and Alexander, and therefore so was she. She looked at their photos and their battered old school books. ("That's a Latin grammar," Rowan said of the one with the blue cloth cover and the gold stamp. "That was Patrick's. He was clever. He was going to the University at Glasgow, but then the war came.")

For years, Kate had thought the war ended in June 1917, because after that date, Rowan had nothing to say about it. But time was a confused concept at Inverash. Every Sunday afternoon, Rowan and she went to the rowan tree at the gate to polish the sixpenny pieces nailed to its bark. In June the blossom hung low in thick creamy clusters and, while Kate polished, Rowan used to pick some and thread it into Kate's hair while she told the story of the sixpences as if for the first time.

"The boys carved their initials there before they went away. There, see? C. A. P., one on top of the other, 1914. And after Charlie and Alex were killed, and Patrick lost, all three in 1917,

my father used to scrape the initials clean of lichen every now
and then. Mother had a sixpence which Charlie had in his
pocket when he was killed. It was new-minted, a 1917 coin,
and somehow she could not bring herself to spend it. And
whenever she got another 1917 sixpence, she could not spend
that either, so she kept them in a jam-jar on the windowsill.
And then one warm June night, two years after the war was
over, she woke to find Father gone from the bed and heard
banging and cursing. He was out at the gate in the moonlight
with the jar of coins, a hammer, and long thin nails, and he was
hammering sixpences into the initials to make them permanent. And with one bang he'd cry 'My sons! My sons!' and
with the next a curse word, and the blossom, all ghostly white
in the moonlight, showered from the tree and lay in his hair
and round his feet. He hammered in a new date too: 1917.
Mother was afraid that night, for he hammered like a devil in
hell, he who had been a tower of strength, never shedding so
much as a tear for his sons, but going about his business as
usual, straight-backed and quiet-spoken. She brought him
back to bed eventually and the floor and the quilt and the
pillows were thick with the little flowers and their heady
perfume. It was days before Mother was able to get all the
blossom shaken out of the bedding, a week before the scent
faded," Rowan said.

And days before it faded from her hair too, Kate remembered. On Sunday nights, after the polishing, she always stood
at the bedroom window, brushing the rowan flowers and
pollen out of her hair. She looked out over the loch, bright
silver in moonlight, or black silk in the dark, and at the lacy
silhouette of the rowan tree at the gate, to try and make out the
sombre gleam of the initials of three boys, two dead and one
lost. Sometimes "A" and "C" and "1914" were obscured by
hanging flowers, but "P" and "1917" were further down the
trunk and winked gently through the warm gloom.

Rowan often stood with her, checking that her hair was
properly brushed and her teeth cleaned before bed, talking
about the boys.

"What do you see out there?" she asked once.

"The tree and shiny sixpences."

"Maybe if you look hard enough you'll see the boys. They're around here somewhere. Charlie and Alex at any rate. Where Patrick is, I cannot tell. He was lost. Missing in action, presumed killed."

While Rowan talked, Kate listened to the quiet darkness, to the lap of the water on the shingle.

"They used to come tearing down the hillside, whooping like apaches, and run along the loch side, laughing. The sound carried for miles across the water – the minister used to say he could hear them in his wee white church on the other side. And when they got to the gate, they scuffled to get in first, leap up, and smack the branches of the tree. Such a sight they were, elbowing one another out of the way. It still makes me laugh."

Kate was a teenager before she realized that Rowan could never have seen the boys playing since she was born long after they were killed. "That's right," Rowan agreed. "I was the result of the night Father hammered in the sixpences, which is how I got my name. I was either Rowan or Despair, my mother always said. Rowan was prettier." She stirred the tea in her cup and smiled. "But all the same, I've heard Charlie and Alex laughing. I've seen them often too, tearing down the hillside. I still do. Never Patrick though."

The verdict of the family was that Rowan was a little crazy but harmless, contaminated by the grief of her parents and thinking their memories her own. Kate never argued the point but she knew Rowan wasn't crazy. On warm summer nights when the loch was a black disc with a yellow moon floating in it, she too sometimes heard the thud of running feet and the silvery giggles of young boys, very faint, as if coming from a long way off. It might have been a dream, or the effect of Rowan's talk, but Kate thought time had no meaning here, for it overlapped and sprawled backwards and sideways and didn't know that its proper place was marching forward in a straight line.

★ ★ ★

Gavin enjoyed being a celebrity, which was why they ate at Café Franz each night. They had been identified as the relatives of the soldier brought in from the cold after ninety years missing; this fact conferred a certain status among the habitués of the Armistice Day ceremonies. Café Franz was the haunt of the British who came with little wooden crosses and poppies and wreaths as gifts for the dead they had come to visit. They huddled round the red-and-white checked tablecloths which covered small round tables, removed their Aran sweaters when the room warmed up, and did their best to relive the Great War. Kate loathed it all.

From floor to ceiling the walls of the café were hung with ancient photographs of smiling boys in khaki and grim-faced men in khaki; worst were the ones, men and boys, who tried to smile beneath their haunted eyes. In khaki. In puttees. In kilts. In British Warms. Even in turbans. Then there were the photos of the gassed, the wounded, the shell-shocked, in trenches, in casualty stations, in ambulances, on trains. Their dead eyes gazed palely down at the company gathered in their honour. Kate could not meet that gaze and fiddled with her knife and fork while Gavin told yet again the story of Patrick's reappearance: the man digging up his garden to make a patio; the sudden summer storm which raged all night; the heavy clay soil which shifted and heaved and thrust up the detritus of war: the bullet casings, a tin cup, a toothbrush, a thin white bone which turned out to be a finger beckoning (how Gavin enjoyed telling that, his hand raised, his finger curled in a summons), a hand emerging, an arm extending, stretching, reaching ...

"Every year it happens," the man in the Manchester United T-shirt said. "The earth pushes them up and we bring them in from the cold." He drained his pint. "They want to be found."

Gavin nodded. "Yes. Patrick came to the surface on the anniversary of the day he was killed – the seventh of September 1917."

There was a moment's respectful silence and then the Man

U fan raised his glass. "And now he'll have a proper burial. Peace at last. Here's to Patrick."

Glasses were drained all round the café. Peace, Kate thought bitterly. Why would Patrick be any more at peace in the little white coffin in Ramparts Cemetery than he had been happed up in the clay in someone's back garden? He had never been at peace; the earth hadn't pushed him up – he had struggled out of his muddy shroud and brought her here to Ieper.

She toyed with her mineral water. No wine for a pregnant lady, as if it mattered. But the leaflets from the doctor's surgery had been quite definite – no alcohol. It was odd how authoritative a leaflet could be, even to a soon-to-be-over pregnant lady.

"… They are all around here. You can feel them. I like to think they know we're here, that they're not forgotten." It was the man from Newcastle speaking. He had a tendency to sentimentalize. "There are times I think of my young great-grandfather, who never lived to see his son. The week before he was born, great-granny woke screaming and saw her husband at the foot of the bed. He appeared out of a stinking brown mist – we reckon that was the mist of cordite and explosives that hung over the Somme valley – and there was a great hole in his chest all gushing with blood. Ghastly pale he was and he leaned forward as if to touch her belly and cried, 'Christ! I wish I'd seen that bairn!' and then disappeared."

And, of course, Kate thought, it turned out that he had been killed – shot in the chest – on the very night he appeared to his wife. All their stories ended like that – with a supernatural punchline, the resolution of longing in a spectral return home.

"And often I wish that I could see him, that one time I'll turn a corner and there he'll be."

Oh, you wouldn't like it if he was, she thought silently.

"Imagine being able to talk to him," Newcastle said wonderingly, "and to ask him what it was really like."

"I don't suppose you'd have much to say to one another after all these years!"

She hadn't meant to speak aloud, or so sharply, but the

words rose up and out like fizz. Fear, she realized, had the qualities of champagne.

The big man continued as if she hadn't spoken. "He'd want to know about the bairn, of course," he said. "And all the other bairns that came after."

It is spring at last, Mum and Dad, even in this place. Imagine my surprise to see bare blasted trees putting out little green buds; and there's a blackbird nesting not twenty yards from where we are entrenched. I hear her every morning, whistling with the important business of sitting on her eggs while the big guns boom with the important business of destruction. Corporal Mackenzie died this morning. A sniper shot. He lived for a few minutes after he fell but did not have much pain. He lay looking up at the sky. "It's spring," he said, surprised. The blackbird was singing and I thought what a hard thing it was to die listening to the happy burbling of the wild birds.

We said a prayer over him and then made tea. The edge was off the wind and the earth warm and stirring. Soon we were laughing and joking. What a force life is, even out here. But my head is full of thoughts which there is not time to write. When I come home, then we'll talk.

Cheer-ho!

Patrick

May, 1917

Suddenly things were unbearable. The stony faces on the walls frowned down at her; Newcastle, who was after all a civil soul, drifted into a reverie; Gavin was trying to catch her eye. She got to her feet and retreated through the door that led into the courtyard where the toilets were. The last of the autumn leaves were thick on the cobbles and crunchy underfoot. She scuffed through them, then was irritated when a gust of wind snatched them up and threw them prickling against her legs. The wind blew from the road that led to the Lille Gate and past the moat which enclosed Ramparts Cemetery, where Patrick would lie.

She had first seen the place from the other side of the moat:
from a distance, the creamy headstones, stalwart on thick
green lawn, looked like a stubby little village huddling under
the trees. At Gavin's insistence they had crossed to go in and
she had posed for a photo at the foot of the Cross of Sacrifice.
The air was sharp with chrysanthemum scent which rose like
thin smoke from the ragged clumps planted at each grave;
sombre in their funeral purples and golds, the flowers sighed
out the bitterness of the dying days of autumn and the finish
of things. Patrick's grave was open and ready to receive him.
And she was here to learn at last what he wanted.

The nights at Inverash were full of sound: the water lapped
and the trees sighed and the owl in the woods to the rear of
the house hooted mournfully. There were whispers too, boys'
whispers, as they slipped out of the back door and into the
woods, looking for badgers, or going down to swim in the
dark, which was strictly forbidden but Mum and Dad slept
deeply. Rowan was always pleased when Kate told her she'd
heard them, and disappointed when Kate was sure there were
only two.

They used to sit in the evening and read the letters, which
were carefully stored in a square metal biscuit tin. Charlie's
and Alex's were short, hoping everyone was as well at home as
they were in France and Flanders, and please to send some
tobacco; but Patrick, the clever one, wrote often and at length:

> ... *Jinty was bringing up the rear when we crawled back into
> the trenches and suddenly Fritz opened fire. Well, the bullets
> pinged off the wire and whizzed into the tin cans, and some
> of them hit Jinty's kilt, and next thing we knew, he was leap-
> ing up and down, flipping his kilt up to keep the smoulder
> off his legs, skirling like a banshee. Talk about a Highland
> Fling! Anyway, the snipers' bullets started falling short. They
> were probably laughing too much to take aim and Jinty got
> back in alive. There wasn't a mark on him, except for a little
> embarrassing singeing.*

Cheer-ho!
Patrick
April, 1917

Kate had told the English teacher about the jokes and laughing when they were studying Wilfred Owen, but the teacher felt that Patrick had rather missed the point if he wasn't doom-laden and star-crossed. Kate thought the teacher had missed the point.

> *The worst thing would have been not keeping my end up. I was more afraid of that than anything else the first weeks. But I'm all right now. When it's time to go over the bags, when the whistles blow, something rises in me like the sap in spring and carries me along. I wouldn't call it courage. In both life and death there is nothing for it but to go forward. So forward it is.*
> *Cheer-ho,*
> *Patrick.*
> *August 1917*

There were letters too from hospitals all over the country in response to the family's enquiries about a soldier who might have lost his memory, or been too ill to know who he was, a Scottish soldier, five foot six, dark-haired, blue-eyed.

"She wrote to hospitals for years. She never gave up hope," Rowan said. "The day he disappeared, there was an advance into autumn mist and gun fog. One minute he was there and the next not and no one saw what happened. So he might have been picked up or captured or lying bleeding in the mud. She was tormented for years by the thought that he might be somewhere. Because living or dead, he must be somewhere. Somewhere."

One night Kate and Rowan sat on the front step looking over the loch – it was too warm for bed or to sit inside – and shared dreams about what might have happened to Patrick. All the endings were happy until the realization that in life they hadn't been silenced them.

"We can only hope it was a clean shot," Rowan said, and went to bed first. Kate looked across at the winking silver coins on the rowan tree. Patrick's looked duller than the other two. She stared – no, it was shining as brightly – then, no it wasn't. It was duller. Then brighter. Then dull again. A shadow? She glanced up at the sky, but it was clear of clouds and full of stars. She stared harder at the coin and it was as if the still air was gathering round it, not darker but thicker. She watched as the sixpence was gradually obscured by air as thick as syrup. She watched and then leaped to her feet and ran inside, locking the door behind her. In seconds she was in her room with the curtains drawn and the light on, but she could not shut out the sound of whispers and low laughter. The boys were on the path to the gate, scuffling, and then someone slapped the tree, and then someone else. And then a third. She flicked back the curtain, but there was nothing to see, only the coins twinkling and showers of blossom falling lightly and silently on to the grass.

Next day, she could hardly bear the eager flare of hope in Rowan's eyes when she was told the story, or the mischief in the eyes of the lost soldier on the mantelpiece.

"Kate!"

Gavin. Impatient. She wondered how long she had been standing here.

"Kate. Aren't you coming back inside? It's cold out here."

"Just getting a breath of fresh air."

"You were rather rude to that man, you know."

He was in the doorway with the light behind him, a bulky faceless shadow with a peevish voice which grated. She turned to face him.

"Was I? They're a bit much sometimes."

"You could show a polite interest."

"You laughed hard enough at the one who's dug a replica trench, complete with sandbags, in his allotment." She paused. "When we got back to the hotel anyway. But I'll allow you were polite and interested to his face."

They were spared an argument by the creak of the door set in the yard wall, then footsteps and the rustle of fallen leaves. Another shadow appeared out of the darkness. She froze. It was in uniform, complete with puttees and soup-plate tin hat, carrying a rifle. The squirming in her stomach was like live eels and she gasped.

"Sorry, hen. Didn't mean to startle you."

A thick Scottish accent, a broad face with a smile like the one on a Hallowe'en lantern. She stood unable to move or speak until he had passed by into the café.

"Kate, you look like you've seen a ghost."

Patrick? His name dropped into her mind like an envelope falling on the mat. Was that Patrick? But no, Patrick was finer-featured, smaller. Gavin was beside her now, patting at her arm.

"Come inside. That was one of the re-enactors. They're here for a sing-song round the piano. Songs of the Great War."

Re-enactors. Of course. After the Armistice Day parade, they were going to march out of Ieper and follow the route the troops took to Messines, living on tins of bully beef and plum jam. They were mad as hatters.

"Their uniforms are exact replicas," Gavin said. He laughed. "Gave you quite a turn, didn't he? Now come inside and join the party. There's a little surprise for you."

He pulled her gently inside, towed her right up to the bar, and stood expectantly, pointing to a place above the gantry. Patrick. The photo from Rowan's mantelpiece, black-framed with a scarlet poppy stuck to one corner.

"I had it copied," he said, "so that Patrick could take his place with the others."

He was waiting for thanks, she knew, but she could not find the words, not when her stomach was heaving and her mouth dry. Patrick stared down at her impishly, the dimple at the end of his grin deeper than she remembered. She could not look away from the face she had avoided for years. Was she imagining a knowing triumph in the clear light gaze? Was she imagining the colour creeping into the face? The blue light flooding the eyes, the pink flushing the skin, the deep black sweeping into the thick dense hair? He was in from the cold, warming up.

Words rattled round inside her skull like raindrops spattering on window glass: *Here I am, here I am. At last, at last, at la-aaa-ssst.* Her skull was transparent and he could see inside, she knew he could, her every thought, her every secret.

"Go away," she muttered. The dimple deepened and the eyes held her gaze. "Go," she said louder, but the piano player was thumping out crashing chords and no one heard her. And Patrick wouldn't go away anyway.

Voices roared into song. "*It's a long way to Tipperary, it's a long way to go . . .*" There were a dozen re-enactors round the piano, standing, slouching, leaning on one elbow as they sang. Lamplight shone on their brass buttons, their buckles, their glossy boots. The sight made her queasy. "Tipperary" was too much to take.

> *Everyone loves to sing that song as we march, Mum. Sing it and think of us and the long straight roads with the big trees growing like spears on either side.*
>   *Cheer-ho,*
>   *Patrick*
>   *August, 1917*

"Gavin – I have such a headache. I think I'll go back to the hotel."

"Playing up a bit, aren't we? Not giving into hormones, are we?"

"I can't speak for you."

He stiffened. "I'll walk you back if you must go."

"It's only across the street. You stay here and . . . sing. I'll be fine."

She saw his hesitation, but he was reluctant to give up his place as centre of attention, as relative of the resurrected hero.

She wriggled through the assembled singers and was out the door before he could follow.

★ ★ ★

Inverash became a place of unease. She took to keeping her curtains drawn and her window closed at night. It was small comfort because then she had to suffer the knowledge that the night air, thick and viscous, was pressing up against the window pane, feeling for a crack to slide through, oozing around the house, searching for a way in, wrapping it in cool heavy darkness, flooding it with a longing for . . . she didn't know what. She didn't want to know.

Rowan scoffed, saying that if Patrick came he would enter through the door like anyone else. It wasn't a helpful reply. Kate found herself awake half the night, listening for a footstep on the gravel path outside, for the click of the old-fashioned latch. In the evenings, she found excuses to avoid the reading of the letters because the air outside was always thicker when they read of his adventures in Flanders, as if the telling drew him closer. She knew he was listening, reliving those days, watching her. It was intolerable.

Rowan was hurt by her early nights and the books she had to read for school, but it couldn't be helped. Patrick wasn't pleased either. Night after night she lay in bed, knowing he was out there. She heard the muffled laughter, the excited whisper-ings like the buzzing of insects, and then the heavy silence when Charlie and Alexander wandered off down the path and left Patrick alone. She never heard him or saw him but knew he was there, waiting. He was the gently insistent tap of the tree branch on the window, not blown by a stray breeze, but regular and rhythmic, guided by someone; he was thick like warm summer air, dense as cat's fur rubbing at her wall, at her window, insistent, gentle, coaxing. He invaded her dreams in the form of a shadowy figure which ran silently into a brown mist and disappeared, and no matter how she peered, she could not see where he had gone. Once she woke to find herself at the window, hand clutching the curtain, ready to draw it back; another time she was in the hall at the front door. Both times she had a struggle to turn away: her hand would not let go of the curtain or the bolt; her feet would not take her away. Instead she listened and dreaded and sensed a smile in the darkness and, without her volition, her hand would reach forward to open, to let in a brownish mist or a lost soldier.

"What do you want?" she whispered each time, wrenching her hand away and holding it tightly behind her back.

No answer but the sigh of the waters of the loch and the whisper of leaves in the night breeze and a silence that listened hard. There was no one there and she did not know what that no one wanted.

Her last summer visit to Inverash was the time she sleep-walked to the parlour and woke up directly in front of the fireplace. He was smiling from the photograph frame, amused. She tried to turn away but was pinned to the floor where she stood while the colour crept into his face and made him seem alive. His head was tilted enquiringly at her. Rowan never believed that she had seen colour seep into the photo, but she had. He was warming up, gathering strength.

The following summer Kate said she was too busy to visit Rowan. And the next and the next. And soon Inverash and its unsettling experiences became part of childhood lore, a dream half forgotten, a nightmare half remembered.

The hotel was fifty yards down the street from Café Franz on the opposite side. Kate headed into the misty night, fishing her room key from her pocket as she went. She was thinking of Rowan and the old woman's hurt at her defection, all the phone calls asking when she would come again, her own guilty irritation at having to fend off the gentle urgings to visit, year after year.

Then came the call she could not ignore. Rowan babbled and wept and made no sense at first. She'd had a visit from a man from the War Graves Commission. Patrick had been found. In a garden in Ieper. He was only bones, but his had been the easiest identification they'd ever had: his St Christopher medal had his name scratched on the back; there was a rotted leather pouch with his initials in brass on it, and inside that an oil-cloth parcel of letters safely wrapped, letters to him from Mother and Father, the address at Inverash still clear in Mother's loopy handwriting. Oh, such a pang she'd felt to see Mother's handwriting again! It had made her cry. Patrick was to be reburied on the day after Armistice Day, in a place called Ramparts Cemetery. She could not go herself at her age, but someone from the family should be there and that person should be Kate who was somehow closer to Patrick than anyone else. She would go, wouldn't she?

Closer to Patrick than anyone else? Her heart thudded against her ribs when she heard that, but there had been nothing to do but agree. An hour after the phone call, Rowan called again.

"I forgot to say. The strangest thing. He came to the surface on the anniversary of his disappearance. The seventh of September. He's come back out of that brown fog. I can hardly bear it – oh, where has he been?"

Gavin had laughed at that. "He was under the earth and had a modern development built over him, and he was lucky not to wind up under the patio or he'd never have surfaced."

7 September. Two months ago. It was around then that Kate had conceived if the dates were right. Suddenly two members of the family had turned up unexpectedly, wanting to make her acquaintance, and neither of them welcome.

Mother, don't worry so. I'll be back, you wait and see. Nothing will keep me from Inverash and you, nothing, especially now that we've lost Alex and Charlie. Third one lucky. Don't fret.
Cheer-ho,
Patrick
6 September 1917

Why did that letter terrify her so? Kate quickened her pace. Perhaps everything would settle once he was properly buried. She went to cross the road and, with a spurt of dismay, realized that she had been so deep in her thoughts that she had over-shot the hotel. She glanced back the way she had come. The mist, silvery under streetlamps and a moon thin as a sixpence, was rising, but she could see that she wasn't even in the right street. She must have turned a corner or gone up a side alley. She stood for a moment, trying to get her bearings. The sky was bitter black and the small moon icily hard. Houses lined the street, their shuttered windows blind and unfriendly. She had no idea where she was. It was not possible to get lost on a fifty yard stretch of road, but lost she was. The sensible thing would be to walk back the way she had come, and yet going back felt wrong somehow. She hesitated. Ahead of her, the mist was sparse and ragged so that she could see patches of building and wall; behind, it was thickening to fog, dense and heavy, dimming the beams from the streetlights to a fuzzy glow. Her insides twisted. The fog was rolling towards her, closing in. It was impossible to stand where she was or go back. She plunged ahead, into the wraiths and wreaths of mist, with a rolling fog at her heels.

Somewhere close by, she could hear a piano playing and singing: "Lili Marlene".

The re-enactors in full cry. So she wasn't so very lost after all. The trouble was that, as she sped along, the music came from behind her, and then from her left, and then it was ahead and she thought she was running towards it. And she was running, skimming along past darkened houses, her feet knowing where to go and herself with no idea where she was. Then the singing faded and she was alone in the foggy dark. With a huge effort, she stopped dead in her tracks. A gate beside her, a neat little wrought-iron gate. And overhanging it, a rowan tree, its clumps of berries still scarlet, brushing cool and hard against her face as she put her hand on the gate. Of course she knew where she was now. Mr Westermann's house. This was the garden where Patrick had been found, where he'd wrenched himself muddy from the clay earth and summoned help with a crooked finger.

She tried to back away but her hand was glued to the gate. Close behind, she heard whispering, an excited buzz, a silvery giggle. She drew closer to the gate to get away from the sound. Her eyes fell on the new flagstones. He had been under there. By the light of the carriage lamp at the door of the house, she could see the neat square of stone, the earth-enware pots of plants precisely placed. One held a holly bush, humped in the dim light in the centre of the patio. She looked at it, felt an excitement as the buzzing behind her grew louder. The holly bush darkened and grew bulkier, took shape. A sleeping man, seated, slumped over his knees. A blanket, a coat, something draped over his head. Rifle in hand. She could see it as plain as day, a rifle pointing downward, a hand clasping it loosely.

In spite of herself, she reached for the latch and opened the gate. She stepped forward into the garden; stepped lightly so as not to disturb him; stepped into a mist thick with the scent of summer rowan blossom and the bitterness of autumn chry-santhemums. A sound like a sigh behind her. In front of her a movement, the shoulders of the huddled figure turning slowly towards her, the rifle scraping on stone, the blanket slipping from the head. Except there was no head. Just shoulders and an obscene knot of tendons and bone rising from between them and a thick, sticky darkness all down the front of the tunic where blood had rushed down. The tendons writhed wormlike and in agony as if they had only just been severed. She closed her eyes, nauseated. Rowan's clean shot. Death must have been instantaneous. Ugly but instant. She clung to that something-to-be-thankful-for. For Patrick there had been no regretful listening to the singing of the wild birds. That was something to be thankful for too. She thought about that rather than the thing before her, then decided it was time to be gone. Eyes still closed, because she couldn't face the torn wriggling tangles of what was left of him again, she took a step back. There was a buzzing in her ear, the pressure of something soft and determined pushing at her back. The fog billowed round her, carrying her forwards, cradling her coldly, carrying her to the slumped man.

She opened her eyes and recognized him at once. The head was in place, the face intact, the dimple deepening at the end of a smile, the eyes blue and gentle, studying her. Oh, her great-great-uncle was young and he was handsome! And he had the family flick of dark hair that tumbled on to the fore-head. Like hers. What a shame it all was, what a shame, the cutting short, the blotting out, the end of things! What an end to humour and courage, to future and plans! A sense of might-have-beens pierced her through and through like a splinter of glass.

He laid his rifle across his knees and extended a hand, touched her midriff lightly. *Oh, Christ, I wish I'd seen that bairn* . . . No, no, that was the Newcastle man's story, not theirs. The hand lay there, lightly, but with a warmth that seeped through her clothes and the layers of flesh and deep inside where something stirred and leaped, feebly but thrillingly. No, she thought, no, and looked down. It's too soon. It can't move yet. But it leaped again. She felt Patrick's gaze heavy on her and raised her eyes to meet his. But he had disappeared. This time she saw a child's face, a little boy's, dark haired and with blue eyes full of rage and tears, the head sunk into the shoulders in despair, the dimple flattened out by a mouth tight with anger and grief. The buzzing at her ear grew more intense and became a hoarse whisper.

"I've nowhere else to go."

She heard the words quite distinctly.

"Nowhere. Nowhere to go. Oh, that bairn . . . that bairn . . . Christ, I wish I'd seen it . . ."

She drew back and the fog parted for her. She was free to go now. She was out of the gate and down the street in seconds, at the steps in front of the hotel in minutes. Across the street the little square windows of Café Franz were golden with light. The piano was still thumping out the songs of war, and the men roaring the choruses the dead men, the nowhere men, used to sing "Keep the Home Fires Burning". How they yearned for home, and fretted over their dead ones.

She hurried upstairs to the bedroom. She wasn't surprised really to find it sweet with the scent of rowan blossom. Patrick, it was clear, though young, was determined to make an impression. She sat on the edge of the bed, her mind empty, unable to think or feel, at least not anything she wanted to think or feel. That was what uncertainty meant. Emptiness. Lack of direction or purpose. You sit and listen to an old song about faraway lads and home and then everything you thought or felt before seems trivial in the face of that desolation of endings. Sentimentality is what Gavin would call it, a feeling to be avoided as it rather got in the way of other things, but what those other things were she wasn't quite sure any more, except that beginnings were more appealing than endings.

She stood up and crossed to the window, breathing in the fragrance of summer blossom and growth Patrick had brought to her all the way from that place of the dead, and the green shoots and the nesting birds. Down the street, the men were gathering outside Franz's place, loudly calling their goodnights. The men in the anoraks and Aran sweaters mingled with the ones in khaki and puttees, laughing and backslapping and promising to meet tomorrow.

One soldier caught her eye. He was leaning against the wall in the circle of light from a street lamp, smoking a Woodbine. She knew it was a Woodbine because that's what the family sent the boys. The tin hat was at a rakish angle, the rifle hung loosely from his hand. She knew who it was. He was looking up at her window, head tilted enquiringly. The men walked past him, unseeing. How annoyed they would be if they ever found out that he had been among them and that they had missed him! Gavin was standing near him, self-important, promising to let his companions read all the letters next day. "So moving," he was saying. "They bring it all to life, make it real."

Patrick flicked his cigarette butt into the gutter and hitched his rifle sling over his shoulder. She waved down at him and he smiled mischief at her from under his tin hat. Something inside her leaped like the sap in spring. As Patrick had written, in both life and death there was nothing to do but go forward, so forward it was. He moved off up the street, going to that somewhere or nowhere which she could not imagine. Gavin passed right by him on the pavement – they almost brushed shoulders. Neither of them looked at the other.

"Cheer-ho, Patrick," she muttered. "I'll be seeing you."

From somewhere far off, she heard a boy's silvery giggle.

What was she going to say to Gavin?

My Moira

Lilith Saintcrow

"This will make you see things, Georgie. Take it."

Moira Staufford pressed the pendant into my cold palm, her fingers slippery with sweat. When she walked quickly away down Hagen Street her hair was a fall of copper-gold in late-autumn sunlight, her strides leggy as always but anxious as they had never been. I remembered braiding that hair on hungover mornings, holding it back while she heaved on drunken nights, and the familiar sharp bite of frustration in my chest made my eyes water.

She got into a long shining black limousine and it pulled away from the curb, inserting itself into the morning traffic with easy grace.

A heavy, antique silver chain held the clawed pendant, its sinuous shape a cross between a lion and a snake. Its eyes looked like chips of diamond, but oddly dark, and the whole thing vibrated in my hand. I stood outside the coffee shop, watching the limo until it vanished. I hadn't seen Moira since college, and I never saw her again.

At least, not alive.

It was all over the papers the next morning. *Billionaire's Wife Dead in Car Crash.* Fiery fatality. Police investigating. Husband distraught, rushing back from a European trip. I stood in

Harly, Withers & Chagg's grey fluorescent-lit break room and stared at the newspaper, my throat dry as rock.

Moira's picture from a charity luncheon grinned in full colour on the front page, right next to a blurred shot of twisted, smoking wreckage. Gooseflesh rose up all over me, nausea tightening my stomach into a ball. There, right below the vulnerable hollow of her collarbone – she never gained much weight – was a silver curve, the top edge of the pendant peeking up over a Chanel suit jacket worth more than I made in a month.

"Hey, Parkes. Can I get the Altman files from you?" Gene Withers, the junior partner, washed out and worn, tugged at his perfectly straight tie, a nervous tic that didn't do him any good in the courtroom. Then again, law school would probably make a nervous wreck out of anyone. Which was why I was just a lowly paralegal. "Or is Ben still using them?"

"I'll check." My voice sounded funny, faint and faraway, a whooshing in my ears. But Gene didn't seem to think so. He just poured himself a hasty cup of overcooked coffee and was gone, his wingtips squeaking a little.

I stood there under buzzing fluorescents, smelling Moira's cedarwood perfume, my purse heavy on my shoulder. I hadn't even set down my briefcase yet. My hands had turned slippery, and I scooped up the front section of the paper. I hid it in my briefcase like a criminal. Just like I'd hidden the pendant in my Chanel knockoff.

The day passed in a blur. Gracie and Emily invited me to lunch, and I think we gossiped, as always, about who was sleeping with whom and which lawyer was the worst to work for. Everyone agreed Chaggs was the worst, and Emily preened.

A smooth glass ball of calm had descended over me. So what if Moira was dead? There was nothing I could do. So what if she'd looked me up, told me she *had* to meet me, and given me what was probably an antique? I'd earned it, hadn't I? I'd written every goddamn paper she ever turned in. I'd driven her home after every drunken party, tagged along whenever she needed the ballast of a plain-Jane friend, cosseted her and basked in her borrowed glow. I'd been the battery so she could shine, and what did it get me?

Two months before graduation she'd run off with some older guy. Probably the same billionaire she ended up with. She was always cut out for it, our Moira.

My Moira. Who left me adrift.

The trip home on the filthy dark subway was the usual, and the elevator in my building was still out of order. So it was four flights up in my heels, my back killing me, and five full minutes of fucking with the locks before I could get into my own little shoebox. I shut the door, flipped the locks, dropped my briefcase, and decided to go for a bath. I left a trail of clothes, banged my elbow on the bathroom door, flipped on the light, and screamed.

Moira's ghost stood in the white glare of my tiled bathroom, a river of burn marks charring one side of her body and blood dripping scarlet over her bloated hands. She was livid-pale, her hair wet, smoke-crisped draggles, and completely naked.

I hit my head on something as I fell, and blacked out for a few merciful seconds. But not nearly long enough. When I woke up, I found out just how much everything had changed.

Traffic whooshed outside. It had started to rain. I held the icepack to my temple. "This is just temporary insanity," I told her. "Probably brought on by stress. You don't exist."

Her blue eyes had turned a murky grey, the whites yellowing and swelling like eggs. Her head lolled drunkenly, and the nakedness was distracting. A short but jagged appendectomy scar sliced up her abdomen, vanishing into the cracking, charred flesh gripping her whole side. I remembered driving her to the hospital through knee-high snow, the doctor swearing in wonderment, her being whisked away to surgery. I'd missed an exam and my grades took a hit, but Moira had pulled through.

Just like always. Even though the infection should have killed her.

"You were the only person I could think of." It was Moira's

voice, certainly . . . but flat and uninflected, a straight line on a heart monitor. "That might help me."

The pendant lay on my secondhand mahogany coffee table, its chain spilling away, a river of brightness. Ice crackled as I shifted the pack against my aching head. "Head trauma. No, stress. Work's been really bad lately."

"You're probably angry. I would be too. I just dropped you for years, and now this. I'm sorry." Her usual apology, meaningless. The blood dripped, coating her hands, bright red gloves. Pearls of smoky water clung to her high firm pallid breasts. The tiny scars from silicone implants were purple-livid, and stippling ran down her back, her buttocks cupped with bruised darkness.

That's where the blood settled, because she was on her back for a while. The thought sent a hot bolt of sourness through me, and I leaned forward, dropping my head. That just made it hurt more. I moaned.

"I look bad, too." She made a short *tsk*ing noise. "All that money spent on maintenance, but once you go over and you can't rest, you start looking like Frankenstein. I'm sorry, Georgie. You were the only choice."

The apologies, again. She must need something. "Shut. Up." I peered at her under one barely opened eyelid. "Am I insane? I've gone round the bend. Loony-bin time."

"Nope." One corner of her mouth twitched. It was a ghost of her famous smile, back when she'd been the redheaded college party terror. "You're sane, you've accepted the Seal. You're seeing my ghost, babydoll. I can't pass on without your help."

"Great," I moaned again. "I should just take your word for it? Tautology, Staufford."

"It's Hannigan now. Or maybe I can take my maiden name back. This qualifies as a divorce." Those clouding eyes fixed on me, and a spark of red lit in their depths. "He killed me, Georgie. My cheating, lying sorcerer of a husband. He wanted the Seal."

"Which is that thing on the table." I eyed its innocent silver gleam, balefully, and wished for a nice big jigger of Scotch.

"Right."

"Sorcerer?" This time I eyed Moira's ghost. The blood dripping from her hands and the water dripping from everywhere else vanished in midair with little popping crackles, a slow steady sound like a loose, sizzling faucet. She, however, stayed nice and solid. Or apparently solid. I didn't want to touch her and find out either way.

Thank God I couldn't *smell* her, too.

A short, very characteristic Moira nod. Water splatted dully from her lank, crisped hair. Her eyebrows were singed, and soot clung to her cheeks. "Right."

"*Right.*" I hauled myself to my cold, bare, shivering feet. "Don't let the door hit you in the ass on the way out, kiddo."

If only it was that easy.

I gave up trying to sleep and switched the light on. She hadn't moved. Still standing there next to my bedroom window, dripping blood that vanished in midair and staring at me with those clouded, accusing eyes.

She could always outwait me. I'd found that out the hard way.

So I went ahead and admitted defeat. "Fine. What am I supposed to do?"

A slow, twitching grin, her purpling lips pulling back from shocking-white teeth. "First things first. Put it on."

"Bring me my purse, then." I pulled down the hem of my tank top.

A roll of those discoloured eyes. "Don't be stupid. I'm a *ghost*, I can't carry your shit."

Which was what I'd wanted to know. "Just checking." So of course I had to get out of my nice warm bed, pad out into the living room, and fish in my purse until I found the pendant. I worked the chain over my sloppy dishwater-brown ponytail. The metal was ice-cold for a brief second before warming, almost obscenely, against me. The pendant fluttered a little, caressing the skin over my breastbone, and the world rippled a little. "Whoa!"

"That's what I thought when I put it on." Moira smiled,

another faint echo of her old devil-may-care grin. "Gramma Staufford's probably rolling in her grave that I didn't spawn a little girl to give it to and ruin *her* life."

You mean, just like you're ruining mine? But I didn't say it. It was no use. She wouldn't see it that way. Moira never did. "So you could see ghosts?"

"Not all the time. Grams died right before midterms, remember? I went to the funeral and my mother had a cow because she couldn't find the Seal. Turns out Grams had taken it off and mailed it to me. Chose me over Mom, and that was not a happy cupcake, let me tell you. I was always Grams's favourite." Moira moved a little, restlessly, the water on her rippling. "You can't die while you're wearing it. But if you have someone in mind, sometimes you can take it off and give it. As a gift. Don't do that unless you're ready to die, though. I'm serious."

"Were you? Ready, I mean?" I touched the pendant gingerly, with one fingertip. Christ, how was I going to wear this all the time? It went with absolutely *nothing*.

"Dying was preferable to being married to Ryan." A shiver went through her. She blurred like a television image, static bursting through her almost-solid outline. "He's a sorcerer, Georgie. He kept *experimenting*. Trying to get it off me, trying to make it obey him. Seeing the dead is the least of its tricks."

"So . . . he reached out all the way from Europe and gave you a car crash?" I grabbed the chenille throw off the back of the ratty old couch an ex-boyfriend had helped me haul home from Goodwill, and wrapped myself up. "Come on, Moira. Give the rest of it."

"I keep telling you, he's a *sorcerer*. Use that great big egg brain of yours, Parkes." She half-turned, staring at the window for once instead of at me. "I helped him get filthy rich, too. The Seal only picks women. Or at least, that's what Grams told me. Ryan was studying it for aeons. He figured out he couldn't hold it, so when Grams died he waited until he knew who it had settled with and swooped down on me. Wined and dined me, and I was stupid enough to fall for it."

"You always did like attention." It was snide, yeah. But I figured I'd earned some snide.

She didn't even register the hit. Just considered it, head cocked sideways and a bead of water trickling down one cheek. "I did, didn't I? Anyway, he was pretty wealthy, but he wanted more. *Lots* more. He knew about how to use the Seal. Called it a Grand Talisman. There's major and minor ones, all tumbling around the world, but the Seal is one of the big players. Gram said it was only for the dead, but there are plenty of . . . other uses. Anyway . . . first we got Ryan filthy stinking rich, then that wasn't good enough. *I* wasn't good enough. He wanted the Seal himself. Only he couldn't get it off me, so . . . do you know what it's like to have a sorcerer on you all the time?" A delicate little shudder. Her tone was still flat, uninflected, and completely eerie. "I wouldn't let him divorce me for a trophy, and he wouldn't divorce me anyway because I had the Seal and he wanted more. That's the thing about sorcerers. Greedy fucks."

It's not just sorcerers, honey. I bet I can find a lawyer who's worse. "You read entirely too much sci-fi growing up."

"Some fantasy novels get it right. Anyway, I started thinking about you. The Seal intimated that it wouldn't mind you, if I *really* wanted to give it up. So I found you. You didn't move very far."

How could I move? I barely had enough energy to tread water. "Neither did you." I scrunched back into the couch, the blanket wrapped securely around me, and I was still freezing. It wasn't an external thing – the cold was way down deep. The pendant warmed, reassuringly, and I forced my fingers away from it with an effort. "So, what is it you want me to do exactly, Moira? It's late and I need my beauty z's."

"Go to bed and get them, then. Now we wait." Her slow smile was all the more chilling because I recognized it. It was the same grin she used to use when contemplating a nasty prank to play on her helpless flavour-of-the-week boytoy. "Ryan will come to you. I'd bet my afterlife on it."

The most disconcerting thing about taking a ghost to work was other people walking through her. Moira grimaced each time, rippling, and I flinched because the pendant would twitch against my skin. Like a little live thing.

Another disconcerting thing? The world was brighter. Literally. I blinked and squinted my way through that first day, and everyone from Emily to Gene to Anderson told me how nice I looked but asked me if there was something wrong, since my eyes kept watering. It took a little time to adjust. Plus, the pendant kept *twitching*. Like an insect, or a little animal settling into a new burrow. And it really did go with nothing in my closet, but nobody noticed it.

Their gazes just slid right over it.

Moira's running commentary on my day was hysterical. Or it would've been, if I could have talked back.

"Jesus Christ," she noted when Anderson leaned over the back of my chair in the meeting room, "looking" at the paperwork in front of me but certainly taking the opportunity to rub against my shoulder. "Please tell me you didn't sleep with this guy? He reeks of Vitalis. Oh, and chlamydia."

I hadn't, and I almost opened my mouth to say so. I settled for giving her a filthy look and she laughed, the blood dripping off her hands snapping out of existence with sharp lightning crackles. A naked woman in a lawyer's office is a distraction and a half. Especially when she's corpse-livid and the discolourations keep spreading through her flesh. Not-flesh. Unflesh. Whatever.

It didn't take long. She died on Tuesday. On Friday I came in to find a blue message slip on my desk, Sharon the receptionist's angry scrawl as familiar as my own handwriting by now.

Ryan Hannigan had called.

"Meet in a neutral place," Moira insisted. So it was the Metropole Hotel, because they had a restaurant and if he was picking up the tab – which I was fairly certain he would – I could do with a steak.

I was seeing my dead college room mate. Cholesterol was the least of my goddamn worries.

Ryan Hannigan certainly didn't disappoint. Trim, tanned, wide-shouldered, in a suit that would have cost me a month's pay (if I'd ever wear black worsted) and dark-eyed, he rose as soon as I approached the table and offered his hand. "Miss Parkes."

"Mr Hannigan." I shook it once, wearing my "pleasant-but-noncommittal" smile. Took my hand back decisively. "I'm a bit surprised by this."

"Yes . . . I'm sorry." He was fetchingly awkward, running his hand back through a shelf of dark hair. "I just . . . Moira. It was a shock."

I sank down, the bald maître d' hovering long enough to drop a napkin in my lap and bustling off. "Thank you for telling me about the memorial service." I tried not to look at Moira, who hovered behind him as he settled in his own chair. Instead of flat disinterest, her entire face had turned predatory, her discoloured eyes suddenly piercing, red sparks burning in their depths. At least she was quiet, for once. "I feel bad," I said, all in a rush. "She . . . it was so sudden, and I hadn't seen her for years—"

"She was good at keeping secrets." He cocked his dark head, and I had the sudden vivid mental image of a shark smiling before it opened wide. "She's standing right behind me, isn't she?"

I swallowed hard. The pendant twitched again, decisively.

"For Christ's sake." His faint smile didn't alter. "You're wearing the Seal. You keep looking up over my head, right where she'd be standing if she wanted to slip a knife between my ribs. Which she'd probably love to do. The dead *lie*, Miss Parkes. Did she tell you that?"

"Never," Moira whispered, leaning over him. "We *never* lie. Don't take the bait, Georgie."

Another hard swallow, my throat dry and slick as a summer windshield. "Mr Hannigan—"

"Ryan. We're past formality, Georgia, wouldn't you say? Do you know you can shut her off? Now that you're wearing the Seal, you can tell her to go away so we can have a leisurely chat over dinner. Just concentrate on making her fade."

Moira leaned forward, taut, the blood crackling as it dripped off her hands. "Georgie—" Another real emotion instead of just flatline.

Fear.

Her eyes bugged, the whites turning even more jaundiced. She faded, static buzzing and blurring her sharp outlines. I stared over Ryan Hannigan's shoulder, letting out a slow whistling breath, my eyebrows coming together.

"Isn't that better?" Ryan leaned back in his chair as a slim Hispanic boy filled our crystal water goblets. A paper-thin slice of lemon floated in mine, twisting as it settled. Like a yellow scarf, or a grimacing mouth.

Moira winked out of existence. The pendant twitched again, and the new sharp colour and clarity in the world intensified. Like I'd been seeing through gauze before putting the necklace on, thinking I had 20/20 because I didn't know any better.

My heart leaped, pounded thinly in my wrists and throat.

"Now." He settled back, watching me with bright, reined interest. "Let's get to know each other a little. I can't use the Seal, but I can teach *you* how to use it. And we can make each other very happy."

She materialized in the middle of my living room, her face squinching up into a twisted, plummy root-shape. She didn't even have to take a breath before starting in on me. "Do you have any idea how *uncomfortable* that is? What did he say to you? What did you *do*? He's dangerous, Georgie. You have no idea how dangerous, and you just threw me under the bus, goddammit—"

I dropped my purse, stalked into the kitchen. Put the paper box of leftovers in the fridge. When I closed the door she was right there, and still going.

"—and we *can't* lie as long as you're wearing the Seal. Jesus Christ, Georgie, when did you start listening to anything a man says? Especially a man like that! *He killed me, Georgie!* Why aren't you listening to me?"

It took her a good ten minutes to wind down. She trailed me

while I undid my hair and stepped out of my shoes. She ranted while I filled the bathtub, and when I slid my clothes off and stepped into the water she shimmered in the steam filling the air. The blood crackled angrily off her hands, and when she flung them around to accentuate certain points, the droplets winked out of existence with tiny red sparks.

I settled back in the water and closed my eyes. The Seal pulsed reassuringly against my chest. Finally, silence ticked through the bathroom. A drop of water plinked from the faucet. For the first time in days, I was thoroughly, blessedly warm.

"Are you finished?" I wiggled my toes. Water rippled.

I cracked an eyelid. She was staring at me, her irises gone muddy, the jaundiced whites bulging, and her lips even more purple. The charring had spread. Her breasts sloped a little, the implants sagging, and there was absolutely no dignity in her nakedness. Not like during college, when she could have walked the length of the entire campus stark naked as a jaybird and nobody would have even sniggered. Her raw, blood-drenched hands hung at her sides, and sudden shame bit me high up in my throat, right where the bitter copper taint of mute rage and failure had lodged since childhood.

"He invited me out to the house on Sunday."

"Georgie—" A faint horrified cricket whisper.

I felt nastily, faintly glad that she was the one looking horrified, instead of me. "We're supposed to drain some of the charge off the Seal so he can use it in his—"

"*Georgie*—"

"Shut *up*, Moira. You brought this to me, I'm going to fucking fix it. The way I fixed every other problem you had in college. I cleaned up after you for *years* and I'm still doing it. I thought I'd gotten away from it." I wiggled my toes again, for punctuation. "Anyway. If I can make you go away, I can make you more solid, right? It's elementary logic."

"I can borrow mass," she whispered. "Yes. For a short time."

This is why I wrote all your papers. You just don't think, do you? Well, of course not. She never *had* to. Everything just fell into

her arms or her lap. Fell – or was sucked in by her sheer unconscious voraciousness.

I made a restless movement. Water slopped against the
sides of the tub. "Well, OK then. Between now and Sunday
you're going to teach me more about using this thing. Just
quit fucking riding me, Moira! I'm not in the mood. The man
makes me feel dirty. If you can't bring me a glass of Chablis
then at least shut up and let me enjoy my bath." I heard the
bitchy whine, softened it up a little by habit. "I mean, Christ.
I've pulled you out of the fire every other time, right? Why
don't you trust me now?"

She was motionless, even the crackles of vanishing blood
oddly muted.

"Georgie?" She spoke faintly, almost in a whisper.

If she dropped *one more thing* on me . . . "What?" I shifted
again. Water lapped. I tried not to think of the charring spreading all over her, the faint reek of burning that was beginning to
permeate the bathroom, *or* the things Ryan Hannigan had told
me. I wanted very hard not to think at all for a little while. Ten
minutes, twenty if I was lucky.

"Thank you."

For the first time, Moira sounded like she meant it, not just
like it was the thing to say when you'd twisted someone's arm.
My eyes opened fully just in time to see her drift through the
door to the hall, slipping through it like smoke. The steak I'd
managed to choke down rose in a hot wad, but I set my jaw
and swallowed hard again.

I'd earned every bite. And I was going to keep earning it.

The limousine arrived precisely at twelve-thirty. Long, sleek,
and black, and I only had a moment's misgiving before climbing in. The newspaper said Moira had died in a silver MG.

The chauffeur was a slightly tubby blondish man in an
uncomfortable-looking suit. "New hire," Moira sniffed. The
seat didn't dimple under her, and the blood crackled away
before it reached the upholstery. "He probably fired Enrique.
I *liked* Enrique."

I wanted to ask how *well* she'd liked him, but kept my mouth shut. Settled back on the seat and watched the city slide by.

"We can go over it again." Was she nervous? She was back to that uninflected flatline, it was hard to tell. "Once you're in the circle, you'll be insulated, but you won't be able to get out. You'll have to concentrate really hard to get me the mass I need while he's distracted."

I nodded, slightly. The smoked-glass partition between me and the driver was half-open, but I could see his dark eyes in the mirror. They were fixed front, and looked dilated.

That was not a good sign.

Both Ryan and Moira swore I couldn't die as long as I had this thing on. I found out I was playing with it again, running my fingers over the fluid curves, the chain sliding warm and soft against my nape.

"Bastard," she hissed, softly. "You know, I probably *bought* this for him. He's nothing without the Seal. He's scared. *Good.*"

It was the only time she didn't sound monotone, when she was telling me how much she hated him. I nodded again, half-closing my eyes. I was glad I'd worn jeans and a T-shirt for this. The boots had good grippy soles, too, and as the limo turned uptown I propped one on the seat and imagined the limo was mine.

The house reared up in a grey wave under an overcast sky. The English gardens were clipped and lifeless, winter settled in to stay for a while. The driveway was pitch-black and newly sealed, and an honest-to-God butler offered to take my coat. I declined, clutching my purse to my side with one elbow as if it might wriggle away, and Ryan Hannigan came down the great sweeping staircase like he was in an MGM musical. I expected to hear the voice of God telling Moses what the hell to do, or for Hannigan to bust out a cane and start tap-dancing, at any moment.

"Thank you, Chilton. I'll take Miss Parkes from here. If you could just leave the week's menu for Cook before you go? Good." Hannigan arrived at the bottom and surveyed me as the butler glided away. "Hello, Georgia. I trust the drive was pleasant?"

"I think your chauffeur's stoned." My palms were hot and slick.

"He's temporary." He'd just stepped out of some European version of *Vogue* – charcoal and black, cashmere pullover and sharply-creased slacks, his dark hair perfect and his smile a white slash. A chunky silver watch gleamed on one tanned wrist. "Especially if you don't like him. We are, after all, going to be working together."

I made a noncommittal noise. All of him was so impossibly vivid, burning with stolen life.

Just like Moira. Two of a kind, both high aces. And what was I? A two or a three of spades. Maybe I could graduate to joker, though, when all this was done.

"He got rid of my grandfather clock," Moira noted, ripples passing through her in bursts. "Probably my dinnerware too, before my body even got cold. *Bastard.*"

I only saw a little of the house, but I liked it. Despite the Eastern thing Hannigan had going on -- cushions and Zen hangings, at least two huge stone Buddhas, and various poor village tchotchkes re-made so rich people could play at being peasants. I searched for something to say. "So, are you a Buddhist and a sorcerer? How does that work?" It sounded stupid, like cocktail-party conversation, and I wished I could rub my palms against my jeans to dry them off, and get rid of the pounding in my head too.

"Buddhism's a technology, Georgia. Not a religion." He liked educating dumb females, his tone said. He liked it a *lot*. He continued, and I quit listening, concentrating on putting one foot in front of the other. The pendant quivered against my skin, nestling close. I could almost see its outlines shifting under my shirt as the lion-dragon-thing moved, flowing in a circle.

"Oh, Christ." Moira rippled some more, drifting after him. "I *hate* that tone of his. And look at him. Hasn't missed a workout, I can tell you *that* much. In between getting rid of all my— oh, no, my O'Keefe's gone!"

Shut up, I wanted to tell her. *You're distracting me.* I followed him through a library, suspecting that most of the leather-bound spines filling the glassed-in shelves were fakes. Interior decorators can do that, books by the yard. I wondered if some of them were magic books, decided not to ask.

"And here is where we make the magic, Georgia." He swept open a pair of heavy mahogany doors, and I followed him through into a circular stone-walled room.

It must have cost a pretty penny, from the star in a circle cut into the floor to the grey-black stone covering walls, ceiling, and floor. Custom-built cabinets and counters ran across one half of the wall's curve, jammed with fascinating things – jars of bones, smoke shifting like liquid inside rows of jewel-glowing bottles, feathers and bits of things, a baleful little obsidian statue of a gargoyle or something that tapped on the glass, furiously, as it shivered and reformed, the cracks vanishing. Ranks of candles stood on twisted iron candelabra, some of them taller than I was, and there was a pleasant spicy smoke-smell from the cloud of incense.

"You're taking this rather well," he remarked as he closed the doors behind me. "I almost thought there would be screaming and fainting."

"I got that all out of the way early." A glass terrarium on the nearest end of the counter held a piebald snake, coiled in on itself and watching with one black-gem eye. I touched the glass and it moved, shifting fluidly just like the pendant. A wave of nausea passed through me. I stood very still until it was gone. "How did you find out about the pendant? The Seal, I mean."

"My family used to own it, until Moira's stole it. That was in Ireland, a long time ago. Hannigans have a distressing habit of breeding only sons, and a man can't hold the Seal. Yet."

Oh. "You think you're going to be the first?"

"I'll settle for working with the woman who *can* hold it. I'm a reasonable man, when I'm met with reasonableness." There was a metallic, scraping sound. I whirled, but he had already punched the sword through my chest.

Right through my heart.

★ ★ ★

The stone floor seared my back. I sat up, choking, and screamed. Blood crusted my lips, and the pendant was a cicatrice of flame. When I ran out of air I scrabbled, my arms and legs not quite working right, my chest on fire, until I hit an invisible wall. It was the edge of the circle, and even though my legs kept going, trying to push me back through it, the air was as solid as steel.

I inhaled sharply, screamed again.

He waited until I ran out of breath again. "I'm sorry. I had to get you into the circle."

Moira flitted through the room, running laps in a weird ghostly way. First she would be standing near the counter, then she'd wink out and show up a couple of feet to the right or left. She kept doing that, hopping around; I clapped a hand to my chest and found a bloody hole in my T-shirt. My bra was ruined, but everything under it seemed just fine.

"—*bastard*—" was all I could get out. I quit screaming. There didn't seem to be any point.

"Exactly." Hannigan nodded. "Precisely. I'm not even a full Hannigan. But I *will* get my hands on that Seal, one way or another. And dear darling Moira just helped me. It's so easy to predict a woman blinded by the lust for vengeance."

"*Georgie* . . ." Moira's voice, faint and far away as she popped in and out of existence. "*I can't get through, Georgie* . . ."

Hannigan straightened. He'd shrugged into a long black robe, and looked like a college student playing graduation at some drunken party or another. His eyes had lit up, and that shark smile was just as wide and white. "If Moira's trying to get through, you can tell her not to bother. She helped me build this room, she knows it's a psychic fallout shelter. She helped me build *everything*, but she wouldn't share the Seal. Now I'll have it anyway."

The pendant was still burning. A thread of smoke drifted up from my T-shirt, perfumed with coppery, roasting blood.

Hannigan stepped back. The candle flames guttered as he raised his arms, the robe brushing back and forth like he carried his own personal wind with him.

"Georgie, you'll have to concentrate... Georgie, I can't get through. Help meeee, Georgieeeeee ..." The burns were spreading up Moira's body as she flickered like the candles.

Oh, holy shit.

Ryan Hannigan began to chant.

It *hurt.* The Seal roared furiously, electricity jabbing through me. Now I know what it feels like to stick your finger in a light socket, lightning coursing through your veins, skyfire burning every nerve.

"Georgie, you've got to concentrate! Georgieeeee—" Moira howled. The candles blossomed with sudden flame, and I screamed again, going into seizure on the floor, blood bursting from my mouth and nose, my heels drumming the stone, a sharp edge in the deep-carved star slicing open my foot – he'd taken my boots off, damn it – and more blood flying, the droplets spattering that invisible wall and hanging.

Hannigan's voice rose, a long yell of triumph shaped in syllables that cut and stabbed, venomous snakes of reddish smoke twisting and glowing around him. The Seal screamed again as it lifted from my chest, but my arm flew up and my fingers cramped around its sinuous curves, forcing it back against my skin.

Even though it hurt. Even though it *burned.*

It wasn't just the Seal. It was Moira, her copper-gold hair lifting on a breeze, laughing as her bicycle ploughed through fallen leaves. Moira in the middle of the night, leaning out of a car window and shouting, lit up like a marquee. Those years we shared the same dorm room and I did the donkey work so she'd drag me along as the plain-Jane friend, those were *my* years, and even if they had sucked everything out of me so I was stuck as a paralegal in a shady-ass firm full of ambulance-chasers instead of having the stones to get through law school on my own, they were still *mine.*

She was still *my* Moira. And this bastard had killed her, chanting in this room while the car bucked and shuddered underneath her and the fuel truck loomed out of the intersection, its brakes failing and the blossom of fire kissing like an angry lover all over her last moments on earth. I *saw* it, clear as day, the Seal burning through me, and I wasn't just concentrating.

I was *furious*.

A thunderclap tore the room apart. The floor underneath me heaved, broken pieces jolting apart and the pressure inside me suddenly easing, bleeding away.

Hannigan's yell of triumph choked off.

Because Moira's bleeding hands were clamped around his throat. She crouched on his chest, his arms flailing ineffectually as the snakes of crimson smokefire heaved around them both, and she *squeezed*.

So did I. But I wasn't squeezing with anything physical. It was my will, an invisible snake inside my head, and even as Moira howled in satisfaction and Hannigan gurgled his last, the Seal *flexed* inside me and my dead college room mate's ghost shredded apart. A burst of cold, clear white light filled the room – the light people talk about when they describe their hearts stopping and the Other Side beckoning.

"*Georgie, nooooooo*—" Moira screamed, a fading train whistle, but the light winked out. The stone room grumbled, like a subway muttering up through pavement, and the smoke took on a sharper, less perfumed tang. I coughed, choking, and heaved myself up to hands and knees.

"M-M-Moi—" I stammered over her name, because I was sobbing.

Now she was truly gone. And so was he.

Monday morning I called in sick and took the ferry.

It was one of those bright clear winter days where the wind comes off the river like a knife and everything sparkles. I stood on the deck in my Goodwill wool peacoat, my belly against the railing, and the fluttering newspaper was whisked up out of my hands.

Billionaire Dead in Mansion Fire, the headlines screamed. They were calling it a double tragedy. It had been a job and a half pulling enough force through the drained Seal to burn that motherfucking pile down, and I didn't like doing it. Still, it was the only thing I could think of, if the police weren't going to come knocking and asking me how I'd strangled him.

Criminals set fires to cover things up all the time. I just had the Seal to make sure it stuck. It was a wonder anything was left of him. The papers didn't say, but I was fairly sure there would just be charred bones.

The pendant glittered unhappily, cupped in my hand. It was drained now, Hannigan had siphoned off a lot of force, and I'd siphoned off even more. If I was going to do this, now was the time. When it was stronger, I wouldn't be able to take it off.

Don't take it off unless you're ready to die.

Well, I wasn't ready to die. Not really. But . . . Jesus Christ, living with this thing was not going to make me a happy cupcake.

And . . . Moira.

The wind scoured my face, drying the tears. I held my arm out, stiffly, drew back, and managed a pretty decent throw. It snapped as it left my hand, the chain biting, and beads of blood welled up on my wrist. Sharp darts of light glinted from it as it somersaulted, grabbing at the wind, the chain suddenly tentacles. But I've got a good aim, and it hit the choppy water and vanished with a twinkle.

A cloud settled over the sun, the colour and richness of the world stolen away again. I made it home without getting run over, took a bath without drowning, and went to bed because I was too fucking tired to care.

Tuesday morning showed up way too early, the alarm shrieking at me. I smashed the sleep button, rolled over, and spent another ten minutes in dreamland. There was something hard under my cheek.

The alarm shrieked again. I groaned, cursed, and punched it off. Turned my lamp on, every muscle protesting. I was sore all over from being stabbed, suffering seizures, and—

A silver gleam. The lion-dragon snarled slightly, and as soon as I touched the warm metal with a trembling finger it shifted, supple curves gleaming. I let out a small sound like I'd been punched and picked it up by the chain, gingerly, holding it away from me.

The Seal swung in tight circles, muttering at me. *You're not gonna get away that easy*, it said, and I was reminded of tagging along after Moira.

Haunting her steps. Now this thing was haunting mine.

It settled against my breastbone like it had never been away, the chain sliding under my hair and the lion-dragon twisting and turning as it rubbed catlike against me. I sat in my bed, listening to the rumble of traffic outside, and hugged my knees. My curtains glowed; I could see every thread in the fabric. Every edge was rich and solid again, not washed-out and dull.

"Moira," I whispered. "Tell me what to do now."

And just like that, the answer occurred. Well, why not? I could almost hear her laughing. It was what Moira would have done. At least, *my* Moira. Not Hannigan's. Not the gaping hole she'd been or the woman she grew into, but the girl I'd thought I . . . loved.

I had enough saved up, and if the Seal could make Hannigan rich it could do the same for me. But I'd do something different. I'd *help* people. I'd find the dead, and close their cases. I'd be a goddamn private eye.

I always wanted to be a superhero.

Forget Us Not

Nancy Kilpatrick

You hear only the crunch as your boots crush snow along this narrow street. A plume of carbon dioxide escapes your nostrils, vaporizing, like a ghost vanishing. Where the smaller ploughs have scraped the sidewalks, crystalline banks form glittering, otherworldly mountains and you scale one to cross the street.

It has been nearly a year since Brian died. A powerful wave of grief crashed over you, and then, within an hour of his demise, leaving grief in its wake, numbness flooded you. You are anaesthetized. A voluntary amnesiac. Now, you merely exist, rather than live, opening your eyes each morning with only a mild curiosity as to whether or not this day will be different. But the days are all the same and much of the time you realize that your waking thought is naïve; hope died with your husband. You are as cold as the dead.

Your brain hurts and you yank the parka's hood down to protect your forehead and daydream about prairie winters. They had been as bad, worse really, longer, that's for sure, but that cold was "dry"; you are just beginning to grasp what "dry" means. Here, it is damp and the thermostat often reads warmer than it actually is. Still, you owe this city. You needed a big change – change or crawl into a grave yourself. "Change is better than a rest," Brian always joked; you wonder if you'll ever truly rest again.

This is the kind of night you remember vividly from childhood. Not the urban landscape, of course. But, from time to time, the present of this place dovetails with recollections of the past. You recognize the silence. That combined with the pristine white leaves you calm on some level. Despite the chill, a small, grim smile turns up the corners of your lips. You intentionally blow a stream of visual air into the night, just to watch it vanish, and think again: how like a spirit departing when the body can no longer contain it!

You reach the mouth of an alleyway close to the corner and a sudden sound cuts the silence, causing you to stop. You pull the furry hood back to listen. Must have been a cat, you think, or it sounded like one. An unhappy cat. Maybe a cat in pain. An image of Ruddie comes to mind and you squeeze closed your eyes for a second and shake your head, not wanting to think about that.

You glance down the alley but the dim lighting reveals nothing. It's far too cold just to stand here so you hurry along and turn left at the corner, heading towards boulevard St Laurent.

Within a block, activity blossoms amidst the swirling white. It is normal for people here to wander around in storms and you have gotten used to going out to meet the necessities of life in all kinds of weather and finding shops, bars, restaurants, every place packed. This, you know, is *not* like Saskatchewan, where home and family is everything. But when family is gone, strangers remain. Brian used to say that strangers are "just friends waiting to happen".

Traffic moves at a snail's pace but the slim Montrealers manage a good clip despite icy sidewalks. You imitate their pace, grateful that you learned to ice skate at the age of five and walking the black-ice streets of Saskatoon felt natural. Montreal is so much further south. When your clients complain about the weather, you often tell them, "This is nothing. You should see life when everything is obliterated!"

The bar you favour is in the Plateau area. It is Saturday night, but early, and you will have enough time to drink yourself comatose before the crowds arrive. Drinking has become your hobby, a comfortable pastime, and Saturday is the only night you can indulge because the office is closed on Sunday. Brian used to say, "Never drink alone, Gena. It can't lead anywhere good." And you don't. You drink with a crowd of strangers who, after all this time, are no closer to being friends.

Anton & James is a large resto-bar, cosy at this hour, and you have come here every weekend without fail for nine months. The bartender places your double Scotch, neat, on the oak bar without your asking, smiles and says, "How it's going?"

"Fine," you say, as you do every Saturday night, the ritualistic words exchanged as if they are a talisman that will ward off bad luck.

You know the bartender's name is Rod – it says so on the pin attached to his shirt. He knows your name is Gena – your credit card gives away this vital statistic. That is enough familiarity, although you sometimes wonder what his life outside this bar is like. Is he married? Does he have a girlfriend? Children? Is this his only job? You also wonder if he wonders about you.

The hours pass, the bar begins to fill, the music is cranked for the night, and you have tossed back the remains of your fifth drink. On cue, Rod rings up your tab and discreetly places the bill before you. Your credit card comes out of your coat pocket; within minutes you have punched in your code and left a generous tip on the hand-held credit card machine. You look in your glass but it is empty, stand on rubbery legs, slip into your coat and Rod says, "See you."

"Yeah. Bye."

And then you are out the door, trudging back up the street which is now as crowded as midday with laughing, energetic bar and club goers. Briefly you think of stopping for something to eat, but the thought of consuming anything solid evokes a touch of nausea and anyway you have soon turned the corner, shutting out the noise and traffic and clubs and restaurants, and eventually you are on your street.

Even before you reach the mouth of the alley, you hear a single, pitiful yowl. From the corner of your eye a dark form darts across your path. Startled, you jump back, skidding on a patch of ice, arms flailing to regain balance. "OK, OK," you gasp, "it's just a cat. Relax."

You glance up the alley but don't see the feline kamikaze. The back lanes of this city are full of strays and it breaks your heart that they live outdoors in such frigid weather. It is the one thing about Quebec that you truly detest, how animals are treated. Back home, there are shelters that take in homeless animals for the cold months, neuter them so they won't procreate and produce more starving strays. Then they try to find homes for the cats and dogs, or at least foster care. Here, there are few shelters and they are all at capacity all the time. This shocking disregard for abandoned pets leaves you horrified. You have always loved animals. You had intended to become a vet, but last year's events resulted in a change of plan. You cannot bear to think of any creature suffering.

By the time you gingerly climb the iced-up metal staircase that leads to your third-floor apartment, you are relieved to be headed indoors. You have the key in the lock when a ferocious shriek fills the night and causes the hair at the back of your neck to stand on end. It sounds like a cat being murdered. Maybe it is the cat that just raced across your path.

You cannot stop yourself. You hurry down the slippery spiral steps and return to the laneway, picking your way along it, making kissy sounds, calling, "Here, kitty. It's OK, I just want to help you," trying to hunt down the poor creature, hoping it's not injured. If you can catch him or her, you'll take the cat in for the night, despite the landlord's "no pets" rule. In the morning, you can get the animal to the vet clinic in the building next to your office for a proper exam and whatever else is needed, then try to find it a home.

But, after four or five passes up and back along the lane, you discover nothing. Maybe, you think, the cat's in heat. But it is the wrong time of year for that. And that cry was not a cat fight either. The sound was bone-chilling, worse than anything you've heard, even from the terrified feral tom that scratched you last month when you tried to pet him. It sounded like a creature being tortured. The thought of it makes your heart beat wildly and your stomach lurch.

It is only later, when you are snuggled in bed, the book you have been attempting to read in your drunken state lying cover-up on the quilt, the vague thought of turning out the light drifting through your mind as you build energy for this gargantuan task before your eyes close for the night, that you hear that screech again. You jolt upright. The cry is almost human. Is a murder taking place? You race to the window and throw it open. Arctic air blasts in, shocking you to wakefulness. Heart thudding, you listen intently but . . . nothing. The street is silent. About to close the window, you see what appears to be a huge dark shadow at the only part of the laneway visible from this angle. The shadow of a cat moves along the wall, but you cannot see the actual animal.

You debate with yourself about getting dressed and going down to hunt for the cat again, but, even inebriated, that strikes you as insane. It is 4 a.m. Tomorrow is your only day off and you have a million chores to do, errands to run. At least it's alive, you rationalize. You will search for it tomorrow.

As you contemplate climbing back into bed, you think that it is curious not having actually *seen* the cat, just the shadow, because from here, you *should* have seen the cat making the shadow. A chill runs through you. You close the window too hard, shivering in the warmth of your bedroom, thinking, yes, you definitely should have seen the cat.

Sunday you are in and out of your apartment half a dozen times, and both coming and going you meticulously search the alleyway. There is no sign of a cat, no paw prints in the snow, no urination marks, no blood or tufts of fur from what might have been a battle. Nothing. The evening is quiet outdoors. Inside, you are trapped in a predictable phone conversation with your mother.

"Gena, I'm worried about you."

"Mom, don't be. I'm fine."

"But you're there all alone. You haven't even made friends."

"I've gotten to know Glenn, the part-time accountant I hired last month. And Rod." You are stretching the truth with both of these men, especially the bartender.

"Are you dating Rod?" your mother wants to know, and you repress a sigh.

"Not exactly. I just see him occasionally."

Your mother knows not to push you and segues to one of her other favourite subjects. "Well, that's nice. I'm glad you're making friends. When are you coming home for a visit? It's been almost a year."

"Maybe in the summer."

"That's a long ways away, Gena. What about Easter?"

"I'm really busy at the office and January to May is tax time, the busiest months. I've got to work six days a week to keep the bills paid."

"Do you need money?"

"No, no, that's not what I mean. I'm doing well, the business is growing, but a year isn't long in accounting and I'm just getting known. I'm trying to build my clientele, get on solid ground. I need to feel secure."

The pause at the other end alerts you to the fact that your mother is about to launch into her third favourite topic and you brace yourself for the onslaught.

"Your dad and I visited the grave last week."

You don't know what to say. What is there *to* say? But, of course, your mother is waiting for a response. "That was nice of you."

"We had to re-cover the rose bush – the wind tore the burlap to bits."

"Thanks."

"Gena, Brian would want you to have a life."

"I know, Mom." You speak too quickly and too sharply and try to think of something to say to ease away from this topic and let you off the phone quickly. You attempt to soften what comes next. "I have a life. I'm doing OK."

"There's some sad news. About Ruddie. He died in his sleep last night, on the blanket you bought him. I thought you should know."

Guilt eats through you like acid. The cat you and Brian loved is dead. You are stunned and something thoughtless erupts from your mouth: "He was an old cat."

Your mother pauses a second. "Ruddie never stopped missing Brian. Or you."

The acid guilt you struggle to keep at bay spreads up your chest to your heart. So much guilt! You must get off the phone. Now! "Mom, I'm sorry, I think that's the doorbell, I have to go. I'll call soon."

Before she can respond, you hang up, feeling new guilt pile on top of the old. The moment your caring mother's voice ceases, unwanted thoughts plague you.

You told yourself that Ruddie would be better off with your parents. He *was* an old cat, and it would have been heartless to put him through the journey across the country and subject him to a new environment. In Montreal, he would not have been able to roam outside the way he could at home. You knew you would be working a lot, building your business; Ruddie would have been alone all the time . . . But no. That is not the whole story . . .

Ruddie appeared the day Brian and I married. As Brian carried me across the threshold of our new house, both of us laughing happily, a sleek, black Hallowe'en cat slipped through the door and wove between Brian's legs. The cat pranced around as if he lived there, tail straight up in the air, purring loudly; he clearly felt at home. Laughing, both of us bent down to pet him at the same time. It was three-way love at first sight. As I took the satiny-furred cat into my arms, his purring ratcheted up a couple of notches. Brian stood looking at the two of us, grinning, then said of the malnourished creature, "I guess we have a furbaby!"

We checked with the previous owners, and our new neighbours, but the cat's home couldn't be traced. It didn't take long to fatten up the hungry stray. Brian named him Ruddie. "For absolutely no reason, but it feels right," he said. I always called him Baby.

Once, while Brian was working in the back of the garden out of earshot planting a line of cedars to cut the wind, I took a tumble down the basement steps, strewing laundry everywhere and twisting my ankle badly. Ruddie arrived at my side, meowing in distress at my pain.

"Ruddie," I groaned, tears leaking from my eyes, "if only you were a dog, I could send you to get Brian."

As if he understood, Ruddie blinked his amber eyes once, turned and bounded up the cellar steps. I heard the cat flap swinging. Within minutes, Brian came at the back door calling my name.

"Down here!"

He found me at the bottom of the steps and sat hugging me while I sobbed.

"Do you think it's broken?" he asked, gently probing the already-swollen joint.

"I don't know if it's broken or sprained, but it sure hurts. It's lucky you came in when you did," I sniffled.

"Ruddie told me something was wrong."

"What?"

"The way he was acting ... spinning in a circle, crying, like he was in pain. I thought he was having a seizure or something. I came in to get you to come outside and have a look at him."

Just then, Ruddie raced down the cellar steps, purring. He pushed his way between us for a group hug, rubbed his head against Brian's upper arm and then against my face. Brian and I laughed and nuzzled Ruddie back. That's when Brian started calling him "St Ruddie the Rescue Kitty. Our personal St Bernard".

With Brian's death, it was the grief in Ruddie's eyes that you could not bear and you know this is the biggest reason why you abandoned your beloved cat. And now Ruddie is gone, and you might be responsible. Did he die of grief? The grief of abandonment? You can understand that; you feel like both the abandoned and the abandoner and wonder why you wake every day, why you haven't just died from a fractured heart.

Ruddie is gone. Another piece of your connection to Brian has disappeared. The world you three shared has vanished. And you are left here, alone.

Sunday night you lay out clothes for Monday, pop a frozen meal into the microwave – some sort of pesto-pasta thing – eat

it, wash up, and think about TV or the Internet but decide not
to bother. You are especially tired, for some reason, the weight
of Ruddie's death on your already heavy shoulders, and bed
looks inviting. You know you sleep too much, but it is hard to
fill waking hours outside of work, and very easy to curl into a
ball beneath the covers.

Even before you change into your nightgown, you hear the
strange, high-pitched shriek and race to the window. There!
The oversized shadow of the cat again, moving along the
alley wall.

Spontaneously, you slip on your shoes, coat, gloves, grab
your door key and hurry out, determined to find this forlorn
waif and bring him in.

No one is on the street, either on foot or in a car. The night
has turned bitterly cold and windy. Yet, as you near the mouth of
the alleyway, the gale-force wind suddenly dies. The stillness
and silence feel unnatural and frighten you. You glance around;
it is as if you have stepped into another reality, a surreal snow
globe where everything has settled. But you feel very unsettled.

Cautiously, you move down the lane calling for the cat.
Every step seems more difficult than the last, as if the air has
thickened, and you do not understand why. An eerie feeling
creeps over you, leaving you sweating. Then, suddenly, you see
him. Ruddie! Turning in circles and crying, waiting for you
under the alley's dim yellow streetlight. You cannot believe it is
Ruddie, and yet you do – you would know your cat anywhere!
Joy surges through you, an emotion you never expected to feel
again. It occurs to you that you have died. You have found
Ruddie and, any second, you will be with Brian again. The
three of you will be reunited!

You rush down the snow-packed laneway. "Ruddie! Baby!"
He stops and his tail shoots straight up into the air and you
hear a familiar meow. You reach him and scoop your beloved
cat into your arms. His silky furry face brushes against your
cheek – so familiar! – and his loud purring grows louder, a
sound you recognize, one that is embedded in your soul, one
you have lived without for a year.

"Ruddie, Ruddie, I've missed you!" you cry, tears spilling from your eyes. "I'm so sorry for everything. Please forgive me."

Your tears become unstoppable and you can no longer control their gushing. Loud sobs rack your body and you can barely breathe from the pain ripping through you. Weakness comes over you and you bend in a crouch, folding in half, as if you have broken in the middle. You feel your soul crack open. You find yourself kneeling, rocking, crying, sobbing calling "Brian", "Ruddie", again and again. Then, strong arms surround you and Ruddie and, finally, the barrier within you gives way, flooding you with grief.

Time has ceased and you do not know how long you have been in this place, suffering a nearly unbearable agony. Only the wind returning and new snow falling bring awareness of where you are coupled with *who* you are. And with that, another realization: Ruddie is gone. Brian is gone. Forever. But you, you are still here.

And suddenly you view yourself through the clarity of returning memories: I am a person who has lost loved ones. Fate decreed that I, the driver, was not killed in the accident, but Brian, who died in my arms, was. There is no reason why I am alive, no real way of understanding why things happened the way they did. The facts stand: it was the other driver's fault. But facts are cold comfort and have meant little. Guilt has been my tortuous anaesthetic, keeping the more painful grief of my loss at bay.

There is no guilt, only grief. Thank you, St Ruddie. Now I can mourn.

Front Row Rider

Muriel Gray

She's not a morning person. Never has been. But lately mornings have become harder than usual. Blinking in the putty-hued square of light from her window she accepts that she has become a cliché, and she can't bear clichés any more than she can bear the assault of the work-day alarm clock. Yet here she is, lying in a corner of her double bed, bought in a moment of optimism never fulfilled, clutching a damp, compressed pillow. What can be more clichéd than the sleeplessness of the haunted?

There is little originality, she thinks, in the troubled creature who nightly thrashes the duvet to the edge of the bed, and hers hangs tantalisingly this morning, as it has on others, waiting to slither from the edge like a linen coin push as she shifts and squirms. Her waking is not gentle, following another night of sweats and nightmares, of falling and screaming and bright lights and hard surfaces, the knowledge presenting itself in the daylight that she won't be able to bear much more of it.

She coughs, out of habit rather than necessity, tugging back the escapee duvet, trying to find solace in its softness, its familiar insulation. Feeling nothing, she huddles and crouches, making a ball of her body like an armadillo expecting trouble.

No part of her even wonders any more. She simply accepts it will happen. Time ticking, days counting, something inevitable approaching. On a good day she asks herself if it might be the same for everyone. Death approaching. The sands running down. Then her heart tells her it's not the same. She won't die an ordinary death in a hospital bed; fixed-smile, grown children at her side, framed by wilting petrol station-bought chrysanthemums. She writhes at the vision she has just conjured. Is that ordinary? Is that desirable? She coughs again, turns, and questions for a moment why she forged an image so dismal.

No matter. She feels certain she will never die a picturesque death. Her future is a blur and not a Norman Rockwell tableau. She has no children, no lover, no life that can be filed under satisfactory. She blinks at the ceiling. Recently painted it offers little Rorschach relief, mocking her with its absence of distraction in peeling patches or dampening blooms. A bland, plain, desert of magnolia, leaving her alone with reality.

She closes her eyes, sighs deeply and gives herself over to the day's simmering fear. She frames the thought by saying the words. Says them in her head and faces the day.

Is he here?

If he isn't here already, then when will he be here? It's the same thought. Every day. On waking. Sometimes the dread cools as the day wears on and she dares to hope. Maybe he isn't here at all. Maybe he's busy somewhere else. Where would that be? Is her haunting unique, personalized, bespoke? Why should it be? What's so special about her? Maybe it's a chain-store haunting. Why shouldn't it be happening at the same time to an Amazonian monkey hunter, a Korean care worker, or an Icelandic property developer? Are they afraid to look people in the eye? Fearful of reflections and shadows? Terrified they will see the face in the crowd, that person who shouldn't be there, who has no right to be there, but who is always, unfailingly, reliably there? What vanity says a ghost is for you alone?

But such musings bring little comfort. The hope of a day without him is always dashed. He will come. Early, late. Day or night. Sooner or later. He will come. She realizes her breath is coming fast, her heart beating too hard. She closes her eyes and composes herself. She can do this. It's a new day and she reminds herself that in this indifferent, enigmatic, ineffable universe, she is lucky to be here.

Without knowing how, she is already at the breakfast table. She stirs her tasteless, colourless cereal, mechanically, without joy. She is at work, staring into the depth of a computer screen, her colleagues moving around her like choreographed dancers. She is in a café, the fat proprietor watching the evening news on the wall-mounted TV, arms crossed over his ample belly. Summer bluebottles drone and bump against the glass. Her coffee and half-eaten of plate of food sit cold in front of her.

The temperature drops. She bows her head in despair. Here it comes. As always, she feels him approaching before she sees him. Many times she's tried not to look. Tried closing her eyes, or reading a book. But like floating gutter leaves sucked down a drain, her gaze is helplessly pulled towards the point of his appearance. So now, against her will, she looks up, a fearful glance from half-closed lids, her breath blowing vapour into cold air that has no right to exist in this summer heat. The café owner shudders and rubs his arm against the sudden icy chill. She waits, heart thumping, but doesn't have to wait long. This time it's fast. He walks swiftly past the grimy café window, left to right, adjusting a jumper knotted round his neck, a bundle of newspapers held beneath his bare arm. That's all. It's over. The room regains its steamy warmth. That brief, tiny glimpse, she knows, was all there will be for the day. Just once. Just enough to drain her, tire her, chill her. Defeated, she heads home.

Each night, before she tumbles into scorched sleep, she tries to relive it, to work out what she did wrong, and each night she knows the answer. She turns over on the pillow, draws her knees to her chest. Face it, she thinks. Face the thing that she dreads, the error she made, the turning in life she took that led to this limbo of low-level terror that hums in the background of her life like an electric fence penning her in.

She shouldn't have bought the photo.

She can watch that day in fast forward now. Picking it apart used to take longer. These nights it lays itself out chronologically like a storyboard. This night, it feels different. The story feels alive. She gets out of bed and walks to the darkened sitting room. Pressing back into the hard, worn sofa, a single table light burning low in the bedroom she left behind, she lets her chin fall to her chest and the playback commences.

Jill talking. You're only forty once. Travelling. A package to Orlando, Florida. All four of them. Just the girls. A theme park birthday. Disney, Universal, Seaworld; the greatest rollercoaster rides on earth.

Forty and fat. Forty and a smoker. Forty and making drinking alone a habit. Forty and never having taken a risk, or climbed a mountain, or run a marathon. Forty and never having been properly in love. At least never loved back. Never ridden upside down in a chair on rails at forty miles an hour. Shorthand. Forty. Never really lived.

The girls gabbling. Shouting advice. Make it change. Make it happen. Turn your life around time. Do those things. Stop watching time tick by. Start living, why don't you, gal?

Details of the holiday, now just fragments of memory in a blender. Laughing, drinking, neon lights and the faux-antique wooden booths of cheap themed restaurants. The girls cackling, ruby-red lips open in constant shrieking mirth in their tireless quest to catch the attention of incurious Americans while she cowers in embarrassment. Look at us. Look at the time we're having. Highways crawling with slowly moving oversized cars. Outsized people, outsized food. You must feel like a super model here, laughs Jill. She laughs too, but wants to cry. "Jesus Loves You" sky-written in vapour from a tiny plane, the disintegrating words floating against an azure Floridian sky. She photographs it. Wishes it were true.

All leading towards the moment. The decision.

Her heart couldn't beat any faster in the queue. The Hulk. The fastest, hardest ride in the park.

Libby makes them stand in line for the front row. Keeps barking statistics. World's tallest cobra roll: 110 feet. Launch lift that shoots you from zero to forty miles per hour in under two seconds. Stop it, she thinks. Stop it, stop it, stop it. Front row seats have a bigger queue. Worth the wait, says Jill. Forty-five, maybe fifty minutes. Every one a hundred hammering heartbeats of panic. She sweats. She trembles. And then . . . the bitches! The rotten, lousy bitches see a gap for three people, two rows back, and dive for it. Squealing with delight. Waving to her as they strand her in that front-row line. Shouting and guffawing. Roaring that they'll see her at the bottom. She's alone. Made to wait for the next ride. Takes a thousand years to come by, arriving, clunking into place like a mechanized abattoir. A couple of sullen Americans behind push her roughly forward on to the row, the seat at the far side already filled by a young man, staring ahead, calm, like he's waiting in a doctor's surgery. Must have boarded from the fast-pass queue on the other side.

It's him.

Alone and waiting.

Ahead, a mountain of rails. A metal serpent waiting to receive its sacrifice.

She hugs her knees tighter. It's time to play the next frame again in her head. Again. Again. She plays it until she knows it by heart, because she knows this matters. Somehow it does.

She's shaking. Nearly crying. She's tried speaking to the American couple, her voice too high, too hysterical to sound casual. But Americans don't make small talk. They tell you to have a nice day if you pay them to, but to those without a name badge on their shirt you might as well be invisible. The big man grunts when she giggles the truth that she's scared. The girl stares ahead, chewing gum like it's a chore.

The coaster car jerks up and then down, bouncing as the automatic harnesses lower, pinning her to the back of the seat. She starts to cry. Silently. More alone than she could ever remember.

She can see his face now, still clear, remembering every detail as he turns slowly to look at her, savouring the memory of his irresistibly sympathetic gaze that follows the fat tear coursing down her cheek until it lands on the restraining bar of the seat. She can see that wide, friendly face, a shadow of stubble around the jaw, round hazel eyes, and a head of thick brown hair cut tight to tame curls. Of course she looks at this face every day in the photo by her bed, but the memory, the real sweet memory, is more vivid than the picture. He was English. She thinks she knows that now. She swallows, climbs back into the moment.

He's smiling. Comforting, gentle. He reaches out his hand, places it on the bloodless, tightly clenched claw that's hers, and speaks, a laugh just beneath the voice, but a kind one. Not Jill or Libby's broken-glass laugh, full of taunts. His hints of mischief and joy.

"You're going to be fine. Just fine."

Then nothing. A void of suffering. Screaming. Pressure. Held back, upside down, body pinned in a vice. Forces working on her, stealing her breath, twisting her gut. But somewhere in the maelstrom of pain, his hand has found hers again, a warm, kind hand, squeezing and reassuring.

And then it's over. She's walking, slowly, like in a dream, weaving unsteadily, sick and sore, to the air-conditioned little booth where a bored Hispanic woman is presiding over photographs of the ride. So dazed she feels she's the only customer, though the ride was full, and the woman leans on her elbow and points with long acrylic talons up at the screens showing digital snaps of every row just disembarked.

There she is. Mouth open in a silent scream, eyes clamped shut, hair flying back, hands gripping the harness. The couple pictured on her left are stony-faced.

And then there's him. He's not looking ahead. He's in profile looking directly at her. What she can see of his face is full of concern. His hand is cupping hers.

There's no hesitation. She buys it. She buys it and now she lives with it. Day and night. On her bedside table from then until now. His face the most familiar in her universe

A man who isn't there.

The first time she saw him after returning home was like a

miracle. It was the best time. Close to joy. Stole her breath away. Oxford Street. A Saturday. His face, unmistakable in the crowd. He looked haggard, world weary, but it was him all right. Her heart in her mouth she ran, and waved, and ran again, but he'd gone. And, oh, the thrill of that moment of recognition. The excitement of that chance sighting. An opportunity to thank him. Who knows? Maybe more than that. A coffee? A reminisce? A laugh? Would he remember her? Did he buy the photo too? Is she somewhere in his life? Maybe not on his bedside table, but dare she hope perhaps on his office desk, or propped up on some shelf full of books? All over the world people cherish their roller-coaster photos taken with strangers they will never see again. Faces glimpsed once then preserved forever. Why not hers? There she would be, the stranger he rode the front row with. She had never wanted anything so much in her life than to catch up with him and put her hand on his arm. But he was gone. His curls lost in the bobbing sea of heads that flowed along the street. She stood for a long time, alone again. Then she went home.

The second time. In the cinema. Too good to be true. Another chance. It must be fate. He left before she could reach him. Then the third. He was on a boat on the Thames. She was on a bridge. When was it? The twentieth time? The fiftieth? The hundredth? When did she wake up and realize that not only can he not see her or hear her when she shouts, screams sometimes, but that maybe, actually, genuinely, he isn't really there at all? Too frightened to call up the theme park, to try and find witnesses to that day, to maybe track down the digital trail of the photo. Too scared in case what she fears turns out to be true. What is he? A spirit? A demon? Worse. A figment of her imagination? She has been beaten. There is no part of her left now that wants to see an alternative photo of her front row ride. A photo in which she is sitting next to an empty seat. So she lives with it. Deals with it.

But tonight she feels different. Tension has been building in her like the close summer air outside. This must come to a conclusion. The burden on her heart is too heavy and tomorrow it will end. She will make it end. She is going to face him, whatever the consequences. She walks back to her bed and curls into her roller-coaster sleep.

Come morning, she waits outside a shop, staring into its dusty window displaying foreign newspapers and bottles of sweet drinks, still and passive, knowing he is coming. No need to look. She keeps her back to the street, and shudders against the cold as she feels him pass by.

A deep breath. This time he won't get away. It's now or never. She walks quickly, weaving in and out of the rush hour crowd folding over his wake. He can't outrun her today. Today her feet have wings. He turns and enters Kings Cross Station. She breaks into a half-run. He's through the turnstile. She has no ticket. She jumps the barrier. Back behind her, maybe someone shouts. Maybe not. She's not sure. She carries on. He's on the escalator. She pushes forward, lightly tripping down the metal stairs, commuters twitching away in dreamy irritation as she brushes by. He turns into the tunnel for the Circle Line. A train is just leaving. The set of his body registers exasperation. He's missed it.

It's the moment. It's now. There's nowhere to run. In just a few moments this will be over. She closes her eyes and sighs. Deep, satisfied. Her eyes open and she calms herself as she walks slowly and deliberately towards him, her breath cooling in the hot, stifling underground air. Everything around her has slowed. The movement of the crowd has been quieted as though caught in treacle. The platform is an eddy in this slug-gish human stream, the passengers at rest, self-absorbed, patient, waiting. His back is to her as he faces the rails, his body tightly flanked on the left by an expressionless man with a rucksack, and on the right by a bespectacled woman, laden with parcels yet attempting to read a book. A train is screech-ing from the tunnel, its lights beginning to bathe the rails. The crowd shifts and pushes behind her in anticipation and she glides forward.

She takes a deep breath, turning it to icy vapour on the exhale, as her heart beats calmly and steadily now. The train stops and the doors open. He shuffles forward, penned between the man and the woman. She moves towards him. Her hand comes slowly, slowly, gently, up from her side. She lays it on his shoulder and the touch is like an electric shock. He halts, his head turns and he looks her straight in the eye.

He's trying to piece together what's happening, but his breath has been punched from his body and he's gasping like a beached fish. Everything has slowed. The noise of the train, the people pushing past him, even the hot, brisk wind of the underground has turned to sluggish, still cold air around his head. The noises of the station sound like a clockwork music box that's wound down.

He's not ill any more. He knows he's not ill. Dr Sutton has told him he's not ill. Today is a big day. The interview is at ten. He's left himself enough time to get there and he's calm, prepared. There's no reason for a panic attack. Especially not today. In fact, there's no reason for an attack at all. He's worked hard, he's focused and he's not anxious. He tries to breathe. Breathe like Dr Sutton showed him how. But he can't. He feels faint.

It's not her. It's impossible. He knows it's impossible, and yet the icy chill of terror is spreading through him like black ink poured into a beaker of water. He wants to look away from those eyes, to tear this freezing hand from his shoulder. But he's solid with fear, immobilized and breathless.

His brain works feverishly to rationalize. It's his fault. This is his fault entirely. He should never have accepted, let alone kept, the photo they sent. It's the familiarity of her face that's making him recreate her so perfectly now in this madness. It has to be. He might have forgotten how she looked if he'd just binned it. It was nearly two years ago. But they meant well, the family. It was loving, not ghoulish, hunting down and retrieving the photo from the theme park after what had happened. They wanted to honour her last great thrill. To remember her. Remember her not as the fat, lonely, quiet girl they'd raised, but as a risk taker. Someone who lived large. A front row rider.

And they wanted to thank him for all he did. What did he do? How did that go again? What order did Dr Sutton say he should remember it in? Her screaming. His laughing. Her screaming again, and again, too much, too shrill, too long, too gurgled for an outburst of joyful abandonment. Then her jerking, and gasping, and slumping. His screaming for help as the ride stopped, and no one coming. Screaming more and more as the harness didn't lift, then, when it finally loosened, grunting and heaving to get the bulk of her sweat-slicked body out of the chair and on to the hard concrete. Still screaming for a doctor, with everyone standing watching as though it were an act. Then putting his mouth to hers, and blowing, and pumping her chest with his palms, and crying, and still shouting for help.

And then slumping himself, realizing she was gone, and he hadn't helped, hadn't saved her. This poor, frightened, lonely stranger. His was the last face she saw. The last hand she held. And now he was here, recreating it all in his crazy brain, just as he was about to start afresh. Sabotaging himself. That's what Dr Sutton calls it.

His anxiety has won. He blinks as he watches his guilty creation lower her hand and listens, numb with horror, as she speaks. She is stern. Almost angry.

"If you follow me on to this train, it won't be fine. It won't be fine at all."

He stays perfectly still. She holds his horrified gaze for a beat then walks past him, steps on to the train, and sits herself gracefully and serenely next to the man with the rucksack. The doors close. The train begins to move away, and as he watches her though the glass she smiles, an expression of release playing in her darkened eyes. She turns her head away from him, lifts a hand and lays it gently over that of the woman with parcels. She disappears with the train into the darkness of the tunnel.

His chill is gone now. He's sweating. His fevered imagination has made him miss the train that today, at 8.50 a.m., could have taken him to a new job and a new chance and a new life. He has no stomach to wait for another.

He weaves slowly and shakily off the platform and heads for the stairs.

He should feel defeated. He should feel insane, a failure, a casualty. But right now as he jostles through the crowds pushing in the opposite direction, he feels strangely elated, light of heart, released and invigorated. Baffled, he takes a breath and gives himself over to the emotion. In the months and years to come he will recall that this instant, these precious few moments of confused elation were to savour and not to fear.

In four and a half minutes' time the man with the rucksack in the train will detonate his bomb.

God Grant That She Lye Still

Cynthia Asquith

It was not until three weeks after I came to live at Mosstone that I first saw her. But most of my new patients had talked to me of Margaret Clewer, the youthful owner of the Manor House. Many shook kindly heads because she was so alone in the world. "Only twenty-two, and without a single near relation!" – but they also spoke of her beauty and charm, and it was with agreeable curiosity that I set out to pay my professional call at what the Mosstone villagers called "the great house".

As I passed through the gateway that I had so often admired from outside, into a large, grey-walled court, the muffled atmosphere of the place seemed to envelop me like a cloak. The very air seemed thicker and more still. It was as though I had stepped out of the everyday world into something cloistered and self-sufficing.

Pigeons fluttered and crooned and plumes of blue smoke rose into the golden air. Absorbing its beauty like a long, lovely draught, I gazed at the exquisite gabled house, with its great mullioned windows and queer twisted chimneys, round which the swallows skimmed.

It struck me then, I remember, that more than any other building I had ever seen, this house appeared to have a face, an actual countenance that might vary like that of a beautiful woman. Yet could any building look more remote, more strikingly aloof?

Time had deposited so much on those mellowed walls; for so many centuries a deep reservoir of life, the house now looked withdrawn from any further participation, as though with gentle repudiation disassociating itself from the present and the future.

My watch told me I had returned from my walk twenty minutes before I was due. Ever since my boyhood I had loved poring over old epitaphs, so I turned into the churchyard, which was only a few yards from the front windows of the house.

Like most village churchyards it was very overcrowded, but the dark red-fruited yew trees shed an air of sombre peace over the clustered graves. Most of these graves were mere uncommemorated grass mounds, but there were also a number of grey lichen-clad tombstones lying and leaning at all angles, and on many of these the name of Clewer was engraved. Evidently innumerable generations of my future patient's family had lived and died here. Most of these long-dead Clewers seemed to have been mourned by appreciative and verbose relations. Nothing that uncouth rhyme and shapeless sculpture could do to preserve the memory of the departed had been omitted. The scriptures had been ransacked for consoling texts, and prose and verse not only lavishly set down the virtues, talents and deeds of those described as "not lost but gone before", but also assiduously struggled to describe the emotions of the bereaved. Only once in all those generations had a strange reticence descended on the Clewer family.

In the corner of the churchyard nearest to the house, directly beneath a darkly presiding yew tree, was a worn, flat stone. Here nothing implored the passing tribute of a sigh. There was only the bare inscription:

Here lyes the body of Elspeth Clewer. Born 1550 – dyed 1572.

And beneath in different lettering the words:

God grante that she lye stille.

This inscription struck me as laconic and queerly worded, so like, and yet so different from, the familiar – *Requiescat in pace*. Could those who buried the dead girl find nothing to praise? Was it too great a strain on their capacity for hope to associate her with peace? Or was the rather piteous supplication "God grante that she lye stille" more for themselves than for her they consigned to the grave?

Idly I wondered whether I should ever know Margaret Clewer well enough to question her about this undesignated ancestress.

It was now time to run from the dead to the living, so I moved towards the home of the Clewers. As I approached the iron-studded door, the air was heavily sweet with the scent of the magnolias. These, as well as wisteria and clematis, clustered thickly over the front of the building, but to my fancy the great house seemed to wear them with, as it were, a shrug of indifference, as though it knew nothing could really enhance its own beauty. The gentle austerity of that beauty humbled me again, and it was with a sense of intrusion that I pulled the bell and heard the responding clang and the bark of an aroused dog.

I don't know what I had subconsciously expected, but the smiling beribboned parlour maid who opened the door seemed incongruous.

"Dr Stone?" she asked. "Miss Clewer is expecting you."

Obedient to her "Come this way, please", I followed her through a large hall in which young people were playing ping-pong and noisy games of cards; the blare of a gramophone triumphing over the confusion of sounds. A heavy door through which we passed cut us off into complete cool silence, and a short flight of shiny black oak stairs, splendidly solid to the tread, led us to the door of my patient's room. The strong evening sun streamed in and it was through a dance of dazzling motes that I first saw her.

She lay on a low wide bed drawn close up to the window, and a Golden Retriever luxuriously sprawled over the flower-embroidered coverlet that was spread across her feet.

I cannot remember how much I took in at first sight: I know the window-shelf and the tables were then, as always, crowded with flowers and great branches cut from trees, and the bed strewn with books, writing materials and needlework.

The shock with which I saw her was not without an element of recognition. Vaguely I had always expected that one day I should see a woman far more lovely than all others. Her hair gleamed in the sunshine, and her translucent face smiled up at me. I thought I should never see anything more beautiful, but I did the next time I saw her, for the variety of her beauty was unending. Changing as the sea changes with the sky, her colouring had its special response to every tone of light, just as her expression varied with every shade of feeling. It was a fluid, unset loveliness, suggesting far more than it asserted.

After this first sight of her, I was often to wonder how I should describe her, supposing I had to reduce my impressions to the scope of words. What, for instance, should I set down if I were asked to fill in her passport? Would she be allowed across frontiers if I described her mouth as normal? Normal! When it was never the same for two consecutive seconds. As for her eyes. I should not even have known what colour to call them. "Eyes too mysterious to be blue, Too lovely to be grey," would not help. Many more than two colours met in those pools of light.

As I entered the room I was to know so well, two canaries in a large golden cage were singing loudly, and l could scarcely hear Margaret Clewer's welcoming words. In her lovely, lilting, but, to my professional ear, definitely nervous voice, before she began to speak of herself, she asked me many questions as to the comfort of my house and my impressions of my new practice. I had almost forgotten in what capacity I was there when she said:

"I've been very silly and strained my heart, I think, over-rowing myself. I've got a craze for very violent exercise. Anyhow, I feel distinctly queer, and my heart seems to beat everywhere where it shouldn't be. And so," she added in her way – how well I was to know that way – of speaking in inverted commas, "my friends insist on my taking medical advice, so perhaps you had better see if my heart is in the right place."

It did not take me long to discover that her heart was severely strained. There was also a very considerable degree of anaemia, and I prescribed three weeks' rest in bed.

My verdict was received with equanimity.

"If I can't row or ride, I'd just as soon remain in the horizontal," she answered gaily. "I shall be quite happy with books and food and friends, and with my beautiful Sheen. Isn't he lovely?" she added, turning the Retriever's golden head towards me.

After paying homage, I asked if there were anyone to whom she would like me to speak about her health.

"Oh, no! I haven't any relations. I haven't anyone to edit me. I'm quite alone."

"But there seem so many people in the house."

"Oh, yes, but they're just visitors. When I said alone, I meant independent. I couldn't bear to be literally alone."

The last words were said with a vehemence that rather surprised me. Her room, with its multitude of books, a violin and several unfinished sketches, seemed to bear evidence of such varied resources, and I had already diagnosed her as a person who would be very good company to herself.

As I shook hands with her, saying I would return the day after tomorrow, I noticed that, for all their brightness, the responsive eyes held a slightly, not exactly hurt, but shall I say initiated expression. In spite of the nervous voice, my first impression had been that here, if anywhere, was one who had not felt the touch of earthly years. This superficial impression was already modified. Had life already bared its teeth at this lovely girl?

"I saw you groping about among the graves," she said, as I reluctantly turned towards the door. "Are you interested in the rude forefathers, in worms and graves and epitaphs?"

"Well, at any rate, I love epitaphs," I replied, "and this is a peculiarly picturesque churchyard. You, yourself, must surely have a weakness for it, as you occupy a room so immediately overlooking it."

"Yes, I am close, aren't I?" She laughed. "No rude forefather could turn in his grave without my hearing him. But this happens to be the room I like best in the house. There isn't any harm in being so close, is there?"

"I can't say I consider it physically unhealthy," I answered professionally.

She smiled her swift, slanting smile. "Are you afraid of my being troubled by ghosts, Dr Stone? Well, if it's a nervous patient you want, I'll see what I can do to oblige you; but first, please put my heart back into the right place."

I told her I would do my best and return the day after tomorrow to report progress.

"Au revoir, then," she said. "And meanwhile, I shall look out for you in the churchyard, you ghoul! You ought to come and see it by night. You can't think how lovely it is in the moonlight, with a great white owl swooping and brushing against the tombstones."

As I turned my back on the beautiful house I found myself walking with a light step. For the first time since I came to this friendless new country a fellow creature had made me aware of myself as a human being. Till then I had been merely the new doctor.

I walked back through the village with a sense of enhanced life. There was now something to which I looked forward.

I visited my new patient three times during the next week. Finding her physical condition very little improved, I decided that some electric treatment would be beneficial, and as I had a portable apparatus, I was able to give the applications in her own room. A long course of this treatment involved many visits, which were the occasion for the most enchanting talks I have ever known. I look back on these summer weeks as the happiest of my life. Day after day I drifted on a stream of delight. She was a magical companion, to me a real Pentecost. Her quicksilver sympathy, the lightning gaiety of her response, her dancing voice, and a way she had of appreciatively echoing one's last words: I suppose it was all these qualities that made me for the first time in my life feel so delightfully articulate. There can never have been a more receptive and therefore stimulating mind. It was as though she understood my thoughts almost before I had decided to put them into words.

There seemed no limitations to her understanding and sympathy. Her supple mind rejected nothing, and her iridescent gaiety was like running water in sunshine, continually flinging off a lovely spray of laughter. How, I wondered, had she found time to read so widely, so richly, to store her astonishing verbal memory? Of herself she spoke very little in any autobiographical way. After weeks of frequent conversation I knew nothing of the events of her life, of her dead parents or of her friends; but almost from the very beginning she showed a tendency to discuss herself psychologically, to expatiate on her character, or rather, on what – to my amusement – she called her lack of character.

I suppose it was about six weeks after my first visit that our conversation took a turn which for me sounded the first faint note of disquiet.

In her usual rather unconcerned voice she said:

"It must be fun to be someone very definite and positive. You can't think how uncomfortable it is to have no personality."

I laughed. "Are you suggesting that you have none? I know of no one of whose personality one is more quickly and lastingly aware."

I'm not fishing," she said, with the slightest tinge of impatience. "I don't mean that I'm too insignificant and colourless to make any impression on other people. I know I'm quite nice to look at; I'm not stupid, and I've plenty of responsiveness. I don't know how to explain, but what I mean is that there is no real permanent essential Me. Of course, I've got plenty of facets, and your presence conjures up a certain *Me* – not too bad a one. Thank you for the self with which you temporarily endow me. But I don't feel any sense of being a separate entity.

No – I can't find any essential core of personality, nothing which is equally there when I'm alone, with you or with other people . . . There's no real continuity. I'm so hopelessly fluid!"

"But, if I may say so," I broke in, "it is that very fluidity of your mind that makes it such a treat to talk to you. We were discussing Keats's letters the other day. Do you remember where he writes: 'The only means of strengthening one's intellect is to make up one's mind about nothing – to let the mind be a thoroughfare for all thoughts – not a select party'? I think—"

"No, no. I don't mean that sort of thing at all. You entirely misunderstand me!" she interrupted, and something in her face made me realize the subject was serious to her and that the characteristic lightness of her manner hid real concern.

"I'm not worrying about my qualifications as a companion," she continued. "You see the difficulty is that I can't talk about myself in a serious voice. I always sound so flippant. But my flippancy is a reflex. I should like to be able to talk to you about myself really melodramatically."

"Please do," I urged. "I'm feeling quite serious."

"I don't expect I'll be able to, but let me try," she said. "I don't want to be a bore, but I assure you it really is nightmarish – this sense of having no identity. You remember the very first time I saw you, I told you that I couldn't bear to be alone?"

"Yes."

"Well, that is because other people seem to a certain extent to hold me together – to, as it were, frame me by, I suppose, their conceptions of me. But often when I'm quite by myself I feel like – like water released from a broken bowl – something just spilling away – to be reabsorbed back into nothingness. It's almost like a temporary dissolution – a lapsing away. Yes, lapsing is the word – lapsing back into nothingness."

"I don't think there is anything so very unusual about your sensations," I said, I fear rather pompously. "I think we all of us at times feel something very like what you describe. It's a mild sort of neurosis, and it's in the nature of every neurosis to give the sufferer a sense of singularity."

"I daresay," she said, and went on as though making up her mind to take a fence. "But then, you see, I have twice had a strangely disturbing experience which has made those sensations I try to describe become a real obsession."

"Experiences?" I echoed. "What do you mean?"

"I'll tell you," she said. "Don't expect a ghost story. I should hate to raise false hopes. It will be difficult to describe these experiences, and I don't expect you'll believe me, but they are true. Anyhow, don't interrupt. Just let me Ancient-Mariner you. The first time was when I was very young – scarcely grown up. Late one evening I was resting on my bed. I was very tired and consequently especially depressed by that curiously disagreeable feeling I have tried to describe – the 'no-identity' feeling. Like any other trouble it is apt to be worse when I am over-tired.

"It was dark and my window, against which the jasmine tapped, was on the ground floor. I slept downstairs then. Suddenly I had that sense we all know of being impelled to look in a certain direction. I turned and saw a dim face pressed against the window – peering through at me. I wasn't exactly frightened – just rather detachedly aware that my heart was thumping. Just then the moon slipped free from a fleece of clouds, so that I could see the face quite clearly. It was my own face!"

"What?" I broke in.

"Yes, Dr Stone. Of that there was no doubt. One knows one's own face. My face was gazing at me – very intently, very wistfully – and, as I stared, whatever it was that was outside shook its head very sadly. I hoped I was dreaming. I shut my eyes, but I couldn't keep them shut, and when I looked up again it was still there, and now it wrung its hands, oh! so mournfully.

"As I have said, it was my own face I saw through the window, but did I – could I – myself look so miserable? I wanted to see myself, my own self – so I got out of bed. I found my knees were trembling and I swayed as I went up to my looking-glass.

"I don't know how to make you believe what I am going to tell you. Don't laugh. It was the most awful shock. I found I could not see myself in the glass. I stared, and stared. I shook the glass. But my reflection was not there. The pictures on the wall, the corner of the cupboard, the bird-cage, all the familiar objects were reflected as usual, but I myself was not there.

"It was still outside, and now it looked as though it were trying to get in – to get back, but could not. Terror came over me, and a feeling of faintness against which I desperately struggled. Dizzily I left my room, dragged myself upstairs and went up to the Chippendale mirror in the drawing room. The wide shining sheet of glass was hopelessly empty of what I sought. What had happened to me that I had no reflection? Surely the thing must be a delusion. Was I insane? I can't describe the state of mind in which I returned to my own room. I scarcely dared open the door. To my infinite relief the face was no longer looking through the window. I strode to the looking-glass. My reflection was there. Except that I looked strangely wan, my face was as usual." She paused. "That was the first time it happened. Shall I tell you about the second time, or do you wish to certify me at once?"

"Go on," I said.

"It was about three years later. I was laid up in bed with a sprained ankle. I had been in a sort of apathy all day and towards evening was assailed by that painful sense of the lack of identity that I have tried to describe. There seemed no string threading the beads of mere moods. I felt without any real opinion, emotion, or impulse, as though I were an actor thrust on to a stage without having been given a single word of his part. Just a sense of complete vacuum. Neither my mind nor my hands were engaged. I was not even consciously looking in any particular direction. Suddenly I found myself rigid and staring. There was a sofa in my room, and on it a form was lying just as I lay on my bed. The form was mine, and again my own face gazed at me – oh! so mournfully. As before, that awful sense of faintness – of ebbing away – came over me, but I just managed to remain conscious. It still lay on the sofa. The face gazed at me with an unforgettable look of sadness. It looked as though it wanted to speak – in fact, the lips moved – but I heard nothing. A hand-mirror lay on a table within my reach, and I forced myself to lift it in front of my face. My dread was realized. I stared into blankness. My face was not reflected. For some time I lay there, now staring hypnotized at what lay on the sofa, now searching the empty mirror. I don't know how long it was before my reflection began mistily and gradually to reappear, flickering in and out until at last it was still and as usual – except that I looked as tired as I felt. Of course I didn't say anything about this to anyone. You are the first person I have mentioned it to. What is your verdict, Dr Stone?"

"I am going to say a very tiresome thing," I replied, with a sense of the futility of my words as I pronounced them. "I think you dreamed both these experiences."

"If you are going to talk like that," she said wearily, "I shall never tell you anything about myself again. You know just as well as I do that I was awake."

"Well," I said, "you may not have been actually physically asleep, but I think this com—"

"If you are going to use the word complex, I shall change my doctor!" she interrupted laughingly.

"I think," I continued, "that you had allowed this – shall we call it – obsession of yours about your lack of continuous personality to weigh so heavily on your subconscious mind that it created a sort of symbolic imagery, which imposed itself on your senses even to the point of definite illusion. It was, so to speak, a fixation of an idea. This sort of phenomenon is quite well known to psychologists. I could give you many examples."

Margaret shook her head sadly. "It's sweet of you to try and reassure me, but I'm afraid I am not convinced. And," she added with darkening eyes, "this thing really troubles me far more than I have been able to convey. I think I told you I felt faint both times? Somehow I knew it was dreadfully important that I should not actually faint. With a desperate effort, I held on to consciousness. I simply didn't dare let myself go and quite slip my moorings. It would be awful to be ousted, wouldn't it?"

"Ousted?" I echoed blankly.

"Well, isn't it rather a risk to leave untenanted bodies lying about? Houses need caretakers." She laughed, but there was no laughter in her eyes.

Before I left her she had dismissed the subject and become her familiar radiant self, and yet never again was I to feel quite untroubled about her.

As for her "experiences", I dismissed them as purely subjective. Anything they might intimate was still for me too far removed in the regions of sheer fantasy. It was something in her voice, when she used the word "ousted", that had made me conscious of a chill. That and the expression in her eyes.

As usual I turned back to look at the house as I went out of the gate. The glow of the fading day warmed its grey austerity, and this evening, to my fancy, it wore an expression positively benign and sheltering.

I did not see much less of my patient after she ceased to be an invalid. Not only did I still give her electric treatment, but she would often ask me to dinner, and the happiest hours of my life were spent in her little sitting room, the most personal room I have ever known. It was like her very shell.

I look back on those magic evenings of that late summer and see them in a golden haze. The white room heavy with the scent of flowers; the Golden Retriever, his plumed tail sweeping from side to side; Margaret in her shimmering beauty; the two of us talking – talking; or Margaret reading aloud, or at her piano playing by heart, gliding from one loveliness into another, characteristically never saying what it is that she is going to play.

She frequently reverted to what she had told me on that day of sudden confidence, but usually very lightly, as though the matter no longer preyed on her mind.

Once she even laughingly referred lo herself as the "absentee landlady". Indeed, from the lulled expression of her eyes, I judged her nerves to be much quieter, and it was a shock to me to realize how easily I had been deceived by the characteristic lightness of her manner. One evening she broke off in the middle of a poem she was reading aloud, and said, "I am feeling very detached from myself this evening – disquietingly detached." She then began to harp on the old theme, dwelling on the affair of her reflection – the "home-made symbol", as we had agreed to call it. Her voice was unconcerned, and in an attempt at reassurance I said something rather perfunctory.

At that she suddenly burst out with wholly unaccustomed vehemence: "From every word you say I know that you do not understand, and that I can never make you understand!"

My chagrin at having failed her must have shown in my face.

"So sorry," she said in her sweetest manner. "How can you be expected to guess that I am serious when I can't help speaking even of these things in my small-talk voice? I am such an involuntary bluffer! But, you see, it happened again last night. But now, for heaven's sake," she broke in on my words of concern, "for heaven's sake, don't let's say another word about Margaret Clewer! Please read to me. I want to get on with my embroidery."

I look back on that evening as the end of a halcyon spell.

The next morning stands out sharply etched on my memory. From then onwards it was through a web of mystification, gradually thickening into horror which baffled belief, that I struggled to preserve my reason.

I had just finished my breakfast when I was told Miss Clewer's maid wished to speak to me on the telephone. I knew Rebecca Park well. She worshipped her mistress, whom she had attended since childhood, and I was sure that, with the instinct of the simple and devoted, she recognized me as a real friend. Her voice was sharp with anxiety.

"Please come quick, sir. I can't wake my mistress this morning, and her sleep don't seem natural."

Ten minutes later I entered the familiar bedroom. Margaret lay in something between a swoon and a sleep. She breathed unevenly and I noticed that her hands were tightly clenched.

No man who loves a woman can see her asleep for the first time without emotion. Something clutched at my heart as I looked at Margaret's unconscious face. I cannot remember whether I had ever actually pictured her asleep. If so I could never have surmised that which I saw. How could closed eyes and lack of colour effect so great though subtle a change in a familiar face? What was it in the expression of those lovely features that was so utterly alien – so disquietingly alien – to the Margaret I loved?

Struck by the coldness of her wrist when I felt her pulse, I told Rebecca to fetch a hot-water bottle, and as we turned back the bedclothes to apply it we both received a shock. Margaret's feet were not only cold, but damp and stained with earth: little lumps of clay soil stuck between the toes. It had been a very wet night.

"She has been walking in her sleep," I whispered to Rebecca. "On no account tell her when she wakes, and please wash all traces from her feet. Quick, before she wakes."

As I bathed her blue-veined temples. Margaret gave a long, shuddering sigh, and very piteously breathed out, "No! No! No!" her voice rising as she pleaded.

As she recovered consciousness and the long lashes lifted, her own expression swam into her eyes like some lovely flower rising to the surface through muddied waters. Her first words were curious, and at the time I wondered whether Rebecca noticed.

"Is it Me?" she said, gazing upwards. Not, as I might have expected – for my presence must have puzzled her— "Is it you?" but "Is it Me?"

I explained my presence, telling her as unconcernedly as possible that I had been sent for because she had fainted.

Her brow contracted and fear looked out of her eyes. As

soon as Rebecca had left the room she spoke in the quick level voice that I associated with her rare confidences.

"It happened again last night."

"What happened?"

"I was pushed out of myself . . . no reflection, nothing. You know I told you before how desperately hard whatever was left of me had to struggle not to faint? Well, this time I fainted. The awful dizziness overcame me. I had to let go." She gave a queer little laugh. "Yes, this time I really slipped my moorings and evidently my faint – as you call it – has lasted an unconscionable time. Not that I know when it was I went off. 'Went off' is the correct expression, isn't it?"

Impressing on Rebecca the necessity for absolute quiet, I started on my professional rounds, but not for one moment in all that busy day did the thought of Margaret leave my mind. An undefined but deep anxiety settled in my heart.

I have already admitted that I loved her. To hope for a return of my love had never entered my head. It did not occur to me that I could lay any claim to so transcendent a being. As soon would I have made a declaration to the moon. Fool that I was! How often I have asked myself whether avowed love might have helped where friendship failed.

At about half-past twelve that night I suddenly awoke, thoughts of Margaret thrumming in my brain. Suppose she were to walk in her sleep again? Might she not injure herself or wake up and be terrified? How could I have risked such a thing happening again without even warning her? Of course I should have arranged for someone to sleep in her room.

I was in my clothes almost before I knew I had decided to go to the Manor House. If I found her walking, I could lead her home in her sleep.

A full moon flooded the house with a strange green beauty. Glancing up at Margaret's window, I was surprised to see it shut on so warm a night. I decided to patrol the courtyard and watch the door in case she should emerge. I trod as softly as possible. Save for the distant bark of the inevitable dog, my vigil seemed unshared. The night was full of an indescribable menace. A low wind crept through the trees and the leaves whispered momentously. Claimed by the moon, the house looked wan and remote, palely repudiating any human allegiance it might seem to concede by daylight.

I was startled by the loud hoot of an owl, a sound I can never hear without a strange stirring as of some forgotten but intense memory. "You can't think how lovely it looks at night with a great white owl sweeping about." I remembered Margaret's words, and obeyed an impulse to enter the churchyard. A white owl almost brushed my cheek as he passed on his blundering flight.

Beneath the transmuting moon the crowded tombstones looked more sharply outlined, far less merged into the green quiet of the long grass. In the day time the atmosphere breathed a sense of acquiescence, as though the oft-repeated text "Thy will be done" had been instilled into the very air, but now the peace of buried centuries seemed disturbed; the consecrated ground to quiver with insubmission. Even the yew trees seemed to bristle. Starkly black, they stood like mutinous sentinels.

As I turned my eyes to the eastern side of the churchyard, I heard myself gasp. In the uttermost corner something white glimmered on the ground. I knew at once what it was. Ten strides brought me to where Margaret, in her long nightgown, lay outstretched across a flat tombstone. Her arms, the hands tightly clenched, were flung out in front; her slim, protesting body writhed. It looked as though she were struggling to rise, but had no power; almost as though some force were drawing her down. I heard a low, piteous moaning, and kneeled to examine her pale, twisted face. The eyes were closed. Her tormented body rolled over to one side, leaving the inscription on the grey lichened stone exposed. As I knelt I involuntarily read the brief words:

Here lyes the bodye of Elspeth Clewer.
God grante that she lye stille.

I recalled my first visit to the churchyard. So it was upon the grave of Elspeth Clewer, the uncommended ancestress who had so aroused my curiosity, that Margaret lay.

"No! No! *No!*" was wrung from her lips, and she writhed as though in anguish.

I raised her gently. Strength was required. It was like lifting a body from a quicksand. Fearful of waking her, I slowly led her home and to her room.

Sheen, the Golden Retriever, greeted me sleepily, but with his usual exquisite courtesy, and when I had laid her on the bed, he gently licked his mistress's white hand.

I watched by her side for some time until her sleep seemed tranquil and normal. Then, in misplaced confidence, I left her alone, except for the dog who lay stretched out his golden length across the bed.

Anxious to see her the next morning, I went round as early as possible, intending to explain my uninvited visit by a wish to alter a prescription. But Rebecca met me in the passage, her honest brow besieged with worry.

"You're a glad sight for sore eyes, Doctor. I was just going to send for you. Miss Margaret's just like she was yesterday – deep drowned in that sleep that don't seem natural. I can't abide to see her like that."

"I think it only means she's very over-tired," I said, anxious to soothe.

"That's as maybe," she answered, unconvinced. "Though what she's done to get so tired, I don't know. And, Doctor, there's something most dreadful's gone and happened. I suppose that dratted cat must have got into my lady's room in the night and forced its way – the cunning brute – into the birdcage, and there's them two sweet little birds, as Miss Margaret sets such store by, lying dead in their blood with their poor little heads torn right off of their bodies. Really, I don't know how to tell Miss Margaret when she wakes. She'll take on so!"

"I'll tell her," I said, as I followed her into the bedroom, hastily adding, "but, for heaven's sake, take away the cage. She mustn't see that awful sight when she wakes."

With little moans of concern the maid hurried away with her gruesome burden.

Margaret lay in deep unconsciousness. Her appearance was in every way the same as on the previous morning. I turned over her limp hand to feel her pulse. Then I heard my heart hammering in my ears. It was as though it had attended and taken in something my mind refused to accept. Soon I felt deadly sick. Self-protection, reason, fought against the evidence of my sight, but in vain. The lovely white hand that I had so often ached to kiss was thickly smeared with red, and sticking between the fingers and thumb was a cluster of blood-stained feathers.

For the first time I knew what it was to shudder with my whole being. Difficult though it was to control my thoughts, prompt action was necessary, and, fetching warm water, I hastily washed all traces from her hand.

Soon afterwards she turned and, struggling through layers of oblivion and subconsciousness, came to herself. Bewilderment showed in her eyes, then relief and welcome.

"What's the matter?" she said, looking at my face. Struggling to hide the shrinking that I felt, I explained my presence and wrote out a prescription.

Margaret looked round the room for her inseparable companion. "Where's Sheen?" she asked.

"He wasn't in here when I come in this morning, Miss," said Rebecca, "and I can't find him nowhere. I've asked everyone, and no one's seen him."

"He must have jumped out of the window," said Margaret. "How queer of him."

At her request I looked out of the window. The flower bed below plainly showed a dog's pawmarks.

"I must get up and go and hunt for him," said Margaret. "I had a horrid dream about him."

She looked deathly pale, quite unfit to leave her bed, but I knew it would be useless to attempt to detain her. I had come to the conclusion that I must tell her of her sleep-walking and insist that she should have a night nurse for a time. I wanted an opportunity to break this to her as unalarmingly as possible, so I reminded her of her promise to call on a farmer's wife and try to persuade the obstinate woman to obey my injunctions and send her crippled child to a hospital. She agreed to come that afternoon.

As I left the house I remembered that I had not told her about the death of the birds: neither had she noticed the absence of their cage.

At three o'clock we started on our two-mile walk across the fields. It was a lovely afternoon, resplendent summer, though a delicious tang in the air hinted at autumn and brought an exquisite pink to Margaret's cheeks. More than ever I was struck by her astonishing look of dewy youth. Like a just opened wild rose her face looked utterly unused, as though it had never harboured any expression save one of vague expectancy. My horrid misgivings began to seem fantastically unreal.

"Have you heard of the cat's crime?" she asked. Her eyes looked like wet flowers and her voice quivered, though characteristically she tried to laugh as she added: "Of all Shakespeare's adjectives, I think the queerest are his 'harmless' and 'necessary' applied to a cat. I adored those little birds."

I murmured sympathy.

"I'm wretchedly worried about Sheen's disappearance, too," she said. "He's never been away from me for even an hour before. He'll go mad with misery without me. Do you think he can have been stolen?"

"I'm quite sure he hasn't," I said emphatically.

I steered the conversation until, as unconcernedly as possible, I told her I had discovered that she was given to the quite common but not to be encouraged habit of sleep-walking.

Consternation flared in her eyes and she flushed painfully. She tried to laugh it off.

"I wonder what my particular 'damned spot' may be. It always is some damned spot that won't 'out' that makes people walk in their sleep, isn't it? Or may it be merely due to unsubmissive food?"

"It's far more often caused by indigestion than by conscience," I said, with a laugh, and I took advantage of this wave of flippancy to float the hospital nurse into the conversation.

To my surprise and relief Margaret promptly acquiesced. In fact, it seemed to me that a look of unmistakable relief flickered across her face. I told her an excellent nurse was just about to leave one of my patients, and that I would engage her to come in that evening.

"You won't need to see her at all during the day," I said. "She'll just sit up in your room at night."

"Oh, I hope she doesn't knit," laughed Margaret. "I don't expect sleep will ever slide into my soul with her sitting there. I shall be the watched pot that never boils! However, no sleep – no walking; so it will be all to the good."

With that we dismissed the matter.

"Now let's forget everything, except this winged hour. It is such a heavenly afternoon!" she exclaimed. "Thank heaven I can always live in the present. I hope you don't think it's dreadful to have a nature like a duck's back?"

She stepped out and the shadow which had overhung her ever since that unexpected outburst in her sitting-room lifted from her. Once more she shone out as the radiant being I had first known. It was impossible not to be infused by her brilliant gaiety, and as her lovely peals of laughter rang out, for the time being my nightmare was almost dispersed. Her inimitable mimicry, delicious raillery and stream of brilliantly garbled quotations almost made me forget the unforgettable. But her radiance suddenly clouded over when I said:

"What an amazing memory you have got!"

"Memory?" she answered almost sharply. "Yes, I admit I have plenty of memory and understanding. But what protection are such merely *receptive* qualities?"

"Protection?" I echoed blankly.

"Well, here we are," she said in evasion, her hand on the farmyard gate. "Now I propose that you stay here, while I go in by myself and twist the good woman round my little finger.

I'm sure your presence would cramp my little finger's style. I'll wish it luck," and pulling off her glove she smilingly held up her tapering, pink-nailed finger. "What's the matter?" she asked uneasily.

I'm afraid an uncontrollable inward shudder must have shown on my face. The last time I had looked at that slender finger, it had been stained with blood, and I could still see the pitiful little feathers that had stuck to it.

"I've got a stitch," I lied. "I'll wait here for your good news. Good luck."

A prey to uninvited thoughts, I leaned against the gate. About five minutes later I heard myself hailed and was delighted to see the gardener with Sheen on a chain. As I patted the beautiful dog's head, he slowly waved his sweeping tail.

"Please, sir," explained the gardener, "the keeper found him in a distant wood, and when he brings him home, Miss Park, knowing where you was goin', she asks me to follow you, thinking Miss Clewer would be that pleased to see him safe."

Delighted to be the bearer of good news, I hurried towards the farmhouse, and was met by Margaret.

"Triumph to my little finger!" she began, but directly I spoke of Sheen her successful mission was forgotten in delight, and she ran towards the gate. "Darling, darling Sheen! How could you leave me?" I heard her eager voice.

Then something so dreadful happened – something so painful, that even now I can scarcely endure to recall it.

As Margaret approached her dog, expecting an exuberant welcome, an unaccountable change came over him. His tail was lowered until it disappeared between his cringing legs, and his whole body shook with unmistakable terror.

"Sheen – what is the matter?"

Her voice was piteous and, looking at her face, I saw it contorted with unbearable suffering.

"It's Me!" she pleaded. "Sheen, it's Me!"

But the dog she had said "would be mad with misery without her" cowered lower and lower as though it would creep through the ground, and his golden coat grew dark with sweat.

"Oh, what did happen last night?" wailed Margaret, and put out her hands to the dog in anguished propitiation.

"Back, miss, back!" shouted the terrified gardener.

The dog's eyes showed white, he howled, snapped wildly in Margaret's direction, and tore at his collar in frantic efforts to escape.

"Take him away!" cried Margaret. "Take him away! I'll go back by the road," and she started off as fast as her swift stride could carry her.

I overtook her, but could think of nothing to say. A terrible constraint lay between us. I looked at her. Tears coursed down her white, strained face and her mortally affronted eyes stared straight in front.

"Unaccountable things, dogs," at last I ventured.

"Unaccountable? Do you think so?" she said sharply. "I wonder." And as she strode on, she clenched her hands till the knuckles stood out white.

A moment later she turned to me as though she were on the point of really speaking, of letting something gush out. She made a little movement with one hand, but then it was as though an iron shutter slid between us, and in a cold formal voice she told me of her successful interview with the farmer's wife. That was all we spoke of. We might almost have been strangers.

The next morning I went to give her some electric treatment. She looked bitterly troubled, but said she liked the hospital nurse, a pleasant, serene-faced young woman. I missed the accustomed twitter of the birds, and the room looked strangely deserted without the beautiful golden dog. I dared not ask about him, and I never saw him again.

With a pang of pity I noticed that all the mirrors had been removed.

"Has that queer thing happened again?" I ventured. "Did you think there was something wrong with your reflection?"

"Don't ask me about that any more," she answered feverishly. "I've finished with all that fanciful nonsense and I never wish to hear it alluded to again. Never, never, never!"

With that a safety-curtain of unhappy reserve fell between us. She seemed to consign herself to the loneliness of utter withdrawal, and from that time onward the shadows settled more and more darkly on her beautiful face.

A few days after her arrival I asked the nurse to come and talk to me about her patient. She had nothing very definite to report, except that, though her charge slept for a fair number of hours, her sleep was very troubled and brought little refreshment. In fact, she always seemed most tired and overwrought in the mornings.

"Of course," the nurse said, "I do think that having no fresh air in the room these stifling hot nights may have something to do with her condition."

"Why," I asked, "do you mean to say she doesn't have the window open in this weather?"

The stubborn summer had blazed out into a last fierce spell of heat, and I was indeed amazed.

"No, sir, I can't persuade her to, and sometimes I can scarcely bear the closeness myself."

I promised to use my influence.

"Then there's another thing," the nurse went on. "Do you think it can be good for anyone in an excited state of nerves to be doing all that rehearsing? If you'll excuse my saying so, sir, I think you should order her to give up those theatricals."

"Theatricals?" I echoed blankly. "What theatricals?"

"I don't know when they're to be, but I know she's very busy rehearsing for them. Whenever she sends me to fetch something during the night, and she's always asking me to fetch some book or something special from the stillroom – not that she ever scorns to use the things when I bring them – well, as I come back, all the way down that long passage, I hear her fairly screaming out her part. Wonderful actress she must be! You wouldn't really think it could be her own voice; no, you wouldn't think such a sweet young lady could produce so horrid a voice. It simply raises my hair – that acting voice of hers does. And, as I was saying, I really can't think it can be good for anyone whose nerves are disturbed to be studying so violent a part."

"Thank you, Nurse. I'll speak about it."

That afternoon I called on Margaret. After some casual talk I said, "I hear you sleep with your window shut. And, you know, you are looking extremely pale. To insist on keeping the window open all the year round may be a foolish fetish, but in this sort of weather, it really is essential."

"If the nurse makes a fuss about that, I won't keep her," Margaret burst out. "How can I leave the window open when it's from there that I feel that awful pressing in – that pressing and pushing away? How can I? Though, heaven knows, it's foolish enough to think it's any use to shut things. If stone walls cannot a prison make, nor iron bars a cage, still less can they make a fortress." Suddenly she seemed to remember herself. "But these are but 'wild and whirring words'," she said, smiling. "I'm so sorry. Please don't pay any attention to them. My disease of quoting grows worse and worse. It's because I have no opinions of my own."

She looked disquietingly excited and my own head swam. "That awful pressing in!" What did she . . . what could she . . . mean? A sense of dreadful menace almost stifled me, and I felt utterly estranged; but something had to be said.

"When are your theatricals to be?" I asked. "I didn't know you were acting."

"Acting?" she repeated. "What do you mean?"

"The nurse tells me she often hears you rehearsing in the night."

She blushed crimson. "Oh, that!" she said. "Oh, yes! You see, I have a silly habit of reciting poetry aloud to myself, and it made me feel self-conscious to know she had overheard me, so I said I was rehearsing for some theatricals."

"I see," I said; but my heart sank at hearing her lie.

Then we spoke of other things, but we were both hopelessly preoccupied, and there was no life in our talk. It was almost forced, and I noted that nearly everything that Margaret said was in inverted commas. Scarcely anything passed her lips that was not a quotation. I had already observed that the more tired, strained or preoccupied she seemed, the more this was the case. When her vitality was lowered it was, to use her own words, as though she had "no opinion, emotion or impulse" of her own, but was merely a thoroughfare for the thoughts of others – as though nothing remained to hold the fort except memory.

I think it was three days later that the nurse, of her own accord, came to report to me again, and told me she considered her patient increasingly nervous and depressed. To my enquiry as to how Miss Clewer was sleeping, she answered: "Very little now." Adding ominously, "And if you ask me, sir, I don't think she wants to go to sleep."

"She's given up the theatricals anyhow, hasn't she?" I asked, in as casual a voice as I could command.

"Given them up, sir? No, I wish to goodness' sake she would. I really can scarcely bear to hear it; the way she screams out her part has thoroughly got on my nerves. As often as I come back along that passage, she's going through it. I know some of her part by heart myself. I don't believe I'll ever be able to forget the queer words."

"What are the words you overhear her saying?" I asked, as indifferently as I could.

"Saying? You wouldn't call it saying if you'd heard her, sir, it's more like yelling. As I was saying the other day, you'd never think such a gentle lady could produce such a terrifying voice. The words that she most often repeats are: 'Let me in! Give way! What can I do without a body? What use are you making of your body? I want it! You clear out! I must be lodged! I must be lodged! I must be lodged!' And the third time she repeats 'I must be lodged', her voice rises to a screech. But whatever's the matter, sir? You've come over as white as a sheet!"

Murmuring that I felt faint and must get some brandy, I told her I would see her in the evening, and left the room.

My legs almost gave way as I went upstairs, and directly I reached my bedroom I turned the key in the lock, though what it was I thought might thus be debarred, God only knows.

With shaking hands, I opened the book I had been reading in bed the night before.

It was a bound copybook, filled with the faded brown of a spidery sixteenth-century writing. Margaret had long given me the freedom of her library, and on a high shelf I had found a manuscript book – a sort of irregular journal kept by an ancestress of hers, also a Margaret Clewer. I had read it far into the night. It was all interesting, and by the final heart-broken entry I had been most vividly and painfully impressed.

Were certain words really as, with horror, I remembered them, or was my memory deceiving my disturbed nerves?

Trembling, I turned the leaves until I came to the words:

So she is dead! Elspeth, our shame, lyes dead. That I should live to thank God that my own child be laid in the churchyarde! A sennight yesterday since they carryed her home after her falle from her horse. A sennight of torment unimagined to us all. The passing of her eville spirit has been a horror past beliefe. The drawing nigh of Death had no softening effect on her violent, eville greedy spirit. Her hold on lyfe was terrible. Breath by breath it was torne from her shattered bodye. So her fierce spirit clung to her beautiful broken bodye, God helpe us all! Could any Death be deep enough to make me to forget how with her last breaths she cryde out: "I won't dye! I won't dye! There is still so much to do! Some way I'll get back! I must get back! My spirit is so unquenched! I must find another bodye. I must be lodged! I must be lodged! I must be lodged!"

The long-dead woman's manuscript slipped from my hand and I struggled to think. Even last night the words of the dying changeling daughter had made me shiver. Now, after what the nurse had quoted, they seared my mind. Elspeth Clewer! I remembered the grey, uncommunicative grave beneath the yew tree. Its bleak reticence had impressed my imagination on my first visit to the churchyard, and now, to my mind's eye, it was forever associated with Margaret's prostrate, writhing body.

God grante that she lye stille! God grante that she lye stille! I snatched at a faint, fluttering hope. Perhaps Margaret was familiar with the journal I had found. If so, its grim contents would be very likely to haunt her. Might not what the nurse mistook for rehearsing have been her quoting it in disturbed sleep?

That evening I found her pale and wild-eyed. I told her of my discovery of the diary and asked if she had ever read it. She disclaimed all knowledge, and this time I knew she spoke the truth. I said it gave a strange account of an ancestress of hers, an Elspeth Clewer. Was it my fancy, or did she draw in her breath at the name?

"Oh! Does it?" she said. "Yes, I've heard of her. Though she died before she was twenty-three, she's the only celebrated member of the Clewer family, for she crowded her short life with every imaginable vice and crime. I believe she was an absolute mythical monster of violence and cruelty: but, as I have often told you, I really don't take the faintest interest in my ancestors."

Two days later, as I sat at breakfast, the front-door bell was so violently pulled that I went to the door myself. The faithful Rebecca stood there, her face mottled with agitation. "Oh, sir! She's been and gone and bolted!"

"Miss Clewer?" I gasped.

"No, sir," she gabbled breathlessly. "That yere nurse, been and gone and offed it – left my poor lamb with no word to no one. Yes, when I comes along this mornin' I finds my lady deep asleep, and, if you please, on the floor there's a tray with broken pieces of cup and saucer and Benger's food slopped all over the carpet. Just dropped out of Nurse's hand, it must have been. And she couldn't be found nowhere; clean gone she was – run off and left all her things behind her. The garden boy, he tells me he seen her tearing round the garden like as though the devil were after her. I looks in at the station, and they said she'd been there a full hour before the first train went, and

looked that queer without no hat nor nothing. And my lady –
she looks to go to your heart this morning – she says she calls
to mind asking Nurse to fetch her a cup of Benger's – and then
she thinks she must have fallen asleep, since she doesn't
remember no more."

Incensed with the nurse, I rang up the London association
from which she came and instructed them to telephone directly
she arrived. Full of foreboding I hurried to the Manor House.
I found Margaret walking up and down in the garden, her face
drawn and set.

"I'm sorry I've frightened your nurse away," she said bitterly.

"Frightened her? You!" I tried to laugh.

"So it seems. A well-trained nurse who drops her tray and
flies from the house must surely be a little upset."

"She must have taken leave of her senses," I said dryly.
"Fortunately I know of an admirable one who happens to be
free now."

"No, thank you. No more nurses for me! I can't say I've found
the last one very reassuring. No, I've just telegraphed to lots of
my friends to come down. I've been too unsociable lately." She
spoke defiantly, and I knew it would be no use to argue.

That afternoon I was rung up by the matron of the Nursing
Association. Nurse Newson had never turned up, but on
enquiry it was found she had gone to her mother, whose telephone number I was given.

"Mrs Newson speaking," answered a painstakingly genteel
voice.

I explained who I was, stating that I wished to speak to her
daughter, whose amazing behaviour demanded explanation.

The voice let itself go, and unmistakable relish in a crisis was
plain through its agitation.

"Oh, sir! I'm afraid you can't speak to my daughter. She's
bad in bed, and doctor says she's suffering from shock and
mustn't be disturbed. Oh, sir! Whatever did happen to make
her take on so, such a sensible, steady girl as she is? She's in
ever such a state! I never did see anyone so upset before, and I
can't get from her what it is she's so scared on – at least nothing

that you would call coherent. And, please sir, she says she's terribly sorry to have let you down, but she couldn't have stayed on – not for any consideration."

Feeling no sympathy, I snapped out: "I never heard of such behaviour. A nurse abandoning a case in the middle of the night? She must be hopelessly hysterical. What possible excuse can she have? Her patient is the most charming young lady."

"Yes, she says the young lady she was engaged for was ever so sweet, but Doctor – I don't understand – she talks so wild – and when I question her, begs me not to ask, but wasn't there *another* young lady?"

Exasperated, I banged the receiver down.

It was necessary to go to the Manor House to give the address to which the nurse's luggage was to be sent. I would have gone in, but two cars were just unloading their freight of visitors. Loud voices echoed in the courtyard, and aggressively young people, brandishing tennis rackets, bounded up the steps towards their hostess, who stood in the doorway, her face resolutely gay.

With a forlorn sense of being cut off from her, and with apprehension heavy on my heart, I stole away. As I looked back at the house, gilded by the setting sun, I almost hated it for its unconcerned beauty.

Two days later I received a note in her strangely variable, but always recognizable, writing. It had no beginning:

> *I am going away . . . I must leave at once. When you get this*
> *I shall be in the train. I could not stay here another night.*
> *Please never ask me to explain. Something unthinkably*
> *dreadful happened last night. I could never dare risk having*
> *anyone to stay here again. Not possibly.*
>
> *Neither can I live here by myself.*
>
> *I don't understand; but, believe me, it's fearful, and I must*
> *go. Oh, God! There are more things in heaven and earth!*
> *I'll write.*
> *Margaret Clewer*

★ ★ ★

She went abroad, and I was glad to know her gone. If life became unutterably dreary, at least my nightmare fears were in abeyance. Naturally I wrote begging for an explanation of her note, but none came. I had many letters from her; but, except for the one line, "I am so glad I came away," they told me nothing. They were merely brilliant descriptions of her travels – little more than inspired *Baedekers*, with scarcely a word to show we had ever been great friends and shared an unacknowledged dread. I wrote to Rebecca to enquire after her mistress's health. Her reply said her young lady seemed well enough, but appeared restless and as though not really enjoying the full life she led.

As the leaves fluttered down, till winter lay like iron over the land, the magical days of that long summer began to assume the golden haze of something dreamed. Often I would go and gaze at her empty home. I began to wonder whether I was ever to see her again. There was even a rumour that the Manor House was to be let on a long lease.

One morning, when an unusually reluctant spring had at last turned the fields to glory, I was surprised to see on an envelope bearing a London postmark the writing that always made my heart leap. I read:

> *I find it quite impossible to keep away any longer. I feel myself irresistibly drawn home, but I shall not sleep in my old room. I shall come back Monday, but shall arrive late. Please come to luncheon Tuesday.*
> Margaret Clewer

Coming home Monday? This was Monday. I should see her in little more than twenty-four hours. The day crept by with unbelievable slowness. To hasten tomorrow I went to bed unusually early.

In the middle of the night I woke up suddenly and with the certainty that I had been aroused by some sound. Yes, there it was again, outside the house. Small pebbles were being thrown up against my window. Expecting an emergency call, I struggled out of sleepiness and looked out of my low window. The moon was full; a tall figure stood below; a white, upturned face gleamed in the silvery-green light. It was Margaret! Her loveliness glimmered in the strange, cold light, but she looked wild, and there was desperate urgency in her voice.

"Quick, quick!" she cried. "I must have your help. I'm so frightened. Quick! Let me in! Let me in! This time I'll tell you everything!"

Snatching my overcoat, I hurried downstairs as quietly as I could for fear of waking my servant, and opened the door.

It was no dream. The white figure stood outside, arms outstretched towards me. A glorious hope leaped in my heart; but, as I advanced, something indescribable looked out of her eyes. With desperate haste her hands moved, and in a second her face was entirely concealed by the chiffon scarf in which they had swathed it.

"Too late! Too late!" she wailed in a changing voice. "Go back, go back, and for God's sake, don't dare to follow me!" The white figure sped away.

Aghast, I started in pursuit, but after a few strides, the swathed, faceless figure turned. At the torrent of words that were shrieked at me in an unknown voice, I stood transfixed, frozen with horror.

Wild, nauseated fear took possession of me. God forgive me, I renounced her. To save my soul I could not have followed another step. I stole back and, drenched in cold sweat, lay shaking on my bed. Sleep never approached me, but I felt too shattered and ill to get up at my usual hour. At ten the telephone rang. Wondering what ghastly intimation was to come, I lifted the receiver.

Margaret's lovely voice slid into my astonished ears. "It's *me*. Please come and see me. They tell me I'm not well." Her own lovely voice that I had not hoped to hear again. Had some monstrous dream imposed itself upon me? Almost I began to think it.

When I reached the Manor House, I asked where Miss Clewer's new room was.

"Just the same as before, sir," replied the parlour maid. "Miss Clewer did give orders for one to be prepared on the other side of the house, but as soon as she came she said she'd go back to her own room."

Rebecca lay in wait in the familiar passage.

"Thank God you've come, Doctor," she whispered. "She seems to be wandering in her mind this morning."

I stole into the room. Margaret, strangely beautiful, but wan and fragile, lay back on a great pillow. She stretched out both hands in welcome. At once I knew that her memory held no trace of last night. She greeted me as though we met for the first time since her departure all those long months ago.

"Rebecca thinks I'm ill," she said. "But I must be a creature incapable of my own distress, because I assure you I feel quite well. And, oh! So, so glad to see my physician!"

Did I say that, after the incident of the dog, I was only once again to see Margaret in her incomparable radiance? Strange that it should have been now, when I was prepared to find her in delirium. But thus it was. Once more she seemed her original, untroubled, sparkling self.

She questioned me about all the Mosstone news and gave irresistibly funny descriptions of people she had met on her travels. All was as I first remembered her, dancing voice, lovely laughter, buoyant, bubbling talk, lightning response, showers of quotations. What had Rebecca meant by describing her as delirious?

But suddenly a change came into her eyes. She clutched at my hands and held them tight. Then she began to, what Rebecca described as, wander. Her voice was solemn.

"As the tree falls, so shall it lie! That is true, isn't it, John?"

John? I had almost forgotten my unused Christian name.

"It is true in every sort of way," she went on, "isn't it, darling? And as that tree lies, so shall it be all through the days of eternity – that's true too, isn't it, John – absolutely true?"

"Yes – yes, of course," I soothed her.

"Oh, John," she went on. "I've just found such a lovely, lovely poem. I didn't know it before. I can't think how I could have missed it. It's by Barnefield. Just listen to the mournful magic of these two lines:

> *"King Pandion he is dead,*
> *All thy friends are lapped in lead'.*

"'Lapped in lead'! Doesn't that make death sound delicious and luxurious? As though to be alive were something very makeshift." She gave a little quick laugh. "'Lapped in lead – lapped in lead'," she repeated, very slowly. "Oh, how lovely and peaceful and untormented! You know that would be the best thing that could happen to me, don't you? The best thing that could happen to your Me. Then *your* Me would be safe."

An urgent summons came, and I had to go to a distant case. Telling Rebecca on no account to leave her for a moment, and that I would get a nurse to come as soon as possible, I hurried away.

It was for a birth that I had been summoned. The baby was as reluctant to enter the world as its mother seemed disposed to leave it, and midnight had already struck when I reached home.

Through all the strain of that endless day I had been haunted by Margaret, and I intended to snatch some supper and hurry back to the Manor House. But before I had sat down the telephone rang. It was Rebecca's voice:

"Come quick, come at once! Miss Margaret seems so weak, as though she couldn't scarcely breathe. I'm speaking from her room. Do—" The voice broke off; it was no longer at the mouthpiece, but I heard it cry out, in deathly terror: "Oh, God, who—" And then the telephone must have been dropped.

No further sound came through. I replaced the receiver, and after a moment's pause rang up the Exchange, in my impatience violently rattling the instrument.

"Number, please? Number, please?" expostulated the

Exchange. I gave the number several times, but there was nothing to be heard beyond the intermittent ringing of an unanswered call . . . I pictured the overturned telephone lying on the floor of Margaret's room. What had happened?

Leaping into my car, I drove to the Manor House. The front door stood wide open, but no one was about. I did not meet anyone on my way to Margaret's room. The whole house was deserted.

What I saw when I approached the bed no one could attempt to describe and keep their reason. It writhed and moaned and seemed to breathe with terrible difficulty. I averted my eyes from the face, and with the automatic professional instinct to preserve life, administered an injection.

The thing on the bed gave a convulsive shudder and I heard the fast, thick breathing of some desperate struggle. Determined not to see the usurper again, I kept my eyes shut. I dared not look! Then there was silence, followed by a gentle sigh.

Something in that gentle sigh impelled me to open my eyes. Ineffable relief flowed over me. Like pure silver rising through primeval slime, the being I loved had struggled through and triumphed over the awful spiritual hideousness of that invasion. It was Margaret's face that smiled at me. Her voice came sweet but hopelessly weak.

"It's all right, darling," she breathed, and in her voice was a tenderness I had never imagined. "It's all right. I've won. It's me, *your* Me. Don't let me give way again. Keep me safe—"

Sure of her haven she gazed at me. Her hand clung to mine, and her lips smiled, but the strain of that final struggle had been too much for the already weakened heart. The eyelids fluttered up once or twice, as her clasp of my hand loosened. Almost inaudibly, but with an ecstasy of glimpsed peace, she breathed out the words: "'Lapped in lead – lapped in lead—'" And something else I could not quite hear. I felt a last little clinging clutch at my hand, and with one or two long sighs the spirit I loved slipped from its beautiful lodging.

Some hours later I left the deserted house, and returned to the emptied world. Gratitude mingled with my grief; my broken heart was at peace, for I knew her to be unassailable. The long dread was at an end.

It is a desolate path I tread, but sometimes, when it seems most steep and bare, there comes, like a gentle wave washing against my tired brain, the soft assuagement of her voice murmuring: "'Lapped in lead – lapped in lead'." And again I hear the promise in the infinite tenderness of her whispered "darling".

What were the words I failed to hear?

I often linger round her empty home. No smoke rises from the twisted chimneys, but pigeons still flutter and croon, and the grey house I once thought so aloof seems to receive me into an atmosphere of benign peace.

The Phantom Coach

Amelia B. Edwards

The circumstances I am about to relate to you have truth to recommend them. They happened to myself, and my recollection of them is as vivid as if they had taken place only yesterday. Twenty years, however, have gone by since that night. During those twenty years I have told the story to but one other person. I tell it now with a reluctance that I find it difficult to overcome. All I entreat, meanwhile, is that you will abstain from forcing your own conclusions upon me. I want nothing explained away. I desire no arguments. My mind on this subject is quite made up, and having the testimony of my own senses to rely upon, I prefer to abide by it.

Well! It was just twenty years ago, and within a day or two of the end of the grouse season. I had been out all day with my gun, and had had no sport to speak of. The wind was due east; the month, December; the place, a bleak wide moor in the far north of England. And I had lost my way. It was not a pleasant place in which to lose one's way, with the first feathery flakes of a coming snowstorm just fluttering down upon the heather, and the leaden evening closing in all around. I shaded my eyes with my hand, and stared anxiously into the gathering darkness, where the purple moorland melted into a range of low hills, some ten or twelve miles distant. Not the faintest smoke-wreath, not the tiniest cultivated patch, or fence, or sheep-track, met my eyes in any direction. There was nothing for it but to walk on, and take my chance of finding what shelter I could, by the way. So I shouldered my gun again and pushed wearily forward, for I had been on foot since an hour after daybreak and had eaten nothing since breakfast.

Meanwhile, the snow began to come down with ominous steadiness, and the wind fell. After this, the cold became more intense, and the night came rapidly up. As for me, my prospects darkened with the darkening sky, and my heart grew heavy as I thought how my young wife was already watching for me through the window of our little inn parlour, and thought of all the suffering in store for her throughout this weary night. We had been married four months, and, having spent our autumn in the Highlands, were now lodging in a remote little village situated just on the verge of the great English moorlands. We were very much in love, and, of course, very happy. This morning, when we parted, she had implored me to return before dusk, and I had promised her that I would. What would I not have given to have kept my word!

Even now, weary as I was, I felt that with supper, an hour's rest, and a guide, I might still get back to her before midnight, if only guide and shelter could be found.

And all this time the snow fell and the night thickened. I stopped and shouted every now and then, but my shouts seemed only to make the silence deeper. Then a vague sense of uneasiness came upon me, and I began to remember stories of travellers who had walked on and on in the falling snow until, wearied out, they were fain to lie down and sleep their lives away. Would it be possible, I asked myself, to keep on thus through all the long dark night? Would there not come a time when my limbs must fail, and my resolution give way? When I, too, must sleep the sleep of death. Death! I shuddered. How hard to die just now, when life lay all so bright before me! How hard for my darling, whose whole loving heart – but that thought was not to be borne! To banish it, I shouted again, and again the echo followed. Then a wavering speck of light came suddenly out of the dark, shifting, disappearing, growing momentarily nearer and brighter. Running towards it at full speed, I found myself, to my great joy, face to face with an old man and a lantern.

"Thank God!" was the exclamation that burst involuntarily from my lips. Blinking and frowning, he lifted his lantern and peered into my face.

"What for?" growled he, sulkily.

"Well – for you. I began to fear I should be lost in the snow."

"Eh, then, folks do get cast away hereabouts fra' time to time, an' what's to hinder you from bein' cast away likewise, if the Lord's so minded?"

"If the Lord is so minded that you and I shall be lost together, my friend, we must submit," I replied; "but I don't mean to be lost without you. How far am I now from Dwolding?"

"A gude twenty mile, more or less."

"And the nearest village?"

"The nearest village is Wyke, an' that's twelve miles t'other side."

"Where do you live, then?"

"Out yonder," said he, with a vague jerk of the lantern.

"You're going home, I presume?"

"Maybe I am."

"Then I'm going with you."

The old man shook his head, and rubbed his nose reflectively with the handle of the lantern.

"It ain't no use," growled he. "He 'on't let you in – not he."

"We'll see about that," I replied, briskly. "Who is he?"

"The master."

"Who is the master?"

"That's nowt to you," was the unceremonious reply.

"Well, well; you lead the way, and I'll engage that the master shall give me shelter and a supper tonight."

"Eh, you can try him!" muttered my reluctant guide; and, still shaking his head, he hobbled, gnome-like, away through the falling snow. A large mass loomed up presently out of the darkness, and a huge dog rushed out, barking furiously.

"Is this the house?" I asked.

"Ay, it's the house. Down, Bey!" And he fumbled in his pocket for the key.

I drew up close behind him, prepared to lose no chance of entrance, and saw in the little circle of light shed by the lantern that the door was heavily studded with iron nails, like the door of a prison. In another minute he had turned the key and I had pushed past him into the house.

Once inside, I looked round with curiosity and found myself in a great raftered hall, which served, apparently, a variety of uses. One end was piled to the roof with corn, like a barn. The other was stored with flour sacks, agricultural implements, casks, and all kinds of miscellaneous lumber; while from the beams overhead hung rows of hams, flitches, and bunches of dried herbs for winter use. In the centre of the floor stood some huge object gauntly dressed in a dingy wrapping-cloth, and reaching halfway to the rafters. Lifting a corner of this cloth, I saw, to my surprise, a telescope of very considerable size, mounted on a rude movable platform, with four small wheels. The tube was made of painted wood bound round with bands of metal rudely fashioned; the speculum, so far as I could estimate its size in the dim light, measured at least fifteen inches in diameter. While I was yet examining the instrument, and asking myself whether it was not the work of some self-taught optician, a bell rang sharply.

"That's for you," said my guide, with a malicious grin. "Yonder's his room."

He pointed to a low black door at the opposite side of the hall. I crossed over, rapped somewhat loudly, and went in, without waiting for an invitation. A huge, white-haired old man rose from a table covered with books and papers, and confronted me sternly.

"Who are you?" said he. "How came you here? What do you want?"

"James Murray, barrister-at-law. On foot across the moor. Meat, drink, and sleep."

He bent his bushy brows into a portentous frown.

"Mine is not a house of entertainment." he said, haughtily. "Jacob, how dare you admit this stranger?"

"I didn't admit him," grumbled the old man. "He followed me over the muir, and shouldered his way in before me. I'm no match for six foot two."

"And pray, sir, by what right have you forced an entrance into my house?"

"The same by which I should have clung to your boat, if I were drowning. The right of self-preservation."

"Self-preservation?"

"There's an inch of snow on the ground already," I replied briefly; "and it would be deep enough to cover my body before daybreak."

He strode to the window, pulled aside a heavy black curtain, and looked out.

"It is true," he said. "You can stay, if you choose, till morning. Jacob, serve the supper."

With this he waved me to a seat, resumed his own, and became at once absorbed in the studies from which I had disturbed him.

I placed my gun in a corner, drew a chair to the hearth, and examined my quarters at leisure. Smaller and less incongruous in its arrangements than the hall, this room contained, nevertheless, much to awaken my curiosity. The floor was carpetless. The whitewashed walls were in parts scrawled over with strange diagrams, and in others covered with shelves crowded with philosophical instruments, the uses of many of which were unknown to me. On one side of the fireplace stood a bookcase filled with dingy folios; on the other, a small organ, fantastically decorated with painted carvings of medieval saints and devils. Through the half-opened door of a cupboard at the further end of the room I saw a long array of geological specimens, surgical preparations, crucibles, retorts, and jars of chemicals; while on the mantelshelf beside me, amid a number of small objects, stood a model of the solar system, a small galvanic battery, and a microscope. Every chair had its burden. Every corner was heaped high with books. The very floor was littered over with maps, casts, papers, tracings, and learned lumber of all conceivable kinds.

I stared about me with an amazement increased by every fresh object upon which my eyes chanced to rest. So strange a room I had never seen; yet seemed it stranger still to find such a room in a lone farmhouse amid those wild and solitary moors! Over and over again I looked from my host to his surroundings, and from his surroundings back to my host, asking myself who and what he could be? His head was singularly fine; but it was more the head of a poet than of a philosopher. Broad in the temples, prominent over the eyes, and clothed with a rough profusion of perfectly white hair, it had all the ideality and much of the ruggedness that characterizes the head of Ludwig van Beethoven. There were the same deep lines about the mouth, and the same stern furrows in the brow. There was the same concentration of expression. While I was yet observing him, the door opened and Jacob brought in the supper. His master then closed his book, rose, and with more courtesy of manner than he had yet shown, invited me to the table.

A dish of ham and eggs, a loaf of brown bread, and a bottle of admirable sherry were placed before me.

"I have but the homeliest farmhouse fare to offer you, sir," said my entertainer. "Your appetite, I trust, will make up for the deficiencies of our larder."

I had already fallen upon the viands, and now protested, with the enthusiasm of a starving sportsman, that I had never eaten anything so delicious.

He bowed stiffly, and sat down to his own supper, which consisted, primitively, of a jug of milk and a basin of porridge. We ate in silence, and, when we had done, Jacob removed the tray. I then drew my chair back to the fireside. My host, somewhat to my surprise, did the same, and turning abruptly towards me, said:

"Sir, I have lived here in strict retirement for three-and-twenty years. During that time I have not seen as many strange faces and I have not read a single newspaper. You are the first stranger who has crossed my threshold for more than four years. Will you favour me with a few words of information respecting that outer world from which I have parted company so long?"

"Pray interrogate me," I replied. "I am heartily at your service."

He bent his head in acknowledgment; leaned forward, with his elbows resting on his knees and his chin supported in the palms of his hands; stared fixedly into the fire; and proceeded to question me.

His enquiries related chiefly to scientific matters, with the later progress of which, as applied to the practical purposes of life, he was almost wholly unacquainted. No student of science myself, I replied as well as my slight information permitted; but the task was far from easy, and I was much relieved when, passing from interrogation to discussion, he began pouring forth his own conclusions upon the facts which I had been attempting to place before him. He talked, and I listened spell-bound. He talked till I believe he almost forgot my presence, and only thought aloud. I had never heard anything like it then; I have never heard anything like it since. Familiar with all systems of all philosophies, subtle in analysis, bold in generalization, he poured forth his thoughts in an uninterrupted stream, and, still leaning forward in the same moody attitude with his eyes fixed upon the fire, wandered from topic to topic, from speculation to speculation, like an inspired dreamer. From practical science to mental philosophy; from electricity in the wire to electricity in the nerve; from Watts to Mesmer, from Mesmer to Reichenbach, from Reichenbach to Swedenborg, Spinoza, Condillac, Descartes, Berkeley, Aristotle, Plato, and the Magi and mystics of the East were transitions which, however bewildering in their variety and scope, seemed easy and harmonious upon his lips as sequences in music. By and by – I forget now by what link of conjecture or illustration – he passed on to that field which lies beyond the boundary line or even conjectural philosophy, and reaches no man knows whither. He spoke of the soul and its aspirations; of the spirit and its powers; of second sight; of prophecy; of those phenomena which, under the names of ghosts, spectres, and supernatural appearances, have been denied by the sceptics and attested by the credulous of all ages.

"The world," he said, "grows hourly more and more sceptical of all that lies beyond its own narrow radius; and our men of science foster the fatal tendency. They condemn as fable all that resists experiment. They reject as false all that cannot be brought to the test of the laboratory or the dissecting-room. Against what superstition have they waged so long and obstinate a war, as against the belief in apparitions? And yet what superstition has maintained its hold upon the minds of men so long and so firmly? Show me any fact in physics, in history, in archaeology, which is supported by testimony so wide and so various. Attested by all races of men, in all ages, and in all climates, by the soberest sages of antiquity, by the rudest savage of today, by the Christian, the Pagan, the Pantheist, the Materialist, this phenomenon is treated as a nursery tale by the philosophers of our century. Circumstantial evidence weighs with them as a feather in the balance. The comparison of causes with effects, however valuable in physical science, is put aside as worthless and unreliable. The evidence of competent witnesses, however conclusive in a court, as for nothing. He who pauses before he pronounces is condemned as a trifler. He who believes is a dreamer or a fool."

He spoke with bitterness and, having said thus, relapsed for some minutes into silence. Presently he raised his head from his hands and added, with an altered voice and manner:

"I, sir, paused, investigated, believed, and was not ashamed to state my convictions to the world. I, too, was branded as a visionary, held up to ridicule by my contemporaries, and hooted from that field of science in which I had laboured with honour during all the best years of my life. These things happened just three-and-twenty years ago. Since then I have lived as you see me living now, and the world has forgotten me, as I have forgotten the world. You have my history. It is a very common one," he continued. "I have only suffered for the truth, as many a better and wiser man has suffered before me."

He rose, as if desirous of ending the conversation, and went over to the window. "It has ceased snowing," he observed, as he dropped the curtain and came back to the fireside.

"Ceased!" I exclaimed, starting eagerly to my feet, "Oh, if it were only possible – but no! It is hopeless. Even if I could find my way across the moor, I could not walk twenty miles tonight."

"Walk twenty miles tonight!" repeated my host. "What are you thinking of?"

"Of my wife," I replied impatiently. "Of my young wife, who does not know that I have lost my way, and who is at this moment breaking her heart with suspense and terror."

"Where is she?"

"At Dwolding, twenty miles away."

"At Dwolding," he echoed, thoughtfully. "Yes, the distance, it is true, is twenty miles; but – are you so very anxious to save the next six or eight hours?"

"So very, very anxious, that I would give ten guineas at this moment for a guide and a horse."

"Your wish can be gratified at a less costly rate," said he, smiling. "The night mail from the north, which changes horses at Dwolding, passes within five miles of this spot, and will be due at a certain crossroads in about an hour and a quarter. If Jacob were to go with you across the moor and put you on to the old coach road, you could find your way, I suppose, to where it joins the new one?"

"Easily – gladly."

He smiled again, rang the bell, gave the old servant his directions and, taking a bottle of whisky and wineglass from the cupboard in which he kept his chemicals, said:

"The snow lies deep and it will be difficult walking tonight on the moor. A glass of usquebaugh before you start?"

I would have declined the spirit, but he pressed it on me, and I drank it. It went down my throat like liquid flame and almost took my breath away.

"It is strong," he said; "but it will help to keep out the cold. And now you have no moments to spare. Good night!"

I thanked him for his hospitality and would have shaken hands but that he had turned away before I could finish my sentence. In another minute I had traversed the hall, Jacob had locked the outer door behind me, and we were out on the wide white moor.

Although the wind had fallen, it was still bitterly cold. Not a star glimmered in the black vault overhead. Not a sound, save the rapid crunching of the snow beneath our feet, disturbed the heavy stillness of the night. Jacob, not too well pleased with his mission, shambled on before me in sullen silence, his lantern in his hand and his shadow at his feet. I followed, with my gun over my shoulder, as little inclined for conversation as himself. My thoughts were full of my late host. His voice yet rang in my ears. His eloquence yet held my imagination captive. I remember to this day, with surprise, how my over-excited brain retained whole sentences and parts of sentences, troops of brilliant images, and fragments of splendid reasoning, in the very words in which he had uttered them. Musing thus over what I had heard, and striving to recall a lost link here and there, I strode on at the heels of my guide, absorbed and unobservant. Presently – at the end, as it seemed to me, of only a few minutes – he came to a sudden halt and said:

"Yon's your road. Keep the stone fence to your right hand and you can't fail of the way."

"This, then, is the old coach road?"

"Aye, 'tis the old coach road."

"And how far do I go before I reach the crossroads?"

"Nigh upon three mile."

I pulled out my purse, and he became more communicative.

"The road's a fair road enough," said he, "for foot passengers; but 'twas over-steep and narrow for the northern traffic. You'll mind where the parapet's broken away, close again' the signpost. It's never been mended since the accident."

"What accident?"

"Eh, the night mail pitched right over into the valley below – a gude fifty feet an' more – just at the worst bit o' road in the whole county."

"Horrible! Were many lives lost?"

"All. Four were found dead, and t'other two died next morning."

"How long is it since this happened?"

"Just nine year."

"Near the signpost, you say? I will bear it in mind. Good night."

"Gude night, sir, and thankee." Jacob pocketed his half-crown, made a faint pretence of touching his hat, and trudged back by the way he had come.

I watched the light of his lantern till it quite disappeared, and then turned to pursue my way alone. This was no longer a matter of the slightest difficulty, for, despite the dead darkness overhead, the line of stone fence showed distinctly enough against the pale gleam of the snow. How silent it seemed now, with only my footsteps to listen to; how silent and how solitary! A strange disagreeable sense of loneliness stole over me. I walked faster. I hummed a fragment of a tune. I cast up enormous sums in my head, and accumulated them at compound interest. I did best, in short, to forget the startling speculations to which I had but just been listening, and, to some extent, I succeeded.

Meanwhile, the night air seemed to become colder and colder, and though I walked fast I found it impossible to keep myself warm. My feet were like ice. I lost sensation in my hands, and grasped my gun mechanically. I even breathed with difficulty, as though, instead of traversing a quiet North-country highway, I were scaling the uppermost heights of some gigantic alp. This last symptom became presently so distressing that I was forced to stop for a few minutes and lean against the stone fence. As I did so I chanced to look back up the road, and there, to my infinite relief, I saw a distant point of light, like the gleam of an approaching lantern. I at first concluded that Jacob had retraced his steps and followed me; but even as the conjecture presented itself, a second light flashed into sight – a light evidently parallel with the first, and approaching at the same rate of motion. It needed no second thought to show me that these must be the carriage-lamps of some private vehicle, though it seemed strange that any private vehicle should take a road professedly disused and dangerous.

There could be no doubt, however, of the fact, for the lamps grew larger and brighter every moment, and I even fancied I could already see the dark outline of the carriage between them. It was coming up very fast and quite noiselessly, the snow being nearly a foot deep under the wheels.

And now the body of the vehicle became distinctly visible behind the lamps. It looked strangely lofty. A sudden suspicion flashed upon me. Was it possible that I had passed the cross-roads in the dark without observing the signpost and could this be the very coach which I had come to meet?

No need to ask myself that question a second time, for here it came round the bend of the road; guard and driver, one outside passenger, and four steaming greys, all wrapped in a soft haze of light through which the lamps blazed out, like a pair of fiery meteors.

I jumped forward, waved my hat, and shouted. The mail came down at full speed and passed me. For a moment I feared that I had not been seen or heard, but it was only for a moment. The coachman pulled up; the guard, muffled to the eyes in capes and comforters, and apparently sound asleep in the rumble, neither answered my hail nor made the slightest effort to dismount; the outside passenger did not even turn his head. I opened the door for myself, and looked in. There were but three travellers inside, so I stepped in, shut the door, slipped into the vacant corner, and congratulated myself on my good fortune.

The atmosphere of the coach seemed, if possible, colder than that of the outer air and was pervaded by a singularly damp and disagreeable smell. I looked round at my fellow passengers. They were all three men, and all silent. They did not seem to be asleep, but each leaned back in his corner of the vehicle, as if absorbed in his own reflections. I attempted to open a conversation.

"How intensely cold it is tonight," I said, addressing my opposite neighbour.

He lifted his head, looked at me, but made no reply.

"The winter," I added, "seems to have begun in earnest."

Although the corner in which he sat was so dim that I could distinguish none of his features very clearly, I saw that his eyes were still turned full upon me. And yet he answered never a word.

At any other time I should have felt, and perhaps expressed, some annoyance, but at the moment I felt too ill to do either. The icy coldness of the night air had struck a chill to my very marrow, and the strange smell inside the coach was affecting me with an intolerable nausea. I shivered from head to foot and, turning to my left-hand neighbour, asked if he had any objection to an open window?

He neither spoke nor stirred.

I repeated the question somewhat more loudly, but with the same result. Then I lost my patience and let the sash down. As I did so, the leather strap broke in my hand, and I observed that the glass was covered with a thick coat of mildew, the accumulation, apparently, of years. My attention being thus drawn to the condition of the coach, I examined it more narrowly, and saw by the uncertain light of the outer lamps that it was in the last state of dilapidation. Every part of it was not only out of repair but in a condition of decay. The sashes splintered at a touch. The leather fittings were crusted over with mould, and literally rotting from the woodwork. The floor was almost breaking away beneath my feet. The whole machine, in short, was foul with damp, and had evidently been dragged from some outhouse in which it had been mouldering away for years, to do another day or two of duty on the road.

I turned to the third passenger, whom I had not yet addressed, and hazarded one more remark.

"This coach," I said, "is in deplorable condition. The regular mail, I suppose, is under repair."

He moved his head slowly, and looked me in the face without speaking a word. I shall never forget that look while I live. I turned cold at heart under it. I turn cold at heart even now when I recall it. His eyes glowed with a fiery unnatural lustre. His face was livid as the face of a corpse. His bloodless lips were drawn back as if in the agony of death, and showed the gleaming teeth between.

The words that I was about to utter died upon my lips, and a strange horror – a dreadful horror – came upon me. My sight had by this time become used to the gloom of the coach and I could see with tolerable distinctness. I turned to my opposite neighbour. He, too, was looking at me with the same startling pallor in his face and the same stony glitter in his eyes. I passed my hand across my brow. I turned to the passenger on the seat beside my own, and saw – oh, Heaven! How shall I describe what I saw? I saw that he was no living man – that none of them were living men, like myself. A pale phosphorescent light – the light of putrefaction – played upon their awful faces; upon their hair, dank with the dews of the grave; upon their clothes, earth-stained and dropping to pieces; upon their hands, which were as the hands of corpses long buried. Only their eyes, their terrible eyes, were living; and those eyes were all turned menacingly upon me!

A shriek of terror, a wild, unintelligible cry for help and mercy, burst from my lips as I flung myself against the door and strove in vain to open it.

In that single instant, brief and vivid as a landscape beheld in the flash of summer lightning, I saw the moon shining down through a rift of stormy cloud – the ghastly signpost rearing its warning finger by the wayside – the broken parapet – the plunging horses – the black gulf below. Then the coach reeled like a ship at sea. Then came a mighty crash – a sense of crushing pain – and then darkness.

It seemed as if years had gone by when I awoke one morning from a deep sleep and found my wife watching by my bedside. I will pass over the scene that ensued and give you, in half a dozen words, the tale she told me with tears of thanksgiving. I had fallen over a precipice, close against the junction of the old coach road and the new, and had only been saved from certain death by lighting upon a deep snowdrift that had accumulated at the foot of the rock beneath. In this snowdrift I was discovered at daybreak by a couple of shepherds, who carried me to the nearest shelter and brought a surgeon to my aid. The surgeon found me in a state of raving delirium, with a broken arm and a compound fracture of the skull. The letters in my pocket-book showed my name and address; my wife was summoned to nurse me; and, thanks to youth and a fine constitution, I came out of danger at last. The place of my fall, I need scarcely say, was precisely that at which a frightful accident had happened to the north mail nine years before.

I never told my wife the fearful events which I have just related to you. I told the surgeon who attended me; but he treated the whole adventure as a mere dream born of the fever in my brain. We discussed the question over and over again until we found that we could discuss it with temper no longer, and then we dropped it. Others may form what conclusions they please – I *know* that twenty years ago I was the fourth inside passenger in that Phantom Coach.

The Old Nurse's Story

Elizabeth Gaskell

You know, my dears, that your mother was an orphan, and an only child; and I dare say you have heard that your grandfather was a clergyman up in Westmorland, where I come from. I was just a girl in the village school when, one day, your grandmother came in to ask the mistress if there was any scholar there who would do for a nurse-maid; and mighty proud I was, I can tell ye, when the mistress called me up, and spoke to my being a good girl at my needle, and a steady, honest girl, and one whose parents were very respectable, though they might be poor. I thought I should like nothing better than to serve the pretty young lady, who was blushing as deep as I was, as she spoke of the coming baby, and what I should have to do with it. However, I see you don't care so much for this part of my story, as for what you think is to come, so I'll tell you at once. I was engaged and settled at the parsonage before Miss Rosamond (that was the baby, who is now your mother) was born. To be sure, I had little enough to do with her when she came, for she was never out of her mother's arms, and slept by her all night long; and proud enough was I sometimes when Missis trusted her to me. There never was such a baby before or since, though you've all of you been fine enough in your turns; but for sweet, winning ways, you've none of you come up to your mother. She took after her mother, who was a real

lady born; a Miss Furnivall, a granddaughter of Lord
Furnivall's, in Northumberland. I believe she had neither
brother nor sister, and had been brought up in my lord's family
till she had married your grandfather, who was just a curate;
son to a shopkeeper in Carlisle – but a clever, fine gentleman
as ever was – and one who was a right-down hard worker in his
parish, which was very wide, and scattered all abroad over the
Westmorland Fells.

When your mother, little Miss Rosamond, was about four or
five years old, both her parents died in a fortnight – one after
the other. Ah! That was a sad time. My pretty young mistress
and me was looking for another baby when my master came
home from one of his long rides, wet, and tired, and took the
fever he died of; and then she never held up her head again,
but lived just to see her dead baby, and have it laid on her
breast before she sighed away her life. My mistress had asked
me, on her death-bed, never to leave Miss Rosamond; but if
she had never spoken a word, I would have gone with the little
child to the end of the world.

The next thing, and before we had well stilled our sobs, the
executors and guardians came to settle the affairs. They were my
poor young mistress's own cousin, Lord Furnivall, and Mr
Esthwaite, my master's brother, a shopkeeper in Manchester; not
so well to do then as he was afterwards, and with a large family
rising about him. Well! I don't know if it were their settling, or
because of a letter my mistress wrote on her death-bed to her
cousin, my lord; but somehow it was settled that Miss Rosamond
and me were to go to Furnivall Manor House in Northumberland,
and my lord spoke as if it had been her mother's wish that she
should live with his family, and as if he had no objections, for that
one or two more or less could make no difference in so grand a
household. So, though that was not the way in which I should
have wished the coming of my bright and pretty pet to have been
looked at – who was like a sunbeam in any family, be it never so
grand – I was well pleased that all the folks in the Dale should
stare and admire, when they heard I was going to be young lady's
maid at my Lord Furnivall's at Furnivall Manor.

But I made a mistake in thinking we were to go and live where my lord did. It turned out that the family had left Furnivall Manor House fifty years or more. I could not hear that my poor young mistress had ever been there, though she had been brought up in the family; and I was sorry for that, for I should have liked Miss Rosamond's youth to have passed where her mother's had been.

My lord's gentleman, from whom I asked as many questions as I durst, said that the Manor House was at the foot of the Cumberland Fells, and a very grand place; that an old Miss Furnivall, a great-aunt of my lord's, lived there, with only a few servants; but that it was a very healthy place, and my lord had thought that it would suit Miss Rosamond very well for a few years, and that her being there might perhaps amuse his old aunt.

I was bidden by my lord to have Miss Rosamond's things ready by a certain day. He was a stern, proud man, as they say all the Lords Furnivall were; and he never spoke a word more than was necessary. Folk did say he had loved my young mistress; but that, because she knew that his father would object, she would never listen to him, and married Esthwaite; but I don't know. He never married at any rate. But he never took much notice of Miss Rosamond; which I thought he might have done if he had cared for her dead mother. He sent his gentleman with us to the Manor House, telling Mr Herry to join him at Newcastle that same evening; so there was no great length of time for him to make us known to all the strangers before he, too, shook us off; and we were left, two lonely young things (I was not eighteen) in the great old Manor House. It seems like yesterday that we drove there. We had left our own dear parsonage very early, and we had both cried as if our hearts would break, though we were travelling in my lord's carriage, which I thought so much of once. And now it was long past noon on a September day, and we stopped to change horses for the last time at a little, smoky town, all full of colliers and miners. Miss Rosamond had fallen asleep, but Mr Henry told me to waken her, that she might see the park and the Manor House as we drove up. I thought it rather a pity; but I did what he bade me, for fear he should complain of me to my lord. We had left all signs of a town, or even a village, and were then inside the gates of a large, wild park – not like the parks here in the south, but with rocks and the noise of running water, and gnarled thorn-trees, and old oaks, all white and peeled with age.

The road went up about two miles, and then we saw a great and stately house, with many trees close around it, so close that in some places their branches dragged against the walls when the wind blew; and some hung broken down; for no one seemed to take much charge of the place – to lop the wood, or to keep the moss-covered carriage-way in order. Only in front of the house all was clear. The great oval drive was without a weed; and neither tree nor creeper was allowed to grow over the long, many-windowed front; at both sides of which a wing projected, which were each the ends of other side fronts; for the house, although it was so desolate, was even grander than I expected. Behind it rose the Fells, which seemed unenclosed and bare enough; and on the left hand of the house, as you stood facing it, was a little, old-fashioned flower-garden, as I found out afterwards. A door opened out upon it from the west front; it had been scooped out of the thick dark wood for some old Lady Furnivall; but the branches of the great forest trees had grown and overshadowed it again, and there were very few flowers that would live there at that time.

When we drove up to the great front entrance and went into the hall I thought we should be lost – it was so large, and vast, and grand. There was a chandelier all of bronze, hung down from the middle of the ceiling; and I had never seen one before, and looked at it all in amaze. Then, at one end of the hall, was a great fireplace, as large as the sides of the houses in my country, with messy andirons and dogs to hold the wood; and by it were heavy, old-fashioned sofas. At the opposite end of the hall, to the left as you went in – on the western side – was an organ built into the wall, and so large that it filled up the best part of that end. Beyond it, on the same side, was a door;

and opposite, on each side of the fireplace, were also doors leading to the east front; but those I never went through as long as I stayed in the house, so I can't tell you what lay beyond.

The afternoon was closing in and the hall, which had no fire lighted in it, looked dark and gloomy, but we did not stay there a moment. The old servant, who had opened the door for us, bowed to Mr Henry and took us in through the door at the further side of the great organ, and led us through several smaller halls and passages into the west drawing room, where he said that Miss Furnivall was sitting. Poor little Miss Rosamond held very tight to me, as if she were scared and lost in that great place, and as for myself, I was not much better. The west drawing room was very cheerful-looking, with a warm fire in it, and plenty of good, comfortable furniture about. Miss Furnivall was an old lady not far from eighty, I should think, but I do not know. She was thin and tall, and had a face as full of fine wrinkles as if they had been drawn all over it with a needle's point. Her eyes were very watchful, to make up, I suppose, for her being so deaf as to be obliged to use a trumpet. Sitting with her, working at the same great piece of tapestry, was Mrs Stark, her maid and companion, and almost as old as she was. She had lived with Miss Furnivall ever since they both were young, and now she seemed more like a friend than a servant; she looked so cold, and grey, and stony, as if she had never loved or cared for anyone; and I don't suppose she did care for anyone, except her mistress; and, owing to the great deafness of the latter, Mrs Stark treated her very much as if she were a child. Mr Henry gave some message from my lord, and then he bowed goodbye to us all – taking no notice of my sweet little Miss Rosamond's outstretched hand – and left us standing there, being looked at by the two old ladies through their spectacles.

I was right glad when they rung for the old footman who had shown us in at first, and told him to take us to our rooms. So we went out of that great drawing room, and into another sitting room, and out of that, and then up a great flight of stairs, and along a broad gallery – which was something like a

library, having books all down one side, and windows and
writing-tables all down the other – till we came to our rooms,
which I was not sorry to hear were just over the kitchens; for I
began to think I should be lost in that wilderness of a house.
There was an old nursery, that had been used for all the little
lords and ladies long ago, with a pleasant fire burning in the
grate, and the kettle boiling on the hob, and tea things spread
out on the table; and out of that room was the night-nursery,
with a little crib for Miss Rosamond close to my bed. And old
James called up Dorothy, his wife, to bid us welcome; and both
he and she were so hospitable and kind, that by and by Miss
Rosamond and me felt quite at home; and by the time tea was
over she was sitting on Dorothy's knee, and chattering away as
fast as her little tongue could go. I soon found out that Dorothy
was from Westmorland, and that bound her and me together,
as it were; and I would never wish to meet with kinder people
than were old James and his wife. James had lived pretty nearly
all his life in my lord's family, and thought there was no one so
grand as they. He even looked down a little on his wife; because,
till he had married her, she had never lived in any but a farmer's household. But he was very fond of her, as well he might
be. They had one servant under them, to do all the rough work.
Agnes they called her; and she and me, and James and Dorothy,
with Miss Furnivall and Mrs Stark, made up the family; always
remembering my sweet little Miss Rosamond!

I used to wonder what they had done before she came, they
thought so much of her now. Kitchen and drawing room, it
was all the same. The hard, sad Miss Furnivall, and the cold
Mrs Stark, looked pleased when she came fluttering in like a
bird, playing and pranking hither and thither, with a continual murmur, and pretty prattle of gladness. I am sure they
were sorry many a time when she flitted away into the kitchen,
though they were too proud to ask her to stay with them, and
were a little surprised at her taste; though to be sure, as Mrs
Stark said, it was not to be wondered at, remembering what
stock her father had come of. The great, old rambling house
was a famous place for little Miss Rosamond. She made

expeditions all over it, with me at her heels; all, except the east wing, which was never opened, and whither we never thought of going. But in the western and northern part was many a pleasant room; full of things that were curiosities to us, though they might not have been to people who had seen more. The windows were darkened by the sweeping boughs of the trees, and the ivy which had overgrown them: but, in the green gloom, we could manage to see old China jars and carved ivory boxes, and great, heavy books, and, above all, the old pictures!

Once, I remember, my darling would have Dorothy go with us to tell us who they all were; for they were all portraits of some of my lord's family, though Dorothy could not tell us the names of every one. We had gone through most of the rooms, when we came to the old state drawing room over the hall, and there was a picture of Miss Furnivall; or, as she was called in those days, Miss Grace, for she was the younger sister. Such a beauty she must have been! But with such a set, proud look, and such scorn looking out of her handsome eyes, with her eyebrows just a little raised, as if she wondered how anyone could have the impertinence to look at her; and her lip curled at us, as we stood there gazing. She had a dress on, the like of which I had never seen before, but it was all the fashion when she was young: a hat of some soft, white stuff like beaver, pulled a little over her brows, and a beautiful plume of feathers sweeping round it on one side; and her gown of blue satin was open in front to a quilted, white stomacher.

"Well, to be sure!" said I, when I had gazed my fill. "Flesh is grass, they do say; but who would have thought that Miss Furnivall had been such an out-and-out beauty, to see her now?"

"Yes," said Dorothy. "Folks change, sadly. But if what my master's father used to say was true, Miss Furnivall, the elder sister, was handsomer than Miss Grace. Her picture is here somewhere; but, if I show it you, you must never let on, even to James, that you have seen it. Can the little lady hold her tongue, think you?" asked she.

I was not so sure, for she was such a little, sweet, bold, open-spoken child, so I set her to hide herself; and then I helped Dorothy to turn a great picture that leaned with its face towards the wall, and was not hung up as the others were. To be sure, it beat Miss Grace for beauty; and, I think, for scornful pride, too, though in that matter it might be hard to choose. I could have looked at it an hour, but Dorothy seemed half frightened at having shown it to me, and hurried it back again, and bade me run and find Miss Rosamond, for that there were some ugly places about the house, where she should like ill for the child to go. I was a brave, high-spirited girl, and thought little of what the old woman said, for I liked hide-and-seek as well as any child in the parish; so off I ran to find my little one.

As winter drew on, and the days grew shorter, I was sometimes almost certain that I heard a noise as if someone was playing on the great organ in the hall. I did not hear it every evening; but, certainly, I did very often; usually when I was sitting with Miss Rosamond, after I had put her to bed, and keeping quite still and silent in the bedroom. Then I used to hear it booming and swelling away in the distance. The first night, when I went down to my supper, I asked Dorothy who had been playing music, and James said very shortly that I was a gowk to take the wind soughing among the trees for music; but I saw Dorothy look at him very fearfully, and Agnes, the kitchen maid, said something beneath her breath, and went quite white. I saw they did not like my question, so I held my peace till I was with Dorothy alone, when I knew I could get a good deal out of her. So, the next day I watched my time, and I coaxed and asked her who it was that played the organ; for I knew that it was the organ and not the wind well enough, for all I had kept silence before James. But Dorothy had had her lesson I'll warrant, and never a word could I get from her. So then I tried Agnes, though I had always held my head rather above her, as I was even to James and Dorothy, and she was little better than their servant. So she said I must never, never tell; and if I ever told, I was never to say *she* had told me; but it was a very strange noise, and she had heard it many a time, but most of all on winter nights, and before storms; and folks did say it was the old lord playing on the great organ in the hall, just as he used to do when he was alive; but who the old lord was, or why he played, and why he played on stormy winter evenings in particular, she either could not or would not tell me.

Well! I told you I had a brave heart; and I thought it was rather pleasant to have that grand music rolling about the house, let who would be the player; for now it rose above the great gusts of wind, and wailed and triumphed just like a living creature, and then it fell to a softness most complete; only it was always music, and tunes, so it was nonsense to call it the wind. I thought at first that it might be Miss Furnivall who played, unknown to Agnes; but, one day when I was in the hall by myself, I opened the organ and peeped all about it and around it, as I had done to the organ in Crosthwaite Church once before, and I saw it was all broken and destroyed inside, though it looked so brave and fine; and then, though it was noon-day, my flesh began to creep a little, and I shut it up, and ran away pretty quickly to my own bright nursery; and I did not like hearing the music for some time after that, any more than James and Dorothy did.

All this time Miss Rosamond was making herself more and more beloved. The old ladies liked her to dine with them at their early dinner; James stood behind Miss Furnivall's chair, and I behind Miss Rosamond's all in state; and, after dinner, she would play about in a corner of the great drawing room, as still as any mouse, while Miss Furnivall slept and I had my dinner in the kitchen. But she was glad enough to come in the nursery afterwards; for, as she said, Miss Furnivall was so sad, and Mrs Stark so dull; but she and I were merry enough; and, by and by, I got not to care for that weird rolling music, which did one no harm, if we did not know where it came from.

That winter was very cold. In the middle of October the frosts began and lasted many, many weeks. I remember one day at dinner, Miss Furnivall lifted up her sad, heavy eyes,

and said to Mrs Stark, "I am afraid we shall have a terrible
winter," in a strange kind of meaning way. But Mrs Stark
pretended not to hear, and talked very loud of something
else. My little lady and I did not care for the frost; not we! As
long as it was dry we climbed up the steep brows behind the
house, and went up on the Fells, which were bleak, and bare
enough, and there we ran races in the fresh, sharp air; and
once we came down by a new path that took us past the two
old, gnarled holly-trees which grew about halfway down by
the east side of the house. But the days grew shorter and
shorter; and the old lord, if it was he, played away more, and
more stormily and sadly on the great organ. One Sunday
afternoon – it must have been towards the end of November
– I asked Dorothy to take charge of little Missy when she
came out of the drawing room after Miss Furnivall had had
her nap; for it was too cold to take her with me to church, and
yet I wanted to go. And Dorothy was glad enough to promise,
and was so fond of the child that all seemed well; and Agnes
and I set off very briskly, though the sky hung heavy and
black over the white earth, as if the night had never fully gone
away; and the air, though still, was very biting and keen.

"We shall have a fall of snow," said Agnes to me. And sure
enough, even while we were in church, it came down hard, in
great, large flakes, so thick it almost darkened the windows. It
had stopped snowing before we came out, but it lay soft, thick
and deep beneath our feet as we tramped home. Before we got
to the hall the moon rose, and I think it was lighter then – what
with the moon, and what with the white dazzling snow – than
it had been when we went to church, between two and three
o'clock. I have not told you that Miss Furnivall and Mrs Stark
never went to church: they used to read the prayers together,
in their quiet, gloomy way; they seemed to feel the Sunday
very long without their tapestry-work to be busy at. So when I
went to Dorothy in the kitchen, to fetch Miss Rosamond and
take her upstairs with me, I did not much wonder when the old
woman told me that the ladies had kept the child with them,
and that she had never come to the kitchen, as I had bidden

her, when she was tired of behaving pretty in the drawing-room. So I took off my things and went to find her, and bring her to her supper in the nursery. But when I went into the best drawing room, there sat the two old ladies, very still and quiet, dropping out a word now and then, but looking as if nothing so bright and merry as Miss Rosamond had ever been near them. Still I thought she might be hiding from me; it was one of her pretty ways; and that she had persuaded them to look as if they knew nothing about her; so I went softly peeping under this sofa, and behind that chair, making believe I was sadly frightened at not finding her.

"What's the matter, Hester?" said Mrs Stark sharply. I don't know if Miss Furnivall had seen me, for, as I told you, she was very deaf, and she sat quite still, idly staring into the fire, with her hopeless face. "I'm only looking for my little Rosy-Posy," replied I, still thinking that the child was there, and near me, though I could not see her.

"Miss Rosamond is not here," said Mrs Stark. "She went away more than an hour ago to find Dorothy." And she too turned and went on looking into the fire.

My heart sank at this, and I began to wish I had never left my darling. I went back to Dorothy and told her. James was gone out for the day, but she and me and Agnes took lights and went up into the nursery first, and then we roamed over the great large house, calling and entreating Miss Rosamond to come out of her hiding place, and not frighten us to death in that way. But there was no answer; no sound.

"Oh!" said I at last. "Can she have got into the east wing and hidden there?"

But Dorothy said it was not possible, for that she herself had never been in there; that the doors were always locked, and my lord's steward had the keys, she believed; at any rate, neither she nor James had ever seen them: so, I said I would go back, and see if, after all, she was not hidden in the drawing room, unknown to the old ladies; and if I found her there, I said, I would whip her well for the fright she had given me; but I never meant to do it. Well, I went back to the west drawing room, and I told Mrs Stark we could not find her anywhere, and asked for leave to look all about the furniture there, for I thought now, that she might have fallen asleep in some warm, hidden corner; but no! We looked, Miss Furnivall got up and looked, trembling all over, and she was nowhere there; then we set off again, everyone in the house, and looked in all the places we had searched before, but we could not find her. Miss Furnivall shivered and shook so much that Mrs Stark took her back into the warm drawing room; but not before they had made me promise to bring her to them when she was found. Well-a-day! I began to think she never would be found, when I bethought me to look out into the great front court, all covered with snow. I was upstairs when I looked out; but, it was such clear moonlight, I could see quite plain two little footprints, which might be traced from the hall door, and round the corner of the east wing. I don't know how I got down, but I tugged open the great, stiff hall door; and, throwing the skirt of my gown overhead for a cloak, I ran out. I turned the east corner, and there a black shadow fell on the snow; but when I came again into the moonlight, there were the little footmarks going up – up to the Fells. It was bitter cold; so cold that the air almost took the skin off my face as I ran, but I ran on, crying to think how my poor little darling must be perished, and frightened. I was within sight of the holly trees, when I saw a shepherd coming down the hill, bearing something in his arms wrapped in his maud. He shouted to me, and asked me if I had lost a bairn; and, when I could not speak for crying, he bore towards me, and I saw my wee bairnie lying still, and white, and stiff, in his arms, as if she had been dead. He told me he had been up the Fells to gather in his sheep before the deep cold of night came on, and that under the holly trees (black marks on the hillside, where no other bush was for miles around) he had found my little lady – my lamb – my queen – my darling – stiff, and cold, in the terrible sleep which is frost-begotten. Oh! The joy, and the tears, of having her in my arms once again! for I would not let him carry her; but took her, maud and all, into my own arms, and held her near my own warm neck, and heart, and felt the life stealing slowly back again into her little, gentle limbs. But she was still insensible when we reached the hall, and I had no breath for speech. We went in by the kitchen door.

"Bring the warming-pan," said I; and I carried her upstairs and began undressing her by the nursery fire, which Agnes had kept up. I called my little lambie all the sweet and playful names I could think of – even while my eyes were blinded by my tears; and at last, oh! at length she opened her large, blue eyes. Then I put her into her warm bed, and sent Dorothy down to tell Miss Furnivall that all was well; and I made up my mind to sit by my darling's bedside the live-long night. She fell away into a soft sleep as soon as her pretty head touched the pillow, and I watched by her till morning light; when she wakened up bright and clear – or so I thought at first – and, my dears, so I think now.

She said that she had fancied that she should like to go to Dorothy, for that both the old ladies were asleep, and it was very dull in the drawing room; and that, as she was going through the west lobby, she saw the snow through the high window falling – falling – soft and steady; but she wanted to see it lying pretty and white on the ground; so she made her way into the great hall; and then, going to the window, she saw it bright and soft upon the drive; but while she stood there, she saw a little girl, not as old as she was, "but so pretty," said my darling, "and this little girl beckoned to me to come out; and oh, she was so pretty and so sweet, I could not choose but go." And then this other little girl had taken her by the hand, and side by side the two had gone round the east corner.

"Now, you are a naughty little girl, and telling stories," said I. "What would your good mamma, that is in heaven, and never told a story in her life, say to her little Rosamond, if she heard her – and I dare say she does – telling stories!"

"Indeed, Hester," sobbed out my child, "I'm telling you true. Indeed I am."

"Don't tell me!" said I, very stern. "I tracked you by your foot-marks through the snow; there were only yours to be seen:

and if you had had a little girl to go hand in hand with you up the hill, don't you think the footprints would have gone along with yours?"

"I can't help it, dear, dear Hester," said she, crying, "if they did not; I never looked at her feet, but she held my hand fast and tight in her little one, and it was very, very cold. She took me up the Fell-path, up to the holly trees; and there I saw a lady weeping and crying; but when she saw me, she hushed her weeping, and smiled very proud and grand, and took me on her knee, and began to lull me to sleep; and that's all, Hester – but that is true; and my dear mamma knows it is," said she, crying. So I thought the child was in a fever, and pretended to believe her, as she went over her story – over and over again, and always the same. At last Dorothy knocked at the door with Miss Rosamond's breakfast; and she told me the old ladies were down in the eating parlour, and that they wanted to speak to me. They had both been into the night-nursery the evening before, but it was after Miss Rosamond was asleep; so they had only looked at her – not asked me any questions.

"I shall catch it," thought I to myself, as I went along the north gallery. "And yet," I thought, taking courage, "it was in their charge I left her; and it's they that's to blame for letting her steal away unknown and unwatched." So I went in boldly, and told my story. I told it all to Miss Furnivall, shouting it close to her ear; but when I came to the mention of the other little girl out in the snow, coaxing and tempting her out and up to the grand and beautiful lady by the holly tree, she threw her arms up – her old and withered arms – and cried aloud, "Oh! Heaven, forgive! Have mercy!"

Mrs Stark took hold of her; roughly enough, I thought; but she was past Mrs Stark's management, and spoke to me, in a kind of wild warning and authority.

"Hester! Keep her from that child! It will lure her to her death! That evil child! Tell her it is a wicked, naughty child." Then Mrs Stark hurried me out of the room; where, indeed, I was glad enough to go; but Miss Furnivall kept shrieking out,

"Oh, have mercy! Wilt Thou never forgive! It is many a long year ago—"

I was very uneasy in my mind after that. I durst never leave Miss Rosamond, night or day, for fear lest she might slip off again, after some fancy or other; and all the more, because I thought I could make out that Miss Furnivall was crazy, from their odd ways about her; and I was afraid lest something of the same kind (which might be in the family, you know) hung over my darling. And the great frost never ceased all this time; and, whenever it was a more stormy night than usual, between the gusts, and through the wind, we heard the old lord playing on the great organ. But, old lord or not, wherever Miss Rosamond went, there I followed; for my love for her, pretty, helpless orphan, was stronger than my fear for the grand and terrible sound. Besides, it rested with me to keep her cheerful and merry, as beseemed her age. So we played together, and wandered together, here and there, and everywhere; for I never dared to lose sight of her again in that large and rambling house. And so it happened, that one afternoon, not long before Christmas Day, we were playing together on the billiard table in the great hall (not that we knew the right way of playing, but she liked to roll the smooth ivory balls with her pretty hands, and I liked to do whatever she did); and, by and by, without our noticing it, it grew dusk indoors, though it was still light in the open air, and I was thinking of taking her back into the nursery, when, all of a sudden, she cried out—

"Look, Hester! Look! There is my poor little girl out in the snow!"

I turned towards the long, narrow windows, and there, sure enough, I saw a little girl, less than my Miss Rosamond, dressed all unfit to be out-of-doors such a bitter night – crying, and beating against the window-panes, as if she wanted to be let in. She seemed to sob and wail, till Miss Rosamond could bear it no longer, and was flying to the door to open it, when, all of a sudden, and close upon us, the great organ pealed out so loud and thundering it fairly made me tremble; and all the more, when I remembered that, even in the stillness of that dead-cold weather, I had heard no sound of little battering hands upon the window-glass, although the Phantom Child had seemed to put forth all its force; and, although I had seen it wail and cry, no faintest touch of sound had fallen upon my ears. Whether I remembered all this at the very moment, I do not know; the great organ sound had so stunned me into terror; but this I know, I caught up Miss Rosamond before she got the hall door opened, and clutched her, and carried her away, kicking and screaming, into the large, bright kitchen, where Dorothy and Agnes were busy with their mince pies.

"What is the matter with my sweet one?" cried Dorothy, as I bore in Miss Rosamond, who was sobbing as if her heart would break.

"She won't let me open the door for my little girl to come in; and she'll die if she is out on the Fells all night. Cruel, naughty Hester," she said, slapping me; but she might have struck harder, for I had seen a look of ghastly terror on Dorothy's face, which made my very blood run cold.

"Shut the back kitchen door fast, and bolt it well," said she to Agnes. She said no more, but gave me raisins and almonds to quiet Miss Rosamond: but she sobbed about the little girl in the snow, and would not touch any of the good things. I was thankful when she cried herself to sleep in bed. Then I stole down to the kitchen, and told Dorothy I had made up my mind I would carry my darling back to my father's house in Applethwaite; where, if we lived humbly, we lived at peace. I said I had been frightened enough with the old lord's organ-playing; but now that I had seen for myself this little, moaning child, all decked out as no child in the neighbourhood could be, beating and battering to get in, yet always without any sound or noise – with the dark wound on its right shoulder; and that Miss Rosamond had known it again for the phantom that had nearly lured her to her death (which Dorothy knew was true); I would stand it no longer.

I saw Dorothy change colour once or twice. When I had done, she told me she did not think I could take Miss Rosamond with me, for that she was my lord's ward, and I had no right

over her; and she asked me, would I leave the child that I was
so fond of, just for sounds and sights that could do me no
harm; and that they had all had to get used to in their turns? I
was all in a hot, trembling passion; and I said it was very well
for her to talk, that knew what these sights and noises beto-
kened, and that had, perhaps, had something to do with the
Spectre-Child while it was alive. And I taunted her so, that she
told me all she knew, at last; and then I wished I had never
been told, for it only made me more afraid than ever.

She said she had heard the tale from old neighbours, that
were alive when she was first married; when folks used to come
to the hall sometimes, before it had got such a bad name in the
countryside: it might not be true, or it might, what she had
been told.

The old lord was Miss Furnivall's father – Miss Grace, as
Dorothy called her, for Miss Maude was the elder, and Miss
Furnivall by rights. The old lord was eaten up with pride. Such
a proud man was never seen or heard of; and his daughters
were like him. No one was good enough to wed them, although
they had choice enough; for they were the great beauties of
their day, as I had seen by their portraits, where they hung in
the state drawing room. But, as the old saying is, "Pride will
have a fall"; and these two haughty beauties fell in love with
the same man, and he no better than a foreign musician, whom
their father had down from London to play music with him at
the Manor House. For, above all things, next to his pride, the
old lord loved music. He could play on nearly every instrument that ever was heard of: and it was a strange thing it did
not soften him; but he was a fierce, dour, old man, and had
broken his poor wife's heart with his cruelty, they said. He was
mad after music, and would pay any money for it. So he got
this foreigner to come; who made such beautiful music, that
they said the very birds on the trees stopped their singing to
listen. And, by degrees, this foreign gentleman got such a hold
over the old lord that nothing would serve him but that he
must come every year; and it was he that had the great organ
brought from Holland, and built up in the hall, where it stood

now. He taught the old lord to play on it; but many and many a time, when Lord Furnivall was thinking of nothing but his fine organ, and his finer music, the dark foreigner was walking abroad in the woods with one of the young ladies; now Miss Maude, and then Miss Grace.

Miss Maude won the day and carried off the prize, such as it was; and he and she were married, all unknown to anyone; and before he made his next yearly visit, she had been confined of a little girl at a farmhouse on the Moors, while her father and Miss Grace thought she was away at Doncaster Races. But though she was a wife and a mother, she was not a bit softened, but as haughty and as passionate as ever; and perhaps more so for she was jealous of Miss Grace, to whom her foreign husband paid a deal of court – by way of blinding her – as he told his wife. But Miss Grace triumphed over Miss Maude, and Miss Maude grew fiercer and fiercer, both with her husband and with her sister; and the former who could easily shake off what was disagreeable, and hide himself in foreign countries – went away a month before his usual time that summer, and half-threatened that he would never come back again. Meanwhile, the little girl was left at the farmhouse, and her mother used to have her horse saddled and gallop wildly over the hills to see her once every week, at the very least – for where she loved, she loved; and where she hated, she hated. And the old lord went on playing – playing on his organ; and the servants thought the sweet music he made had soothed down his awful temper, of which (Dorothy said) some terrible tales could be told. He grew infirm too, and had to walk with a crutch; and his son – that was the present Lord Furnivall's father – was with the army in America, and the other son at sea; so Miss Maude had it pretty much her own way, and she and Miss Grace grew colder and bitterer to each other every day; till at last they hardly ever spoke except when the old lord was by. The foreign musician came again the next summer, but it was for the last time; for they led him such a life with their jealousy and their passions that he grew weary, and went away, and never was heard of again. And Miss Maude, who had always meant to have her marriage acknowledged when her father should be dead, was left now a deserted wife – whom nobody knew to have been married – with a child that she dared not own, although she loved it to distraction; and living with a father whom she feared, and a sister whom she hated.

"When the next summer passed over and the dark foreigner never came, both Miss Maude and Miss Grace grew gloomy and sad; they had a haggard look about them, though they looked handsome as ever. But by and by Miss Maude brightened; for her father grew more and more infirm, and more than ever carried away by his music; and she and Miss Grace lived almost entirely apart, having separate rooms, the one on the west side, Miss Maude on the east – those very rooms which were now shut up. So she thought she might have her little girl with her, and no one need ever know except those who dared not speak about it, and were bound to believe that it was, as she said, a cottager's child she had taken a fancy to. All this, Dorothy said, was pretty well known; but what came afterwards no one knew, except Miss Grace, and Mrs Stark, who was even then her maid, and much more of a friend to her than ever her sister had been. But the servants supposed, from words that were dropped, that Miss Maude had triumphed over Miss Grace, and told her that all the time the dark foreigner had been mocking her with pretended love – he was her own husband; the colour left Miss Grace's cheek and lips that very day for ever, and she was heard to say many a time that sooner or later she would have her revenge; and Mrs Stark was forever spying about the east rooms.

One fearful night, just after the New Year had come in, when the snow was lying thick and deep, and the flakes were still falling – fast enough to blind anyone who might be out and abroad – there was a great and violent noise heard, and the old lord's voice above all, cursing and swearing awfully – and the cries of a little child – and the proud defiance of a fierce woman – and the sound of a blow – and a dead stillness – and moans and wailings dying away on the hillside! Then the old lord summoned all his servants, and told them, with terrible oaths, and words more terrible, that his daughter had disgraced herself, and that he had turned her out of doors – her, and her child – and that if ever they gave her help – or food – or shelter – he prayed that they might never enter Heaven. And, all the while, Miss Grace stood by him, white and still as any stone; and when he had ended she heaved a great sigh, as much as to say her work was done, and her end was accomplished. But the old lord never touched his organ again, and died within the year; and no wonder! For, on the morrow of that wild and fearful night, the shepherds, coming down the Fell-side, found Miss Maude sitting, all crazy and smiling, under the holly trees, nursing a dead child – with a terrible mark on its right shoulder. "But that was not what killed it," Dorothy said; "it was the frost and the cold – every wild creature was in its hole, and every beast in its fold – while the child and its mother were turned out to wander on the Fells! And now you know all! And I wonder if you are less frightened now?"

I was more frightened than ever; but I said I was not. I wished Miss Rosamond and myself well out of that dreadful house for ever; but I would not leave her, and I dared not take her away. But oh! How I watched her, and guarded her! We bolted the doors, and shut the window-shutters fast, an hour or more before dark, rather than leave them open five minutes too late. But my little lady still heard the weird child crying and mourning; and not all we could do or say could keep her from wanting to go to her, and let her in from the cruel wind and the snow. All this time, I kept away from Miss Furnivall and Mrs Stark, as much as ever I could; for I feared them – I knew no good could be about them, with their grey hard faces, and their dreamy eyes, looking back into the ghastly years that were gone. But, even in my fear, I had a kind of pity – for Miss Furnivall, at least. Those gone down to the pit can hardly have a more hopeless look than that which was ever on her face. At last I even got so sorry for her – who never said a word but what was quite forced from her – that I prayed for her; and I taught Miss Rosamond to pray for one who had done a deadly sin; but often when she came to those words, she would listen, and start up from her knees, and say, "I hear my little girl plaining and crying very sad – Oh! Let her in, or she will die!"

One night – just after New Year's Day had come at last, and the long winter had taken a turn, as I hoped – I heard the west drawing-room bell ring three times, which was the signal for me. I would not leave Miss Rosamond alone, for all she was asleep – for the old lord had been playing wilder than ever – and I feared lest my darling should waken to hear the spectre child; see her I knew she could not. I had fastened the windows too well for that. So, I took her out of her bed and wrapped her up in such outer clothes as were most handy, and carried her down to the drawing room, where the old ladies sat at their tapestry-work as usual. They looked up when I came in, and Mrs Stark asked, quite astounded, "Why did you bring Miss Rosamond there, out of her warm bed?" I had begun to whisper, "Because I was afraid of her being tempted out while I was away, by the wild child in the snow," when she stopped me short (with a glance at Miss Furnivall), and said Miss Furnivall wanted me to undo some work she had done wrong, and which neither of them could see to unpick. So, I laid my pretty dear on the sofa, and sat down on a stool by them, and hardened my heart against them, as I heard the wind rising and howling.

Miss Rosamond slept on sound, for all the wind blew so; and Miss Furnivall said never a word, nor looked round when the gusts shook the windows. All at once she started up to her full height, and put up one hand, as if to bid us listen.

"I hear voices!" said she. "I hear terrible screams – I hear my father's voice!"

Just at that moment, my darling wakened with a sudden start: "My little girl is crying, oh, how she is crying!" and she tried to get up and go to her, but she got her feet entangled in the blanket and I caught her up; for my flesh had begun to creep at these noises, which they heard while we could catch no sound. In a minute or two the noises came, and gathered fast, and filled our ears; we, too, heard voices and screams, and no longer heard the winter's wind that raged abroad. Mrs Stark looked at me, and I at her, but we dared not speak. Suddenly Miss Furnivall went towards the door, out into the ante-room, through the west lobby, and opened the door into the great hall. Mrs Stark followed, and I durst not be left, though my heart almost stopped beating for fear. I wrapped my darling tight in my arms, and went out with them. In the hall the screams were louder than ever; they sounded to come from the east wing – nearer and nearer – close on the other side of the locked-up doors – close behind them. Then I noticed that the great bronze chandelier seemed all alight, though the hall was dim, and that a fire was blazing in the vast hearth-place, though it gave no heat; and I shuddered up with terror, and folded my darling closer to me. But as I did so, the east door shook, and she, suddenly struggling to get free from me, cried, "Hester! I must go! My little girl is there; I hear her; she is coming! Hester, I must go!"

I held her tight with all my strength; with a set will, I held her. If I had died, my hands would have grasped her still, I was so resolved in my mind. Miss Furnivall stood listening, and paid no regard to my darling, who had got down to the ground, and whom I, upon my knees now, was holding with both my arms clasped round her neck; she still striving and crying to get free.

All at once, the east door gave way with a thundering crash, as if torn open in a violent passion, and there came into that broad and mysterious light the figure of a tall old man, with grey hair and gleaming eyes. He drove before him, with many a relentless gesture of abhorrence, a stern and beautiful woman, with a little child clinging to her dress.

"Oh, Hester! Hester!" cried Miss Rosamond. "It's the lady! The lady below the holly trees; and my little girl is with her. Hester! Hester! Let me go to her; they are drawing me to them. I feel them – I feel them. I must go!"

Again she was almost convulsed by her efforts to get away; but I held her tighter and tighter, till I feared I should do her a hurt; but rather that than let her go towards those terrible phantoms. They passed along towards the great hall-door, where the winds howled and ravened for their prey; but before they reached that, the lady turned; and I could see that she defied the old man with a fierce and proud defiance; but then she quailed – and then she threw her arms wildly and piteously to save her child – her little child – from a blow from his uplifted crutch.

And Miss Rosamond was torn as by a power stronger than mine, and writhed in my arms, and sobbed (for by this time the poor darling was growing faint).

"They want me to go with them on to the Fells – they are drawing me to them. Oh, my little girl! I would come, but cruel, wicked Hester holds me very tight." But when she saw the uplifted crutch she swooned away, and I thanked God for it. Just at this moment – when the tall old man, his hair streaming as in the blast of a furnace, was going to strike the little, shrinking child – Miss Furnivall, the old woman by my side, cried out, "Oh, Father! Father! Spare the little, innocent child!" But just then I saw – we all saw – another phantom shape itself, and grow clear out of the blue and misty light that filled the hall; we had not seen her till now, for it was another lady who stood by the old man, with a look of relentless hate and triumphant scorn. That figure was very beautiful to look upon, with a soft, white hat drawn down over the proud brows, and a red and curling lip. It was dressed in an open robe of blue satin. I had seen that figure before. It was the likeness of Miss Furnivall in her youth; and the terrible phantoms moved on, regardless of old Miss Furnivall's wild entreaty, and the uplifted crutch fell on the right shoulder of the little child, and the younger sister looked on, stony and deadly serene. But at that moment the dim lights, and the fire that gave no heat, went out of themselves, and Miss Furnivall lay at our feet stricken down by the palsy – death-stricken.

Yes! She was carried to her bed that night never to rise again. She lay with her face to the wall, muttering low, but muttering always: "Alas! Alas! What is done in youth can never be undone in age! What is done in youth can never be undone in age!"

Among the Shoals Forever

Gail Z. Martin

"Even for Charleston, it's too many damn ghosts to ignore." Sorren, my patron and mentor, leaned back in his chair.

"We're in one of the most haunted cities in the New World," Uncle Evann replied. "What's a few more 'haints' when we've got so many?" He shrugged. "I never reckoned ghosts were really any of our business."

Sorren gave Uncle Evann a look that managed to convey both exasperation and affection. "They become our business when they're bound here by dark magic," Sorren said. He swirled the red liquid in his goblet, liquid I knew for certain was blood. The glow from the fireplace added colour to Sorren's pale complexion, but could never warm his skin. He might have let out a long sigh, if he still needed to breathe. Instead, he looked from Uncle Evann to me.

"And it becomes Dante's business when pirates are involved," he said with a hint of a smile that just slightly exposed the tips of his elongated eye teeth.

He had me at "pirates". "Yeah," I said with a glance at Coltt, my partner in crime. "Whatever it is, count us in."

Sorren was the silent partner behind the curio shop in Charleston run by my Uncle Evann. Three years ago, when Coltt and I had been the only survivors of a pirate raid on our small fishing village, we'd taken our stolen ship and fled to

Charleston, hoping Uncle Evann could give us sanctuary. We'd killed the pirates who had murdered our families, and had a haunted necklace to show for it, one that I knew for a fact was evil. I thought Uncle Evann would know what to do with it.

As it turned out, Uncle Evann's shop, Trifles and Folly, was more than it appeared. Sorren was one of a small, secret group of mortals and immortals pledged to keeping dangerous magical objects out of the hands of those who might misuse them. Sorren and Evann kept an ear open whenever objects with unusual pasts came up at auction, or were part of an estate being distributed. One way or another, Sorren made it his business to take those objects out of circulation. Evann handled the legal acquisitions. Coltt and I now took care of the rest.

Sorren stretched out his long legs, and watched the fire burn as he spoke. "Felicity Reynolds Barre disappeared on a voyage from Bermuda to Boston almost a year ago."

I frowned. "Sloan Barre's daughter?" Sloan Hampton Barre was a scion of an old Boston family with numerous business ties in every port city of the seaboard, including Charleston.

Sorren nodded. "The same. It appears her ship was overtaken by pirates. There were no survivors found, nor bodies recovered. That would suggest that the passengers were either killed and thrown overboard—"

"Or taken to sell in the brothels and sugar cane plantations of the Indies," I finished, distaste clear in my tone.

"Precisely," Sorren replied. "Normally, I'd say there was nothing we could do except offer a prayer for the young woman's soul. But it appears that Miss Barre was exceptional beyond just her family connections. She was given an antique cameo brooch by a young man named Islwyn Lawry, a brooch that her family believed had occult power. Lawry, it seems, convinced her that it had the power to protect the wearer, and Miss Barre never took it off."

My expression darkened. "Was Islwyn Lawry any relation to Galoshin Lawry, the gent with the fondness for black magic we went after a while back?"

Sorren chuckled. "Islwyn is Galoshin's son, but he had a big row with his father several years ago, and by all accounts didn't approve of his father's schemes or the way he used his power. Islwyn gave the cameo to Felicity when she set sail to return to Charleston, as a token of his love. It appears they had made plans to marry when she returned to Bermuda."

"But she never did," I murmured. "So the cameo wasn't as powerful as Islwyn hoped."

Sorren frowned. "Or perhaps it didn't work in quite the way he expected. Barre made a special trip to Charleston, and he came to Evann several nights ago, referred by a trusted mutual friend. Need I say that Trifles and Folly is not among his usually frequented establishments? The good man believes he is being haunted by his daughter's ghost. She comes to him in his dreams, wearing the cameo around her neck, begging for something, but she doesn't speak."

"Grief makes people see strange things, even in a city as haunted as Charleston," I replied.

"If Barre were the only one to see the girl's apparition, I might agree," Sorren replied. "But there have been reports up and down the Battery of the same ghost, a young woman in a blue gown with upswept hair and a fine cameo at her throat."

I crossed my arms. "I'm not sure what Barre expects us to do about it. If the cameo were cursed, it's probably at the bottom of the ocean by now. Unless it's shown up in Uncle Evann's shop."

Uncle Evann shook his head. "I've had no cameos brought in for quite some time," he replied. No matter how vast the store's inventory, Uncle Evann knew every piece. The storefront was crowded with antiques and curios from around the world, while in the back rooms, Evann and Sorren dealt with the dark magic items that found their way – legally or not – into Evann's possession. Some of those dark items were destroyed, while Sorren passed others along to his network of secret operatives for safekeeping. Although the parlour was warm from the fire, I shivered. I'd handled several of those dark items myself, and I knew their power. One damned

necklace had already tried to kill me; I had to admit I was sceptical of searching for another.

"If she's showing up as a ghost, that makes it pretty clear
what happened to her," Coltt said. "But the cameo is probably
off the coast of Bermuda. What can we do?"

Sorren took another sip of blood. "I believe the cameo is
here, in Charleston. And I believe both the appearance of
Felicity and the unusual ghostly activity are linked." He leaned
forward and met my gaze. "I have a strong feeling that we've
got a necromancer here in the city, and I fear what we've seen
is just the beginning."

The only things I like less than pirates are necromancers.
Then again, maybe I should qualify that statement, since in the
eyes of the Navy, Coltt and I are technically pirates. I prefer to
think of us as paranormal privateers, chartered by Sorren and
his murky band of relic-snatchers, helping the good guys by
plundering the bad ones. I avoid the Navy because I don't
think they'd understand the distinction.

"So who's our necromancer?" I asked.

Sorren shook his head. "Don't know yet. But I'm certain
whoever it is has focused his power in the Battery. That seems
to be the nexus of the disturbances."

I let out a low whistle. "That's one wealthy necromancer."
The Battery was a row of some of the finest houses in
Charleston, so named because it fronted the harbour just
behind the city's port defences. The rainbow-hued homes,
reminiscent of mansions in the Caribbean islands, had long
been the preserve of the wealthiest and most prominent citi-
zens in the city. Sorren knew how to navigate in that company,
but it didn't come naturally to country boys like Coltt and me.

"As luck would have it," Sorren said, with a hint of a smile
indicating that luck had little to do with it, "there's going to be
a grand ball at the home of a dear friend of your Uncle Evann's.
Everyone from the Battery will be there, as well as the folks
who live south of Broad Street. And so will you," he said,
looking straight at me.

"Are you coming, too?" I asked, not sure whether Sorren

could hear the uncertainty in my voice. Pirates I could handle. Old-money aristocrats I found much more frightening, on a whole different level.

Sorren chuckled. "I'm a bit too well known in certain circles," he said. "There will be more than one esteemed reverend of the church in attendance who might find my presence . . . unsettling."

"They'll balk at a vampire and not a bloody necromancer?" Coltt broke in. "How's that?"

Sorren gave an eloquent shrug. "Necromancers have a pulse. I don't. Unlike the undead, necromancers and their sort have survived for centuries hiding in plain sight, usually among the most privileged and pious."

"I guess I'd better dust off the company manners," I said resignedly. Give me a good sword fight any day over a social event. Both are battles, but one is at least honest about it.

"I've trained you better than that," Sorren chided. And it was true. Under his tutelage, I had mingled among the wealthiest and most powerful men in the former colonies, with them none the wiser to the charade. And usually, while I mingled, Coltt was busy thieving in the darkened rooms upstairs.

"The ball will keep the Battery's residents occupied, and it's very likely they'll give their servants the night off, so it should be easy for Coltt to slip into the houses and look for clues to the whereabouts of our necromancer," Sorren added.

"And what kind of clue is that?" Coltt demanded. "Perhaps a sign that says 'Ring bell for the necromancer' or some such?"

"You're the best thief in the New World," Sorren replied smoothly, and added, "trained by the best thief in the Old World," with a hint of pride, tugging at his collar to indicate himself. "I have full confidence in your abilities to find our man."

"Just make sure this necromancer likes fancy dress balls," Coltt said darkly. "I don't have your strength or Dante's magic. I'm not the man for a fight."

I personally knew that, when his back was against the wall,

Coltt could be utterly ruthless in battle, but I also knew that the memories of those few awful times weighed more heavily on him than they did on me. Maybe it meant Coltt was a nicer person than I am. Or maybe I'd just lost so many of the people I cared about that I no longer worried about God keeping score.

"The ball is tomorrow night," Sorren replied. "I've had an associate get me the plans to as many of the great homes as he could; Coltt will no doubt find them useful. Evann's probably already gotten his hands on the guest list and been to his sources for news. And as for you, Dante" he said, with a glance in my direction, "a haircut and a shave might be in order. I've taken the liberty of having a new outfit delivered to your rooms. I believe you'll look quite acceptable in it."

I sighed. Sorren had taught me long ago that the best spies looked good enough to fit in and unremarkable enough not to be remembered. I feared it was my lot in life.

The next night, Evann and I headed out. We were dressed like aristocrats, with a carriage and driver (thanks to Sorren) that rivalled the best in the city. Coltt had caught a rental coach as far as Meeting Street, where he would walk the rest of the way to attract the least notice. Evann and I intended to have our driver let us out by the main door, but someone's coach horse had bolted, and the street in front of the mansion was a tangle of people, policemen and panicked horses, so we had our man let us out on Church Street just a block or so from the Battery, with instructions to pick us up in the same place afterwards.

The ball was just beginning to get lively when we arrived. "Welcome, gentlemen," said the servant who met us at the door to take our cloaks. "You've arrived just in time." He dropped his voice conspiratorially. "The musicians have warmed up and the crowd is lively, but the sideboard is still full, if you hurry," he said with a wink.

He turned away just as I saw a button fall from my cloak. I bent to retrieve it, and saw a small, intricate design at the outside corner of the stone step. It was a symbol of some sort, drawn in a yellow, chalky powder, very small, as if not to attract notice. My button fell next to it, so I couldn't avoid seeing it, although otherwise, I would never have looked down. I stood, and, for an instant, saw a look of stark fear cross the servant's face, until his mask of genial welcome slammed back into place. *Odd*, I thought, vowing to ask Sorren about it later.

"Evann! How good of you to come!" I looked up to see Eudora Hallingsworth, the doyenne of the Battery, holding out her arms to greet Evann with a prim kiss on each cheek. Mrs Hallingsworth was descended from the families whose names matched the streets and plantations of Charleston, as close as we got in these post-colonial days to local royalty.

"Honoured to be your guest," Evann said, making a low bow and kissing her hand with a rakish raise of his eyebrows.

Eudora Hallingsworth chuckled. "Really, Evann! Such a show you make," she protested, clearly thrilled at the attention. "And who is this with you?"

Evann turned to me with a flourish. "My nephew, Dante Morris, of the Virginia Morrises."

Mrs Hallingsworth smiled indulgently at me. "Pleased to make your acquaintance. Your family has an illustrious reputation."

I smiled along with the ruse. "You're too kind, m'lady," I replied. Yes, my family name was Morris, and yes, I was from Virginia, but otherwise Evann had led the dear lady woefully astray. My father was a fisherman in a poor coastal village, not a planter aristocrat. But if privateering hadn't already damned my soul, I doubted another lie or two would tip the balance.

"You simply must try the roast duck," Mrs Hallingsworth said, leading us into the ballroom, where musicians had already struck up a lively reel. "One of the servants will get you a cup of punch, and you can't overlook Cook's benne seed wafers." Her attention turned to me with the eye of a mother.

"And you, Dante, shouldn't waste another minute when the band is playing. Come with me. I'll introduce you to the prettiest young ladies in South Carolina!"

Evann and I were swept into the high spirits of the ball. It seemed to me that, for a curio-shop owner, Evann seemed to know everyone who was anyone in Charleston's notoriously cliquish upper society, and they treated him with the fondness usually reserved for an elderly, quirky relative. After Mrs Hallingsworth had made my introduction, I was accepted as an approved and eligible bachelor, and managed to dance with the daughters of some of the most powerful men in the city. I was certain those same men would be horrified to know that their coddled darlings were waltzing with a pirate.

All the while, I kept my senses keen to magic. While more than one of the blue-blooded young ladies made me tingle, it had nothing to do with the supernatural. To my surprise, I picked up its traces on several of Charleston's movers and shakers. Not water magic, but other forms of power. Land magic, not surprising given Charleston's planter heritage. Charisma beyond the norm, good for swaying others to see things your way. Attraction magic, which led to the gathering of friends, power and money.

I chanced a look at the black-frocked Anglican priest who was engaged in a lively discussion in the corner. What might the good Father have to say if he knew just how many of his parishioners had more than a hint of magic to them?

Waltzing was a good excuse to circle the room without being obvious. I could keep my eyes on my attractive partner, while my magic swept over the bystanders as we circled past. Most of the people didn't register at all with me, meaning that they were what they appeared to be and no more. But twice, as my partners and I passed the back corner of the room, my powers gave me an uncomfortable jolt, a wave of alarm.

"Thank you for this dance," I said, favouring Sarah, my latest dancing partner, with a deep bow.

"The pleasure was all mine," she drawled. She was so good at innocent flirtation that I knew it was a skill honed of long practice.

I murmured an excuse about needing more punch, and found a reason to go the long way back to the sideboard. I passed within a few feet of the place where my magic had jolted me, slowing as much as I dared to get a look at its source.

The elderly gentleman had his back to me at first, but he turned as I walked past, and I wondered if he sensed something, too. He had a shock of untamed white hair over bushy eyebrows and a furrowed face. His hazel eyes had a wary glint, and his lips were pressed tightly together, jaw set. In his prime, he might have been a tall man, but age had hunched him. I shook my head to clear it. No, it wasn't age that made his shoulders slump. In my mind's eye, my magic eye, I saw him clutching a chest against him, hunched over it to protect it with his body, to hide it from view. His eyes met mine, and I got a very nasty frisson down my spine. I was pretty sure I'd found our necromancer, and at the moment, I'd bet that he was wondering whether my magic posed him any threat.

"Dante! There you are!" Mrs Hallingsworth's greeting was music to my ears. Our hostess took my elbow and steered me away from the old man, whose gaze, I was sure, followed me as I headed in the opposite direction. "I'd like you to meet my niece."

"I'm embarrassed to ask," I said, doing my best to look chagrined, "but I couldn't place the older gentleman in the other corner. Should I know him?"

Mrs Hallingsworth chuckled. "I should say not – unless you're a pirate! That's Judge Heinrich Von Dersch. He served as the king's highest magistrate in Bermuda before he moved to South Carolina on the eve of the war, and he's been an absolute bulwark against piracy on the high seas. He'll tell you that he's hanged over three hundred pirates himself, and I believe him." She cast a backwards glance. "He's a stern fellow, but then, who wouldn't be in his position?"

My hostesses's words were gracious, but I could feel a tinge of fear. My good Mrs Hallingsworth had a generous dollop of magic in the form of charisma, though she probably didn't know it and would be horrified to find out that her "charm" was indeed charmed. I was willing to bet that the tingle of fear she felt came from the feel of Judge Von Dersch's magic: dark, grasping, and vengeful.

I spent much of the next hour engaged in light conversation with Mrs Hallingsworth's lively niece Isabella. To my delight, Isabella was well-read, educated in the classics, and had travelled extensively abroad. She also shared her aunt's charisma, which was difficult to resist, even when I knew it to be magic. Alas, I also knew any prospects there were doomed from the start, though I was reluctant to say good night when Uncle Evann came to collect me for the drive home.

A different servant brought us our cloaks. As we left, I made a point to look down at the step where I had seen the chalked symbol. It had been rubbed out.

"I want to look at something," I said to Evann as soon as the door closed behind us. I led him around the house, bending low so as not to be seen out of the windows, an eye on the foundation stones of the great house.

"Look there," I said in a whisper, drawing his attention to another of the intricate, graceful marks. Gingerly, I touched it. Magic quivered beneath my fingertips, of a sort I couldn't readily identify. I slipped my fingertips together, puzzled. The marks seemed to have been made in a mixture of cornmeal and ash. Strange.

"There's another one over here," Evann said quietly. It was a different symbol, but of the same sort, and we found them at intervals all around the foundation stones, and a few more at the entrance to the servants' kitchen.

When we were safely back on the street, I turned to Evann. "What did you make of all that?" I asked, interested to hear his thoughts before I shared my own.

"You're the one with the magic," Evann replied. "I was just there to get you in the door."

I chuckled. "Forced to eat fine food and drink fine wine and be flirted with by some of the richest widows in the city."

Evann sighed. "I do what I must for the cause." He sobered. "As for those marks, I know I've seen something like that before, but not often. I'll see what I can find when I get back to the store." He gave me a sideways glance. "How about you? Did you pick up anything, or were you too addled by the beautiful ladies?"

"Considering that their fathers would line up to challenge me to a duel if they had any idea who had danced with their daughters, I'd say my attraction was tempered with a cold splash of common sense," I said. "But they were pretty, weren't they?"

"Focus, Dante."

It was my turn to sigh. "As you wish. Yes, I picked up on something besides the symbols. There was an old man in the corner. Miserable-looking person, not exactly the life of the party. I saw a couple of the men talking briefly to him, but most people gave him a wide berth, and the servants did their best to stay out of his way entirely."

"Judge Von Dersch," Evann replied. "And what did your magic say?"

"He's hiding something," I answered, carefully sifting through my impressions. "I think he's able to put a glamour on his magic, to make it seem different than it is. I sensed . . . falseness." I paused again, thinking. "There was a feeling of doom around him, and the oddest thing was, I could swear it waxed and waned over the course of the evening. I barely noticed him when we arrived, but a few hours later his magic seemed to fill the room so that I could scarcely think. It gradually got better, but I wondered how many of the other guests with a hint of magic felt the same thing."

"Between eighth and ninth bells, I noticed that the good Judge was standing completely alone," Evann said. "I was watching him, too, but for a different reason. Sorren didn't want me to mention it before we came, didn't want to prejudice your read on the evening, but he thinks the judge is our necromancer."

I shuddered. "I think you're right." I glanced up at the darkened windows of the other homes along the Battery. "What do you think Coltt's found?"

Evann gave a crafty smile. "I don't know what's he's

discovered, but I do know the judge's house was at the top of his list to explore."

We hustled along with our capes drawn close against the autumn wind. As we passed the entrance to one of the many small, narrow alleyways, my magic tingled. I've got water magic, and I'm strongest when I'm at sea, but close to the bay I could feel the pull of its power, and I knew from prior experience that spirits could feel it, too. Evann hadn't been kidding about Charleston being one of the most haunted cities in the former colonies. New Orleans might rival us, maybe. Both are gracious cities built on rivers of blood and a world of human suffering. The rich folks choose not to remember, but the spirits never forget.

A shot rang out at close quarters. Evann grabbed me and shoved me against the wall, and we waited, but there were no running footsteps, no shouts for the police. Exchanging a worried glance, Evann and I straightened our clothes and ventured away from the shelter of the wall, daring to peer down the narrow alley.

"Have you seen him?" The voice startled me. I looked more closely, and saw a young man standing in the shadows. My eyes narrowed, and I looked with my magic instead of merely sight. The man's outline glowed faintly with a light blue nimbus. Now that I took a closer look, I could see that he bore a fatal chest wound, unfortunately not uncommon in the alleyways of Charleston. Dozens of headstrong young men met their untimely deaths at the hands of an aggrieved rival and a fast bullet in the side streets of the Holy City. But only one had bothered to hail us.

"Who are you looking for?" I asked, expecting the shade to be searching for his killer.

"The death mage."

That brought Evann and me up short. "What do you mean?" I said carefully, although I certainly had a good idea.

"Can't you feel him? You've got a touch of magic to you. There's a hocus who binds souls to the tide. The spirits run from him, those who can. But the girl can't get away."

Evann and I exchanged glances. "What girl?" I asked.

"Are ye deaf?" the spirit asked, shaking his head. "Can't you hear her wailing? She's a pretty lass in a blue dress with a fancy brooch, and she sobs something fierce."

"Where have you seen her?"

"Up and down the Battery. Mostly at high tide in the night."

High tide. Odd for that to come up again so soon. Not a coincidence, I was sure of it.

"I've been looking for that girl," I said cautiously. "Her name is Felicity Barre. Her family is very worried about her. Do you know anything else that might help me set her free?"

The ghost seemed to take my measure. "Maybe. I know someone who knows a lot about spirits and hocus. She's the one who told me I'm doomed to die in the same damned duel night after night until I put things right. She might could help you."

"Much obliged," I murmured. The ghost turned, and Evann and I followed him down the narrow alley. We wound through the back streets of Charleston, a world apart from the glittering ball we had just left. These were dark, dank streets even the harbour's burly longshoremen feared to tread. They were the province of Charleston's slaves, and they were not generally a welcome place for people like Evann and me, or for our guide, had he still been mortal.

I could feel eyes watching us as we passed the abysmal slave quarters. It was after 10 p.m. curfew, and few bondsmen would risk the beating that could come if they were found in the streets after the bells rang. I could feel the suspicion that greeted us, and the fear. There was magic, too, strange and powerful, from somewhere far away, utterly outside of my own experience.

"By the way, I'm Ellison," the ghost said over his shoulder. "Ellison Hawking-Muir the Third." He paused. "My friends used to call me Hawk."

"Nice to meet you, Hawk," I said. "How did you come to be in a duel?"

"I was called out because I danced with the wrong girl at a

party, and she told her brother I had somehow insulted her," Hawk replied. "I hadn't meant to. I tried to apologize. But her brother wouldn't have it, and demanded a duel for her honour. Stupid game. Turns out, he was a member of that secret duelling society. Probably trumped up a reason to call me out. He'd already shot four men dead before me. I didn't stand a chance."

"I'm sorry," I told Hawk. I'd heard about Charleston duels, a pastime of rich, spoiled young men with more money than sense. It didn't surprise me that duelling would be just another form of one-upmanship, only a game that left the loser dead instead of just humiliated. "What happened to your murderer?"

Hawk gave a sharp, bitter laugh. "Happened? Nothing happened. Not for a while." The ghost dropped his voice, although I was pretty sure I was the only one who could hear him. "Until he came back to the alley for another duel. I could see he'd picked another easy mark, like I'd been. Poor fellow must have borrowed the gun; he could barely tell the butt from the barrel."

"And?" I asked, sure there was more to the story.

Hawk glanced at me over his shoulder, his lips pressed in a tight, pained smile. "Just as the guy who had challenged me sighted to aim, I tackled him. Went right through him. It made him shiver, and it threw off his aim. He missed, and the poor fellow he'd challenged was so frightened he managed to squeeze off a shot and got lucky. Took my murderer through the shoulder, and he bled to death before his buddies could do anything about it. The other guy ran off as fast as he could." Hawk didn't look as smug as I'd expected him to. Instead, he just looked sad. "But I'm still here."

Finally, Hawk stopped in front of an old slave cabin. I hesitated, unsure of what to do. Walking up and knocking didn't seem like a good idea. Before I could ask Hawk what came next, the door opened and an old woman dressed in white stood in the doorway.

"That's Mama Nadege," Hawk whispered. "Tell her I brought you."

"Mama Nadege?" I managed, finding my throat had gone dry. "I'm supposed to tell you that Hawk brought me here. It's about the weeping ghost."

Mama Nadege looked me up and down, and then she did the same to Evann. When she spoke, I could see that her gaze was fixed just off to my right, where Hawk's ghost stood. "Well, of course Hawk brought you. He's right with you, plain as day." Her voice was thick as gumbo, heavy with the consonants of the islands and somewhere else I couldn't place.

"Come in then. The neighbours won't bother you none, not now that they know you're here to see me," she added, with a glance towards the darkened buildings behind us.

We followed Mama Nadege into her house. The air was heavy with the smell of incense and candle smoke. Mama Nadege was a big woman, swathed in a white, loose gown. Her hair was tied up in a kerchief, and I couldn't tell her age from her face. Her eyes were what drew me. Black eyes, dark as her skin, like deep pools for drowning. Her magic flowed around me, almost smothering in its intensity, but my power sensed no threat. She was curious, and intrigued. And I had the unsettling feeling that she had been expecting us.

Her small cabin was hung with brightly coloured block-printed cloths and filled with candles, clay figures, crude stuffed, dolls, and carved wooden images. Lanyards of shells, beads and dried plants festooned everything.

"You're a mambo," Evann said.

Mama Nadege smiled. "Mambo asogwe," she replied.

Evann turned to me. "She's a high priestess of voodoo."

I'd heard that term before, but I hadn't associated it with Charleston. "I thought voodoo only happened in New Orleans," I replied.

Mama Nadege laughed, a deep chuckle that resonated. "Oh, there be voodoo in Charleston, all right. My mama was born in Haiti, where we know how to talk to spirits. She was brought to New Orleans and sold there, but her mistress married a man from Charleston and brought my mama with her. She raised me in the power. She wasn't the only one he brought here from New Orleans, either. Oh, no, child, the voodoo is all around you. You're just too pale to notice," she said, and laughed heartily at her own joke.

She sobered and looked at me again, and I felt tendrils of her magic gliding over my skin. I fought the urge to shiver. "You've got some power," she murmured, her consonants smooth as a spicy roux. "Considerable power. Why'd it bring you to me, child?"

Evann gave me the barest hint of a nod, letting me know it was safe to tell the truth, or at least most of it. "I'm trying to stop a necromancer. He's got a dark magic object, and my master sent me to take it back from him, put it somewhere it can't hurt anyone."

She eyed me carefully. "You're nobody's slave," she said, walking slowly around me. "You might not own those fancy clothes, but you're a freeman, sure enough." She began to shake her head. "Uh, uh, uh," she murmured. "Only one kind of man be your master. You serve a nightwalker, am I right?"

"Nightwalker" seemed close enough to vampire to accept without quibbling. "Yes."

"Mr Sorren?"

I tried to hide my astonishment. "Yes."

Mama Nadege relaxed, and smiled broadly. "Well, why didn't you say so?" She gestured towards two chairs near the fireplace. "Sit down. Tell Mama what you know, and what you need to know."

I told her about the missing girl, and how she might be the weeping woman Hawk told us about. Mama Nadege listened as I recounted the ball and the encounter with Judge Von Dersch, and rocked back and forth in her chair without saying anything. "There's one more thing," I added. "I saw a marking by the doorway. I don't think I was supposed to see it. The man who took my coat looked afraid when I noticed it, like it might cause trouble." I paused. "Afterwards, Evann and I walked around the house, and a whole series of markings were made on the foundation stones. They were made of cornmeal and ash."

Mama Nadege nodded knowingly. "Oh, trouble it would cause, that's for sure." She bent down and drew on the hard dirt floor of her cabin with a stick, tracing an elaborate symbol very like the one by the door of the Hallingsworth house. "Did it look like this?"

I nodded. "That's one of the marks. There were others."

Mama Nadege sat back up. "Those are veves. Powerful magic. They can open the gateway to the spirits, bring one of the loa, the Invisibles, across to guide us. Someone took a risk to try to protect that house."

"If the . . . veves . . . are there for protection, how did Judge Von Dersch get in, if he really is a necromancer?" I asked.

Mama Nadege shook her head. "Someone did his best to protect that house. Risked a whippin', or worse, if he got caught. But it's for nothin'. Takes a mambo to chalk veves with power. Those were just pretty marks. Sure wouldn't stop a necromancer none." She gave me an arch look. "I notice it didn't stop you from walking right in, either."

I hadn't thought of that. "No, ma'am," I replied. "It didn't." I paused. "Have you heard the weeping girl? Seen the spirits?"

Mama Nadege began to rock again, and closed her eyes. "Oh, yes. I've seen her. I've seen all of them. Like a cloud of witnesses they are, all around us. And I'll tell you something: all of them was wronged. Oh, most of them were pirates and thieves, like the judge say. Most of 'em deserved hangin', they did indeed. But they didn't deserve what happened after. And that girl, she didn't deserve nothin' like that."

"Like what?" Evann asked, leaning forward.

"Most white folks 'round these parts like Judge Von Dersch because he's a hangin' judge. Had a reputation in Bermuda for hangin' more pirates than any judge alive. And he ain't stopped hangin' them since he came to Charleston. No, siree. But he don't just hang them. He makes sure the bodies get thrown in the oyster shoals. That's a place of the damned, those shoals. Tide comes in and out through them, never fully dry and never fully wet. Those souls, they ain't never gonna get no rest in a buryin' place like that. They are doomed to suffer for eternity. Ain't no one, not even pirates, deserves that, and there ain't no judge but the Almighty right to pass that kind of sentence. But Von Dersch does."

"Why?" I asked, intrigued and horrified. "Why would he care what happens to them after they're dead?"

Mama Nadege shook her head. "You're as green as you are white, son. This magic is new to you, ain't it?"

I tried not to bristle. "I've had magic all my life," I replied. "But no real schooling in it, until I met Sorren. I've got a lot to learn."

My answer seemed to satisfy Mama. "That you do, son. Well, here's your lesson for tonight. A necromancer draws power from enslaving spirits. Not just killing . . . slaving. I imagine you can guess how I feel about somethin' like that."

I swallowed hard. For all her power, Mama Nadege herself was owned as property by one of Charleston's wealthy families. It didn't take much imagination to guess that she'd take a dim view of any slaver, before or after death. "I imagine I can," I said quietly. Another thought came to me, and I dared to look up at Mama Nadege.

"If you knew Von Dersch was a slaver, why didn't you do something yourself?"

Mama Nadege began to laugh, but it wasn't a pleasant sound. "Oh, I did do something, child. I marked veves – powerful veves – around the places my people live. Those cabins out there, they're the safest place in Charleston. He has no power, not in my alley. But how you reckon an old slave woman gonna come up against a judge, 'specially when all the masters favour him? Uh-uh. All I'd get is dead, and then who's gonna protect my people?" She leaned forward. "But I can help you, if you're of a mind to do it. That I can. And I've got some powerful friends myself."

I exchanged a glance with Evann. This might be the best chance we were going to get. "All right, I said. "What do I need to do?"

"You need to get into that Judge's house, and find his object of power. By himself, his magic is weak. I know this. It's not his magic makes him so strong, it's some dark object he has; bad thing, very bad. You get in there, you gonna find that he keeps something from all of the souls he's bound – a reminder. I bet he's got somethin' belonged to the poor girl, too. How she got mixed up with him, I don't know, but she got stuck, like the others. You go in there, you make it right, hear me? You be like Moses and let those poor slaved souls go free."

I drew a deep breath. It wasn't as if I hadn't figured it would come to this, but hearing Mama Nadege say it made it entirely too real. "Sorren had someone scouting the houses," I said finally. "He might have learned something we can use. I'd like to talk with him – and with Sorren – before we do anything."

Mama chuckled. "You think I was gonna send you out tonight? Uh-uh. These things take time. I have to call the power. I have to talk to my loa, my guides. I know who I'm gonna call to help us, just the spirits who will want to see this man get what he deserve. You come back to the alley tomorrow night; mind it be an hour before low tide. Very important – because those souls, they be bound on the shoals. When the tide is high, his power is high. Tide go out, he's weaker. That's the time to strike.

"You get Hawk to bring you back here. My people know Hawk. They'll leave you alone if you're with him. You leave it to me. I'll get you into that house – and out, too, maybe."

I didn't like the way that sounded, but it was probably the best I was going to get. Hawk saw us out to the end of the alley. "Thanks," I said, not sure what to say to the ghost.

Hawk shrugged. "If you can help that girl, I'll do what I can for you. I'm stuck here because I was stupid. I deserve what I got. But her – I don't think she did anything wrong."

I nodded. "I'll see what I can do," I said, feeling less sure of just what could be. Evann and I walked to where we were supposed to meet the carriage. To our surprise, it was still waiting for us.

"Get in." The voice from inside the carriage was Sorren's. I tried to hide my surprise as Evann and I climbed inside. Coltt was there, too. It made for a crowded ride.

"I had time to get into most of the houses on my list before your little party wound down," Coltt said. "But there was one house I couldn't enter. Wasn't the locks – I can pick them. It was dark magic, and I couldn't break it."

"Let me guess," I said with a look towards Evann. "Judge Von Dersch's house."

Sorren gave a cold smile. "I thought you might come to that conclusion."

"We found something else out," said Coltt. "About Felicity."

I looked up with interest. "And?"

"Sorren did some research on the old court cases Judge Von Dersch handled. There was a case about six months after Felicity went missing where an entire pirate crew was seized and brought to trial. They were found guilty and hanged, but here's the interesting part. The records say there was a woman aboard. She was dressed like a trollop and too drunk to give testimony, so they hanged her along with the pirates as the ship's whore."

A cold shiver went down my back. "If she'd been their prisoner for months . . . been dishonoured . . . she might not have been in her right mind by the time they found her," I said quietly.

"Or the pirates might have kept her liquored up to make sure she couldn't tell anyone who she was," Coltt put in solemnly. "But it would explain what happened to her."

"And why her ghost hasn't been able to rest," I finished.

I looked at Sorren. "You know anything about a mambo named Mama Nedege?"

"Mambo asogwe," he replied. "In magic, distinctions matter." Sorren paused. "So she found you?"

"I would have said we found her, but yes, we've met."

Sorren chuckled. "More like, she led you to her. Mama's very powerful. But she can't go up against the judge on her own for the same reason I couldn't confront him at the ball tonight. The risks of exposing what we are outweigh the possibility of being able to win. That's why we need someone like you."

I grimaced. "So I've been told." Sorren and Coltt listened closely as Evann and I recounted our evening. I ended with Mama's offer to help get me past the wardings that had stopped Coltt. Sorren nodded sagely.

"If anyone can do it, she can," he replied. "Let's get you home. You've got a long day tomorrow."

I met Hawk at the end of his alley just before 2 p.m., when the tide would be lowest. In the daylight, it was more difficult to see him, but when Hawk stepped into the shadows, he was nearly as clear as he had been last night. Hawk's fatal duelling wound was as raw as the first time I'd seen him, but if it still gave him pain, he did not show it. Instead, he seemed as excited as a ghost can be about the day's work.

"Where's your other friend?" Hawk asked, looking for Evann.

"Coltt and Evann have the house staked out. They saw the judge leave this morning for court. He shouldn't be home until around four p.m."

I followed Hawk back to Mama Nadege's cabin. The other slave homes were empty, their occupants presumably about their daily business. Mama sat on the steps of her cabin, weaving a sea-grass basket and singing. Around her were sea grass baskets of all sizes and shapes, beautiful objects with intricate patterns, woven with the touch of a master.

"You like my baskets, huh?" Mama greeted me. "Now that I'm old, this is what the master has me do all day. When I've made the ones Master needs for the household, I can make as many as I can to sell for myself down in the Slave's Market."

"They're beautiful," I replied, looking at the array of designs.

Mama Nadege laughed, a deep belly laugh. "Oh, you just looking at the surface, child. Stretch out your magic, and see what it tell you."

I did just that, and my eyes grew wide. The baskets weren't just beautiful, they were tinged with power. Magic to bring luck, to win love, to keep relationships harmonious, to prevent food from spoiling. "Household" magic my mother would

have called it, often not respected as much as the great magics
to affect weather or turn the tide of battle. Yet, as my mother
always reminded me, such small magics were the warp and
woof of our lives, and without them we would be much poorer.
"Do your buyers know?"

Mama let her head fall back and gave another deep laugh.
"What, you think I'm crazy, child? No one knows why, they
just think my baskets are lucky as well as strong. Make them
feel good when they own one, make their food last longer,
make their house happier. Then they come back and buy more,
and get more lucky." She gave a crafty grin. "And the more of
these baskets Master have, the more he like me. The nicer he
be to my people." She chuckled.

When this is over, if I live through it, maybe I'll be back for
one of those baskets, I thought. Something for protection, or
to make the ladies notice me.

Mama held out a woven basket that looked like a cylinder
with a matching lid. "I made this for you, child," she said, and
her dark eyes grew serious. "To take into that house where
you're goin'. When you find that thing your master wants, you
put it in there, and my magic will keep it still. Mind you don't
open the lid once it's in there and check on it. You keep that lid
shut tight, and what you find will go to sleep."

"Thank you," I said. I'd been wondering how I was going to
get whatever-it-was out of the house, and I sincerely hoped it
would fit in Mama's basket.

She stood and waved for me to follow her into her cabin.
"Mind where you step," she cautioned, and I looked down to
see two intricate veves etched in the dirt near the centre of her
small house. To the side lay a skin drum and several guttered
candles. Three candles, black, purple and silver, still burned.

"We worked the magic last night," Mama said, and I could
see that she looked very tired. "I called to the loas, the spirits. I
asked them for guidance. Ghede came to me. Powerful loa.
Loa of death and resurrection, huh. The right spirit for this
job, no? Ghede is also the patron of vampires. I think he knows
just what we doin', don't you think? Ghede Nibo came to me.

He helps the spirits cross over, and he especially care for spirits below the water."

She set her hands on her hips, pleased with herself. "Huh. I think we got the right loa, that for sure. We fed him and gave him rum and let him smoke his cigars, and when he be all happy and satisfied, I ask him for your protection, to get those poor souls out of that house. Ghede Nibo, he say yes. That be powerful magic on your side, child.

"Here, you take this, too." She held out a charm woven of sea grass that hung on a leather strap. The sea grass had been darkened to a red brick colour, and as I held it in my hand, some of the powder that stained it coloured my palm. "This veve, it's for Ghede Nibo. Help you take his magic with you."

"Thank you for the charm," I said, fastening it around my neck. "But Coltt said the house was warded against entry. How will I get in?"

Mama gave a toothy smile. "I'm getting to that, child. We raised two loa last night. Ghede Nibo be one of them. Papa Legba is the other. Papa, he holds the doorway between us and the loa. Papa Legba, he will take you to the house and open a passage for you through the magic. What happens inside is up to you. When you find the object that gives the judge his power, you put it in my basket, seal it tight. If you can free the spirits, Ghede Nibo say he will help them cross over. The loa will wait outside. Once you're inside the house, child, you be on your own."

I shivered, but nodded. "Let's go. I want to be in place at low tide, when the judge's power is weakest."

"I have business down by the Slave's Market, and then I'll go to the oyster beds. I'll call to Yemanja, mother of the sea, to set those souls free. Slaving them in her waters is an affront to her. Find what that judge holds over those souls and break the bond, and Yemanja will set them free." She nodded to a pile of bloody feathers in the corner that had once been a chicken. "I've done sacrifice to Lady Yemanja. She'll hear me."

Mama met my gaze. "When you're done, come back to the alley. Papa Legba will show you the way. I will keep the candles burning for you, give you my blessing." She reached into the folds of her voluminous white dress and brought out a small bag. It was made of leather, and bulged with whatever was inside, tied off with purple and black string.

"You take this. It's a gris-gris bag. Very powerful. Put it in your shirt, over your heart. Keep it with you. It will give you power."

I made a slight bow, though my heart was thudding at the idea of what I was about to do. "Thank you, Mama Nadege."

She held her hands out over me in a gesture of blessing. "Come back safely, child. And set those spirits free."

Hawk walked back with me to the end of the alley, though in the sunlight he was difficult to see. At the end of the alley, an old man waited with a dog. He was a very dark man, and a half-smoked cigar hung from one corner of his mouth. A wide-brimmed straw hat kept me from seeing his eyes. He leaned on a crutch on his left side. The dog sat quietly beside him, watching me. I'd probably passed old black men who looked just like him a hundred times in the streets of Charleston, but I knew for certain I hadn't passed him. Even at a distance, I could feel the waves of power that rippled from him. I didn't know what he was, but I was certain of one thing: he wasn't human.

The old man waved for me to follow him, and set off at a faster pace than I would have thought possible towards Judge Von Dersch's house.

I could feel the wardings around the house before we reached it. Cold, evil power. No wonder people crossed to the other side of the street when they passed. Even without magic, the house had a bad feel to it. And I was going in alone.

Evann was staked out down the street, with a big hat that hid his features. He leaned against a wall, reading a newspaper, but I knew he was keeping watch to make sure the judge didn't return. Evann gave me a nod that might have been just friendly, but it was his all-clear signal. Coltt wasn't in sight, but I knew he was watching the back of the house, and if he'd seen something, he'd be out front along the sea wall, smoking a pipe.

I followed Papa Legba and his dog into the narrow alley

between the houses. The wardings pressed on my magic horribly, screaming in my head for me to leave. I could see the
warding like a dark film around the house. Papa Legba raised
a hand, and there was silence in my mind. A doorway opened
in the dark wardings, and I stepped through. Mama Nadege
said Papa Legba would help me get out again, and I certainly
hoped he understood that part of the plan. I had my veve
charm and Mama's basket, and although I didn't doubt her
magic, in my belt was a loaded pistol. Taking a deep breath and
clutching the sea-grass basket, I stepped over the wardings.

I'd been afraid that I would need Coltt's skill at picking locks,
but it turned out that the judge put a lot of confidence in his
wardings. The locks on his house were easy enough for me to
get open, with a little jiggling from Coltt's picks and a nudge
from my magic. I glanced up at the sky. The day had grown
cloudy, and now it looked as if a storm were brewing. I opened
the side door and stepped inside.

The interior of the house was gloomy. Blinds were drawn
closed over many windows, and a thick layer of dust lay everywhere. Cobwebs cascaded in the corners, filled with the dead
husks of the spiders that dared intrude on the judge's sanctuary. Grey sheets covered the furniture, slipcovered as if the
owner had gone off for an extended trip. Yet we knew that the
judge still resided here. Maybe "lived" wasn't the word.
Nothing seemed to live within these walls.

The odour of mildew and the stale air made me cough.
Beneath it was a strong smell of camphor. I had entered
through the piazza, and now made my way into the parlour.
Faded curtains shrouded the windows, letting through only
dim rays of light. On the slipcovered furniture, boxes, scrolls,
books of all kinds and sizes and metal tins were piled haphazardly several feet above the cushions. More boxes, crates,
barrels and tins were stacked in every corner of the room,
leaving only a few narrow paths. Here and there, I saw
discarded pieces of clothing and old rags. I had the mental
image of a dragon's lair, and a large black dragon coiled atop a
mound of bleached bones and mouldering treasure. Judging

by the dust, none of the judge's collections had been touched in years.

On shelves all around the parlour I saw small glass boxes. Most of them were filmy with dust; none looked as if they had been opened or moved in a long time. There were dozens of them: on the bookshelves, atop the side tables, on the mantle above the fireplace. I vowed to take a closer look on my way out.

I touched the veve on the strap at my throat for luck, and moved further into the house. It was dark enough that I lit a small candle lantern that sat on a side table. With the draperies pulled tight, I wasn't worried that I'd been seen by neighbours. The candle's glow was comforting, and I moved deeper into the gloom.

The next room was a library. Shelves ranged all the way to the ceiling, several feet above my head. There were hundreds of leather-bound books; not surprising for a scholar and a judge. But on every shelf were three or four of the glass boxes, and here and there small urns. I struggled to remember where I had seen urns like that before, and then I remembered. One or two such urns had come into Uncle Evann's shop. Cremation urns. I shuddered. Somewhere in the house, I could hear the deep, regular ticking of a large clock, and it seemed to echo my pounding heart.

I reached out with my magic. My touch was cautious, checking for magical traps. I was astounded to see the room lit as if with captured stars as every one of the glass boxes began to glow.

I looked closer at one of the boxes on the shelf nearest me, and had to blow on it to clear away enough dust to see inside. A button from a man's coat lay in the box and a few strands of hair. I backed up a step as my magic touched the box. A wave of anger hit me like a punch in the jaw. I had a glimpse of a man in worn and stained clothing, wearing a tattered coat with buttons like the one in the glass box. He looked like a brigand, and I was glad I hadn't met him in a dark alley. Quickly, I turned my attention to the next box. Inside was a meerschaum pipe, stained with tobacco from long use, a sailor's comfort. With it, also, were a few strands of hair.

I gaped at the shelves, understanding what I had found. By holding on to a possession of each condemned man and a few strands of hair, Judge Von Dersch had been able to tap into the power of the souls bound to eternal torment in the oyster shoals. There were boxes everywhere I looked, and I was certain that if I counted them, I would find three hundred glass cases, one for every damned soul on whom Judge Von Dersch had passed sentence.

I let my magic gently skim across the shelves. The clock's ticking grew louder as I moved around the library, and then I saw it – a large, graceful Morbier clock in an ornate cabinet. The cabinet of the clock was gently curved, wider at the top for the clock face, slim at the top of the body, then swelling to where the pendulum hung, and wider still at the feet. The cabinet was a dark Oriental lacquer, and it was covered with carvings and symbols I did not recognize.

I looked closer, and realized how the clock resembled the rough outlines of a human form. Even the terms for its parts, face, body, foot, made it sound human. I looked closer, then recoiled as my magic brushed against it. The clock resonated with power, a dark magic that hissed and sang at the very edge of my consciousness. I stared at it. The clock was as tall as I was, far too large to fit in Mama Nadege's basket.

Then I saw the pendulum. A bronze disc the size of a dinner plate swung back and forth, suspended by a long metal shaft. On the shaft were three gems: a shattered moonstone, a white opal and a garnet, all unlucky. I dared another flicker of magic and realized that the clock was not the locus of power; the stones in its pendulum were. Those I could fit in my basket.

From somewhere nearby, I heard a woman weeping. I looked up, and saw that one of the hundreds of boxes seemed to be glowing more brightly than the others. I climbed atop a desk for a better look, and caught my breath.

Inside was a black cameo brooch with a raised white image of the three Fates. Beside it was a lock of blonde hair. My magic touched the box, and unlike the anger and rage that had responded from the other boxes, this box spoke only of mourning and loss. In my mind's eye, I saw an image of a young woman dressed in a fashionable gown. I felt the energy of the box surge towards me, and images overwhelmed me. A storm at sea, leaving a ship derelict in the water. Discovery by a ship of "rescuers" who turned out to be pirates, ruffians who killed the crew, looted the ship's hold and carried off their treasures, including the young woman.

I tried to turn my head or close my eyes as I felt the ghost's memories forced upon me, memories of being cruelly used and badly beaten, plied with strong liquor to ensure that she offered no resistance. Then another rescue gone wrong, this time when the pirates were captured by the Navy. Dressed in a strumpet's abandoned finery, groggy from the rum and the beatings, she had been incoherent, unable to convince the sailors that she was a victim and not one of the brigand crew. The vision ended abruptly, with the snap of a gallows trapdoor.

I reeled back, covering my face with my hands, tears streaming down my face. There was no doubt that I had found Felicity Barre.

I heard the whispered curses and distant threats of the spirits trapped in the boxes around me as the clock's tick-tock rhythm seemed to grow louder with each heartbeat. The pirates' souls shouted and mocked, swearing in the vilest terms as if I had somehow enabled their torment. Then I heard a woman's voice as clearly as if she had bent low to whisper in my ear.

"Stop the clock and shatter the cases, and he loses his power."

Which to do first? Did the clock bind the souls, or did the trapped spirits power the clock's magic?

I set down the lantern and looked around the room for something to use to shatter the boxes. My gaze rested on a pole that stuck out from amidst the clutter. I grabbed it and pulled, setting off a small avalanche of papers and scrolls. I jumped back, careful to move the lantern so it wouldn't tip.

The pole came free in my hand, a whaler's harpoon. I took a deep breath and drew my pistol, holding the harpoon in my left hand.

I fired into the face of the clock, striking it squarely in the centre pin that bound the hands to the mechanism inside. A bloodcurdling shriek filled the air, the sound of something that had never been remotely human. With my left hand, I brought the harpoon down hard on the nearest shelf, smashing the glass boxes. Again and again my harpoon raised and lowered, sweeping the boxes to the floor, or shattering them where they sat. I took particular pride when the heavy shaft of the harpoon flung Felicity's box to the floor and it shattered, sending the cameo brooch to land near my feet.

Spirits swirled around me, angry and shrieking as the trapped pirates gained a measure of freedom. Without the clock's ticking, the room was otherwise still, but only for a heartbeat.

A blast of freezing air swept through the library, sending papers flying and clouding the room with dust. The same overpowering presence I had felt at the ball when I'd passed Judge Von Dersch now filled the room, and its power reached for me, enraged. The judge might not have returned in the flesh, but some segment of his power knew that his sanctuary had been violated, and like a large, black shadow, it stretched towards me, menacing and deadly.

I cast about with my magic for a weapon, since my pistol would do no good against this foe. I grabbed Felicity's cameo and threw myself towards the clock, wresting the pendulum from where it hung in the shattered clock case. The shadow's icy fingers brushed my skin, but I eluded its grip and stumbled, prising the gems free from their attachment to the pendulum. Mama Nadege's basket was just out of reach, and the shadow was circling to come at me again from an angle that would not require crossing paths with Mama Nadege's spirit catcher.

The shadow lurched towards me as I lunged for the basket. My foot kicked the piles that were precariously balanced on one of the old chairs, sending them sliding in a rush towards the floor, and knocking over the candle in the lantern.

The dry old papers caught fire quickly, and I knew that the crowded, cluttered rooms were a tinderbox. The shadow moved swiftly, and caught my ankle as I tried to scramble clear. Its touch was icy, far colder than even a vampire's undead grip. I struggled to remove the lid from the sea-grass basket without dropping either the gems or Felicity's cameo. The harpoon had fallen beside me, and my pistol was lost somewhere amid the mess.

I kicked at the shadow, but the black tendrils held me tightly. Just a few feet away, more scattered papers caught fire, and the room was beginning to fill with smoke. I grabbed at the leg of a large, overstuffed sofa to keep the shadow from dragging me backwards, but with one hand holding on, I couldn't manipulate the basket.

Outside, I heard rain lash the roof. The cameo beside me flared with brilliant light, and Felicity's ghost materialized, interposing itself between me and the deadly shadow. The air in the stuffy, smoky room began to move, gently at first, and then with the intensity of a captured windstorm. Before I had a chance to gather my thoughts, I saw a cloud of faces in the swirling air, and from the wild wind, the figures of the hanged pirates began to stream towards the shadow of the judge's power. I reached out with my water magic, and grabbed the nearest available source of power, the rain that beat down outside the mansion. I threw a burst of power against the shadow and felt its grip loosen, just as the cloud of spirits descended on the judge, shrieking and wailing. The shadow let go of my ankle and I rolled free, twisting off the lid of the sea-grass basket and thrusting the three gems inside, then slamming the lid down again.

I climbed to my feet, coughing and wheezing. I grabbed Felicity's cameo in one hand and the harpoon in the other, shoving the basket under my arm. Perhaps it was already too late. Smoke filled the room, making it impossible for me to see which way led out.

The house trembled as if shaken to its foundations. I could hear the thud of books falling from the shelves and the crash of glass as, in the other rooms, the glass spirit boxes smashed to the floor. My eyes were streaming tears from the smoke and it was growing difficult to breathe. Fire had spread to the old velvet draperies and the overstuffed furniture. Without a way out, I was sure to join the spirits I had just freed.

A dog barked frantically. Ahead of me, just visible in the smoke, I saw the shape of a large black dog. It barked again, then turned and trotted a few feet, turning again as if to make sure I had seen it. I staggered towards the dog, who jumped up and walked a few feet further, pausing to wait until I came close enough to see it before moving further.

The house rocked again, and I could hear the creak of old beams and the crash of plaster. Whatever I'd destroyed seemed to have been holding the whole damned house together, and the floor began to buckle and lurch beneath my feet. The insistent barking of the black dog kept me focused; drawing me through the smoke even as my lungs burned and skin began to blister from the heat.

Stumbling and coughing, I followed the barely visible dog, and when I could not see him, I followed the sound of his barking. Finally, I reached the door I had entered by and managed to fall more than step out, still holding tight to the basket and the cameo. I let the harpoon fall, unable to see well enough to strike at an enemy.

Rain pelted me, and I felt the sting of hail. Magic convulsed around me, and for a moment I was trapped between the crumbling house behind me and the dark wardings. The black dog stood next to me, still barking. For a moment, we were in the eye of the storm, and then there was silence. I felt as if I were suspended in midair, and then I came crashing down on to the grass, landing on one shoulder so as not to lose the precious items clutched in my white-knuckled hands.

"You've done good, son." I looked up into the wizened face of the old black man who had led me here, into the depthless eyes of Papa Legba. The black dog stood beside him, and I could have sworn it was smiling. Coltt and Evann rushed towards me, abandoning their disguises. It seemed as if everyone in Charleston had gathered, and perhaps they had. Houses on the Battery don't collapse in a puff of smoke every day. On the edge of the crowd I caught a glimpse of a figure dressed in white, and I knew that Mama Nadege had done her part, calling on the sea loa to free whatever part of the trapped spirits' essence was bound to the oyster shoals. In the crowd, just for a heartbeat, I thought I saw a pretty young woman in a blue dress, her hair caught back in an elegant twist. She smiled at me, and then turned, and vanished.

"Let's get you out of here, before there are too many questions." It was Evann's voice, and he and Coltt helped me to my feet. I looked around, but Papa Legba and the black dog were gone. Still dazed from the fight, I let them lead me through the back alleyways until we were far enough away to call for a carriage without attracting attention. Evann made me strip off my sooty jacket, and Coltt took the sea-grass basket, holding it tight with both hands. I slipped Felicity's cameo into my pocket, and the carriage whisked us back to Trifles and Folly.

Late that night, when I had gathered my wits, I returned to the alley where I'd met Hawk. He was waiting with a sad smile. "Did you find her?" he asked.

I nodded. "You deserve part of the credit. You brought me to Mama Nadege."

Hawk shrugged. "Did you free the ghosts?"

"I think so. They attacked whatever energy the judge sent to stop me, and then the whole building collapsed. Sorren told me that the judge dropped dead of a heart attack at the bench in his courtroom at the time the house fell. The pieces in the basket, and Felicity's brooch, will go into safekeeping, somewhere no one else can use them."

Hawk looked at me sadly. "I guess that's it then."

"You did me a good turn. You helped me free a woman's soul, and helped me stop a powerful necromancer. Didn't Mama tell you that you had to make things right before you could leave the alley? Maybe that counts." I removed the veve that I'd worn around my neck, and placed it in the crossroads at the end of the alley. I blinked, and there stood Papa Legba and his dog. Papa nodded to me, and then he turned his attention to Hawk.

"Come along, son. Best you be moving on."

Hawk glanced at me with a look of astonishment and gratitude, and then hurried after Papa Legba and the black dog. When I blinked again, the alley was empty except for me. The veve was gone, too. I patted the gris-gris bag that still nestled over my heart, and began to walk home. In the distance, I heard the faraway joyful bark of a large dog, and I smiled.

Afterward

Edith Wharton

I

"Oh, there *is* one, of course, but you'll never know it."

The assertion, laughingly flung out six months earlier in a bright June garden, came back to Mary Boyne with a sharp perception of its latent significance as she stood in the December dusk, waiting for the lamps to be brought into the library.

The words had been spoken by their friend Alida Stair, as they sat at tea on her lawn at Pangbourne, in reference to the very house of which the library in question was the central, the pivotal "feature". Mary Boyne and her husband, in quest of a country place in one of the southern or south-western counties, had, on their arrival in England, carried their problem straight to Alida Stair, who had successfully solved it in her own case; but it was not until they had rejected, almost capriciously, several practical and judicious suggestions that she threw it out: "Well, there's Lyng, in Dorsetshire. It belongs to Hugo's cousins, and you can get it for a song."

The reasons she gave for its being obtainable on these terms – its remoteness from a station, its lack of electric light, hot-water pipes, and other vulgar necessities – were exactly those pleading in its favour with two romantic Americans perversely in search of the economic drawbacks which were associated, in their tradition, with unusual architectural felicities.

"I should never believe I was living in an old house unless I was thoroughly uncomfortable," Ned Boyne, the more extravagant of the two, had jocosely insisted; "the least hint of 'convenience' would make me think it had been bought out of an exhibition, with the pieces numbered, and set up again." And they had proceeded to enumerate, with humorous precision, their various suspicions and exactions, refusing to believe that the house their cousin recommended was *really* Tudor till they learned it had no heating system, or that the village church was literally in the grounds till she assured them of the deplorable uncertainty of the water supply.

"It's too uncomfortable to be true!" Edward Boyne had continued to exult as the avowal of each disadvantage was successively wrung from her; but he had cut short his rhapsody to ask, with a sudden relapse to distrust: "And the ghost? You've been concealing from us the fact that there is no ghost!"

Mary, at the moment, had laughed with him, yet almost with her laugh, being possessed of several sets of independent perceptions, had noted a sudden flatness of tone in Alida's answering hilarity.

"Oh, Dorsetshire's full of ghosts, you know."

"Yes, yes; but that won't do. I don't want to have to drive ten miles to see somebody else's ghost. I want one of my own on the premises. *Is* there a ghost at Lyng?"

His rejoinder had made Alida laugh again, and it was then that she had flung back tantalizingly: "Oh, there *is* one, of course, but you'll never know it."

"Never know it?" Boyne pulled her up. "But what in the world constitutes a ghost except the fact of its being known for one?"

"I can't say. But that's the story."

"That there's a ghost, but that nobody knows it's a ghost?"

"Well – not till afterward, at any rate."

"Till afterward?"

"Not till long, long afterward."

"But if it's once been identified as an unearthly visitant, why hasn't its signalement been handed down in the family? How has it managed to preserve its incognito?"

Alida could only shake her head. "Don't ask me. But it has."

"And then suddenly—" Mary spoke up as if from some cavernous depth of divination "—suddenly, long afterward, one says to one's self, '*That was it?*'"

She was oddly startled at the sepulchral sound with which her question fell on the banter of the other two, and she saw the shadow of the same surprise flit across Alida's clear pupils. "I suppose so. One just has to wait."

"Oh, hang waiting!" Ned broke in. "Life's too short for a ghost who can only be enjoyed in retrospect. Can't we do better than that, Mary?"

But it turned out that in the event they were not destined to, for within three months of their conversation with Mrs Stair they were established at Lyng, and the life they had yearned for to the point of planning it out in all its daily details had actually begun for them.

It was to sit, in the thick December dusk, by just such a wide hooded fireplace, under just such black oak rafters, with the sense that beyond the mullioned panes the downs were darkening to a deeper solitude: it was for the ultimate indulgence in such sensations that Mary Boyne had endured for nearly fourteen years the soul-deadening ugliness of the Middle West, and that Boyne had ground on doggedly at his engineering till, with a suddenness that still made her blink, the prodigious windfall of the Blue Star Mine had put them at a stroke in possession of life and the leisure to taste it. They had never for a moment meant their new state to be one of idleness; but they meant to give themselves only to harmonious activities. She had her vision of painting and gardening (against a background of grey walls), he dreamed of the production of his long-planned book on the "Economic Basis of Culture"; and with such absorbing work ahead no existence could be too sequestered; they could not get far enough from the world, or plunge deep enough into the past.

Dorsetshire had attracted them from the first by a semblance of remoteness out of all proportion to its geographical position. But to the Boynes it was one of the ever-recurring wonders of the whole incredibly compressed island – a nest of counties, as they put it – that for the production of its effects so little of a given quality went so far: that so few miles made a distance, and so short a distance a difference.

"It's that," Ned had once enthusiastically explained, "that gives such depth to their effects, such relief to their least contrasts. They've been able to lay the butter so thick on every exquisite mouthful."

The butter had certainly been laid on thick at Lyng: the old grey house, hidden under a shoulder of the downs, had almost all the finer marks of commerce with a protracted past. The mere fact that it was neither large nor exceptional made it, to the Boynes, abound the more richly in its special sense – the sense of having been for centuries a deep, dim reservoir of life. The life had probably not been of the most vivid order: for long periods, no doubt, it had fallen as noiselessly into the past as the quiet drizzle of autumn fell, hour after hour, into the green fish-pond between the yews; but these back-waters of existence sometimes breed, in their sluggish depths, strange acuities of emotion, and Mary Boyne had felt from the first the occasional brush of an intenser memory.

The feeling had never been stronger than on the December afternoon when, waiting in the library for the belated lamps, she rose from her seat and stood among the shadows of the hearth. Her husband had gone off, after luncheon, for one of his long tramps on the downs. She had noticed of late that he preferred to be unaccompanied on these occasions; and, in the tried security of their personal relations, had been driven to conclude that his book was bothering him, and that he needed the afternoons to turn over in solitude the problems left from the morning's work. Certainly the book was not going as smoothly as she had imagined it would, and the lines of perplexity between his eyes had never been there in his engineering days. Then he had often looked fagged to the verge of illness, but the native demon of "worry" had never branded his brow. Yet the few pages he had so far read to her – the introduction and a synopsis of the opening chapter – gave evidences of a firm possession of his subject, and a deepening confidence in his powers.

The fact threw her into deeper perplexity, since, now that he had done with "business" and its disturbing contingencies, the one other possible element of anxiety was eliminated. Unless it were his health, then? But physically he had gained since they had come to Dorsetshire, grown robuster, ruddier, and fresher-eyed. It was only within a week that she had felt in him the indefinable change that made her restless in his absence, and as tongue-tied in his presence as though it were *she* who had a secret to keep from him!

The thought that there *was* a secret somewhere between them struck her with a sudden smart rap of wonder, and she looked about her down the dim, long room.

"Can it be the house?" she mused.

The room itself might have been full of secrets. They seemed to be piling themselves up, as evening fell, like the layers and layers of velvet shadow dropping from the low ceiling, the dusky walls of books, the smoke-blurred sculpture of the hooded hearth.

"Why, of course – the house is haunted!" she reflected.

The ghost – Alida's imperceptible ghost – after figuring largely in the banter of their first month or two at Lyng, had been gradually discarded as too ineffectual for imaginative use. Mary had, indeed, as became the tenant of a haunted house, made the customary enquiries among her few rural neighbours, but, beyond a vague "They do say so, ma'am", the villagers had nothing to impart. The elusive spectre had apparently never had sufficient identity for a legend to crystallize about it, and after a time the Boynes had laughingly set the matter down to their profit-and-loss account, agreeing that Lyng was one of the few houses good enough in itself to dispense with supernatural enhancements.

"And I suppose, poor, ineffectual demon, that's why it beats its beautiful wings in vain in the void," Mary had laughingly concluded.

"Or, rather," Ned answered, in the same strain, "why, amid

so much that's ghostly, it can never affirm its separate existence as *the* ghost." And thereupon their invisible housemate
had finally dropped out of their references, which were numerous enough to make them promptly unaware of the loss.

Now, as she stood on the hearth, the subject of their earlier
curiosity revived in her with a new sense of its meaning – a
sense gradually acquired through close daily contact with the
scene of the lurking mystery. It was the house itself, of course,
that possessed the ghost-seeing faculty, that communed visu-
ally but secretly with its own past; and if one could only get
into close enough communion with the house, one might
surprise its secret, and acquire the ghost-sight on one's own
account. Perhaps, in his long solitary hours in this very room,
where she never trespassed till the afternoon, her husband *had*
acquired it already, and was silently carrying the dread weight
of whatever it had revealed to him. Mary was too well versed
in the code of the spectral world not to know that one could
not talk about the ghosts one saw: to do so was almost as great
a breach of good breeding as to name a lady in a club. But this
explanation did not really satisfy her. "What, after all, except
for the fun of the frisson," she reflected, "would he really care
for any of their old ghosts?" And thence she was thrown back
once more on the fundamental dilemma: the fact that one's
greater or lesser susceptibility to spectral influences had no
particular bearing on the case, since, when one *did* see a ghost
at Lyng, one did not know it.

"Not till long afterward," Alida Stair had said. Well, supposing Ned *had* seen one when they first came, and had known
only within the last week what had happened to him? More
and more under the spell of the hour, she threw back her
searching thoughts to the early days of their tenancy, but at
first only to recall a gay confusion of unpacking, settling,
arranging of books, and calling to each other from remote
corners of the house as treasure after treasure of their habitation revealed itself to them. It was in this particular connection
that she presently recalled a certain soft afternoon of the previous October, when, passing from the first rapturous flurry of

exploration to a detailed inspection of the old house, she had pressed (like a novel heroine) a panel that opened at her touch, on a narrow flight of stairs leading to an unsuspected flat ledge of the roof – the roof which, from below, seemed to slope away on all sides too abruptly for any but practised feet to scale.

The view from this hidden coign was enchanting, and she had flown down to snatch Ned from his papers and give him the freedom of her discovery. She remembered still how, standing on the narrow ledge, he had passed his arm about her while their gaze flew to the long, tossed horizon-line of the downs, and then dropped contentedly back to trace the arabesque of yew hedges about the fish-pond, and the shadow of the cedar on the lawn.

"And now the other way," he had said, gently turning her about within his arm; and closely pressed to him, she had absorbed, like some long, satisfying draft, the picture of the grey-walled court, the squat lions on the gates, and the lime-avenue reaching up to the highroad under the downs.

It was just then, while they gazed and held each other, that she had felt his arm relax, and heard a sharp "Hullo!" that made her turn to glance at him.

Distinctly, yes, she now recalled she had seen, as she glanced, a shadow of anxiety, of perplexity, rather, fall across his face; and, following his eyes, had beheld the figure of a man – a man in loose, greyish clothes, as it appeared to her – who was sauntering down the lime-avenue to the court with the tentative gait of a stranger seeking his way. Her short-sighted eyes had given her but a blurred impression of slightness and greyness, with something foreign, or at least unlocal, in the cut of the figure or its garb; but her husband had apparently seen more – seen enough to make him push past her with a sharp "Wait!" and dash down the twisting stairs without pausing to give her a hand for the descent.

A slight tendency to dizziness obliged her, after a provisional clutch at the chimney against which they had been leaning, to follow him down more cautiously; and when she had reached the attic landing she paused again for a less definite reason, leaning over the oak banister to strain her eyes through the silence of the brown, sun-flecked depths below. She lingered there till, somewhere in those depths, she heard the closing of a door; then, mechanically impelled, she went down the shallow flights of steps till she reached the lower hall.

The front door stood open on the mild sunlight of the court, and hall and court were empty. The library door was open, too, and after listening in vain for any sound of voices within, she quickly crossed the threshold, and found her husband alone, vaguely fingering the papers on his desk.

He looked up, as if surprised at her precipitate entrance, but the shadow of anxiety had passed from his face, leaving it even, as she fancied, a little brighter and clearer than usual.

"What was it? Who was it?" she asked.

"Who?" he repeated, with the surprise still all on his side.

"The man we saw coming towards the house."

He seemed honestly to reflect. "The man? Why, I thought I saw Peters; I dashed after him to say a word about the stable-drains, but he had disappeared before I could get down."

"Disappeared? Why, he seemed to be walking so slowly when we saw him."

Boyne shrugged his shoulders. "So I thought; but he must have got up steam in the interval. What do you say to our trying a scramble up Meldon Steep before sunset?"

That was all. At the time the occurrence had been less than nothing, had, indeed, been immediately obliterated by the magic of their first vision from Meldon Steep, a height which they had dreamed of climbing ever since they had first seen its bare spine heaving itself above the low roof of Lyng. Doubtless it was the mere fact of the other incidents having occurred on the very day of their ascent to Meldon that had kept it stored away in the unconscious fold of association from which it now emerged; for in itself it had no mark of the portentous. At the moment there could have been nothing more natural than that Ned should dash himself from the roof in the pursuit of dila-tory tradesmen. It was the period when they were always on the watch for one or the other of the specialists employed about the place; always lying in wait for them, and dashing out at them with questions, reproaches, or reminders. And certainly in the distance the grey figure had looked like Peters.

Yet now, as she reviewed the rapid scene, she felt her husband's explanation of it to have been invalidated by the look of anxiety on his face. Why had the familiar appearance of Peters made him anxious? Why, above all, if it was of such prime necessity to confer with that authority on the subject of the stable-drains, had the failure to find him produced such a look of relief? Mary could not say that any one of these considerations had occurred to her at the time, yet, from the promptness with which they now marshalled themselves at her summons, she had a sudden sense that they must all along have been there, waiting their hour.

II

Weary with her thoughts, she moved towards the window. The library was now completely dark, and she was surprised to see how much faint light the outer world still held.

As she peered out into it across the court, a figure shaped itself in the tapering perspective of bare lines: it looked a mere blot of deeper grey in the greyness, and for an instant, as it moved towards her, her heart thumped to the thought, "It's the ghost!"

She had time, in that long instant, to feel suddenly that the man of whom, two months earlier, she had a brief distant vision from the roof was now, at his predestined hour, about to reveal himself as *not* having been Peters; and her spirit sank under the impending fear of the disclosure. But almost with the next tick of the clock the ambiguous figure, gaining substance and character, showed itself even to her weak sight as her husband's; and she turned away to meet him, as he entered, with the confession of her folly.

"It's really too absurd," she laughed out from the threshold, "but I never *can* remember!"

"Remember what?" Boyne questioned as they drew together.

"That when one sees the Lyng ghost one never knows it."

Her hand was on his sleeve, and he kept it there, but with no response in his gesture or in the lines of his fagged, preoccupied face.

"Did you think you'd seen it?" he asked, after an appreciable interval.

"Why, I actually took *you* for it, my dear, in my mad determination to spot it!"

"Me – just now?" His arm dropped away, and he turned from her with a faint echo of her laugh. "Really, dearest, you'd better give it up, if that's the best you can do."

"Yes, I give it up – I give it up. Have *you*?" she asked, turning round on him abruptly.

The parlour maid had entered with letters and a lamp, and the light struck up into Boyne's face as he bent above the tray she presented.

"Have *you*?" Mary perversely insisted, when the servant had disappeared on her errand of illumination.

"Have I what?" he rejoined absently, the light bringing out the sharp stamp of worry between his brows as he turned over the letters.

"Given up trying to see the ghost." Her heart beat a little at the experiment she was making.

Her husband, laying his letters aside, moved away into the shadow of the hearth.

"I never tried," he said, tearing open the wrapper of a newspaper.

"Well, of course," Mary persisted, "the exasperating thing is that there's no use trying, since one can't be sure till so long afterward."

He was unfolding the paper as if he had hardly heard her; but after a pause, during which the sheets rustled spasmodically between his hands, he lifted his head to say abruptly, "Have you any idea *how long*?"

Mary had sunk into a low chair beside the fireplace. From her seat she looked up, startled, at her husband's profile, which was darkly projected against the circle of lamplight.

"No; none. Have you?" she retorted, repeating her former phrase with an added keenness of intention.

Boyne crumpled the paper into a bunch, and then inconsequently turned back with it towards the lamp.

"Lord, no! I only meant," he explained, with a faint tinge of impatience, "is there any legend, any tradition, as to that?"

"Not that I know of," she answered; but the impulse to add, "What makes you ask?" was checked by the reappearance of the parlour maid with tea and a second lamp.

With the dispersal of shadows, and the repetition of the daily domestic office, Mary Boyne felt herself less oppressed by that sense of something mutely imminent which had darkened her solitary afternoon. For a few moments she gave herself silently to the details of her task, and when she looked up from it she was struck to the point of bewilderment by the change in her husband's face. He had seated himself near the farther lamp, and was absorbed in the perusal of his letters; but was it something he had found in them, or merely the shifting of her own point of view, that had restored his features to their normal aspect? The longer she looked, the more definitely the change affirmed itself. The lines of painful tension had vanished, and such traces of fatigue as lingered were of the kind easily attributable to steady mental effort. He glanced up, as if drawn by her gaze, and met her eyes with a smile.

"I'm dying for my tea, you know; and here's a letter for you," he said.

She took the letter he held out in exchange for the cup she proffered him, and, returning to her seat, broke the seal with the languid gesture of the reader whose interests are all enclosed in the circle of one cherished presence.

Her next conscious motion was that of starting to her feet, the letter falling to them as she rose, while she held out to her husband a long newspaper clipping.

"Ned! What's this? What does it mean?"

He had risen at the same instant, almost as if hearing her cry before she uttered it; and for a perceptible space of time he and she studied each other, like adversaries watching for an advantage, across the space between her chair and his desk.

"What's what? You fairly made me jump!" Boyne said at

length, moving towards her with a sudden, half-exasperated laugh. The shadow of apprehension was on his face again, not now a look of fixed foreboding, but a shifting vigilance of lips and eyes that gave her the sense of his feeling himself invisibly surrounded.

Her hand shook so that she could hardly give him the clipping.

"This article – from the *Waukesha Sentinel* – that a man named Elwell has brought suit against you – that there was something wrong about the Blue Star Mine. I can't understand more than half."

They continued to face each other as she spoke, and to her astonishment, she saw that her words had the almost immediate effect of dissipating the strained watchfulness of his look.

"Oh, *that*!" He glanced down the printed slip, and then folded it with the gesture of one who handles something harmless and familiar. "What's the matter with you this afternoon, Mary? I thought you'd got bad news."

She stood before him with her indefinable terror subsiding slowly under the reassuring touch of his composure.

"You knew about this, then – it's all right?"

"Certainly I knew about it; and it's all right."

"But what *is* it? I don't understand. What does this man accuse you of?"

"Oh, pretty nearly every crime in the calendar." Boyne had tossed the clipping down, and thrown himself comfortably into an arm-chair near the fire. "Do you want to hear the story? It's not particularly interesting – just a squabble over interests in the Blue Star."

"But who is this Elwell? I don't know the name."

"Oh, he's a fellow I put into it – gave him a hand up. I told you all about him at the time."

"I daresay. I must have forgotten." Vainly she strained back among her memories. "But if you helped him, why does he make this return?"

"Oh, probably some shyster lawyer got hold of him and talked him over. It's all rather technical and complicated. I thought that kind of thing bored you."

His wife felt a sting of compunction. Theoretically, she deprecated the American wife's detachment from her husband's professional interests, but in practice she had always found it difficult to fix her attention on Boyne's report of the transactions in which his varied interests involved him. Besides, she had felt from the first that, in a community where the amenities of living could be obtained only at the cost of efforts as arduous as her husband's professional labours, such brief leisure as they could command should be used as an escape from immediate preoccupations, a flight to the life they always dreamed of living. Once or twice, now that this new life had actually drawn its magic circle about them, she had asked herself if she had done right; but hitherto such conjectures had been no more than the retrospective excursions of an active fancy. Now, for the first time, it startled her a little to find how little she knew of the material foundation on which her happiness was built.

She glanced again at her husband, and was reassured by the composure of his face; yet she felt the need of more definite grounds for her reassurance.

"But doesn't this suit worry you? Why have you never spoken to me about it?"

He answered both questions at once: "I didn't speak of it at first because it *did* worry me – annoyed me, rather. But it's all ancient history now. Your correspondent must have got hold of a back number of the *Sentinel*."

She felt a quick thrill of relief. "You mean it's over? He's lost his case?"

There was a just perceptible delay in Boyne's reply. "The suit's been withdrawn – that's all."

But she persisted, as if to exonerate herself from the inward charge of being too easily put off. "Withdrawn because he saw he had no chance?"

"Oh, he had no chance," Boyne answered.

She was still struggling with a dimly felt perplexity at the back of her thoughts.

"How long ago was it withdrawn?"

He paused, as if with a slight return of his former uncertainty. "I've just had the news now; but I've been expecting it."

"Just now – in one of your letters?"

"Yes; in one of my letters."

She made no answer, and was aware only, after a short interval of waiting, that he had risen, and, strolling across the room, had placed himself on the sofa at her side. She felt him, as he did so, pass an arm about her, she felt his hand seek hers and clasp it, and turning slowly, drawn by the warmth of his cheek, she met the smiling clearness of his eyes.

"It's all right – it's all right?" she questioned, through the flood of her dissolving doubts; and "I give you my word it never was righter!" he laughed back at her, holding her close.

III

One of the strangest things she was afterward to recall out of all the next day's incredible strangeness was the sudden and complete recovery of her sense of security.

It was in the air when she woke in her low-ceilinged, dusky room; it accompanied her downstairs to the breakfast-table, flashed out at her from the fire, and re-duplicated itself brightly from the flanks of the urn and the sturdy flutings of the Georgian teapot. It was as if, in some roundabout way, all her diffused apprehensions of the previous day, with their moment of sharp concentration about the newspaper article – as if this dim questioning of the future, and startled return upon the past, had between them liquidated the arrears of some haunting moral obligation. If she had indeed been careless of her husband's affairs, it was, her new state seemed to prove, because her faith in him instinctively justified such carelessness; and his right to her faith had overwhelmingly affirmed itself in the very face of menace and suspicion. She had never seen him more untroubled, more naturally and unconsciously in possession of himself, than after the cross-examination to which she had subjected him: it was almost as if he had been aware of her lurking doubts, and had wanted the air cleared as much as she did.

It was as clear, thank Heaven! as the bright outer light that surprised her almost with a touch of summer when she issued from the house for her daily round of the gardens. She had left Boyne at his desk, indulging herself, as she passed the library door, by a last peep at his quiet face, where he bent, pipe in his mouth, above his papers, and now she had her own morning's task to perform. The task involved on such charmed winter days almost as much delighted loitering about the different quarters of her demesne as if spring were already at work on shrubs and borders. There were such inexhaustible possibilities still before her, such opportunities to bring out the latent graces of the old place, without a single irreverent touch of alteration, that the winter months were all too short to plan what spring and autumn executed. And her recovered sense of safety gave, on this particular morning, a peculiar zest to her progress through the sweet, still place. She went first to the kitchen garden, where the espaliered pear trees drew complicated patterns on the walls, and pigeons were fluttering and preening about the silvery-slated roof of their cot. There was something wrong about the piping of the hothouse, and she was expecting an authority from Dorchester, who was to drive out between trains and make a diagnosis of the boiler. But when she dipped into the damp heat of the greenhouses, among the spiced scents and waxy pinks and reds of old-fashioned exotics – even the flora of Lyng was in the note! – she learned that the great man had not arrived, and the day being too rare to waste in an artificial atmosphere, she came out again and paced slowly along the springy turf of the bowling green to the gardens behind the house. At their farther end rose a grass terrace, commanding, over the fish-pond and the yew hedges, a view of the long house-front, with its twisted chimney-stacks and the blue shadows of its roof angles, all drenched in the pale gold moisture of the air.

Seen thus, across the level tracery of the yews, under the suffused, mild light, it sent her, from its open windows and hospitably smoking chimneys, the look of some warm human presence, of a mind slowly ripened on a sunny wall of experience. She had never before had so deep a sense of her intimacy with it, such a conviction that its secrets were all beneficent, kept, as they said to children, "for one's good", so complete a trust in its power to gather up her life and Ned's into the harmonious pattern of the long, long story it sat there weaving in the sun.

She heard steps behind her, and turned, expecting to see the gardener, accompanied by the engineer from Dorchester. But only one figure was in sight, that of a youngish, slightly built man, who, for reasons she could not on the spot have specified, did not remotely resemble her preconceived notion of an authority on hothouse boilers. The newcomer, on seeing her, lifted his hat, and paused with the air of a gentleman – perhaps a traveller – desirous of having it immediately known that his intrusion is involuntary. The local fame of Lyng occasionally attracted the more intelligent sightseer, and Mary half-expected to see the stranger dissemble a camera, or justify his presence by producing it. But he made no gesture of any sort, and after a moment she asked, in a tone responding to the courteous deprecation of his attitude: "Is there anyone you wish to see?"

"I came to see Mr Boyne," he replied. His intonation, rather than his accent, was faintly American, and Mary, at the familiar note, looked at him more closely. The brim of his soft felt hat cast a shade on his face, which, thus obscured, wore to her short-sighted gaze a look of seriousness, as of a person arriving "on business", and civilly but firmly aware of his rights.

Past experience had made Mary equally sensible to such claims; but she was jealous of her husband's morning hours, and doubtful of his having given anyone the right to intrude on them.

"Have you an appointment with Mr Boyne?" she asked.

He hesitated, as if unprepared for the question.

"Not exactly an appointment," he replied.

"Then I'm afraid, this being his working-time, that he can't receive you now. Will you give me a message, or come back later?"

The visitor, again lifting his hat, briefly replied that he would come back later, and walked away, as if to regain the front of the house. As his figure receded down the walk between the yew hedges, Mary saw him pause and look up an instant at the peaceful house-front bathed in faint winter sunshine; and it struck her, with a tardy touch of compunction, that it would have been more humane to ask if he had come from a distance, and to offer, in that case, to enquire if her husband could receive him. But as the thought occurred to her he passed out of sight behind a pyramidal yew, and at the same moment her attention was distracted by the approach of the gardener, attended by the bearded pepper-and-salt figure of the boiler-maker from Dorchester.

The encounter with this authority led to such far-reaching issues that they resulted in his finding it expedient to ignore his train, and beguiled Mary into spending the remainder of the morning in absorbed confabulation among the greenhouses. She was startled to find, when the colloquy ended, that it was nearly luncheon-time, and she half-expected, as she hurried back to the house, to see her husband coming out to meet her. But she found no one in the court but an under-gardener raking the gravel, and the hall, when she entered it, was so silent that she guessed Boyne to be still at work behind the closed door of the library.

Not wishing to disturb him, she turned into the drawing-room, and there, at her writing table, lost herself in renewed calculations of the outlay to which the morning's conference had committed her. The knowledge that she could permit herself such follies had not yet lost its novelty; and somehow, in contrast to the vague apprehensions of the previous days, it now seemed an element of her recovered security, of the sense that, as Ned had said, things in general had never been "righter".

She was still luxuriating in a lavish play of figures when the parlour maid, from the threshold, roused her with a dubiously worded enquiry as to the expediency of serving luncheon. It was one of their jokes that Trimmle announced luncheon as if she were divulging a state secret, and Mary, intent upon her papers, merely murmured an absentminded assent.

She felt Trimmle wavering expressively on the threshold as if in rebuke of such offhand acquiescence; then her retreating steps sounded down the passage, and Mary, pushing away her papers, crossed the hall and went to the library door. It was still closed, and she wavered in her turn, disliking to disturb her husband, yet anxious that he should not exceed his normal measure of work. As she stood there, balancing her impulses, the esoteric Trimmle returned with the announcement of luncheon, and Mary, thus impelled, opened the door and went into the library.

Boyne was not at his desk, and she peered about her, expecting to discover him at the bookshelves, somewhere down the length of the room; but her call brought no response, and gradually it became clear to her that he was not in the library.

She turned back to the parlour maid.

"Mr Boyne must be upstairs. Please tell him that luncheon is ready."

The parlour maid appeared to hesitate between the obvious duty of obeying orders and an equally obvious conviction of the foolishness of the injunction laid upon her. The struggle resulted in her saying doubtfully, "If you please, madam, Mr Boyne's not upstairs."

"Not in his room? Are you sure?"

"I'm sure, madam."

Mary consulted the clock. "Where is he, then?"

"He's gone out," Trimmle announced, with the superior air of one who has respectfully waited for the question that a well-ordered mind would have first propounded.

Mary's previous conjecture had been right, then. Boyne must have gone to the gardens to meet her, and since she had missed him, it was clear that he had taken the shorter way by the south door, instead of going round to the court. She crossed the hall to the glass portal opening directly on the yew garden, but the parlour maid, after another moment of inner conflict, decided to bring out recklessly, "Please, madam, Mr Boyne didn't go that way."

Mary turned back. "Where *did* he go? And when?"

"He went out of the front door, up the drive, madam." It was a matter of principle with Trimmle never to answer more than one question at a time.

"Up the drive? At this hour?" Mary went to the door herself, and glanced across the court through the long tunnel of bare limes. But its perspective was as empty as when she had scanned it on entering the house.

"Did Mr Boyne leave no message?" she asked.

Trimmle seemed to surrender herself to a last struggle with the forces of chaos.

"No, madam. He just went out with the gentleman."

"The gentleman? What gentleman?" Mary wheeled about, as if to front this new factor.

"The gentleman who called, madam," said Trimmle, resignedly.

"When did a gentleman call? Do explain yourself, Trimmle!"

Only the fact that Mary was very hungry, and that she wanted to consult her husband about the greenhouses, would have caused her to lay so unusual an injunction on her attendant; and even now she was detached enough to note in Trimmle's eye the dawning defiance of the respectful subordinate who has been pressed too hard.

"I couldn't exactly say the hour, madam, because I didn't let the gentleman in," she replied, with the air of magnanimously ignoring the irregularity of her mistress's course.

"You didn't let him in?"

"No, madam. When the bell rang I was dressing, and Agnes—"

"Go and ask Agnes, then," Mary interjected. Trimmle still wore her look of patient magnanimity. "Agnes would not know, madam, for she had unfortunately burned her hand in trying the wick of the new lamp from town—" Trimmle, as Mary was aware, had always been opposed to the new lamp "—and so Mrs Dockett sent the kitchen maid instead."

Mary looked again at the clock. "It's after two! Go and ask the kitchen maid if Mr Boyne left any word."

She went in to luncheon without waiting, and Trimmle presently brought her there the kitchen maid's statement that the gentleman had called about one o'clock, that Mr Boyne had gone out with him without leaving any message. The kitchen maid did not even know the caller's name, for he had written it on a slip of paper, which he had folded and handed to her, with the injunction to deliver it at once to Mr Boyne.

Mary finished her luncheon, still wondering, and when it was over, and Trimmle had brought the coffee to the drawing-room, her wonder had deepened to a first faint tinge of disquietude. It was unlike Boyne to absent himself without explanation at so unwonted an hour, and the difficulty of identifying the visitor whose summons he had apparently obeyed made his disappearance the more unaccountable. Mary Boyne's experience as the wife of a busy engineer, subject to sudden calls and compelled to keep irregular hours, had trained her to the philosophic acceptance of surprises; but since Boyne's withdrawal from business he had adopted a Benedictine regularity of life. As if to make up for the dispersed and agitated years, with their "stand-up" lunches and dinners rattled down to the joltings of the dining-car, he cultivated the last refinements of punctuality and monotony, discouraging his wife's fancy for the unexpected; and declaring that to a delicate taste there were infinite gradations of pleasure in the fixed recurrences of habit.

Still, since no life can completely defend itself from the unforeseen, it was evident that all Boyne's precautions would sooner or later prove unavailable, and Mary concluded that he had cut short a tiresome visit by walking with his caller to the station, or at least accompanying him for part of the way.

This conclusion relieved her from farther preoccupation, and she went out herself to take up her conference with the gardener. Thence she walked to the village post office, a mile or so away; and when she turned towards home, the early twilight was setting in.

She had taken a footpath across the downs, and as Boyne, meanwhile, had probably returned from the station by the

highroad, there was little likelihood of their meeting on the
way. She felt sure, however, of his having reached the house
before her; so sure that, when she entered it herself, without
even pausing to enquire of Trimmle, she made directly for the
library. But the library was still empty, and with an unwonted
precision of visual memory she immediately observed that the
papers on her husband's desk lay precisely as they had lain
when she had gone in to call him to luncheon.

Then of a sudden she was seized by a vague dread of the
unknown. She had closed the door behind her on entering,
and as she stood alone in the long, silent, shadowy room,
her dread seemed to take shape and sound, to be there
audibly breathing and lurking among the shadows. Her
short-sighted eyes strained through them, half discerning
an actual presence, something aloof, that watched and
knew; and in the recoil from that intangible propinquity
she threw herself suddenly on the bell-rope and gave it a
desperate pull.

The long, quavering summons brought Trimmle in precipi-
tately with a lamp, and Mary breathed again at this sobering
reappearance of the usual.

"You may bring tea if Mr Boyne is in," she said, to justify
her ring.

"Very well, madam. But Mr Boyne is not in," said Trimmle,
putting down the lamp.

"Not in? You mean he's come back and gone out again?"

"No, madam. He's never been back."

The dread stirred again, and Mary knew that now it had
her fast.

"Not since he went out with – the gentleman?"

"Not since he went out with the gentleman."

"But who *was* the gentleman?" Mary gasped out, with the
sharp note of someone trying to be heard through a confusion
of meaningless noises.

"That I couldn't say, madam." Trimmle, standing there by
the lamp, seemed suddenly to grow less round and rosy, as
though eclipsed by the same creeping shade of apprehension.

"But the kitchen maid knows – wasn't it the kitchen maid who let him in?"

"She doesn't know either, madam, for he wrote his name on a folded paper."

Mary, through her agitation, was aware that they were both designating the unknown visitor by a vague pronoun, instead of the conventional formula which, till then, had kept their allusions within the bounds of custom. And at the same moment her mind caught at the suggestion of the folded paper.

"But he must have a name! Where is the paper?"

She moved to the desk, and began to turn over the scattered documents that littered it. The first that caught her eye was an unfinished letter in her husband's hand, with his pen lying across it, as though dropped there at a sudden summons.

"My dear Parvis—" who was Parvis? "—I have just received your letter announcing Elwell's death, and while I suppose there is now no farther risk of trouble, it might be safer—"

She tossed the sheet aside, and continued her search; but no folded paper was discoverable among the letters and pages of manuscript which had been swept together in a promiscuous heap, as if by a hurried or a startled gesture.

"But the kitchen maid *saw* him. Send her here," she commanded, wondering at her dullness in not thinking sooner of so simple a solution.

Trimmle, at the behest, vanished in a flash, as if thankful to be out of the room, and when she reappeared, conducting the agitated underling, Mary had regained her self-possession, and had her questions pat.

The gentleman was a stranger, yes – that she understood. But what had he said? And, above all, what had he looked like? The first question was easily enough answered, for the disconcerting reason that he had said so little – had merely asked for Mr Boyne, and, scribbling something on a bit of paper, had requested that it should at once be carried in to him.

"Then you don't know what he wrote? You're not sure it *was* his name?"

The kitchen maid was not sure, but supposed it was, since

he had written it in answer to her enquiry as to whom she should announce.

"And when you carried the paper in to Mr Boyne, what did he say?"

The kitchen maid did not think that Mr Boyne had said anything, but she could not be sure, for just as she had handed him the paper and he was opening it, she had become aware that the visitor had followed her into the library, and she had slipped out, leaving the two gentlemen together.

"But then, if you left them in the library, how do you know that they went out of the house?"

This question plunged the witness into momentary inarticulateness, from which she was rescued by Trimmle, who, by means of ingenious circumlocutions, elicited the statement that before she could cross the hall to the back passage she had heard the gentlemen behind her, and had seen them go out of the front door together.

"Then, if you saw the gentleman twice, you must be able to tell me what he looked like."

But with this final challenge to her powers of expression it became clear that the limit of the kitchen maid's endurance had been reached. The obligation of going to the front door to "show in" a visitor was in itself so subversive of the fundamental order of things that it had thrown her faculties into hopeless disarray, and she could only stammer out, after various panting efforts at evocation, "His hat, mum, was different-like, as you might say—"

"Different? How different?" Mary flashed out at her, her own mind, in the same instant, leaping back to an image left on it that morning, but temporarily lost under layers of subsequent impressions.

"His hat had a wide brim, you mean? And his face was pale – a youngish face?" Mary pressed her, with a white-lipped intensity of interrogation. But if the kitchen maid found any adequate answer to this challenge, it was swept away for her listener down the rushing current of her own convictions. The stranger – the stranger in the garden! Why had Mary not thought of him before? She needed no one now to tell her that it was he who had called for her husband and gone away with him. But who was he, and why had Boyne obeyed his call?

IV

It leaped out at her suddenly, like a grin out of the dark, that they had often called England so little – "such a confoundedly hard place to get lost in".

A confoundedly hard place to get lost in! That had been her husband's phrase. And now, with the whole machinery of official investigation sweeping its flash-lights from shore to shore, and across the dividing straits; now, with Boyne's name blazing from the walls of every town and village, his portrait (how that wrung her!) hawked up and down the country like the image of a hunted criminal; now the little compact, populous island, so policed, surveyed, and administered, revealed itself as a Sphinx-like guardian of abysmal mysteries, staring back into his wife's anguished eyes as if with the malicious joy of knowing something they would never know!

In the fortnight since Boyne's disappearance there had been no word of him, no trace of his movements. Even the usual misleading reports that raise expectancy in tortured bosoms had been few and fleeting. No one but the bewildered kitchen maid had seen him leave the house, and no one else had seen "the gentleman" who accompanied him. All enquiries in the neighbourhood failed to elicit the memory of a stranger's presence that day in the neighbourhood of Lyng. And no one had met Edward Boyne, either alone or in company, in any of the neighbouring villages, or on the road across the downs, or at either of the local railway stations. The sunny English noon had swallowed him as completely as if he had gone out into Cimmerian night.

Mary, while every external means of investigation was working at its highest pressure, had ransacked her husband's papers for any trace of antecedent complications, of entanglements or obligations unknown to her, that might throw a faint ray into the darkness. But if any such had existed in the background of Boyne's life, they had disappeared as completely as the slip of paper on which the visitor had written his name. There remained no possible thread of guidance except – if it were indeed an exception – the letter which Boyne had apparently been in the act of writing when he received his mysterious summons. That letter, read and reread by his wife, and submitted by her to the police, yielded little enough for conjecture to feed on.

"I have just heard of Elwell's death, and while I suppose there is now no farther risk of trouble, it might be safer—" That was all. The "risk of trouble" was easily explained by the newspaper clipping which had apprised Mary of the suit brought against her husband by one of his associates in the Blue Star enterprise. The only new information conveyed in the letter was the fact of its showing Boyne, when he wrote it, to be still apprehensive of the results of the suit, though he had assured his wife that it had been withdrawn, and though the letter itself declared that the plaintiff was dead. It took several weeks of exhaustive cabling to fix the identity of the "Parvis" to whom the fragmentary communication was addressed, but even after these inquiries had shown him to be a Waukesha lawyer, no new facts concerning the Elwell suit were elicited. He appeared to have had no direct concern in it, but to have been conversant with the facts merely as an acquaintance, and possible intermediary; and he declared himself unable to divine with what object Boyne intended to seek his assistance.

This negative information, sole fruit of the first fortnight's feverish search, was not increased by a jot during the slow weeks that followed. Mary knew that the investigations were still being carried on, but she had a vague sense of their gradually slackening, as the actual march of time seemed to slacken. It was as though the days, flying horror-struck from the shrouded image of the one inscrutable day, gained assurance as the distance lengthened, till at last they fell back into their normal gait. And so with the human imaginations at work on the dark event. No doubt it occupied them still, but week by week and hour by hour it grew less absorbing, took up less space, was slowly but inevitably crowded out of the foreground of consciousness by the new problems perpetually bubbling up from the vaporous cauldron of human experience.

Even Mary Boyne's consciousness gradually felt the same lowering of velocity. It still swayed with the incessant oscillations of conjecture; but they were slower, more rhythmical in their beat. There were moments of overwhelming lassitude when, like the victim of some poison which leaves the brain clear, but holds the body motionless, she saw herself domesticated with the Horror, accepting its perpetual presence as one of the fixed conditions of life.

These moments lengthened into hours and days, till she passed into a phase of stolid acquiescence. She watched the familiar routine of life with the incurious eye of a savage on whom the meaningless processes of civilization make but the faintest impression. She had come to regard herself as part of the routine, a spoke of the wheel, revolving with its motion; she felt almost like the furniture of the room in which she sat, an insensate object to be dusted and pushed about with the chairs and tables. And this deepening apathy held her fast at Lyng, in spite of the urgent entreaties of friends and the usual medical recommendation of "change". Her friends supposed that her refusal to move was inspired by the belief that her husband would one day return to the spot from which he had vanished, and a beautiful legend grew up about this imaginary state of waiting. But in reality she had no such belief: the depths of anguish enclosing her were no longer lighted by flashes of hope. She was sure that Boyne would never come back, that he had gone out of her sight as completely as if Death itself had waited that day on the threshold. She had even renounced, one by one, the various theories as to his disappearance which had been advanced by the press, the police, and her own agonized imagination. In sheer lassitude her mind turned from these alternatives of horror, and sank back into the blank fact that he was gone.

No, she would never know what had become of him – no one would ever know. But the house *knew*; the library in which she spent her long, lonely evenings knew. For it was here that the last scene had been enacted, here that the stranger had come, and spoken the word which had caused Boyne to rise and follow him. The floor she trod had felt his tread; the books on the shelves had seen his face; and there were moments when the intense consciousness of the old, dusky walls seemed about to break out into some audible revelation of their secret. But the revelation never came, and she knew it would never come. Lyng was not one of the garrulous old houses that betray the secrets entrusted to them. Its very legend proved that it had always been the mute accomplice, the incorruptible custodian, of the mysteries it had surprised. And Mary Boyne, sitting face to face with its portentous silence, felt the futility of seeking to break it by any human means.

V

"I don't say it *wasn't* straight, yet don't say it *was* straight. It was business."

Mary, at the words, lifted her head with a start, and looked intently at the speaker.

When, half an hour before, a card with "Mr Parvis" on it had been brought up to her, she had been immediately aware that the name had been a part of her consciousness ever since she had read it at the head of Boyne's unfinished letter. In the library she had found awaiting her a small neutral-tinted man with a bald head and gold eye-glasses, and it sent a strange tremor through her to know that this was the person to whom her husband's last known thought had been directed.

Parvis, civilly, but without vain preamble – in the manner of a man who has his watch in his hand – had set forth the object of his visit. He had "run over" to England on business, and finding himself in the neighbourhood of Dorchester, had not wished to leave it without paying his respects to Mrs Boyne; without asking her, if the occasion offered, what she meant to do about Bob Elwell's family.

The words touched the spring of some obscure dread in Mary's bosom. Did her visitor, after all, know what Boyne had meant by his unfinished phrase? She asked for an elucidation of his question, and noticed at once that he seemed surprised at her continued ignorance of the subject. Was it possible that she really knew as little as she said?

"I know nothing – you must tell me," she faltered out; and her visitor thereupon proceeded to unfold his story. It threw, even to her confused perceptions, and imperfectly initiated vision, a lurid glare on the whole hazy episode of the Blue Star Mine. Her husband had made his money in that brilliant speculation at the cost of "getting ahead" of someone less alert to seize the chance; the victim of his ingenuity was young Robert Elwell, who had "put him on" to the Blue Star scheme.

Parvis, at Mary's first startled cry, had thrown her a sobering glance through his impartial glasses.

"Bob Elwell wasn't smart enough, that's all; if he had been, he might have turned round and served Boyne the same way. It's the kind of thing that happens every day in business. I guess it's what the scientists call the survival of the fittest," said Mr Parvis, evidently pleased with the aptness of his analogy.

Mary felt a physical shrinking from the next question she tried to frame; it was as though the words on her lips had a taste that nauseated her.

"But then – you accuse my husband of doing something dishonourable?"

Mr Parvis surveyed the question dispassionately. "Oh, no, I don't. I don't even say it wasn't straight." He glanced up and down the long lines of books, as if one of them might have supplied him with the definition he sought. "I don't say it *wasn't* straight, and yet I don't say it *was* straight. It was business." After all, no definition in his category could be more comprehensive than that.

Mary sat staring at him with a look of terror. He seemed to her like the indifferent, implacable emissary of some dark, formless power.

"But Mr Elwell's lawyers apparently did not take your view, since I suppose the suit was withdrawn by their advice."

"Oh, yes, they knew he hadn't a leg to stand on, technically.

It was when they advised him to withdraw the suit that he got desperate. You see, he'd borrowed most of the money he lost in the Blue Star, and he was up a tree. That's why he shot himself when they told him he had no show."

The horror was sweeping over Mary in great, deafening waves.

"He shot himself? He killed himself because of *that*?"

"Well, he didn't kill himself, exactly. He dragged on two months before he died." Parvis emitted the statement as unemotionally as a gramophone grinding out its "record".

"You mean that he tried to kill himself, and failed? And tried again?"

"Oh, he didn't have to try again," said Parvis, grimly.

They sat opposite each other in silence, he swinging his eyeglass thoughtfully about his finger, she, motionless, her arms stretched along her knees in an attitude of rigid tension.

"But if you knew all this," she began at length, hardly able to force her voice above a whisper, "how is it that when I wrote you at the time of my husband's disappearance you said you didn't understand his letter?"

Parvis received this without perceptible discomfiture. "Why, I didn't understand it – strictly speaking. And it wasn't the time to talk about it, if I had. The Elwell business was settled when the suit was withdrawn. Nothing I could have told you would have helped you to find your husband."

Mary continued to scrutinize him. "Then why are you telling me now?"

Still Parvis did not hesitate. "Well, to begin with, I supposed you knew more than you appear to – I mean about the circumstances of Elwell's death. And then people are talking of it now; the whole matter's been raked up again. And I thought, if you didn't know, you ought to."

She remained silent, and he continued: "You see, it's only come out lately what a bad state Elwell's affairs were in. His wife's a proud woman, and she fought on as long as she could, going out to work, and taking sewing at home, when she got too sick – something with the heart, I believe. But she had his bedridden mother to look after, and the children, and she broke down under it, and finally had to ask for help. That attracted attention to the case, and the papers took it up, and a subscription was started. Everybody out there liked Bob Elwell, and most of the prominent names in the place are down on the list, and people began to wonder why—"

Parvis broke off to fumble in an inner pocket. "Here," he continued, "here's an account of the whole thing from the *Sentinel* – a little sensational, of course. But I guess you'd better look it over."

He held out a newspaper to Mary, who unfolded it slowly, remembering, as she did so, the evening when, in that same room, the perusal of a clipping from the *Sentinel* had first shaken the depths of her security.

As she opened the paper, her eyes, shrinking from the glaring headlines "Widow of Boyne's Victim Forced to Appeal for Aid", ran down the column of text to two portraits inserted in it. The first was her husband's, taken from a photograph made the year they had come to England. It was the picture of him that she liked best, the one that stood on the writing-table upstairs in her bedroom. As the eyes in the photograph met hers, she felt it would be impossible to read what was said of him, and closed her lids with the sharpness of the pain.

"I thought if you felt disposed to put your name down—" she heard Parvis continue.

She opened her eyes with an effort, and they fell on the other portrait. It was that of a youngish man, slightly built, in rough clothes, with features somewhat blurred by the shadow of a projecting hat-brim. Where had she seen that outline before? She stared at it confusedly, her heart hammering in her throat and ears. Then she gave a cry.

"This is the man – the man who came for my husband!"

She heard Parvis start to his feet, and was dimly aware that she had slipped backward into the corner of the sofa, and that he was bending above her in alarm. With an intense effort she straightened herself, and reached out for the paper, which she had dropped.

"It's the man! I should know him anywhere!" she cried in a voice that sounded in her own ears like a scream.

Parvis's voice seemed to come to her from far off, down endless, fog-muffled windings.

"Mrs Boyne, you're not very well. Shall I call somebody? Shall I get a glass of water?"

"No, no, no!" She threw herself towards him, her hand frantically clenching the newspaper. "I tell you, it's the man! I *know* him! He spoke to me in the garden!"

Parvis took the journal from her, directing his glasses to the portrait. "It can't be, Mrs Boyne. It's Robert Elwell."

"Robert Elwell?" Her white stare seemed to travel into space. "Then it was Robert Elwell who came for him."

"Came for Boyne? The day he went away?" Parvis's voice dropped as hers rose. He bent over, laying a fraternal hand on her, as if to coax her gently back into her seat. "Why, Elwell was dead! Don't you remember?"

Mary sat with her eyes fixed on the picture, unconscious of what he was saying.

"Don't you remember Boyne's unfinished letter to me – the one you found on his desk that day? It was written just after he'd heard of Elwell's death." She noticed an odd shake in Parvis's unemotional voice. "Surely you remember that!" he urged her.

Yes, she remembered: that was the profoundest horror of it. Elwell had died the day before her husband's disappearance; and this was Elwell's portrait; and it was the portrait of the man who had spoken to her in the garden. She lifted her head and looked slowly about the library. The library could have borne witness that it was also the portrait of the man who had come in that day to call Boyne from his unfinished letter. Through the misty surgings of her brain she heard the faint boom of half-forgotten words – words spoken by Alida Stair on the lawn at Pangbourne before Boyne and his wife had ever seen the house at Lyng, or had imagined that they might one day live there.

"This was the man who spoke to me," she repeated.

She looked again at Parvis. He was trying to conceal his disturbance under what he imagined to be an expression of indulgent commiseration; but the edges of his lips were blue. "He thinks me mad; but I'm not mad," she reflected; and suddenly there flashed upon her a way of justifying her strange affirmation.

She sat quiet, controlling the quiver of her lips, and waiting till she could trust her voice to keep its habitual level; then she said, looking straight at Parvis: "Will you answer me one question, please? When was it that Robert Elwell tried to kill himself?"

"When – when?" Parvis stammered.

"Yes; the date. Please try to remember."

She saw that he was growing still more afraid of her. "I have a reason," she insisted gently.

"Yes, yes. Only I can't remember. About two months before, I should say."

"I want the date," she repeated.

Parvis picked up the newspaper. "We might see here," he said, still humouring her. He ran his eyes down the page. "Here it is. Last October – the—"

She caught the words from him. "The twentieth, wasn't it?"

With a sharp look at her, he verified, "Yes, the twentieth. Then you *did* know?"

"I know now." Her white stare continued to travel past him. "Sunday the twentieth – that was the day he came first."

Parvis's voice was almost inaudible. "Came *here* first?"

"Yes."

"You saw him twice, then?"

"Yes, twice." She breathed it at him with dilated eyes. "He came first on the twentieth of October. I remember the date because it was the day we went up Meldon Steep for the first time." She felt a faint gasp of inward laughter at the thought that but for that she might have forgotten.

Parvis continued to scrutinize her, as if trying to intercept her gaze.

"We saw him from the roof," she went on. "He came down

the lime-avenue towards the house. He was dressed just as he is in that picture. My husband saw him first. He was frightened, and ran down ahead of me; but there was no one there. He had vanished."

"Elwell had vanished?" Parvis faltered.

"Yes." Their two whispers seemed to grope for each other. "I couldn't think what had happened. I see now. He *tried* to come then; but he wasn't dead enough – he couldn't reach us. He had to wait for two months; and then he came back again – and Ned went with him."

She nodded at Parvis with the look of triumph of a child who has successfully worked out a difficult puzzle. But suddenly she lifted her hands with a desperate gesture, pressing them to her bursting temples.

"Oh, my God! I sent him to Ned – I told him where to go! I sent him to this room!" she screamed out.

She felt the walls of the room rush towards her, like inward-falling ruins; and she heard Parvis, a long way off, as if through the ruins, crying to her, and struggling to get at her. But she was numb to his touch; she did not know what he was saying. Through the tumult she heard but one clear note, the voice of Alida Stair, speaking on the lawn at Pangbourne.

"You won't know till afterward," it said. "You won't know till long, long afterward."

A Silver Music

Gaie Sebold

Inspector Gairden turned up the collar of his coat as a steam velocipede puffed and churned its way past him, filthy water spraying up from beneath its wheels. Its driver hunched under a bowler and greatcoat, rain shedding down his back; its single passenger was no more than a smoky shape behind the yellowed glass. Gairden scowled at the red-glass lantern that marked its retreat.

He crossed the road, picking his way among the puddles. A dead goblin, about the size of a terrier, swollen-bellied, lay face down in the gutter, its tail wavering in the water. He sighed. The things were a damn nuisance, but he had a lingering fondness for them. Some of the lesser sidhe seemed to be adapting to the city, thriving on its debris; others ended like this.

Gairden stood in front of the looming bulk of the Rheese Manufactory. The place roared and fumed in the darkness; shadows moved in the high windows, paper silhouette puppets against a brutal white glare. Rain, snagged by the light, plummeted like steel needles. A rhythmic thudding jarred the paving under his feet. He walked past the great gates to the side door.

Set into the stone surround was the brass opening of a speaking tube supported by two plaster cherubs. Below it, mounted in an elaborately decorated brass surround, a doorbell bore the stern injunction: "Press".

Inspector Gairden did so.

"Yes?" A muted buzz, stripped of gender, emerged from the tube.

"Inspector Gairden," he said, wondering how he sounded to his hidden interlocutor. Less like a machine, he hoped.

"One moment, please."

It was, in fact, a good few moments before someone opened the door, by which point rain was trickling steadily off the brim of the inspector's hat.

"Apologies for keeping you, sir. Terrible night." The man beckoned him in. He was a lean fellow in a workman's uniform of heavy canvas trousers, woollen waistcoat and plain shirt with the sleeves held back by leather bands. His hands were stained with black and brown on the fingers and palms. "Please follow me. It's up three flights. Sorry for the climb, but the lift isn't working."

"May I take your name?"

"Oh, sorry, sir. I'm the foreman. Lassiter. Ben Lassiter." He shook his head. "Awful thing, it is. Got everyone very shaken. We shall have to be very careful, the next few days, that there aren't accidents. Nothing like bad nerves for making people careless."

"Do you have many accidents?" Gairden raised his voice over the noise.

"Not so many in the last five years, since poor Jamie joined us. We do get accidents, yes. But when it happens . . . the machines, they're not *malevolent*, if you see what I mean."

Lassiter glanced through the archway as they passed the factory floor, where the great levers and pistons rose and fell in relentless rhythm, regular as the pumping of a giant heart, the scurrying workers tiny and doll-like. "I suppose so." Had the machines been malevolent, Gairden would have felt . . . not sympathy, but some capacity for understanding. That was how he worked: by trying to sense something about the hearts, the minds, the spirits of those involved in a case. There was none of that, with a machine.

"The idea of someone actually—" Lassiter wiped his mouth. "Well, it's not the same, you see."

"No, you're right, it isn't. You knew the young man, then?"

"Oh, everyone knew young Jamie, sir. Not to speak to, so much; he kept himself to himself, you know. But he was a nice lad when you could get him to notice you existed."

"Preoccupied, was he?"

"You could say that, sir, yes. A bear for his work, he was."

"An asset to the firm, then."

"Oh, I don't think it would be too much to call him a genius, Inspector. We shall be very sorry to lose him." There was, the inspector thought, the slightest possible emphasis on the *we*.

The iron stairway shuddered to the regular thudding; bright curls of shaved metal and fragments of dirt jumped about their feet as they climbed. Smells of hot metal and steam surrounded them. Glittering dust hung in the air.

"What was his position here?" Inspector Gairden said.

"Assistant Deviser, sir."

"And who was he assistant to?"

"That'd be Mr Rheese, sir. The owner."

"I see."

The noise lessened slightly as they moved higher. They stepped into a corridor; heavy wooden doors, gas lamps hissing in their lily-petal shades. Lassiter hurried his steps; Gairden speeded up to stay with him.

Lassiter glanced up and down the corridor; pushed open a door. "In here, sir. It's pretty bad, but I suppose you've seen worse, in your line of work."

Tiny limbs, their sizes carefully graded, hung on the walls. Jars of eyes stared in all directions. A music box stood with gaping lid, the dancer on top poised forever *en pointe*. Neatly arrayed in trays, on hooks, in boxes, were levers, wheels, cogs. Brass and copper, glass and steel. A vice gripped the edge of a workbench like a parrot waiting for a snack; against one wall was a bed, narrow as a coffin, the sheets and one rough blanket tucked in with an almost military precision.

If it had been a burglary, it was an exceptionally neat one. There was nothing out of place, except the body. It – *James*

Wishart, Gairden reminded himself, not just *the body*, never just *the body* – lay face down on the floor.

There wasn't much left of his head.

He was dressed much like the foreman. One hand was outflung, as though reaching for something; the other hand lay at his side, with the palm turned up; it had the same staining as he had noticed on Lassiter's hands. There was something particularly pathetic about it, that strong young hand, darkened and callused with work, lying curled like a sleeping child's. A watch had slipped from his waistcoat pocket and lay flattened, a ruined mess of cogs and metal and glass.

Gairden kneeled down. From the mash of brutally shattered bone and the overlapping sprays of red, it seemed he had been hit not just once, but several times. This close, Gairden was enclosed in the raw stench of blood, the sleek smell of machine oil . . . and a faint, junipery trail of gin.

Something lay in the mess, glittering. Inspector Gairden picked up the tiny brass cog, delicate as a snowflake. Perhaps it was from the watch. "Did he drink?"

"Jamie? Never saw him with anything stronger than a cup of tea, sir."

"Hmm. Is anything missing?"

"Not that I can see, sir."

It was cold; the fire in the grate had long died to ash and cinders. All the fire-irons were in place. It seemed the murderer had both provided his weapon, and taken it away again.

"Lassiter!"

Inspector Gairden looked up. A man was standing in the doorway, regarding the scene with his mouth twisted in distaste.

"Is this the inspector? I thought I told you to bring him to my office?"

Lassiter straightened his shoulders and stared at the opposite wall. "Sorry, sir," he said. "Forgot."

The man hurried forward. "My dear sir, I do apologize. I'd hoped to have a chance to prepare you." He was a burly fellow, what Gairden thought of as a beefsteak man; flushed face girdled with expansive mutton-chop whiskers; smelling of tobacco and pomade. He too had black smudges on his fingers. "Ghastly, quite ghastly."

Gairden got to his feet. "Yes. This is his workshop?"

"Indeed. It's a dreadful business. Lassiter, do get back to the floor; they're bad enough at the moment. They need your eye on them."

"Sir."

"I may need to speak to you again," Gairden said quietly.

"Of course, sir." Lassiter disappeared.

Even as he did so, there was a pause in the thudding, a shiver of silence, then a long metallic screech, and shouting. "Oh, no," mutton-chop whiskers moaned. "As though things weren't bad enough."

"Problem, sir?" Gairden said.

"Goblins in the damn machinery, I swear. I'm sorry, I didn't introduce myself. Tobias Rheese. I'm the owner, for my sins. I say, could we go elsewhere? It's just that—"

"Well, sir, I do need to look around a little."

"Oh, I suppose you do." Rheese glanced at the body, then away, swallowing. "When can we get things decently dealt with?"

"As soon as I'm done."

Gairden worked his way along the battered, deep-drawered oak table that stood against the back wall; he took a pencil from his pocket and used it to lift the edges of papers and charts. He brushed his gloved fingers over the teeth of cogwheels stacked in a box; looked at the tools hanging on their hooks, clean and orderly. He opened a drawer to find it full of papers – technical drawings by the look of them – labelled in a neat, small hand. *A new method for the construction of a speaking tube. Improvements to the ratchet key. Clockwork mechanism for use in an instructive and educational child's toy.*

"Do be careful, there's a good chap. Those papers . . . well, of course, I haven't had time to go through them, but there may be important things in there," Rheese said.

"Of course, sir. Can you tell if anything's been taken?"

"I don't know. It's possible."

The second drawer refused to open easily; something was jammed in the slide. Gairden worked at it with his fingers until it came free. A scrap of paper. A word, *Lalika*, in that same neat hand. A smooth curve, disappearing off the edge of the paper, with an elongated oval within it. That was all. Gairden looked at it, then laid it on the desk.

Above his head, the mantle of one of the gas lamps suddenly flared up with painful brilliance. Gairden blinked. There was a *pop*, and the lamp went out.

He heard Rheese swear under his breath. When he turned, the man seemed to have lost more colour than the dimmer light could account for, and his broad forehead gleamed beneath his pomade-glossed curls. "Could we get out of here? Please?"

"Just one more moment, sir."

Gairden looked around, letting his eyes lose focus. Sometimes, concentrating on the detail hid the story the place had to tell you. Though here, he felt at a distinct disadvantage; it was a place built for machines, not people. Machines did not have stories, or motive, or a past.

Gairden was a man out of his time, and knew it. He had grown up in a world that still went hand in hand with the mystical, but the cities expanded, the woods diminished, and the grind and roar of machines ate into everything. When Gairden was a child, goblins had stolen eggs from his parents' hens and shouted rude remarks when he'd chased them from the garden; now, if he saw one, it had died a poisoned death in the gutter or sat sickly and moaning in a cage in some private menagerie. Naiads abandoned the polluted rivers; the fey retreated deep into the heart of the green. Gairden was a man whose job consisted of shining a light on darkness, yet he loathed the idea of a world of mindless mechanism, where there was only glaring light and stark black; where nothing danced and glimmered in the shadows.

He looked at the gleaming tools of polished wood and brass, the drawers with their shining handles, the neat stacks of books and papers; that narrow, empty bed.

"Well, sir," he said, "I think that's it for the moment. I'll need to ask you a few questions, if it's quite convenient."

"By all means, come with me." Rheese closed and locked the door as Lassiter watched.

"What do I do about—" Rheese gestured to where Jamie Wishart lay, hidden now.

"Our fellows will come to take him away; he'll have to remain with us until this is resolved, of course. Have his family been informed?"

"I don't think he has any. My father took him out of the workhouse, and he wasn't married. This way, Inspector."

Reese's office bore some resemblance to a gentlemen's club that Gairden had had occasion to visit during an investigation the year before. It was, like Rheese, plumply furnished, the lights rosy-shaded and fringed, the desk topped with rich red leather. Designs for intricate machinery were scattered on the surface; thick black lines ran through one of them. He wasn't as tidy as his assistant; papers lay all about the place, as did drinking glasses, an apple-core, a pot of boot-black, a picture of a young woman and a small boy ... Rheese motioned Gairden to sit in one of the deep leather chairs and shuffled the papers into a drawer, leaving black smudges on some of the designs.

"So little time these days," he said. "Since the old man retired, I've barely had a moment to work on my own designs." He looked at his hands, frowned, and wiped them on a cloth. "Damn muck gets everywhere." He poured himself a brandy from one of a set of rather fine decanters of heavy cut crystal. He motioned the stopper in Gairden's direction. "For yourself?"

"Very kind of you, sir, but no."

Rheese sat himself in the chair behind the desk. "Wouldn't want you to think I'm the sort of fellow who always has his nose in the bottle, but a thing like this, well, I have to confess, my nerves are twisted up like clock springs."

"Was it you who found him, sir?"

"No, it was Lassiter. He came pounding on my door, yelling

about blood and murder. And when I saw . . . well, sent for you chaps, obviously."

A clock suddenly chimed, a loud discordant run of notes. Rheese jolted so badly half the brandy he'd just poured spilled down his wrist.

"Sir? Is everything all right, sir?" Gairden said, getting to his feet.

Rheese waved him back down, gulped brandy and tugged at his collar. "Yes, yes."

Gairden glanced at his watch. "It seems your clock is out of time, sir."

Rheese glared at the clock. "So it is. What's the use of a clock that doesn't tell the right time, I ask you?" he said. "Or any machine that refuses to work. Not a bit of use. That's what."

"Sir?"

"Sorry, Inspector. It's been a trying day."

The clock sat on a small ornate table draped with a fringed, green velvet cloth, and something lay just beyond it, glimmering softly.

"Oh," Rheese said, "she's not working either. But I shall have her going, see if I don't."

Gairden peered. His eyes, bemused, sorted through the soft gleam of metal. The long sliver of shine, a leg; the rounded arch, a foot. Some sort of automaton, in polished brass, tumbled in the corner like a drunk. Or a corpse.

"Do you like automata, Inspector?" Rheese said, topping up his brandy.

"Not really my style of thing, sir."

"People are wild for them; the more elaborate, the better. There's a mechanical chamber orchestra that's been all over the papers."

"Oh, I may have seen something, yes."

"That's what people like. But they're clumsy, you know, the mannequins. The way they move . . . everyone's trying for something more human. It's not easy."

"No, I don't suppose it is. Now, Mr Rheese, do you have any idea who might have attacked Mr Wishart?"

"Well—"

"Sir?

"We make frivols, Inspector. Amusements. Toys. Toys are all innocence, you'd think, but there's no harder business than this. Espionage goes on all the time. We take precautions, but someone could have got in, especially during the shift change, with a couple of hundred people going in and out."

"You think Mr Wishart might have disturbed someone in the act of stealing his designs?"

Rheese swallowed the last of the brandy. "We've been doing very well. People notice."

"Yes," Inspector Gairden said. "And I understand that Mr Wishart was an exceptionally talented young man."

"Hah. He was well enough, I suppose, but really, Inspector, he was a boy from the workhouse when all's said and done. I was giving him what education I could, of course. Trying to make him useful, for m' father's sake."

"Oh, I understood he was something like a genius," Gairden said.

"If he'd been that, Inspector, don't you think someone would have tried to bribe him away, rather than murder him?"

Gairden felt the hairs on the back of his neck stir. He turned his head, convinced someone had come into the room. But the door remained firmly shut. A death-rattle sound came from the clock, and a thick final *clunk*. He glanced at it; its stilled and silent face was somehow reminiscent of a cadaver. He turned back to Rheese, who shuddered and tipped more brandy down his throat.

"There is that, of course, sir," Gairden said. "If they'd known about him. Did he have many friends?"

"I don't know, Inspector. Well, he would hardly have brought them here; this is a manufactory, not a club, what?"

"What about enemies?"

Rheese shrugged. "There's the Children of Lud, of course. Wretched fellows."

"The machine-breakers? Have you had trouble with them?"

"Not for some time, but they're still about; well, you'd know, Inspector, wasn't some fella arrested for it just the other week?"

"Not in my jurisdiction, sir. And I hadn't heard of them going as far as murder."

"It's not a great leap, though, is it, Inspector, between attacking a man's property and attacking his person, don't you think?"

Gairden, who rather thought it was, chose not to answer. "Do you know if Mr Wishart had any problems with the other workers, sir?"

Rheese rubbed at his whiskers. "Not that I know of, but they will have their rows and jealousies, you know. My father gave him his own workshop, and so forth. I suppose not everyone likes to see a boy from the workhouse do well, eh? But Lassiter'd know better than I."

"I'll need to talk to them."

A whistle blew, long and loud, cutting over the thud-thud-thud of the machines.

"Well, then, you'd be just in time to catch them coming off shift, if we go now. I'll get Lassiter to gather them up." He picked up the speaking tube that dangled from the wall by his desk, and removed the stopper. "Hello? Amabelle? Tell Lassiter to hold the workers back; the inspector needs to speak to them." He stoppered the tube and got to his feet.

"So you kept them to their work, sir, once Mr Wishart was discovered?" Gairden asked.

"Couldn't stop the machines, not for something like this."

"No. Under what circumstances would the machines be stopped?"

"If there's an accident, obviously, then. Oh, and when Her Majesty, bless her, passed on. All the manufactories stopped for an hour for the funeral."

"Yes, I remember. Well, I needn't keep you from your work, sir, if you're happy to let me talk to them."

"By all means. Yes, I must get on. I'll be doing the boy's work as well as my own, now." For a moment his heavy face quivered with genuine emotion, though what precisely that emotion was, the Inspector couldn't tell.

The workers, taken all together, were a pallid, weary

collection, like nothing so much as dolls that had been left out in the rain by a careless child. There were a hundred and fifty of them; Gairden did what he could to narrow it down. Most, simply enough, had come in, gone to their machines and had not looked up except when they took their meal break; most ate in the refectory, where they now huddled. Several seemed upset; four or five women were sniffing and lending handkerchiefs, some of the men had their heads together, muttering. A few glanced longingly at the windows or gazed sullenly at the floor, showing nothing but a dull resentment at being kept past their time. The new shift were already at the benches; the machines thudded relentlessly on.

Gairden stood in front of them and coughed. "Ladies and gentlemen, I won't keep you a moment. I'm sure you've all heard that Mr Wishart was killed this evening. We hope to find whoever did it as soon as possible. If any of you have seen anything, or noticed anything at all out of the way, however small, please come and tell me. I'll be in the wages office for as long as I'm needed." He'd dealt with factory workers, and factory owners, before, so he added; "If you'd rather not do it here, you may find me at the Thrall Street station. Just ask for Inspector Gairden."

A low murmur rippled through them; a few looked at each other. No one stood.

Gairden made his way to the wages office; a solemn box of a place, its mahogany cupboards sternly locked. It rather put him in mind of an expensive coffin. Though a coffin, he thought, would probably be quieter.

There was a knock on the door. "Come in," Gairden said.

It was Lassiter. "You said you'd like to speak to me again, sir?"

"Ah, yes. Do sit down, Mr Lassiter."

A machine stood on a table in the corner. Gairden could not make it out: it was gleaming black, painted with floral bouquets, and had a series of small white buttons attached to steel arms that disappeared inside the machine. Each of the buttons bore a letter or a number.

"That's one of the new caligraphs, sir."

"And what does that do?"

"It makes letters on paper; very even, just like printed type. You press the keys."

Gairden looked at the machine with distaste. The lettering of a human hand, be it hasty scrawl or copperplate or the awkward, childlike printing of the barely literate, connected one to the writer. Handwriting had, on occasion, helped him solve a case. What could one tell from the printing of a machine, every letter identical, no matter who pressed the keys? He turned his back on it, and sat down.

The noise of the machines was slightly muffled here, but still reverberated through the very walls, calling soft answering clicks from somewhere inside the caligraph.

"Well, Mr Lassiter? Can you tell me about how you found Mr Wishart?"

"I was on the way up to discuss a plan he had, for a new safety device. He'd been promising it for a while . . ." Lassiter looked down, and tugged at a loose thread on his sleeve.

"There were difficulties?"

"He'd get distracted. He had a wonderful mind, sir, no doubt of it. But he did get distracted."

"I see. So, on this particular evening?"

"I just went up to give him a bit of a nudge, as it were. And when I got there, there he was, poor fellow."

"Did you hear or see anything? Did anyone pass you on the stairs?"

"I took the lift, sir. It was working fine then. The corridor was empty when I got out."

"Did you hear anything?"

"There was some shouting, I took it to be outside in the street. And then I did hear something. But it wasn't a sound a person would make, it was like a long note on a fiddle, drawn out; a sort of a wailing, but not anything from a mouth, or a throat."

"And then?"

"And then . . . well, have you ever dropped a copper pot,

Inspector? There was that sort of sound. Like lots of copper pots, falling. It struck me something was up, that there'd been an accident, so I hurried, but when I got around the corner . . ." he shrugged. "The door was open, and I went in, and there was poor Jamie."

"And whatever you heard falling?"

"No idea about that, sir. There was nothing there when I got to the room."

"Did you touch anything . . . move anything?"

"I went close, to see if there was anything to be done. Foolish, I suppose. I could see straight away that his poor head was quite stoved in. I hope I didn't do wrong?"

"No, not at all."

"There was something else, sir."

"Yes?"

"It'll sound odd, sir, but I could have sworn I heard music, just before. Only it could just be the machines."

"I'm afraid I don't follow you?"

"It's the noise, see, sir. Sometimes when I leave I can still hear them, even in my sleep. They put odd noises in one's head. But normally it's ringing, or a sort of buzz; what I heard, it sounded like proper music, like you'd hear down at the concert halls, only . . . well, like all the instruments were made of silver." Lassiter gave him a sidelong glance, looking a little flushed. "Sounds fanciful, I'm sure."

To Gairden, it sounded as though the man had heard fey music, though the fey had a notorious dislike of the manufactories, and rarely ventured into the cities at all. And though they could be dangerous, they tended to be subtle; simply breaking a man's head open like an egg was hardly their style. Or perhaps the machines had had an unfortunate effect on Lassiter, had driven him a little mad. It would hardly be surprising.

"Music, and then shouting. Well, thank you. I shall keep it in mind. Oh, Mr Lassiter?"

"Sir?"

"Have there been problems with the Children of Lud? Anything Mr Rheese might not know of?"

Lassiter stiffened a little; his face became wooden. "Not had any of that manner of thing, sir, no. I don't believe there's many of 'em still about. And of course if we had, I'd be obliged to report it to Mr Rheese."

"Of course. Tell me, do you drink gin at all?

"Wouldn't touch it, sir. We've lost some good workers to gin; I won't have them in if they smell of it. It's sneaky, wretched stuff and makes for accidents."

"Hmm. Thank you, Mr Lassiter. I think that will be all."

The next person to knock at the door was a young woman with strong dark curls escaping from beneath her headscarf. The glow of outdoor work had not quite faded from her skin, and she lacked the grey starveling look so many of the workers had; her arms were solid with muscle, her shoulders broad and strong. Her eyelids were swollen.

"Good evening, miss. Did you have something you wished to speak to me about?"

"Yes, sir."

"Could I take your name?"

"Mattie Drewrey, sir."

"Thank you. And what was it you wanted to tell me?"

"There was someone with him." She was biting her lip, her eyes brimming. "Oh, if I could get my hands on her ..."

Gairden took a clean handkerchief from his pocket; he always kept several about him. "Now, don't fret yourself. Whoever did this was a dangerous person; it's just as well you didn't meet them, eh? Her, you say?" He handed Mattie the handkerchief.

She took it, and blew her nose. "Yes, sir."

"And what did she look like?"

"I didn't see much, sir. I'd gone out, for a breath, see. We don't take our food at the machines, so we get a little time, a few minutes to eat, and I like to go outside."

"Even when it's raining?"

"I was brought up on a farm, sir; you don't hide from a bit of rain when there's stock to be tended. Anyway, I happened to look up at Jamie ... at Mr Wishart's window."

"Was that something you did often?"

She flushed, and lifted her chin. "So what if I did? He needed someone to look after him, did Jamie."

"I'm sure. And what did you see?"

"They were dancing. He'd barely look at you, sir, he was that shy; took me six months before he'd so much as bid me good morning, and there she was, bold as you please, with his arms about her, *dancing*!" Her fingers clenched in her lap.

"Could you make her out?"

She shook her head. "With the rain, and all; the window was wet, and there was smoke from the street. But I saw the shape of them, whirling about. Shameless, it was. Some opera-house floozy, you mark my words."

"You think this woman was involved in Mr Wishart's death?"

She shrugged. "All I know is she was there. And they're strong, those dancers, you ever seen them? Muscles like my uncle Jed, some of them. Maybe she wanted money, and he wouldn't give her any."

Rattattarattattarattatta! Gairden knocked his chair over as he leaped to his feet. Mattie shrieked.

The caligraph's keys were moving, the letters blurring up and down, faster and faster, until, with a *clunk*, they stopped. Several of the metal arms had become entwined, forcing some of the keys into a tight bunch, *g* and *h* and *y* and *t* and *b*. The machine quivered like a dog, and was still.

Mattie was on her feet, her hands clamped to her face. "Oh, sir, it's Jamie!"

"Or," said Gairden, "the vibrations of the machines set the thing to rattling, and now it's tangled itself up. Well, I shan't touch it; I'll leave it to someone who knows how."

"There's no paper," Mattie said. "If there'd been paper in it, he might have written a name."

"Well, there wasn't," Gairden said. "It's just a machine. Now, Mattie, did you hear anything? After you saw this woman?"

"No, sir." She glanced anxiously at the jammed caligraph. "But I was back at the bench by then, so I wouldn't have heard much."

"And you didn't see her go in or out?"

"No. If I had, I'd have had something to say to her!"

"Thank you. You get on home, miss. And if you think of anything more, you come and tell me, just as I said."

Mattie left, still glancing at the caligraph. Gairden glowered at it. "Well," he said, "is that you, Mr Wishart? Still messing about with machines? You'd be better giving me a clue, you know, rather than frightening that girl half out of her wits."

He glanced around, feeling a little foolish, but nothing answered him.

As he left he saw a live goblin hunched over the corpse in the gutter, tugging at the wet fur, and whimpering. "Too late, old fellow," Gairden muttered. Even love could not animate the dead. Though he'd heard things, about the fey ...

He returned to his lodgings tired and chilled through, but restless. Once he had hung up his greatcoat by the fire, to steam itself dry, he paced his rooms, straightening a picture here, sliding a book even with its fellows there. He thought about Jamie Wishart; his mechanisms and his narrow bachelor bed. He thought about Lassiter, and Rheese, and Mattie Drewrey. About machines and goblins. About steam and blood. The portrait of a young woman, hair that looked almost too heavy to bear piled upon her fragile head and descending in thick curls about her delicate neck, watched him with a solemn stare. At one point he turned to it. "Well, Esther? What do you think? All this business with music and dancing, that's more your area than mine. You always liked to dance, while you had the strength for it." But tonight Esther had no answers for him.

He went to turn his coat, and felt in the pockets; a scrap of paper, and a tiny cog. The paper with the word *Lalika* on it. He frowned; he was sure he had left it on the table. How had it come to be in his pocket? He looked at it again, crumpled and torn where it had been caught in the drawer slide. Now he thought back, there hadn't been any other papers in that drawer that seemed to have their corners missing.

So whatever this had been part of, it was no longer there.

Someone had taken it out, perhaps in a hurry, wrenching at it. Leaving behind this fragment. And now the fragment had come home with him, along with one tiny cog; tiny yet slightly too big to have been part of the broken watch. Everything else in the office was so neat, so carefully tidied away; a place for everything, and everything, except this little glittering snow-flake of metal, in its place. Well, anyone could lose or discard something so tiny. And yet, there it had been, close to the body. Stained, in fact, with the young man's blood. Gairden rubbed his thumb over it; brown flakes came away.

"Stains . . ." he said. "I wonder what stains their hands. Dyes, perhaps. I must remember to ask Lassiter."

Perhaps Wishart had been working on something; a project of his own, Lassiter had said. Perhaps whoever came in had grabbed not only the papers, but Wishart's latest mechanism.

Possibly Rheese had been right about espionage; tomorrow, he would go to the patent office. And to the theatre, too; he felt a sting of pleasure at the thought. Maybe he would even buy a ticket; it was a long time since he had done such a thing.

Wishart hadn't done such things at all, according to Lassiter. Wishart had spent his life among machines, without family, seemingly without friends. Gairden looked out into the rainy night, and shook his head.

The next day other things intervened: a kidnapping (that might, in fact, be a running-away), a suicide, and the thousand mundanities of the working day; by the time Gairden could have got to the patent office, it was shut. He did make time to have the broken watch looked at by a watchmaker of his acquaintance: Adelle Brigley, a cosy-looking woman of middle years. Her workshop, unlike Jamie Wishart's, was an Aladdin's cave of glittering confusion in which she never, to Gairden's continuing astonishment, seemed to have the slightest trouble finding what she wanted. She poked at the ruined mechanism and held fragments up to the lamplight. "It was a nice piece. A Lockwood and Greene. Engraved inside the lid."

"Is the engraving visible?"

"Some of it . . ." She screwed a jeweller's glass into her eye and peered. "To Jamie . . . something . . . occ . . . probably occasion . . . and two numbers, a two and a one, I think. An 'm'. Then two 'e's. I can't make out the rest."

"A birthday gift," Gairden said. "On the occasion of his twenty-first, I imagine."

"Perhaps."

"An expensive one?"

"Depending on one's means, Inspector. Not an extravagant purchase for a well-off man, but a tidy enough price."

"And is it all there?"

She prodded. "The hands are missing, maybe some other pieces. It'd take a deal of mending."

"Thank you," he said.

"Not at all. Will you take a cup with me, Inspector Gairden? You look chilled."

"No, thank you. More to do yet."

"You work yourself very hard," said Adelle, shaking her head at him.

He smiled, and paid her her usual honorarium, then made his way to the theatre nearest to the Rheese manufactory. It seemed a sensible place to start; murder often had a small circumference.

Among smells of powder and greasepaint and dust and sweat-stained satin and weary feet, he questioned dancers and doormen. None had heard of Jamie Wishart, though plenty had heard of Rheese. None knew of anyone who might have visited the manufactory.

Of course, the fact of someone dancing did not necessarily indicate a professional dancer; his own dead Esther, a postmistress, had loved to dance. When she could no longer dance herself, she liked to sit and watch, and encouraged him to dance with other women. *I like to see you*, she'd said. One in a million, Esther. Not a jealous bone in her.

"The girl, Mattie," Gairden said, to Esther's portrait that night, "had a soft spot for young Mr Wishart. Now, a bludgeoning . . . that's not a woman's murder, as a rule. But she's a strong lass. And got a temper, too, you could see it. Enough of one to stove his head in, though? For love? Is that love, Esther?

"And what about Lassiter? There's something going on there; the way he pokered up. I think I shall be looking at some old reports tomorrow. And the watch . . . I've a thought about the watch, Esther. We shall see. That poor boy . . . what a lonely life, and a dreadful end. If he was dancing with someone, I hope he enjoyed it."

After another day of fruitless enquiries at theatres, and the reading of dusty crime reports in faded handwriting, and damp feet, and frustration, Gairden was wrapping his scarf about his throat prior to leaving the station, the rain having given way to fog thick and chilly as ectoplasm. There was a commotion at the door, and Mattie Drewrey, the curls that escaped her scarf dewed with droplets, her cheeks flushed, was waving at him over the head of the duty sergeant.

"Miss Drewrey?"

"Oh, Inspector, you've got to come! There's been such things going on!"

"Now, Miss Drewrey, why don't you come into my office and tell me what you mean?"

"I can't, sir, it might have stopped by the time we got back – soon as I realized it was something out of the way, I ran straight out to tell you!"

"To tell me what?"

"It's Jamie . . . Mr Wishart . . . He's been making ever such a fuss."

Weariness retreating, Gairden followed Mattie Drewrey through the fog-drifted streets.

The gates were open; the workers coming off shift milling and chattering with those coming on. Outside the entrance doors to the building, the crowd swirled, paused, like water caught in an eddy. Lassiter, the foreman, was standing by the doors; his voice carried clearly over the chatter. "Now, come on, just be patient, it'll be sorted out. Those of you about to start your shift, you might as well come in and wait in the warm."

Gairden realized, finally, what was different; though until now it had seemed of a piece with the weather.

It was quiet. The churn and rumble of a passing velocipede underlined the silence; the paving stones lay quiet beneath his feet. No wonder he could hear Lassiter so easily: the machines were not running.

He excused himself and pushed through the crowd, conscious of eyes on him as he worked his way to the front. "Trouble, Mr Lassiter?"

"Oh, Inspector." Lassiter ran his hands through his hair. "Sorry, sir, I don't know if anyone'll be able to speak with you just at the moment, we've a bit of a problem."

"So I see. Can you tell me what exactly has happened?"

"Bloody sabotage! That's what's happened!" Rheese appeared behind Lassiter. His face was flushed, and a distinct odour of brandy was now incorporated with those of cigars and pomade.

"Perhaps I could take a look, sir?" Gairden said. Mattie was still beside him, her hands clasped in front of her, her eyes darting from one man to the other.

"You have any knowledge of machines, Inspector?"

"No, sir, but I've dealt with a saboteur or two, in my time."

"Hah. You'd best come in, then."

"What, exactly, happened?" Gairden asked, walking among the machines.

"Nothing, that's the thing of it, sir," Lassiter said.

"It's not *nothing* if the damn machines stop!" Rheese said. "Do you know how much this is going to cost me?"

"What I mean, sir," Lassiter said, with a deference tinged with weariness, "is that we can't find a *reason*. We can't find a slipped gear or a thrown cog, not a thing that would account for it. And even if there was, for one set, it wouldn't affect the rest. *All* the machines have stopped."

"When did this happen?" Gairden said.

Lassiter glanced up at the great clock on the wall. "About forty minutes ago, sir. Just on six."

"And was anything happening at the time?"

"No, sir. I was just talking to Mr Rheese about what we should do for Jamie's funeral."

"There are arrangements for that kind of thing, aren't there?" Rheese said. "Wouldn't you fellows sort that out?"

"We can do, sir," Gairden said, "if, as you say, he had no one else to do the thing decently."

Rheese nodded, and turned away.

Gairden prowled among the silent machines. There was nothing here; nothing but mechanism, waiting with donkey patience to move again. Cautiously, he ran his fingers over rivets and pistons. There was a suggestion of warmth in the metal; the room itself was still warm with the motion now stilled. Yet why, with donkey stubbornness, had it stopped? He could see nothing, feel nothing, that suggested the fury or the calculated disruption of the saboteur. The great levers stood poised above his head like guns at the salute.

"Nothing," he said, returning to the others.

"It's Jamie," Mattie Drewrey said stubbornly. "He's trying to tell us who murdered him."

"Don't be ridiculous, girl!" Rheese said; but he glanced about him uneasily.

"He's not going the clearest way about it, then," said Gairden.

Even as he spoke there was a great hissing sigh, and a creak, and a rumbling, and the levers began to move.

"Well!" Lassiter said. "There's a turn-up. Shall I get the workers started, Mr Rheese?"

Rheese was staring at the machines with a kind of glum fury. "Yes, yes," he said. "Get them working while they can. Who knows when everything will stop again?"

"When you're done, Mr Lassiter," Gairden said, "I'd like a word, if you please."

"Of course, sir."

The wall clock, which, unlike the machines, had kept going, chimed the hour. Gairden looked at it, and frowned.

Lassiter came to the wages office as before. He looked tired, the deep lines either side of his mouth pulling it down. Gairden

realized that the man was younger than he had first thought –
it was those lines that made him look more than his age, and a
sort of weary watchfulness.

"Now, Mr Lassiter," Gairden said. "I was going through old
reports today, and I found something that troubled me."

"Sir?"

"Yes. You used to be one of the Children of Lud."

Lassiter sighed, his shoulders slumping. "I did, sir, yes."

"You were arrested for vandalism. Attacking a steam loom."

"I was."

"And now you're a foreman in a leading manufactory.
Explain this to me, if you please."

"What's to explain, sir? I was young. I lived in the country; I
knew a lot of folks being put out of work by the machines;
there was a deal of excitement about it all, a deal of revolution-
ary talk. Then I got myself in that bit of trouble. My mother
bailed me out, it took most of her savings, then she sat me
down and, oh, did she ever give me a talking to." His mouth
tilted upwards, briefly, at the memory. "She said she was never
wasting good money on such foolishness again, so I'd better
sort myself out. I had a good think. I realized the world was
changing, Inspector. If I wanted to be any good in it, I needed
to swim with the tide, not against it. I couldn't stop the
machines, but if I worked, I could learn about them. And
where I am now, I can do a bit of good; work on safety improvements, do my best to get the workers treated decently. The
world's changed. You can't go backwards, sir."

"That seems a very solid turnaround, Mr Lassiter."

"It was make my way or starve, sir, I decided to make my
way the best I could."

"You're very concerned for the safety of your workers."

"Yes, sir, I am."

"Did you resent Mr Wishart's distraction? You were waiting
for safety devices to be finished, and he was working on some
project of his own."

"It was no good getting impatient with Jamie, Inspector.
He'd just give you that smile and show you some wonderful

new thing he was working on. He was like a boy, really. And you'd have about given up, and then he'd come running in with whatever you'd asked for, often better than you'd asked for, and barely stop to show you how it worked before he'd be off to do something else." Lassiter looked down at his hands. "I'm good with machines, I've learned to be, but I had nothing on Jamie. He had a kind of passion in him. He talked about his devices in such a way . . . as though they were real before he'd even made them, as though they were just waiting for him to find the right way . . ." Lassiter blinked. "Did you ..."

"What is it?"

"I thought I heard something. There it is again."

Now he was listening, Gairden could just make it out, the faintest silvery shimmer of sound, winding through the thudding rhythm of the machines.

"That's what I heard, sir, that night," Lassiter whispered. "Like that, only stronger, with more of a beat to it."

It was barely a sigh, Gairden thought, among the brutal clangour of the machines, not so much music as music's shadow. A voice without strength or words, yet so sad, so terribly mournful. Barely had he heard it before it faded.

Now there was only the blunt endless thudding of the steam hammers audible. Lassiter was staring into the distance, like a man who had caught a glimpse of a sorrowful memory. Gairden cleared his throat. "Was Jamie working on something like an instrument?" he said. "Mr Rheese mentioned a mechanical orchestra."

Lassiter blinked, and came back to himself. "Oh, there were a dozen and one things, sir, but recently he'd been keeping whatever it was to himself. He'd promised to show me when he was finished. He said it would be the most wonderful thing. It always was, of course." Lassiter rubbed his forehead.

"Mattie Drewrey thought she saw someone up there – someone dancing with Mr Wishart."

"She did? Well, no one passed me sir, as I said, but it's a rambling place. I suppose there *could* have been someone up there. It doesn't sound like Mr Wishart, though. He wasn't one for that sort of thing, hanging about stage doors and such. He worked a great deal. Slept up there as often as not. Don't know when he'd have had time to meet young ladies."

"No. Oh, one last thing . . . what are those marks on your hands?"

"Oh, dyes, varnishes, such like. They fade, sink into the skin, you know, but there's always the next thing, and you're covered again."

"Thank you, Mr Lassiter."

Gairden went back up to the workshop. There was still a stain on the floor; a fine layer of the glittering dust that hung in the air of the manufactory was beginning to layer itself over everything, making the room with its closed secretive drawers, its miniature limbs and tools and eyes, look like some uncanny half-remembered dream.

Gairden stood in the middle of the floor, avoiding the stain, turning slowly; letting his gaze travel.

Something glittered; something seemed to fall through the air. He glanced up, thinking there was a leak in the roof, but the ceiling was unmarked. He looked down, and there, by the door, was another of those tiny cogwheels – this one of a silvery-blue metal. He moved, and picked it up.

Out in the corridor another faint glittering fall, almost too fine to see; in the glow of the wall lamps it fell like a tiny burning star, landing outside the door of Rheese's office.

It was locked; he was sure it was locked, but under the touch of his fingers the lock snicked back and the door swung open.

Gairden walked in. He would have some explaining to do if Rheese turned up. He stood with his head cocked, waiting, but it seemed that whatever had led him here had run out of steam.

There were papers on the desk again. One quick glance, and he would be gone.

Designs. Toys. A doll, a metal bird. Drawings in a swift, meticulous hand; another hand, heavier with the pencil. Thick lines scored through notes. Half-legible scrawls in the margins. *Nonsensical. How can this work?*

A brown, crinkled stain on the edge of the paper. Gairden sniffed. Brandy.

And beneath the desk were a pair of shoes. Waiting for the bootboy to pick them up for cleaning? They looked very clean already. Polished to a gleam.

Gairden glanced behind him, then picked up the shoes and turned them over.

The soles were smooth, grimed with the dust of the factory floor. If they had trodden in blood, it was no longer there. But something glimmered where the sole met the shoe. Something small and bright. With the tip of his pencil, he levered it out from the seam.

A tiny golden arrow, the weapon of a miniature Cupid. Gairden bounced it on his palm, put the shoe back where he had found it, and left.

The patent office was a great, brown, shuffling, rustling wasp's nest of a place; off the central hallway with its noble domed ceiling and tall imperious counters were dozens of tiny rooms, crammed and choked with paper. Inspector Gairden, after a number of increasingly wearisome enquiries, misdirections, and misunderstandings, found himself in one of these, confronted by a small, tweedy, harassed man with thinning hair and a sore-looking nose. "You wish to examine a patent?" The man rubbed his nose and sneezed. "Excuse me, sir. It's the dust. Which one would you wish to see?"

"I wouldn't," Inspector Gairden said. "I merely wish to be informed about any *new* patent applications. Should they arise."

"Oh, I see. Well, if you've the authority ..."

"I have, yes." He pointed to his authorization papers which were, in fact lying on the man's desk; Gairden was tempted to snatch them back up before they disappeared in the great forest of paper that lay all about them. He found himself wondering how many trees had died, to provide these birth certificates of yet more machines.

"The thing is, Inspector, we can get more than a hundred a week. You want to know about all of them?"

"As many as that?"

"Oh, yes, sir. Anything from a new type of propelling pencil to a flying machine."

"Ah." Gairden tapped his chin. "Mannequins, then. Dolls, automata, things of that nature. And anything with the name Lalika."

"Lalika?" The patent officer shook his head. "Fanciful."

"Oh, and while I'm here, I'd like to see any recent applications in the name of Wishart. J. Wishart."

"That would be with the Ws," the patent officer said. He sighed, and got up from his chair with the air of a man much put upon, and disappeared among towering stacks of paper, muttering: "Doubleyou, doubleyou . . . How recent, Inspector?"

"The last six months, say."

"Hmm. No . . . no, there's nothing. Oh, that's odd …"

"What's odd?"

The patent officer reappeared, clutching a brown manila file. "Well, there's one application, at least five years old. Nothing after that. Looks like old Frobisher's handwriting – he retired last month. Came into some money, unexpected, and moved abroad."

"Did he indeed? Then I'd like to see all the applications he worked on before he had such an unusual stroke of good fortune."

"But …"

Gairden looked around at the tottering piles of paper. "I'm sure you don't throw anything away, do you? Find them. I'll wait."

The sound of the machines thrummed through Rheese's office, like a heartbeat. The level of brandy in the decanter had fallen; the levels in all the others stayed the same. They gleamed like great flaunting jewels. Gairden stood by the table; Rheese sat, as usual, behind his desk.

"I'm glad to hear you have some information," he said. "Do feel free . . . and pour me one while you're about it."

"Do you have gin, Mr Rheese?"

Rheese paused for a moment. "Wouldn't have put you down for that type, Inspector."

"You do keep it, though?"

"Well, yes, for the staff, you know, or traders. Can't stand the stuff meself. Did you want—"

"No, thank you, sir. I think the decanter may be chipped, in any case."

There was a silence. "Really?" Rheese said. "Why would you think that?"

"Because I think it may have been used as a murder weapon, Mr Rheese."

There was a faint clinking noise, then an odd, crystalline buzzing. The tray on which the decanters stood had begun to vibrate, a rhythmic resonance, silvery and strange.

Rheese rubbed his hands together, with a dry rasping sound. "A murder weapon? Really?"

"I don't like machines, Mr Rheese. I don't like the world's obsession with them. But Jamie Wishart did. He loved them. And he put that love into what he made." Gairden moved to the window, and looked out into the rain. A tiny persistent ringing made him glance down, and he realized that the latch of the window, too, was resonating, beating against the frame like the clapper of a bell. "You applied for a number of patents, did you not, Mr Rheese?"

"I . . . what? Yes. Of course I did. Where is that damned noise coming from?"

"Your father applied for a number, too. A man of great talent, Mr Matthew Rheese. He invented several mechanisms of some significance, I understand."

"Yes . . . yes, he did. What is this to do with the matter at hand?"

"He was fond of Jamie, wasn't he?"

"Really, Inspector …"

"He gave him the job, and the workshop. He even gave him a watch, for his twenty-first birthday. That must have jarred on you."

"Father had a soft spot for lame dogs, Inspector."

"But Jamie Wishart wasn't a lame dog, was he? Your father recognized that. I wonder if the boy had a touch of the other, a strain of the fey to him; I suppose we'll never know. Either way, Jamie Wishart was a genius. You aren't, Mr Rheese."

"How dare you?" Rheese exclaimed. "What do you know about it?"

Gairden pinned him with his gaze.

"Until Jamie came along, you hadn't applied for a single patent. The patents you applied for after that weren't yours. The inventions weren't yours. They were all Jamie Wishart's. He was too busy making what he loved to realize that you were stealing from him."

"Now look, Inspector, that's complete—" Rheese pushed himself out of the chair, his cheeks flushed, his teeth bared.

"Sit down, Mr Rheese." Gairden's voice was cold as metal.

Rheese slid back into his chair. "Nonsense! No one will ever believe a word of it."

"They'll believe the patent applications, Mr Rheese. You got careless towards the end, once your father was out of the way. You didn't bother copying the original designs; they're still in Jamie's hand, though the applications are in yours."

"I was doing it as a favour to him! The boy had no business sense ..."

"It's enough for people to start looking very carefully. Looking at why the patent officer, Aloysius Frobisher, suddenly became very comfortably off, just before he retired abroad."

"You can't prove anything."

"Oh, I can," Gairden said. "Boot polish, in your office? I wondered why a man such as you was polishing his own shoes. I realized the stains on your fingers had left smudges – those on Lassiter's are ingrained. He didn't smear the door when he touched it – you did. His fingers are dark with dye – yours were stained with boot-blacking. But you polished the surface, Mr Rheese, and forgot the sole. Not a bad metaphor, is it? You stamped on Jamie's watch. A childish gesture; the poor man was already dead. I found the minute-hand in the stitching of your shoe. She led me to it, I believe."

"Who?"

"Yes, I can prove one murder. Proving the second ..."

"But there wasn't ... I mean—" Rheese's voice was getting ever louder, as though trying to drown out the soft uncanny music that now seemed to shiver in the very walls.

"You took the gin with you," Gairden said. "Did you think you might have trouble, getting him to give up this particular patent? Did you plan to get him drunk? He never touched the stuff, but you didn't know that. You didn't know him at all. I wonder if anyone did."

Gairden moved away from the window, towards the table where the clock stood, humming with resonance, even though it was broken, shivering with a kind of life.

"You found them together, dancing. He'd created something you never could. Something extraordinary; something that would make you a rich man. But this time, he wouldn't let you take out a patent, would he? What he'd created was more than just a mechanism to him. It was a true labour of love.

"You argued. And the gin was in your hand. A little must have leaked from around the stopper when you swung it at his head, again, and again, and again. I knew it wasn't a regular burglary, you see. Someone there merely to steal his designs, they wouldn't have been angry enough to hit him so many times, poor fellow. But you, Mr Rheese, you hated the mind in his skull, that genius mind you could never match. You had to destroy it. His refusal to give her up was just the excuse you needed.

"When Jamie fell, she fell, too; Lassiter heard her, though he didn't know what he'd heard. Something in her broke when Jamie died. She wailed, like a long note on a violin, and then she fell." Gairden leaned over, keeping one careful eye on Rheese, and took hold of what lay behind the clock, and pulled it upright.

The automaton drooped against his shoulder like a tired child. She was beautiful in her cool inhuman way. Her face was a smooth shining oval, her eyes elongated teardrops of blue glass. "He called her Lalika," Gairden said. "I thought it was his ghost that was trying to speak to me; it was the girl, Mattie, who put that into my head. But it wasn't Jamie's ghost. It was hers.

"She was the one who stopped your machines, not Jamie – he wouldn't have stopped them for himself. She made them stop for an hour, because that's what you do when someone dies. And because she knew you would never show him that much respect."

"You're insane."

"He'd made better than he knew – better than you or I understood. I can't see you hang for her murder, Mr Rheese, but I'll do my best to see you hang for Jamie Wishart's. Please don't try to leave, I have officers downstairs."

The decanters stilled on the tray. The window latch ceased to ring. The clock gave one last ghost chime, and fell silent. Out of the air a handful of tiny, glimmering cogwheels fell about the two men, frail as butterflies, landing without a sound. Then there was nothing but the relentless, hammering pulse of the great machines.

It was well attended, for the funeral of a boy from the work-house. At least half the factory workers were there, the place having been closed for the day; and there was an old man with a look of Tobias Rheese about him, who stood, grim and silent, leaning on his cane, watching as the six sweating bearers laboured to carry the coffin with dignity to the waiting grave.

Inspector Gairden, who had also attended, braced himself when the old man approached him. "You'll be the inspector."

"Yes, sir."

"I'm Matthew Rheese. A dreadful business." He glanced at the grave, where the diggers were now scooping earth on to the coffin with wet thuds. "One wonders where one went wrong."

Gairden said nothing. What was there to be said?

Rheese nodded, as though he had replied. "A heavy coffin," he said. "Jamie was slight."

"Sir."

"You did the right thing, Inspector. Jamie was the only one she'd dance for, after all." He turned and walked away, with slow, painful dignity.

Gairden followed, turning his collar up against the rain.

A velocipede stood at the gates. "Cab, sir?"

"No, thank you," Gairden said, but laid his hand briefly on the side of the velocipede. The gleaming metal was as warm as flesh.

He turned away towards the station, and as he did so he thought he heard a run of notes, a sound like music played on instruments of silver, music to dance to, fading into the rain.

Biographies

Kim Lakin-Smith is the author of *Tourniquet: Tales from the Renegade City* (Immanion Press, 2007) and *Cyber Circus* (Newcon Press, 2011). Her fantasy and science-fiction short stories have appeared in *Black Static*, *Interzone*, *Celebration*, *Myth-Understandings*, *Further Conflicts*, *Pandemonium: Stories of the Apocalypse*, and other magazines and anthologies. Kim is a regular guest speaker at writing workshops and conventions.

Sarah Pinborough is a horror, thriller and YA author who has had more than ten novels published. Her next release, *The Chosen Seed* (Gollancz, January 2012), is the last of The Dog-Faced Gods trilogy, which has now been optioned for a television series. Her third urban fantasy YA novel, *The London Stone* (Gollancz, June 2012), will be published under the name Sarah Silverwood and is the last of The Nowhere Chronicles. After this come *Mayhem* and *Murder* from Jo Fletcher Books at Quercus. Her short stories have appeared in several anthologies and she has a horror film, *Cracked*, currently in development. She has recently branched out into television writing and is currently writing for *New Tricks* on the BBC. Sarah was the 2009 winner of the British Fantasy Award for Best Short Story, and has three times been shortlisted for Best Novel. She has also been shortlisted for a World Fantasy

Award. Her novella *The Language of Dying* (PS Publishing) was shortlisted for the Shirley Jackson Award and won the 2010 British Fantasy Award for Best Novella.

Kelley Armstrong is the *New York Times*-bestselling author of the Women of the Otherworld paranormal suspense series and Darkest Powers YA urban fantasy trilogy. She grew up in Ontario, Canada, where she still lives with her family. A former computer programmer, she's now escaped her corporate cubicle and hopes never to return.

Mary Elizabeth Braddon (1835–1915) was the author of more than eighty novels. Today she is chiefly remembered for the furore which her best-selling potboiler *Lady Audley's Secret* (1862) engendered, but M. E. Braddon (eventually Mrs Maxwell) wrote novels and plays; contributed essays, short stories, and poems to such high-circulation periodicals as *Punch* and *The World*; and edited the two literary magazines most closely associated with the Sensation Novel, *Temple Bar* and *Belgravia*. In the 1860s, the decade that was the high-water mark of Sensation, M. E. Braddon wrote at least twenty novels, sometimes at the rate of three per year, while bearing six children of her own and raising them together with six step-children.

Caitlín R. Kiernan is the author of several novels, including *Daughter of Hounds*, *The Red Tree*, and *The Drowning Girl: A Memoir*. She is a prolific short-fiction author – to date, over 200 short stories, novellas, and vignettes – most of which have been collected in *Tales of Pain and Wonder*; *From Weird and Distant Shores*; *To Charles Fort, With Love*; *Alabaster*; *A is for Alien*; and *The Ammonite Violin & Others*. *Two Worlds and In Between: The Best of Caitlín R. Kiernan*, Vol. 1, was released by Subterranean Press in October 2011, and her next collection, *Confessions of a Five-Chambered Heart*, will be released (also by Subterranean) in 2012. Kiernan is a four-time nominee for the World Fantasy Award, an honoree for the James

Tiptree Jr Award, and has twice been nominated for the Shirley Jackson Award. Born in Ireland, she lives in Providence, Rhode Island.

Mary Elinor Wilkins-Freeman (1852–1930) was born in Randolph, Massachusetts, the daughter of strict orthodox Congregationalists. She began writing stories and verse for children as a teenager, and her work quickly saw print. She wrote more than two dozen volumes of published short stories and novels. She is best known for two collections of stories, *A Humble Romance and Other Stories* (1887) and *A New England Nun and Other Stories* (1891). In April 1926, Freeman became the first recipient of the William Dean Howells Medal for Distinction in Fiction from the American Academy of Arts and Letters. She died in Metuchen and was interred in Hillside Cemetery in Scotch Plains, New Jersey.

Sarah Langan is the author of the novels *The Keeper, The Missing,* and *Audrey's Door*. She is currently finishing her fourth book, *Empty Houses*. Her work has garnered three Bram Stoker Awards, an ALA Award, a *New York Times Book Review* editor's pick, a *Publishers Weekly* favourite book of the year selection, and been optioned by The Weinstein Company for film. She lives in Brooklyn with her husband, daughter, and rabbit.

Elizabeth Massie is a Bram Stoker Award- and Scribe Award-winning author of horror novels, short horror fiction, media tie-ins, mainstream fiction, historical novels, poetry, and non-fiction. Most recent works include *Homegrown* (a mainstream novel from Crossroad Press), *Playback: Light and Shadow* (an e-novella from Random House, prequel to the 2012 horror film *Playback*), and *Sundown* (a collection of horror shorts from Necon E-Books.) Massie lives in the Shenandoah Valley with illustrator Cortney Skinner. She is the founder of Hand to Hand Vision and Circle of Caring on Facebook. She likes snow and hates cheese.

Alex Bell was born in 1986 in Hampshire. Her contemporary supernatural mysteries are published by Gollancz, and her YA comic fantasies are published by Headline. She has travelled widely, is a ferociously strict vegetarian and generally prefers cats to people.

Alison Littlewood lives in West Yorkshire, England, where she hoards books, dreams and writes fiction – mainly in the dark fantasy and horror genres. Alison has contributed to *Black Static, Dark Horizons, Not One of Us* and the charity anthology *Never Again*. Her debut novel, *A Cold Season*, will be out early in 2012 from Jo Fletcher Books at Quercus. Visit her at www.alisonlittlewood.co.uk.

Nina Allan's stories have appeared regularly in the magazines *Black Static* and *Interzone*, and have featured in the anthologies *Catastrophia, House of Fear, Best Horror of the Year #2* and *Year's Best SF #28*. A first collection of her short fiction, *A Thread of Truth*, was published by Eibonvale Press in 2007, followed by the story cycle *The Silver Wind* in 2011. Twice shortlisted for the BFS and BSFA Award, Nina's next book, *Stardust*, will be available from PS Publishing in autumn 2012. An exile from London, she lives and works in Hastings, East Sussex.

Lisa Tuttle made her first professional sale forty years ago with the short story "Stranger in the House" – now the title story in *Stranger in the House*, Vol. 1 of her collected supernatural fiction, published by Ash-Tree Press. Perhaps best known for her short fiction, which includes the International Horror Guild Award-winning tale "Closet Dreams", she is also the author of several novels, including *The Pillow Friend, The Mysteries* and *The Silver Bough*, as well as books for children and non-fiction works. Although born and raised in America, she has been a British resident for the past three decades, and currently lives with her family in Scotland.

Nancy Holder is a multiple award-winning, *New York Times* bestselling author (the Wicked Series.) Her two new YA dark fantasy series are Crusade and Wolf Springs Chronicles. *Crusade: Vanquished* and *Wolf Springs Chronicles: Hot Blooded* are on the shelves now. She has won four Bram Stoker Awards from the Horror Writers Association, as well as a Scribe Award for Best Novel (*Saving Grace: Tough Love*). Nancy has sold over eighty novels and a hundred short stories, many of them based on such shows as *Highlander, Buffy the Vampire Slayer, Angel,* and others. She lives in San Diego with her daughter, Belle, two Corgis, and three cats. You can visit Nancy online at www.nancyholder.com

Yvonne Navarro lives in southern Arizona, where by day she works on historic Fort Huachuca. She is the author of twenty-two published novels and well over a hundred short stories, and has written about everything from vampires to psychologically disturbed husbands to the end of the world. Her work has won the HWA's Bram Stoker Award plus a number of other writing awards. Visit her at www.yvonnenavarro.com and look her up on Facebook, to keep up with interludes in a crazy life that includes a military spouse, three Great Danes, a people-loving parakeet named BirdZilla, painting, and lots of white zinfandel and ice cream.

Mary Cholmondeley (1859–1925) was the eldest daughter and third child of a family of eight, and from an early age made up stories to tell to her brothers and sisters for their entertainment. She began to write seriously in her late teens and her first novel was *Her Evil Genius*, followed by *The Danvers Jewels* in 1886. In 1899 Mary's best-known novel *Red Pottage* was published and caused something of a sensation at the time because of its pointed satire. In addition to novels, Mary wrote essays, articles and short stories.

Marion Arnott is a teacher working in Scotland and a writer when she can be. Her work has appeared in *Peninsular Magazine,*

QWF, *West Coast*, *Northwords*, *Books Ireland*, *Hidden Corners*, *Chapman Magazine*, *Scottish Child*, *Solander*, *Crimewave 4& 6*, *Year's Best Fantasy and Horror 2002*, *Best British Mysteries*, *The Alsiso Project*, *Elastic Press Book of Numbers*, *Nova Scotia*, *New Scottish Speculative Fiction*, *Elastic Press Book of Extended Play*, *Hayakawa Mystery Magazine* (Japan), *Roadworks* magazine, *Midnight Street* and *Scottish Momentist Fiction 2006*, and her collection, *Sleepwalkers* (Elastic Press, 2003). She won the Philip Good Memorial Prize for Fiction (QWF), CWA Short Dagger, and has been shortlisted for the same award twice more. She was also nominated for the British Fantasy Society's Best Short Story Award.

Lilith Saintcrow is the author of several urban fantasy and (as Lili St Crow) YA series. She lives in Vancouver, Washington, with her children and several other strays.

Award-winning author **Nancy Kilpatrick** has published eighteen novels, two hundred short stories, one non-fiction book, and has edited a number of anthologies including *Evolve: Vampire Stories of the New Undead* (2010) and *Evolve Two: Vampire Stories of the Future Undead* (2011). Upcoming books include a graphic novel, *Nancy Kilpatrick's Vampyre Theater* (Brainstorm Comics); as editor, the anthology *Danse Macabre: Close Encounters With the Reaper*; and a new collection of her short fiction and novellas *Vampyric Variations* (both from Edge SF&F Publishing). Check her website for details (www.nancykilpatrick.com) and she invites you to join her on Facebook.

Muriel Gray is a writer and broadcaster. From an early career as an illustrator, then exhibition designer in Scotland's National Museum of Antiquities, she carved out a career in the media as a well-known television and radio presenter before forming her own production company, which became the biggest independent in Scotland. Her passion for horror and fantasy is lifelong, and in addition to publishing several non-fiction books, her three novels, *The Trickster, Furnace,* and *The Ancient,* are all supernatural thrillers. Stephen King described the latter as "scary and unputdownable". She has written many short stories for anthologies and comics, and is currently finishing a script for a horror film, beginning production in 2012, entitled *Behind You.* She lives in Scotland with her family.

Cynthia Asquith (1887–1960) is best known as an early anthologist of supernatural tales, persuading many of her literary friends to contribute stories to her books. She was also a writer of ghost stories. The daughter of the 11th Earl of Wemyss, and daughter-in-law of British prime minister Herbert Asquith, she worked for many years as secretary to J. M. Barrie, creator of Peter Pan, who left his literary estate (except for Peter Pan) to her upon his death.

Amelia B. Edwards (1831–1892) was a journalist, novelist, and noted Egyptologist in her time. She was also an active supporter of the Suffrage movement. The daughter of an army officer turned banker and an Irish mother, Amelia was home schooled for most of her childhood. Her first published work, the poem "The Knights of Old", was written when she was just seven. A friend of Charles Dickens, many of her short stories were published in his magazines, notably the Christmas annuals. Among her many novels were *The Ladder of Life, Half a Million of Money,* and *Lord Breckenburg.*

Elizabeth Gaskell (1810–1865) was a Victorian novelist, born in London, the daughter of a Unitarian minister. In 1832 she married William Gaskell, and they settled in the industrial city of Manchester. Motherhood and the obligations of a minister's wife kept her busy. However, the death of her only son inspired her to write her first novel, *Mary Barton,* which was published anonymously in 1848. It was an immediate success, winning the praise of authors such as Charles Dickens and Thomas Carlyle. Dickens invited her to contribute to his magazine *Household Words,* where her next major work, *Cranford*, appeared in 1853. *North and South* was published the following year. Gaskell's work brought her many friends, including the novelist Charlotte Brontë. When Charlotte died in 1855, her father, Patrick Brontë, asked Gaskell to write her biography, *The Life of Charlotte Brontë*. Gaskell died on 12 November 1865, leaving her longest work, *Wives and Daughters*, incomplete.

Gail Z. Martin is the author of *The Summoner, The Blood King, Dark Haven* and *Dark Lady's Chosen* (The Chronicles of the Necromancer series). She is also the author of The Fallen Kings Cycle from Orbit Books with *Book One: The Sworn* and *Book Two: The Dread*, and the upcoming Ascendant Kingdoms Saga. For book updates, tour information and contact details, visit www.ChroniclesoftheNecromancer. com. Gail is the host of the Ghost in the Machine Fantasy Podcast, and you can find her on Facebook, GoodReads, BookTour, BookMarketing.ning, Shelfari and Twitter. She blogs at www.DisquietingVisions.com. She is also the author two non-fiction series. The Thrifty Author's Guide series (Comfort Publishing) includes *Launching Your Book Without Losing Your Mind* and *Author Web Sites that Wow Readers and Impress Reporters*. The 30 Day Guide Series (Career Press) includes *30 Days to Social Media Success* and *30 Days to Online PR & Marketing Success*. Gail's short fiction has been featured in two anthologies: *Rum and Runestones* from Dragon Moon Press and *The Bitten Word* from New Con Press.

Edith Wharton (1862–1938) belonged to an aristocratic New York family with ancestry dating back three centuries. In 1885 she married Teddy Wharton, who was twelve years older than she was. Between 1900 and 1938, Wharton wrote many novels and wrote many ghost stories. The publication of *The House of Mirth* in 1905 marked the true beginning of her literary career. She continued to publish rapidly, producing, among others, *Ethan Frome* in 1911. Wharton continued writing until her death in 1938. She is buried in the American Cemetery at Versailles.

Gaie Sebold was born in the US, lives in South East London, and works for a social change charity. She has had several short stories and a book of poetry published. Her debut novel *Babylon Steel* is due out from Solaris in January 2012. She has been known to run around in woods hitting people with latex swords and declaim poetry in public, though not usually at the same time. She gardens inefficiently, reads obsessively, and is currently working on a novel collaboration with her partner, writer Dave Gullen, along with rather too many other projects. She is gradually being crowded out of her living room by plants. www.gaiesebold.com.